Patricia Rice

Evil Genius

Evil Genius

Patricia Rice

Copyright © 2010 Patricia Rice
First Publication:
Book View Cafe, July 2011
Createspace, January 2014

ISBN 978 1 61138 341 6

All rights reserved. No part of this book may be reproduced in any form or by an electronic or mechanical means including information storage and retrieval systems—except in the use of brief quotations in critical articles or reviews—without permission in writing from the author.

The characters and events portrayed in this book are fictitious. Any similarity to real persons, living or dead, is coincidental and not intended by the author.

Cover design by Mandala

Chapter One

In which EG and Nick arrive bearing trouble.

MY NAME is Ana, and I'm a doormat.

I'm also one of the best virtual assistants in the world, if you'll pardon my modesty. Being a virtual assistant and a wuss often go hand in hand. Most of us are introverts who prefer to work in cyberspace because human nature is messy and unpredictable and computers aren't. My excuse is that my family is messier than most and so far beyond volatile as to establish whole new spectrums of the definition, so being their doormat involves a great deal of mud and muddle that I couldn't take anymore.

So four years ago, I left my family half way around the world, and I never had reason to believe they had interest in finding me until the day my doorbell rang. At the time, I lived and worked in the basement of a Victorian tenement in Atlanta. Expecting the usual FedEx or UPS delivery, I ran up to the foyer, blinking to adjust to the sun filtering through the dirty transom before opening the door. Even though she stood right before me, I still couldn't believe my eyes.

The last time I had seen EG, she was only five. I had fiercely missed my eccentric half-siblings, but once I developed the gumption to quit enabling my mother's dysfunctional lifestyle, I had no choice but to walk out on them.

Since escaping, I've been practicing hard to overcome my doormat tendencies. Granted, it may not seem that way since I'm small and dark and work at blending in, but in my world, invisibility is a defensive position. After twenty years with my flamboyant, nomadic, mother and half-siblings, I treasured the anonymity I'd achieved since my declaration of independence. Invisibility allows me to be myself, giving me hope of establishing a normal life, with a real home someday.

I'm not angling for sympathy, but growing up as the responsible eldest of a family of drama queens, I felt responsible for their welfare, which required more assertiveness and the best therapists my mother's government health plan could afford. It took me twenty-six years to conquer my need to act as mother-hen. And apparently, four for my family to find me again.

If I was as good a virtual assistant as I thought, I wouldn't have been so surprised when EG appeared like a raven of doom that late August afternoon.

"I've brought my own bed," she announced the second I opened the basement door.

In the gloom of the boarded up sidelights, I stared down at her shiny black hair. Since she was only nine, she was still shorter than me.

"EG?" My reaction times were a little off due to lack of use. "How did you get here?"

As far as I was aware, my mother never crossed the Atlantic. Panicked questions like *How long were you on an airplane alone?* and *Who died?* ran rampant, but expressing weakness was not a wise idea when it came to my family.

EG favored me to some extent, with long, straight black hair, slender build, and a mind like a steel trap. Unlike me, she wore her hair in bangs that hid her Irish-green eyes, although EG might be the only one of us who is pure American. I smothered an unexpected urge to hug her, except EG wouldn't have understood a genuine demonstration of love. We'd been raised to be detached citizens of the world. We air-kissed but never hugged.

From beneath the long fringe, EG regarded me incredulously. "Lost a few IQ points since last we met?" she asked, proving my point. She dragged in a wheeled Pullman nearly as big as she was. "The Hungarian Princess gave me her credit card to buy schoolbooks, and whoops, I guess I accidentally booked a plane ticket instead. You know, if you rented that empty apartment upstairs, we wouldn't have to share the coal cellar."

My family was used to EG's ability to answer questions before they're asked and solve problems before we know we have them. Unfortunately, the rest of the world found it a little disconcerting. Our mother, Magda— referred to as the Hungarian Princess for her fairy tales about our background— once had a boyfriend who invented the Evil Genius sobriquet after EG nailed him as a gambling addict just before he ran off with Magda's last divorce settlement. EG's real name is Elizabeth Georgiana.

"I didn't know another apartment was available or that I needed a new one," I said, letting her roll her own bag. "Did anyone come with you?"

There hadn't been anyone on the sidewalk. I checked. Brought up as we had been, we learned to take precautions—and not necessarily against bad guys. Lost nannies, unpaid taxi drivers, even a camel could have waited on my doorstep.

"Nick will be here shortly." Sidestepping my question, she shoved her bag down the stairs and let it explode on the antique Persian carpet I'd spent a month's wages on at a flea market. It was the genuine thing, centuries old, frayed, worn, and I'd had high hopes of one day having a real home to put it in. I might as well have hoped the carpet would fly.

As promised, EG's suitcase explosion produced an inflatable mattress and air pump along with her hoard of books, two pairs of shorts, a silk robe that looked like a cast-off of our mother's, and some T-shirts.

"I figured you'd need my help when Nick got here," EG continued, gathering up her books and neatly arranging them in a stack beside the textbooks on my computer table. The textbooks were left over from an assignment that was as yet unfinished—mainly because my client had disappeared. At least he'd had the decency to pay his bill in advance.

I surveyed the clutter rearranging my neat cave. Her books were old hardcovers with faded writing that I'd probably have to explore to make certain none of them said something like *Sorcery Made Easy*.

"Nick hasn't the attention span to find me," I told her, although it came out more question than statement.

EG, like me, had led a nomadic life, never knowing whether we'd be stationed in mud huts or palaces from one day to the next. Loosely speaking, our mother was part of the government diplomatic corps, a foreign correspondent, and/or a camp follower, depending on what man she was with that year. All of us were well versed in the cheapest way to travel to Marrakesh. Still, that a nine-year-old had taken the time and found the resources to locate me when my mother had not made me very, very uneasy.

I gathered up EG's clothes and heaved them back in the suitcase that would have to serve as her dresser. "Nick disapproves of my lifestyle," I told her. Or lack thereof. As a VA, I stayed safely inside four walls. I communicated with fascinating people who lived exciting lives, without the necessity of bandaging bleeding torsos or chasing baboons out of the kitchen—services my family had been known to require. "I can't imagine why Nick would want to find me."

"Because his latest lover stole his car and ran off with his hair stylist, and he's depressed and has nowhere else to go." EG plopped her skinny, jeans-encased rear in my computer chair and began accessing her e-mail. All in black, she looked like a miniature me. I even recognized her avoidance technique. She was hiding something. My insides knotted as I imagined all the disasters my brilliant half-siblings could incur.

Magda had named us after royalty. I assume Magda was on a Russian kick when she named her two eldest. I'm Anastasia. Nicholas is four years younger than me. Nick was named after the late czar, rather appropriately as it turned out. He possesses the royal *savoir-faire* Prince Charles lacks.

I didn't ask how EG knew he was on the way here. It's a waste of time asking. She just knew and the sooner one accepted it, the easier it was to move forward.

To outsiders, it might sound as if my family is totally weird, but look at the statistics. Most families end in divorce these days. Single-parent homes are the rule, not the exception. It's just that in our family, we're all overachievers, and we had our exceptional mother to thank for that. Had we actually possessed the wealth of royalty—or at least the American equivalent—we would have been lauded as the next generation of Kennedys, capable of running the country or corporate boardrooms. Instead, Magda expressed her ambition and overcompensated with powerful men and numerous offspring.

I was already hyperventilating, imagining the disasters that would divert EG and Nick to my doorstep. Having my most lucrative client disappear leaving a mysterious e-mail message about *envelopes, poison, top hats, and pow* was as much insanity as I was willing to tolerate.

"Look, this area crawls with drug dealers. It isn't safe for either of you," I said, as if EG needed to be told what she no doubt already knew. "What did her Highness do to set you off?"

Pecking away at my keyboard, EG hit the *Send* button and probably notified the entire planet of my whereabouts. "I'm out for summer vacation, and she wants to visit the ski slopes of Switzerland with the sheik. Since we're temporarily homeless..."

She didn't have to finish. I knew the routine by heart. Our mother loved to live like the royalty she claimed to be, but the crown jewels were long since pawned, and nannies could only be paid by men with better-paying positions than Magda's. Not that we ever knew precisely what her position was. I gave up asking long ago.

"Set up your bed," I agreed in resignation, once more returning to the role of family doormat. I didn't want to talk to Magda, but even I realized I'd have to let her know EG was safe. "The cupboard is bare. I have to run to the grocery if you're staying."

EG shrugged and waved me off.

None of this was really the kid's fault. The schism had always been between my mother and me. I believed in homes, security, and routines. Magda was a staunch advocate of chaos.

In rusty caretaking mode, I tugged on my running shoes, grabbed my shoulder bag, and jogged up the stairs and out the tall front door, making mental grocery lists.

Another sister would have felt guilty for leaving a nine-year-old in a run-down apartment house riddled with druggies and psychotics. I was confident EG would have erected an elaborate security system and conned, coerced, or otherwise convinced an alarm company to arm it before I returned. That wasn't just EG's genius. It's what our family's lifestyle had trained us to do. We are the future—prepared for any event from nuclear holocaust to Martian invasion. Of course, the commonplace, like going to the supermarket or living in houses, eluded the rest of my family. That had always been my job.

I longed to pound out my frustration on the punching bag at my favorite gym down the street, but I didn't trust EG alone in my apartment *that* long. A good run would have to suffice.

* * *

EG breathed a sigh of relief now that she was inside the apartment. Ana might huff and puff, but everyone in the family knew she was the safe haven they could rely on. It had been a little scary when Ana had dropped out of sight, but the Oracle had been extremely helpful in locating her after EG had quizzed a search engine.

She didn't know who Oracle was, but the instant she'd explained her problem, his e-mails had given her Ana's screen name. Their computer geek brother, Tudor, had helped trace it. Nick had instructed her on the best methods of transportation since she'd never been in the States before, although she had an American passport because her parents were born here.

The last time EG had seen Ana, she'd been only four or five, but she distinctly remembered the visit. Magda had dumped several of the younger kids at the Italian villa where Ana had moved after she'd declared her independence and run off with her new computer. At the time, Magda had signed on for some African junket as a newspaper correspondent. Or spy, but no one ever said that aloud. Whatever, she'd needed a nest to leave her cuckoos in.

Magda had left a nanny to help Ana out, but the nanny had a tendency to smoke pot in her off hours, which seemed to be 24/7. Ana had come home to find the kitchen stove on fire and the stoned nanny admiring the blaze.

Grinning, EG recalled the image of her petite sister as heroine that she'd cherished over the years. Four years ago, Ana had been growing out her bangs. She'd pulled the odd lengths of her shorter hair back by little butterfly barrettes that marched across her scalp in single-file lines. She'd been barefoot and in some gauzy ankle-length skirt, looking no older than a teenager. Walking into the kitchen, Ana had morphed from caretaking sister to berserker in two seconds flat. She'd competently slammed a cover over the flaming pan, grabbed the stoned nanny by the arm, and with a nonchalance that had left EG open-mouthed, flipped the nanny off the balcony into the patio umbrellas and shrubbery below.

She'd then taken them all out for Italian ices while the smoke cleared.

Of course, the nanny had threatened criminal action, and Ana had been evicted from her apartment for almost setting the building on fire. Ana hadn't blamed anyone for the episode. She'd just efficiently packed them all up and found a new home until Magda returned, and then Ana had disappeared for good.

EG wanted to be Ana when she grew up.

Even in her adoration, EG knew she was imposing on her sister's limited goodwill. But Ana was the only hero she knew.

She desperately needed a hero right now.

With a click of the keys, EG switched the computer to the MSNBC website to check the latest headlines and tried not to cry when she read the top story.

* * *

I couldn't say if it was instinct or luck that caused me to take the long route to the grocery. With my size, I look like a victim, but in my first few months of living in downtown Atlanta, I'd firmly corrected that impression. I now had an unspoken pact with the local street thugs — they disappeared when they saw me coming, and I didn't send their mamas photos of what they'd been doing. Life was good.

Besides, I didn't expect trouble on a steamy August afternoon. Most people had the sense to stay indoors until night cooled the city streets. I was grappling with my frustration with my feckless mother and still contemplating stopping to kick box a few rounds to work it off, when the jeering young punks on the street corner ahead of me raised all my protective antennae. Without EG's warning of Nick's potential arrival, I might have turned down a side street and avoided a confrontation.

On second thought, given my need to punch something, probably not. I might be a doormat for my family, but I have an attitude twice my size as a result.

"I trust you're stopping a purse snatcher," I called loudly enough to be heard over the taunts.

Most people would think one diminutive white female in baggy black T-shirt and capris from Goodwill wouldn't be heard or listened to in a fight involving hulking adolescents in a salute to the street's ethnic diversity, and they might be right. That's why I carried a cap gun in my purse that sounded like a rocket launcher.

I pulled the trigger.

The thugs with enough brains left to connect noise with danger jumped three feet off the ground. The ones familiar with my dirty fighting glanced over their shoulders, grimaced, and melted down an alleyway, leaving the last baggy-pants combatant and his victim revealed.

"Greetings, Ana!" Nick shouted—well, *gaily*. He really was a cheerful fellow, even when provoked by hoodlums with no fashion sense. "Would you be so kind as to explain to this bloke that I need to keep my necklace?"

Nick's father is a British lord. That didn't give him an excuse to adopt a posh accent since he mostly grew up with the rest of us, with only an occasional interim in one of those expensive all-male Brit public schools. Still, he sounded good. I'd missed that barmy accent.

Grinning in appreciation at recognizing Nick and the show that would follow, I crossed my arms over my insignificant chest, cap pistol prominently displayed, and waited for the last wiseass to wise up and depart.

Apparently on a coke downhill slide, the thug popped his blade and glared menacingly at me. "Cute, real cute," he sneered.

"I know." I smiled big and fluttered my lashes and Nick almost cracked up. In the decades of protecting my family in foreign lands, I'd learned that coolness in the face of bullies showed them we were as crazy as they were. Took them aback and gave me time to figure out an escape. "Take my brother's necklace, and he turns mean."

The thug laughed and turned his back on me. Big mistake, but one I had counted on. As did Nick.

He'd learned a new move or two since we'd learned basic judo from a master. A little *tae kwan do* was my guess. Whatever. Nick hit first, showing off by swinging agilely to kick the punk with an upper thrust of his heel. Going for the balls is usually a bad option—the target is too small. But Nick knew what he was doing. We'd had lots of practice, after all.

The guy bent in two to protect his valuables, bringing him down to my level. I bopped him on his do-rag with the cap pistol, and he toppled, howling.

My therapists tell me I may have a few repressed anger issues. I'm cool with that.

Nick stepped on his attacker's wrist and captured the knife, flipping it closed and slipping it into his pocket in one smooth move.

A crowd of young punks watched from across the street. If this had been some gang initiation, our victim was lucky he failed. Maybe he'd live to grow up and be a lawyer. If it wasn't an initiation, we were about to be set upon.

"Just like old times," I murmured, spinning around to jog toward the apartment with Nick on my trail. At least he'd been bright enough to leave his luggage elsewhere.

"And you're looking more like Magda with every passing year," he agreed in his own oblique way. "What is that you're wearing? Pajamas? Why don't you wear something to flaunt what you have instead of hiding behind that abysmal disguise?"

"What, and repeat Magda's mistakes?" I asked in incredulity, reaching for my keys as we approached the apartment door. "I don't need the attention, thank you very much."

"Some things never change," he agreed with good humor. "Do you ever intend to grow up and quit competing with her?"

"I've changed," I declared. "I'm working on the important stuff inside and not the superficial stuff on the outside. I don't need to compete with anyone."

"Tell me another one, Dr. Faustus."

He looked good today, as usual. We both have our mother's angled cheekbones, but Nick inherited her blond hair as well. I don't remember his father, but he apparently had a firm square jaw with a nice cleft that he passed on. And Nick got the height in the family as well. I figured him for movie star material, but he had absolutely no memory for words. He did, however, possess an aptitude for mathematics that served him well in Monte Carlo.

"I like to believe I'm on the side of the angels," I countered. "Cover my back."

"Turned chicken since last we met?" he taunted, scanning the street, while I undid the locks.

If I didn't know him so well, I'd take that as a reference to my refusal to compete with my mother, but Nick isn't that deep. He was referring to the punks behind us.

"Until today, I'd taught them to leave me alone. It would have been nice to keep it that way." I let him into the foyer and secured the bolt behind us before taking the stairs down to my rooms.

Showing her training, EG had already made herself at home. She'd borrowed my extra set of sheets to make up her air mattress, tucked her suitcase under my cot, and was pigging down my raspberry yogurt.

"Hey, Eezhee." Nick slurred the initials into a Slovakian name. "It really is like old times, isn't it? How long have you been mooching off the czarina?"

I left them to catch up and did my usual introverted disappearance by retreating to my inner sanctum. My family hadn't been here for an hour, and already I was a marked target in the neighborhood. This was not an unusual development.

On my own, I might have fought the odds just to keep from moving again. I liked the old Victorian I'd made my home these last few years. Admittedly, my two-room coal cellar wasn't the most gracious home in the world, but it was mine, and I treasured the few possessions I'd collected. I liked my antique iron bedstead with the flowers painted on it, and the copper and black Persian rug with the moth holes. They were *mine*, and I'd worked hard to earn them.

But until I knew what to do about EG, I needed a safe house, and this wasn't a neighborhood for kids, especially one like EG who got in trouble by opening her mouth.

As usual when I had some hard thinking to do, I sat down at my laptop. Writing was a recommended anger management technique that I hadn't practiced enough. As soon as I poured my frustration into these pages, my brain started whirring.

The first thing I acknowledged was that we'd just made ourselves targets for every gang member in the area. The humiliation of being beaten by a pip-squeak and a gay male model would incite the hoodlums like rabid gunslingers. They'd have to come after us just to prove they were still top dogs.

I'd been through this enough times to know it was fruitless hoping trouble would go away. Once the rabble discovered my family's eccentric propensities, we were hounded into either retaliation or escape. Not for the first time, I wished my family were normal with a huge house someplace safe and boring where we could live in peace.

I didn't follow that thought to its logical conclusion immediately, because in my family, it wasn't a logical conclusion. No, the next step of logic was to wonder again why EG and Nick had arrived on my doorstep on the same day and conclude that my first intuition had been right. Something was vastly wrong.

Had I kept typing, I might have reached the right solution sooner, but the realization that I'd been scammed drove me out of my seat and back to the front room again.

"All right, no more evasions." I waited in the doorway, hands on skinny hips, trying to look formidable. "I want a good explanation of why you're here."

Nick had the experience to look suitably innocent. EG didn't. She shoved a spoonful of my raspberry yogurt into her mouth to cover up, but I had two decades of practice over her. I snatched the cup away and pointed at the door.

"I get the whole story or I'll put you on the first train to D.C. and your dad if you don't spill." This last was directed at EG. Nick could take care of himself.

EG's lower lip trembled, and Nick sighed in resignation. Another woman would have felt guilty yelling at a crying kid, but I crossed my arms to hold in my gut-wrenching dismay and gazed at my half brother for explanation.

Nick shrugged. "Don't you ever read the newspapers?"

"Why? They only make me want to walk the street carrying a sign saying *Repent or the world shall end tomorrow.*" I hadn't buried myself in the basement just to avoid family. There was a whole world out there that I would avoid if I could. That way, I could live with the fantasy that the rest of the universe contained sane people, and it was only my piece of it that was nuts.

EG went to my computer, hit a few keys, and called up a news channel. There, in big bold letters I couldn't miss, was the headline: SENATOR TEX HAMMOND A SUSPECT IN AIDE'S MURDER.

Tex was EG's dad.

Chapter Two

Ana visits the ancestral home and ends up talking to a lawyer

THE KNOWLEDGE that the family I loved and hadn't seen in five years had tracked me down so I could solve a murder brought me to the logical solution I'd failed to reach earlier. I'd always believed my younger half-siblings belonged with their influential fathers, but I'd never had the money to ship them half way around the world to whatever distant outpost they inhabited.

Suddenly, I realized even their ambitious fathers might be questionable as caregivers. A senator accused of murder? That was a new low even for us.

EG had followed Tex's career for as long as she was able to spell his name, which was to say from about the age of one. She idolized the man. Nobody said geniuses were any less stupid than the rest of us.

Watching EG's heartbreak, I kicked myself for not seeing the obvious sooner. I wasn't the only one who needed a permanent home. We needed a safe harbor—together—when the world turned on us. I was already reaching for my crusader's helmet.

Maybe it was realizing that the senator was in D.C. and that EG would want to go to him that made me wake up to what I should have seen before—why shouldn't the man who'd let the Hungarian Princess loose upon the world support his progeny's progeny in their time of trouble? Magda might be chronically bankrupt, but I knew from research that my grandfather wasn't. And Grandfather Maximillian lived in D.C.

How sweet was that?

In all the years we traipsed around Europe and Asia and Africa, Magda had never mentioned her father except in fairy tales of kings and queens and lost princesses. I hadn't seen him since before Nick was born. My memory of him was dim, but as far as I was aware, our grandfather had never exhibited any interest in us since we'd left D.C. But that was a minor consideration in my moment of determination. I *remembered* my grandfather's house. It was huge. And surrounded by equally large and secure residences. It was the ideal safe haven.

All I had to do was show him the wisdom of taking in his own kin before Magda turned them into terrorists. Or their fathers turned them into murderers. For my family, confronting a rich old stranger was as natural as sunrise.

I reached into the refrigerator for the raspberry muffins. Both EG and Nicholas followed my every move as if I could solve world peace and hunger at the same time.

I handed each of them a muffin. "I'm not rowing this boat alone. If you want me to help, then we're all in it together." Figuring they were old enough to handle them, I laid down the ground rules.

They waited expectantly, not having a clue as to what I was talking about but apparently willing to find out.

"Our grandfather will know the truth about the senator," I announced. "Book bus tickets to D.C. and start packing."

If silence could be frozen, I'd accomplished it. They hadn't known Maximillian existed.

* * *

"You're going to regret this," EG warned for the thirty-millionth time since we'd left Atlanta. She was hunched up with her arms wrapped around her skinny knees between me and Nick in the back seat of the taxi as it maneuvered D.C. traffic. The cab had no working a/c, and clouds of exhaust fumes and hot August humidity mixed with our anxious perspiration into a decidedly unwholesome atmosphere.

I was still astonished that sophisticated Nick was willing to accept my terms. I'd made him promise to handle nanny duties, using the excuse that I was the only one in a position to make a living at the moment. Have laptop, will travel, and all that. Apparently he really was depressed, or as curious about our past as I was. He'd agreed without a qualm.

"It's time we met our grandfather," I insisted over EG's pessimistic attitude. "We can't live like vagabonds forever. You need a real home." That's what I'd wanted when I was EG's age, but then, I wasn't on quite the same genius level. Maybe geniuses didn't need homes, but at nine, even EG couldn't live alone.

I had a small nest egg that might have set us up elsewhere, but if we had to be in D.C., my money wouldn't last long. D.C. is an expensive town. I was still ambivalent about helping Tedious Tex, EG's dad, but I was bouncing with excitement at the idea of someone else contributing to the family effort.

Grandfather had come to mind first, but now that we were here, Tex had a lot to account for as well. The man paid child support, but to my knowledge, he'd never otherwise acknowledged the existence of his brilliant daughter. I could easily believe a parent that pathetic guilty of murder, but he was EG's father. *She* wouldn't believe it. She was still a kid who wanted to love her charismatic dad. The grass-is-always-greener syndrome, I called it. Most children of separated parents suffer from it.

"You haven't heard from Grandfather in how many years?" she asked. "You should have given me time to do the research."

Grandfather Maximillian had been alive and well when I'd checked at

Christmas. At the time, I'd been lonely and dreaming of family, but I hadn't acted on my foolish dreams beyond research. Sentimentality is so not me.

I wasn't about to house my half-siblings in Atlanta for the time it would take to run a full inquiry into our grandfather. There had been a bus leaving within hours of Nick's arrival, and I'd made certain we were on it. Uprooting myself—again—required determination.

"If we live here, you could go to a real school," I interjected, knowing the school argument would divert her from her gloomy prognostications.

"I do not need a school," she grumbled, but the subject silenced her as anticipated.

I was feeling apprehensive enough without her wet blanket attitude.

I was curious about our grandfather, of course, but I figured anyone who had fathered our mother wasn't the kind of stable authority figure little kids needed. Given what I'd learned in my research, I had him pegged for Mafia.

I also assumed my mother would never have left a luxurious nest if it was available, so there had to be a major flaw in the household, even though I had this vague memory of his home as a welcoming shelter. I'd just been three at the time and recalled the house only because I adored the heavy bronze spaniels guarding the fireplace. I'd never been allowed to have pets, so I must have thought of them as real dogs.

That Magda hadn't mentioned her father's name in a quarter of a century was proof enough that returning to the ancestral home was akin to opening Pandora's box.

I don't remember a grandmother, and our mother's bedtime stories tended to end in the tragic death of the beautiful Hungarian queen, so I had to assume she was out of the picture.

"You should have checked the address again before we left," Nicholas murmured as the taxi cruised down a narrow street of historic D.C. mansions. Half of them looked like foreign embassies—the substantial kind with turrets and enough brick and stone to pave a path to heaven. Or hell. We gaped like hayseeds. I don't know about EG and Nick, but my mind boggled at the idea of Magda coming from one of those castles. Maybe she really was a princess.

"I think God must live here," Nick continued in awe, echoing my impression.

"Or George Washington," EG muttered.

Admittedly, the sense of history contained in the towering Gothic Victorians and eccentric Romanesque Revival houses was overwhelming, but unlike my siblings, I felt at home here. Maybe it was the familiar urban landscape of belching buses and tacky commercial signs that welcomed me. I just knew the old houses whispered security. Maybe in my heart of hearts I longed for the home that three-year-old child in me remembered.

"The man has lived here for over seventy years. Why would he move now?" I asked, dismissing their fears as if I had none. Big sisters are supposed to be reassuring.

"I can give you at least three reasons," EG replied. "And if you had given me even half a second to check—"

"I don't care if he's dead, or in a nursing home." I didn't inquire into the third possibility. The first two were scary enough. "The fact remains, we are his only living kin. Whatever Magda did to him shouldn't be blamed on us. I'm sure he'll learn to appreciate our talents."

Nick snorted at the reference to "talents" but generously refrained from a cocky remark for EG's sake. "I can't believe we *really* come from a background like this," he said with a measure of awe as he gazed up at the historic mansions.

Our ensuing silence evoked our agreement. We'd really thought the "coming from wealth" part of Magda's story was simply a line in her well-embellished fairy tale.

"By George, if he lives alone in one of those, he won't even know we're in the house." Recovering, Nicholas smoothed a blond swathe of hair off his forehead, straightened his square shoulders, and morphed into his Prince Charming mode. It's positively amazing how he does that. "These places are large enough to house a circus."

"Which they will, if we move in," I murmured as the taxi pulled up to the curb.

The houses on this block were more urban and less awesome, but we stopped in front of an impressive brown brick Italianate mansion complete with square tower, gingerbread gables, and a covered porch. Unlike many of the townhouses around it, it was on a corner and set off slightly from its neighbor by an alley. I recognized the black wrought iron fence overgrown with ivy and the green marble Chinese lions guarding the steps. I had nicked the ball beneath one paw with a croquet mallet.

In disbelief and astonishment, I realized I had once actually *lived* in a mansion.

Funny, how memories come pouring back when primed by a familiar sight or smell. I'd never pegged myself as a sentimental person, but gazing up at that ugly house as Nick paid the taxi driver, I was practically choking on a lump of nostalgia. We'd checked our luggage at the bus station until we knew what kind of reception waited for us. I was half inclined to return to the taxi and catch the next bus out. On my own, running away had always been the best strategy.

Did I really want to know why we had been banned from the Garden of Eden?

"I told you so," EG gloated as I froze at the gate.

I drew a deep breath and took confidence from my geek shield of denim jumper and tight French braid. As a teenager, I'd adopted the quiet confidence of Princess Leia as my role model, but the braid was just to keep my waist-length, black Irish hair out of my face. Chin high, I strode up the short walk to wallop the brass knocker against a mahogany door. I wasn't letting a house intimidate me, even if it was larger than the high school I almost graduated from.

I'd ordered EG to wear her blue jeans and a white T-shirt so she looked like a normal nine-year-old and not a tiny Goth, but I hadn't been able to persuade her to put her long black hair in pigtails. Nicholas looked his usual spectacular James-Bondish self, although the yellow ascot was a dead give-away that he was as nervous as I was. What could I say? He deserved his armor as much as I did. We had good reason to hide behind stereotypes.

No one answered my knock.

"The shrub border has been weeded and watered," Nick noted. "Someone lives here."

"Not Grandfather," EG warned—again.

"It's our ancestral home. We have a right to visit." I slammed the knocker in a rapid tattoo that should have echoed through the Halls of Montezuma.

I could hear air conditioning running inside. A place like this had to have servants.

"May I help you?" a voice intoned from the intercom hidden behind a pot of pothos cascading from a sphinx head near the door. I calculated the sphinx as a bronze original and not one of those cheap plaster things adorning Atlanta garden walls. I had an eye for historic detail developed over a lifetime of drooling over other people's houses.

"Anastasia Devlin here," I informed the disembodied voice. "I wish to see my grandfather."

Nicholas elbowed me, and EG scowled, but I didn't see any purpose in terrifying the old guy by telling him a regiment of Magda's offspring was at the door.

The silence following my announcement was striking. I opted for the fantasy of imagining a supercilious butler progressing through marble hallways, dusting the woodwork in his anxiousness to garner the approval of the prodigal grandchild.

"There are no grandfathers present," the voice finally replied, striking a blow to my comfortable reverie.

I am not normally a combative person. I say please and thank you when called upon. But there were times my Irish temper blew the top of my head—

Seeing the gleam in my eye, Nicholas grabbed my elbow and jerked me down the stairs. "Come along. We can take a hotel room and discuss this."

EG scampered for the gate without waiting.

I shook him off and returned to slam the knocker again. "What have you done with my grandfather?" I shouted at the sphinx, rattling the door.

And I was serious. I *remembered* this house. I remembered a tall man with thick pepper-and-salt hair and a bristly mustache, and I wanted his hugs back again. If these monsters had done anything to my grandfather, I'd make them pay. Tears actually stung my eyes as I slammed the knocker, and disappointment and grief spilled into the fury. I wanted my childhood back.

I knew I couldn't have it, but EG deserved a real childhood with kitchen tables and schools and laughing friends. No kid ought to be brought up as I had. I would claw the face off the damned sphinx to give EG the home she needed. This home. Ripped from my subconscious, it had become my reason for living. To hell with Magda and whatever argument had taken us out of our grandfather's life. *I* intended to change all that.

All right, so I had a lot fermenting in the murk of my subconscious, and denial was my middle name. No one ever said therapy helped.

"Maximillian no longer lives here," the voice intoned again in an accent more posh than Nick's. "He passed on two months ago."

EG gave her "I told you so" shrug, sat down on the gate step, and began searching the three-inch band of lawn for four-leaf clovers. I knew she'd been covertly hoping her hitherto unknown relative might help Senator Tex, but EG was not only smart, she's a cynic. My heart bled watching her give up hope.

Apparently as affected by her plight as I was, Nicholas stepped up to the intercom, shot his cuffs to the proper width from his coat sleeve as if someone could see him, and purred with his best British accent, "Then I suggest you open the door to his heirs, or we will be forced to consult with our attorneys."

The plural was a nice touch. *Attorneys,* as if we had an entire firm at our disposal. Nick had learned a few useful things in his ritzy schools besides how to discern sexual proclivity in the object of his interest.

If I could have packaged the silence that followed, I'd use it the next time Magda breezed through to tell me I needed a man. Such splendidly evocative stillness would quell a magpie.

To my amazement, one massive door creaked open. In its place appeared a stiff, barrel-chested man several heads taller than me. Graying hair, of indeterminate age, and his clothing of impeccable tailoring, he could have been a foreign diplomat.

I recognized him. "Mallard!" The name leaped to my tongue from the primeval ooze of my subconscious. *I had come home.* I immediately stifled that nonsense, but I couldn't crush the excitement as I stood there idiotically awaiting a joyous welcome.

Mallard gazed uncomprehendingly at me in my nondescript denim, then to Nick, who had opted for aristocratic nonchalance. I doubted that he could see EG at the gate, fortunately.

"I beg your pardon," he replied with a frozen expression. "Do I know you?"

"I'm Anastasia," I repeated, foolish hopes neatly doused. "I put the nick in the Chinese lion, remember?" The gargoyles were staring at me reproachfully. "Why did no one notify us of Grandfather's death?"

"Mallard, the door is open," a mechanical voice proclaimed from the interior. "Do you need assistance?"

Looking as if he'd swallowed hot coals, Mallard glanced over his shoulder, back to me, and heaving a mighty sigh, stepped out of the way. "We have visitors, sir."

I brushed past, grateful to be out of the sticky heat and in the cool dimness of a long corridor. No wonder I had a penchant for dark basements. I'd spent my formative years in a mausoleum. I immediately traversed the marble floor to the doorway of the front parlor. The bronze spaniels were still there, and my heart did a little pitter-patter of happiness. I almost expected my grandfather's voice to call for me. He'd had an accent, I remembered now. Hungarian, perhaps?

"I don't accept visitors," the disconnected voice responded—definitely not Grandfather's gruff baritone.

Now that I was inside, the voice was less mechanical and more male, but it contained as much inflection as a robot's.

The confidence that I was on home turf intensified. The voice was the usurper. I walked straight up to the brass speaker in the wall as Nick and EG entered. "Then you may leave," I said with the quiet authority I had to have learned from someone other than my excitable mother. "I will call the executor of my grandfather's estate and demand an explanation of your presence."

I would like to have known how that bear of a man died, but I was saving the big guns for last. Questions like that were fraught with emotions, and I wasn't skilled at dealing with them.

It was far easier to calculate that if our grandfather had died only two months ago, an estate the size of his couldn't have been *legally* disposed of without notifying his descendants.

Mallard looked as if he might expire at any moment. Unable to perform such unbutlerish acts as screaming or stamping his foot, he tugged on his stiff collar and turned purple during the ensuing silence.

I ran my finger over the eighteenth-century drop-leaf hall table and nodded approval at the lack of dust. As if I owned the place—which I was quite certain we should since I'd done the research and knew my grandfather had no other family—I swept into the Victorian parlor to inspect further. It hadn't changed an iota. It still smelled of must, my grandfather's hair pomade, and stale cigars. I'd never been homesick a day in my life, but I felt the tug of nostalgia now.

"I purchased the house from the estate the day it appeared on the market," the cold voice informed us through the speaker in the hall. "I suggest you depart the premises and invade Brashton's territory if you require explanations."

I raised my eyebrows at Mallard, who tugged even harder at his collar. "The executor," he whispered.

"You won't find him," EG said. Apparently having overcome her earlier fear now that she could see we wouldn't be met with armed Nazis, she dropped onto the plush horsehair sofa, causing an explosion of dust in the fading sunlight seeping past the maroon velvet draperies.

Alarmed by EG's warning since she seemed to be batting a thousand, I stuck out my hand to Nicholas. Understanding my gesture, Nick handed over his cell phone. Avoiding contact with my family meant I'd never seen the purpose in owning any additional means of privacy invasion — like cell phones. Besides, I never went anywhere to need one.

"The full name of the firm?" I asked of the air.

The disembodied voice ignored me. The owner was no doubt calling security or the cops. I disliked dealing with authority, but I'd done it enough times to know how, so I wasn't particularly scared. I was simply trying to tamp down the swirl of memories and anxieties and the overpowering longing not to be ejected from this house that I *knew* was meant to be ours.

Ever efficient, Mallard produced a business card from a file in the hall table drawer. If I hadn't grown up in a series of strange situations, this disastrous conclusion to our journey might have alarmed me. But living with my chameleon mother all these years had taught me that all is not as it seemed, which developed my healthy sense of curiosity.

Even dysfunctional childhoods could be useful.

Settling into a high-backed wing chair by the window, I pulled on a drapery cord to let in daylight. I didn't mind basements, but this room was suffocating with all the heavy velvet and horsehair. The furniture was huge and overpowering. Two of me could fit into the chair.

As if I had all the time in the world, I regally punched in the telephone number on the card and worked my way through the phone tree until I had the extension for one Reginald Brashton the Third. A secretary answered. I gave my name and grandfather's and asked for the executor of his estate. An awkward silence followed.

For the first time in my life, I disliked silence.

After putting me on hold, she returned. "Let me put you through to Mr. Johnson."

I assumed she'd made a frantic call while she had me on hold. This couldn't be good. EG's bored expression said she knew it wasn't good, but she'd bide her time while I proved it. She'd discovered a shelf of ancient tomes by the mantel, so she was making a good show of not caring if I made an idiot of myself.

Nicholas wasn't in sight. Neither was Mallard. Presumably, he'd followed Nick to protect the silver.

"Blackwell Johnson," a frosty baritone said into my ear. "May I help you?"

I repeated the routine in my best virtual assistant voice. I didn't often have to use telephones, but I knew the clipped tones that commanded respect. Having lived around the world, I had no regional accent to label me, and business-like sentences worked better for me than my mother's purring flattery. Granted, she could squeeze papaya juice out of barnacles with her charm, but it also came accompanied by voluptuous curves, Slavic cheekbones, and slanted, long-lashed eyes that promised naughty sex.

I might have the cheekbones and the eyes, but seduction had never been my style. I had long ago decided I wanted respect for who I am and not what I look like. Darned good thing since I looked like a twelve-year-old shrimp.

The baritone on the other end of the line cleared his throat. "Ah, Miss Devlin. We have been unable to reach you. Or any of your family. It's only recently been ascertained that Reginald had not yet notified you."

I waited. I could hear the nervousness in his voice. This wasn't going to be pretty, but it might be entertaining. He knew who I was. After years of anonymity, recognition was almost pleasing.

I was still struggling with the concept that Grandfather had died. I mourned the loss of the mustached figure in my memory. He couldn't have been much more than seventy. Why hadn't I come here sooner? Look at how much I had wasted, how much I might have learned, had I pulled myself out of my self-centered world. And now it was too late. What else had I lost while hiding?

Rationally, I knew why I hadn't come here, and that Grandfather was more guilty than I in the avoidance department, but that didn't alleviate the pall of sorrow and raw guilt.

"Could you please tell me how my grandfather died?" I asked, surprising even myself.

"A debilitating illness. He had been incapacitated for some time. I believe there were several factors, including heart failure." The lawyer tried to sound soothing and sympathetic, but he failed utterly. He was hiding something. I was certainly in a position to recognize avoidance when I heard it.

The very real possibility that my grandfather had left his estate to the King of Mulgravia or Catholic charities or some such had occurred to me the instant I'd heard of his demise. As much as my instincts told me that this house ought to be ours, I didn't intend to torment myself with it until I had the facts. But I wanted the facts, *now*. Blackwell Johnson had said he'd been looking for us. It must be for a reason, and I was frantically praying the house was it.

"We will need your credentials, of course," the attorney stalled.

"My mother is Magda Maximillian Devlin Bullfinch Hostetter..."

EG produced an address book from her backpack, and I read the list of my mother's various married names with aplomb, concluding with "the only child of Rathbone Maximillian and owner of this house where I'm standing. I can produce a birth certificate and passport, of course, but at the moment I am in the awkward position of defending my right to stay in my grandfather's home. I wish to know at once why his direct descendants weren't notified as required by law and how the estate could be sold without our knowledge."

Johnson cleared his throat again, but before he could speak, the disembodied voice intervened—this time from a black marble lamp near the chair where I was sitting. "It seems we have a problem." The intruder's phrasing expressed no emotion, but his tone possessed a sumptuous male wrath that appealed to the female fury in me.

I glared at the lamp and waited for the lawyer to spit it out.

"It seems we have a problem, Miss Devlin," echoed from the cell phone. I rolled my eyes. EG waited expectantly. Even Nicholas returned, sipping from an eggshell china cup imprinted with royal purple and gold, his pinkie finger delicately extended. Mallard followed with a silver tea tray of goodies.

We'd found our natural habitat—a mansion with a butler to take care of us and antiques to pawn.

"It seems the estate's executor cannot be found," said the attorney, "and we cannot locate his files for the Maximillian property."

"I paid cash for the house, free and clear," the lamp intoned ominously, as if he could hear every word said.

Cash? For a house like this? Furnished? Bullhockey.

"Under contract law, a purchase made in good faith is valid, and it is up to the wronged party to prosecute the criminal and recover the stolen proceeds," the lamp recited.

I remembered that from an on-line contract law class I'd taken when establishing my business. That didn't mean I had to believe it. I can be an optimist when it serves my interest.

"My grandfather's executor sold the house without our permission?" I inquired, trying to sort out their wildly conflicting statements.

While I waited for explanation, I idly toted up the sum of the antiques in the parlor. I was certain they were the same ones that had been there in my childhood. Why would anyone move into a mansion like this and not bring their own furniture?

I calculated the furnishings alone would pay for a nice snug cottage in a small town in Georgia. I might know antiques, but I couldn't hazard a guess as to how much an entire mansion in D.C. might command.

More throat clearing on the other end of the line. I waited. "According to the bank, the Maximillian estate has been cleared from the books and the moneys disbursed," Mr. Johnson finally admitted.

"*Disbursed?*" The Catholics win again? Or maybe Grandfather was generous and left it all to the homeless. That ought to include me. And just about all of his grandchildren. I sure hadn't seen a check.

"Possibly inappropriately disbursed," Johnson murmured apologetically. "We cannot determine."

Chapter Three

A deal is struck and an assignment is given.

THE LAMP remained funereally silent, perhaps in respect for the massive blow I'd just taken. We may have inherited millions but it was all gone? In two months? *Gone?*

An earthquake couldn't have been more shattering. I knew. I'd survived one.

After verifying with the attorney that the children of Magda Maximillian—not Magda herself—appeared to be sole heirs to the estate, I made an appointment to speak with Blackwell Johnson in person the next day. I handed the cell phone back to Nick, trying not to shake too hard. I stared at the faces watching me expectantly.

I was too devastated to even want to kick something. Probably because the only thing in the room deserving a kick was me.

I'd learned to deal with disappointment in my life. It's no big deal. You dust yourself off and move on. I'd done it dozens of times—on my own. I'd never had the hopes and dreams of someone else depending on me. I watched the curiosity die out of EG's eyes and the anticipation fade from Nick's lips, and I knew why Magda kept deserting us. She couldn't handle the responsibility for all our lives and futures. She could barely handle her own.

But I had spent a lifetime proving I wasn't my mother. Reginald Brashton the Third, lawyer thief, would be mud beneath my feet shortly. And I would take extraordinary pleasure in rubbing his face in it.

I spoke to the lamp. "Mr. Graham, might I have a moment of your time?" I had learned his name from the lawyer: Amadeus Graham. At least he was a real human being and not a computer ensconced in the attic somewhere.

"No," the voice replied curtly. "The house is legally mine, and I wish you to leave."

He might be right, but I didn't want to argue the point until better armed. Besides, we had nowhere to go. My instinct for survival insisted that possession was nine-tenths of the law, and commandeering other people's houses was what our upbringing had taught us.

"I need access to a computer," I replied calmly. Never let them see your fear. It was surprisingly easier to talk to a marble lamp than a real human being. "I can settle this matter quite amicably once I locate my grandfather's executor."

The lamp didn't reply.

EG and Nick watched me with fascination. We hadn't seen each other in a few years, and I'd never been prepossessing. My denim jumper and black cotton shirt hid any womanly attributes, and my feet barely reached the floor. Despite my thirty years, I dare say I looked like Barbie's wicked younger sister. They had every right to be doubtful.

"With the proper equipment, I can locate Mr. Brashton," I told EG and Nick as much as the dismissive Mr. Graham. "If I could set up my laptop here, I would be able to find him within a week."

"Absolutely not." The voice remained adamant. "This is a private home and not a hotel. You will leave at once."

He sounded formidable enough to have bodyguards descending on us. I tried to keep a stiff upper lip instead of shivering in my sandals. At least he couldn't see me, and I could sound bigger than I am.

"I am an excellent research analyst," I insisted. "If we are forced to leave here, I will find a library computer and research the legality of the deed to this house and the owner's suspect acquisition of an estate meant to support homeless children." I could also exaggerate on a moment's notice.

I had no idea which statement stirred our host's interest. I simply knew I achieved the result I intended. No bodyguards heaved us out.

"You are skilled at computer research?" the lamp base asked. I could hear the doubt and wondered if he had a camera in the ceiling.

"I have credentials from the Association of Virtual Assistants and references from numerous clients," I agreed. "Have you need of a skilled assistant?"

Thunderous silence. I could almost hear lightning strike and clouds clash. I wanted to meet Mr. Graham. Any man who could create such evocative silences was my kind of person.

EG had gone wide-eyed. I could see her fighting hope, and my heart pinged. I would have this house and everything in it, now. For her. Although what she really needed was a father.

It must be hell to be a real mother.

"I need quiet in which to conduct my research," he intoned ominously, although I thought I detected curiosity behind his Wizard of Oz act.

I tried to picture the mysterious Mr. Graham, but I could see only my grandfather's face in here. I had no recollection of how my grandfather amassed his fortune, but I'd seen enough mansions and rich old men to picture his replacement. And judging by some of my clientele, if this old man needed a research assistant, he was probably a fusty antiquarian hunkered down in his rotting library, scribbling away with a quill pen at some obscure theory on the origin of *Culicidae* and their correlation with the plagues referred to in *Exodus*, Chapter Eight. Or if he's into prophesy, maybe even *Revelations*. I was liking my creative image already.

Or he could be like my missing corporate client and want me to research textbook publishers and media conglomerates. Boring, but more lucrative than the professorial types.

"We are an extremely quiet family," I responded. Not that I had a clue if Nick and EG had learned to stifle their dramatic tendencies. "I insist on order while I am working," I added for good measure.

It wasn't that I was adept at lying. It's just that I'd changed my persona so often that almost everything was the truth, in the past or the future. I was sure we could be quiet and organized if we wished.

"Give me references," he demanded.

That's always a bit tricky since many of my clients preferred their privacy, and I knew them only by their e-mail addresses. But I had several who had agreed I could use their names. I gave them to the lamp base and held my breath.

I would have turned purple if I hadn't let it out again. The lamp didn't immediately respond. EG, Nick, and I stared at each other wordlessly in the subsequent silence.

"Your credentials are impeccable." Returned to mechanical mode—even if it did sound a trifle grudging—the voice intruded on our tense thoughts some minutes later.

He had a computer—and wielded a communication network to rival mine. Interesting.

"I have several research tasks you might perform in return for the use of the first floor for the next week while you pursue estate matters," he continued with a tone of snide arrogance that raised my hackles. "If you cannot accomplish them, you will have to leave."

"And if I accomplish them, may we stay longer if it's necessary?"

"That's unlikely. Do not disturb me for any reason."

I don't think the speaker system actually clicked off, but it might as well have. The sound went dead, and I knew he wasn't listening. Did he mean it was unlikely that I'd accomplish his tasks? Or that he'd let us stay? Or both? I didn't see him as the nice old antiquarian anymore.

Nick grinned in relief. EG looked suspicious, but she looked suspicious on a good day. I swallowed my anxiety and assumed an attitude of assurance.

"We'll need to send for our luggage," I told them. "I'll look for a place to set up my laptop until the Dell arrives. Nick, check out the bedrooms. Mallard, are there linens or do we need to provide them?"

I was more comfortable with crisp authority than sentimental claptrap. My brain had served me far better than my heart all these years. I refused to show relief. This was my house. I just had to prove it. Once I had Reginald Brashton nailed to a wall and the intruder in the attic on the run, I would have time to find out if Senator Tex had been messing around with his aides.

Researching the good senator's peccadilloes wasn't just a cynical penchant of mine. He was, after all, still married to another woman when he and my mother created EG—which is why he never acknowledged her existence except with a monthly check from some company he owned.

Tex was a real rounder, and the aide he was suspected of murdering was female. Had he decided to cover up the hanky-panky with homicide this time?

* * *

A week. A blooming week in which to locate a sneaky, conniving, larcenous lawyer with millions at his fingertips. This was Tuesday.

Nick retrieved our belongings from the bus station, and I had my laptop, but I was too overwhelmed to do more than stare at it as night settled in.

Had our host cared to inspect the rest of his newly acquired home, he might have noticed that the only bedroom on the first floor had been converted from a large front salon. It contained a towering carved headboard and ancient mattress our grandfather had apparently used after he lost the ability to climb the stairs. None of us was prepared to take the bed he might have died in.

There was a small suite off the basement kitchen that Mallard occupied. After EG commented on the lovely quaintness of his quarters, Mallard had been so kind as to inform us that the elusive Mr. Graham lived alone and never left the third floor. Not inhibited, we immediately hied ourselves to the second story family floor and spread out. It was only going to waste as it was.

EG latched onto a hexagonal room in the turret at the far end of the main corridor. Robin's egg blue with fireplace, bookshelves, and twin beds, it might have been a cozy nest for a child at one time. If we regained ownership, I suspected the room would be painted black and decorated in early Gothic. If this house could really be ours, I would happily buy a stuffed bat to begin the transformation.

Nick moved into what had obviously been a lady's suite with a graceful poster bed, gleaming Queen Anne highboy—the colonial hand-carved original and not a copy—and a lovely old Chinese silk carpet in rose and sage. Any antique dealer in his right mind would trade his entire stock for the contents of that room alone. Nicholas had exquisite taste.

I was of a more practical nature. I hunted down a room with updated wiring and a telephone. I could set up my main office in the library downstairs, where I wouldn't disturb our landlord during the day, but I didn't sleep much. I needed my laptop accessible at night.

I assumed the room I chose was once my grandfather's office. It had a huge federal-style desk in front of a window overlooking the street, floor-to-ceiling bookshelves along one wall, and navy leather wing chairs in front of a fireplace framed in hand-painted Delft tile. And blessedly—it had an Aeron chair I could adjust to my size. I scavenged through the other rooms until I found a daybed that Nick and I could move. My suitcase and some empty oak file drawers would suffice as dresser. I didn't want to usurp an entire suite in a house that wasn't mine. Yet.

Cat hair littering an upholstered velveteen chair had me sneezing, so I had that hauled out. I hoped the cat had preceded my grandfather into death. I was allergic to the things.

Setting up my laptop on that wide old desk, looking out on the streetlight-lit night outside as my grandfather had no doubt done for decades, I settled in as if I had come home.

Since I'd never really known a home, I shook off the sentiment, flipped on my computer, and checked the telephone access. To my surprise and delight, my wireless icon lit up. Graham had installed a sophisticated system that recognized my computer's network with ease. And he apparently meant for me to use it since it required no password. Technology is my friend. I immediately set up firewalls and passwords.

Next, I logged on and scanned the day's news stories to be certain Senator Hammond hadn't been arrested. Mindy Carstairs was the name of the murdered aide. From all reports, she was an upright citizen, a divorcee with a history major and wealthy parents who'd contributed to Tex's campaign fund. Business as usual. Her body was found in a Dumpster near Tex's office after her disappearance at the beginning of August. Rumors of Tex's philandering ways were mentioned, but if moral turpitude could indict a U.S. Senator, Congress would be operating on half-staff all the time. Hammond seemed safe enough for now.

I began my basic research into Brashton's whereabouts—following the money. Swiss bank accounts were passé. The Swiss had been berated so ruthlessly for their stupidity in hiding Nazi funds that they'd tightened regulations. The same couldn't be said of Third World countries like the islands scattered across the Caribbean. My bet was on the islands. Lawyers aren't known for their originality. It took time to determine which islands allowed secret accounts.

By the time my eyelids grew heavy and I was prepared to try out the elegant silk daybed, I'd located Brashton's social security number and accessed his curriculum vitae, not to mention his credit records. Brashton had left town owing the Earth and probably a few planets.

Our grandfather had apparently done business with the Brashton, Johnson, and Terwilliger firm since the beginning of time. My nemesis— young Reginald the Third— had only recently acquired access to the

Maximillian account after a decade of working in his father's office, and then only after Brashton Junior's death. That fact spoke volumes to a cynical mind like mine. Grandfather had been isolated by the death of his trusted friend and his own illness, leaving him ripe for picking by avaricious scum. I should have been there for him.

Before I shut down, an instant message popped on my screen from one *Oracle*. "Do you find the system satisfactory for your needs? Graham."

Oracle? I stared at Graham's screen name in disbelief and a modicum of fright. I knew the word from Greek myth and comic books. It also happened to be the screen name of the client whose e-mail had started bouncing several months ago, after leaving me with that cryptic memo about poison and top hats.

I *hate* coincidences.

With a degree of trepidation, I hit the menu to find Oracle's e-mail address. Screen names are simply the monikers that people assign themselves for use by their friends in instant messaging. They are easily duplicated. The country was rife with teenage boys calling themselves *Sprmn* and *Spidey*.

E-mail addresses are specific to the person, just like a snail mail address. Graham's e-mail address belonged to one AG911 through the local telephone company network—a very basic, non-suspicious address for a man named Amadeus Graham. It bore no resemblance to my former client's address. Our landlord just had a comic book mentality, or given my assumption of his antiquated age, he may even have read Greek myth.

I saved his screen name and e-mail address and typed, "Adequate, thank you."

The network was far more than adequate. Tonight I'd accessed mainframes that any normal DSL line would have crashed into. With a little work, I could usually wiggle into almost any computer, but he had direct access. I suspected a government satellite hook-up. Fascinating. And probably illegal.

No point in letting him know I knew that though. I liked to keep my talents to myself. Catching people off guard is an excellent form of self-defense. I had to wonder why he'd decided to let me research when he had such technology at his fingertips, but I wasn't arguing with him.

I switched the computer off and completely disconnected it. I didn't need my client files accessed by a computer spook.

I fell asleep that night and dreamed of burning stakes, villainous laughter, and an oracle who handed me a stone Palm Pilot through a thunder cloud.

I wished I knew what the message was on that stone screen, but hieroglyphics weren't my specialty.

* * *

"School starts next week," Nicholas commented from behind the folds of the morning newspaper.

Mallard had set the formal dining table with china made in Poland prior to World War I. I admired the hand-painted gilding on cobalt blue, and checked the maker's mark on the bottom of my teacup before filling it with an exquisite keemun steaming in the Sevres teapot.

One of the benefits of living Magda's charmed life was that we're quite comfortable in palaces of splendor. One of the drawbacks was that we all had champagne tastes and beer pocketbooks.

"I don't need school," EG muttered through a mouthful of toast slathered with a private label gooseberry jam. Apparently believing that simple statement sufficient to end the subject, she didn't emerge from behind the heavy leather-bound volume in which she'd buried her nose.

"You have to have a degree before anyone will hire you." I corrected her assumption. "Even if Grandfather left us money and I locate it, it will be divided so many ways that you'll still have to work for a living."

Nicholas lifted a skeptical eyebrow but didn't question aloud. Unlike EG, Nick knew the value of our surroundings. It gave one reason to question the source of our landlord's wealth if he paid cash for all this, but that wasn't a subject to be discussed while under his roof.

"I came here to help my father," EG stated with surliness from behind her book.

"You won't help him by being uneducated." I had strong feelings on the subject, for good reason.

"How did your search go last night?" Nick inquired to divert us before war could break out. He's the family peacemaker. "Found Brashton yet?"

"I only had time to lay the groundwork. I'll begin the real digging today."

"Not immediately, Miss Devlin," intoned the silver candelabra in the center of the table.

Well, now I knew why we were eating in this echo chamber instead of the sunny little breakfast room.

"You have an assignment for me, Mr. Graham?" I could have ranted about invasion of privacy or any number of topics on the tip of my tongue, but I chose to start the day in civility.

"I've taken the liberty of installing a new system in the library," the ornamental base intoned. "Yours will be inadequate to the task. You'll find the particulars on the desk."

Again, that silent click indicating the voice had switched off. I glared at the candelabra and debated remaining where I was and consuming the delicious breakfast Mallard had so thoughtfully provided, but curiosity is my besetting sin. He'd provided a computer system overnight? Did the good fairies live here? Or had we entered the Twilight Zone?

As if awaiting a signal from me, EG and Nick both stood up and followed me out. For all we knew, the Mysterious Graham could be running an international smuggling ring, and my assignment could be to locate the next ship carrying gold from Liberia.

I wasn't entirely certain I'd turn it down if it meant leaving this house.

I sighed in awe at the monster dual screen LCD monitor set on the library table at a height ideal for my petite stature. The cost of one of those babies could pay the first semester of EG's college education.

The monitor frame was a translucent cobalt and a thing of beauty. The ergonomic keyboard with glittering blue function keys, some of which even I couldn't identify, was so perfectly matched to my hand span that I wanted to adopt it, give it a name, and a lap pillow.

Had I thought all this had been provided specially just to suit me, I would have kissed Amadeus Graham. But Magda is the one who falls for the shiny gewgaw trick. Not me.

There were no paper files on the table. I clicked the keyboard and the system flickered to life in full Technicolor and Surround Sound.

A financial statement on a firm called Edu-Pub opened with the click of a wireless mouse. I frowned at the accounting babble, closed the document, and opened the next.

The picture of a slightly Oriental male frowned back at me. Thin dark hair, round face, round eyes instead of slanted, and a small goatee, he could have been anyone from a prince to a pauper.

Beneath the photo was the caption "Sak Thai Pao, employee, Edu-Pub."

The instant message appearing in front of the photo read "Find him."

Chapter Four

Researching a thief and toying with a lawyer

I DIDN'T much care if Pao was a terrorist or the next Messiah. I didn't care if Graham wanted to laud or assassinate him. I simply needed to stay in this house until I located the thief who had stolen our inheritance. And I wanted to start immediately.

"What about my dad?" EG demanded. "How will you help him if you're looking for this guy and the thief, too?"

"Tex has lawyers. He's not in jail," I answered without much enthusiasm. Tex had never been one of my favorite people. "I'll see what I can find out from the police files. Right now, we need to think about getting you into school." I hit Google and input Pao's name.

Typing away at the keyboard, I didn't look over my shoulder at the lack of a smart reply. I doubted that Magda had ever sent EG to a real school. The kid was probably terrified. "Nick, if we're staying, can you handle enrolling EG?"

"Piece of cake," he said with a verbal shrug, "after I catch up to her to wring the name of her last school out of her."

I glanced up. EG had apparently disappeared at the first mention of school. I was amazed the curtains weren't billowing from her rush to escape. "Threaten to keep her from books until she spills," I suggested.

"I'm thinking she'll be off to her father if we do," he pointed out, logically enough.

"I'm thinking Tex has enough trouble, and he'll bounce her out on her head if she tries." Which was the reality of our vagabond life. We were intruders anywhere we went.

"Don't go looking at me for the official father figure of the family," Nick warned, "We're mixed up enough as it is."

"You're telling me?" I asked in agreement, before calling up search engines. Nick was the closest thing to a best friend I'd ever had, but I'd forgotten his existence—and our family angst—by the time he stalked out.

Pao either had a lot of cousins or he was an extremely well known man. I found three thousand five hundred forty-eight references to the name on my favorite search engines—most of the references were in languages that didn't use the English alphabet. After all the years of travel, I was a pretty good linguist with the spoken word, but I didn't know the Arabic alphabet. I could read enough Indo-European languages to grasp whether most sites were relevant, but these were hieroglyphics to me. Now I knew what my dream was telling me.

None of the references mentioned Edu-Pub. Very interesting. I dug deeper and decided to follow the largest path which seemed to nail him as a Cambodian theologist. Yeah, right.

I soon learned that Cambodians speak nineteen different languages, the most common called Central Khmer, with a smattering of Mandarin and other combinations that I couldn't translate. The country was predominantly Buddhist and Muslim. I e-mailed requests to my various identity networks in search of visas, driver licenses, birth certificates, and the assorted accoutrements of modern living, then worked my way through any English-speaking sites on the search list. Anyone who has ever seen the asininity that Google can turn up in a search will appreciate my patience.

I found nothing useful under the English language sites and began on the Edu-Pub angle. I reached a dead-end immediately. Their website was specious. It didn't exist in any public corporate forum that I could immediately determine, but I had their financial statement. I sent a copy to another VA who worked with an accountant and asked for a translation.

While I waited for a reply from my Cambodian contacts, I started hunting for my favorite shyster. My appointment with Reginald the Thief's partner wasn't until later that afternoon, but I wasn't wasting any time.

Given that the payments on Reginald's brand new Mercedes were four months past due and his mortgage company was threatening foreclosure, I was pretty certain I wasn't the only one hot on his trail. I also uncovered two convictions for possession of drugs and an outstanding warrant for the sale of illegal substances. My guess was that Papa Reginald had bought Reginald the Lesser out of jail the first two times, but daddy—my grandfather's attorney—had bitten the dust by the time of The Lesser's third arrest. It looked like Reggie's wife filed for divorce after the first conviction. Who in their right senses would name their daughter Araminta? The name gave me visions of a horse-faced woman in pearls. Old money. Had Reggie run through it all?

While I was poking around, I checked on Tex to be certain nothing new had turned up overnight. The D.C. cops moved at a snail's pace. According to the news reports, the murder victim's fingerprints had been found in the senator's library. Go figure. The woman had *worked* for Tex. Did the cops think she wore gloves? One witty reporter thought it important that Ms. Carstairs had been wearing Manolo Blahniks when her body was discovered. Just because her shoes cost as much as two weeks' salary didn't mean she'd paid for them with blackmail proceeds or that Tex had bought them for her. Working women knew where to find bargains.

My bet was on Ms. Carstairs' ex-husband, but the only mention of him was that he'd been verifiably out of town at the time of her death.

Grumbling at the media's lack of imagination, I returned to Brashton the Thief and worked through the better part of the afternoon. I was in the middle of rifling through his mortgage company's on-line files when the front door banged open with a crash that rattled the porcelain on the mantel.

I could hear EG screaming at Nick all the way down the hall. This was not the way to make our landlord happy.

"They want to put me in fourth grade!" EG shouted, flopping on the worn brown leather sofa after flinging open the library door with a crash that probably left a hole in the paneling.

"That's what you get for not studying," I muttered, scanning the mortgage file before someone realized it was open.

"That's what she gets for not having any school records." Nick sauntered in carrying a cup of Starbucks. "If you're really good on that thing, you'll locate her medical records. They won't let her in at all without proof she's had her rabies shot."

"Vaccinations," EG corrected scornfully. "And I can tell you where to find them. But I won't."

"Then I'll make some up and you'll go to fourth grade. Now go away and let me work." I was starting to remember why I'd run away from my family. It's hard to concentrate when Masterpiece Theater is playing in your front room.

"I'll run away again!" EG shouted, leaping up and heading toward the library door. "If you won't help my dad, I don't have to stay here and be treated like a moronic baby."

"That's how you get treated if you behave like one," Nicholas hollered down the hall after her, although the clatter of EG's shoes on the stairs probably drowned him out.

Anxious about hanging onto the roof over our heads, I could almost hear the disapproval emanating from a lamp base. Grandfather's downstairs desk chair was too large for me, but most things were. I sat back and waited, holding my breath. Sure enough, our landlord's dry voice broke the silence following EG's flight.

"I could arrange to have her sent to school in Taiwan if that will ensure peace."

As I feared, we'd awakened the sleeping tiger. Signing off on the useless mortgage file, I tried to think of something pacifying to say. "Thank you for the offer," was the best I could do under the circumstances, and even it sounded sarcastic. Which it was. "I'll locate her records and see that she doesn't create any further outbursts."

"Taiwan might be easier." The voice issued from a sleek console on the table—a genuine intercom. "But you won't be here next week, so it's no concern of mine."

A light went out on the intercom's switchboard. I studied the buttons but couldn't determine if it worked both ways. No point in stirring the old hornet by testing it.

"We will not be out of here," I murmured under my breath as I went after Magda's little brat. "That third floor is going to be *mine*."

The door to EG's room was locked. She'd chosen the only room in the whole house with a key in the door.

"Use my laptop to locate your school records," I told her through the oak panel. "If you can do that, I might consider an alternative school." Not that I had a clue how to find any school, but as I've said, I have a soft spot for EG. She really did belong in high school.

Angry silence was the only response. Shrugging, I returned downstairs. I'd given her a choice. If she didn't want to take it, that was her problem. I might be as close as our family came to normal, but no one ever said I was maternal.

I found Nicholas ensconced on an elegant gold damask sofa in front of the maroon draperies in the parlor, knees crossed and polished shoe bouncing, sipping his Starbucks while perusing a real estate magazine. A copy of *Playgirl* was on the coffee table in front of him.

"You've been a busy lad." I picked up another of the real estate magazines he'd strewn across the neatly arranged *Architectural Digests* on the coffee table. "I think we need to hire a lawyer to sue the lawyers."

"I'm not without resources. I'll make a few phone calls." Nick's professionally shaped eyebrows rose to his hairline as he perused a page. "Here's a house just down the street. You don't even want to know what they're asking for these urban monstrosities. I say we go straight to the attorney general's office and file a complaint against the spider in the attic."

"This is D.C., Magda's home ground. She probably *dated* the attorney general. Just ask around for a good lawyer, preferably one who moved here after she left. We'll know better what to do after we talk to the incompetents who let Reginald the Thief sell our inheritance."

He studied my baggy black capris with disapproval. "Not wearing those, I trust?"

"Of course not." I didn't give him a chance to question further. I worked at home. Career dressing wasn't part of my expense budget. "I've told EG to find her school records. Are you still planning on hanging around until I can finish this job? I could use some back-up."

"You could use a life, a wardrobe, and a haircut, not necessarily in that order," he said, looking me up and down with a superior air intended to make me crawl into a hole.

I was aware that I did not meet my elegant brother's sartorial standards, but then, I didn't need his approval. I was the self-supporting one around here. "I asked only because I can find our money faster if you can keep an eye on EG and help me poke around on Tex. If not, I can probably call on Patra." Even our mother had refrained from naming her third oldest child after the Queen of the Nile, but the shortened form was bad enough.

"Patra's in Greece and I'm here." Nicholas returned to his magazine. "Go get dressed. I can't wait to hear what you'll do to Blackwell Old Boy."

Reassured, I swung around and nearly bounced off Mallard's boiled shirtfront. Or did he have a plaster mold beneath that old-fashioned cutaway? I rubbed my nose and backed up.

With a tsk of disapproval, he removed the real estate brochures from the artistic display of glossy magazines. He poked the *Playgirl* with distaste as if he couldn't bear to touch it. "We do not serve refreshments in the formal parlor," he intoned, eyeing Nick's foam coffee cup.

Nick didn't glance up from his magazine. "That's all right, old fellow. I served myself."

I escaped before learning the outcome of that fray. I was in terror of being thrown out on our ears, but teaching my egocentric family to behave wasn't happening in this millennium.

In honor of the occasion, I donned my denim jumper and a black T-shirt—the most fashionable attire in my wardrobe. Since Nick disapproved of my plain braid, I wrapped it in a more formal fashion at the back of my head. I never wore cosmetics, but I have naturally long lashes and red lips. Why waste money on emphasizing looks when it's my brains I want recognized? I know, my therapists had a word or two to say about my denial of my mother's genes, but therapists have weird fixations.

I tried to sneak down the front stairs and out the door with no one noticing. Of course, Nicholas and EG both popped out from across the hall, and Mallard arrived to open the door.

"Just as I thought." Nicholas sighed and rolled his eyes. "Mallard, keep an eye on the brat for us, will you? We have a meeting with Maximillian's attorneys, and I believe I need to add the necessary *savoir faire*."

Clapping on an English style straw hat with turned down brim, he offered his arm to me. "You either go with me so you look as if you have a keeper, or you wear something respectable."

"Oh, and I'm sure you'll impress them," I mocked in retaliation. "Lawyers *so* listen to clients in pink ascots, especially when they perfectly match your pink suspenders."

"Braces," he replied in his best plummy British accent. "There's a dear now, out you go. Cheerio, Mallard! Don't let our little pet plunge into any rabbit holes while we're gone."

The weird thing is, Nick can pull this off without anyone blinking an eyelash, as if tall handsome Brits go about with diminutive dorks on their arms all the time. Life is so unfair. He's younger, dumber, and far less respectable than I am, but he's the one everyone treats with approval.

I pulled my arm away as he opened the taxi door. "I've been managing on my own for a decade," I reminded him.

"Righto, and you do it so well." He shoved me into the back seat and climbed into the front to check out the gorgeous Greek driver.

Deciding to treat Nick as a younger, obnoxious sister, I crossed my arms and didn't speak a word until we arrived at the impressive brick offices of Brashton, Johnson, and Terwilliger. I wasn't sure Nick noticed my silence. He and the taxi driver were having a voluble dialogue on the nightlife in Adams-Morgan compared to that of DuPont Circle. Nick was far more cosmopolitan than I, and it sounded as if he'd found his niche in the city already.

"Did you have time to make any phone calls while I dressed?" I demanded as we hit the sidewalk in front of the elegant Georgetown office, and I paid for the cab.

"I did." He pushed open the faux wood door with the fake brass knocker that let us into the lobby. "I have the name of an attorney that should make these farts sweat," Nick murmured as we approached the receptionist. "Not that I've been able to reach him, mind you."

"I'll reach him." I memorized the name of the law office scribbled on the scrap he handed me. I didn't recognize the attorney's name, which was good. I wanted a counsel completely independent of the Maximillian family—unlike this firm of Amberzombie and Twitch.

The haughty receptionist led us down a corridor of thick carpet, elegantly striped wallpaper, and closed doors. The place reeked of Establishment. Our guide had sized us up and kept her distance as if we were dog poop on her step.

"Mr. Johnson—Mr. Maximillian and Miss Devlin," she announced, opening one of the many closed doors.

I did mention that Magda didn't marry Nick's father, didn't I? Whether she intended it or not, he now bore our grandfather's last name for lack of any other.

Blackwell Johnson rose to greet us as we were ushered in. "I'm sorry we must meet under such sad circumstances. Your grandfather will be sorely missed."

"You were a friend of his?" I asked, keeping my eyes downcast as I sat in the Federal-blue, satin-upholstered chair he offered. I wouldn't mind an intelligent exchange of information about my grandfather, but instinct told me this man's knowledge was as false as his smile. And the corner of his eye twitched. I tried not to smirk at the aptness of my epithet for the firm.

Peering through lowered lashes, I studied Johnson. Fifties, I'd wager, portly from too much fine living. Artificially tanned. Styled silver hair. Botox to iron out wrinkles. His father was probably the original Johnson in the firm's name. Old money, expensive country club, no doubt lived across the river in Alexandria and never saw a city street closer than from the window of his limo. I didn't like him, so my decorous behavior was as false as he was.

"I met Rathbone several times," the attorney replied. "Eccentric upon occasion, but one of the old school. There should be more like him."

"Right. The world needs more men who ignore their offspring," I agreed pleasantly. "A matriarchal society has many advantages." If one's mother wasn't Magda, the Hungarian Diva.

Lounging beside me in an identical chair, Nick snickered. Except in math, he wasn't our family's brightest bulb, but he was smart enough to let me handle the show.

I got to the point. "Do you have a copy of our grandfather's will?"

"Right here." Johnson tapped a legal-sized envelope but didn't hand it over. "Various stocks to charity, the house, its contents, and substantial investments to the descendants of Magda Maximillian."

"Have you made any attempt to contact us?" I inquired dulcetly.

"I've only just begun." He sounded evasive, as well he should if he's sitting on a multi-million-dollar embezzlement suit. "I can find no permanent addresses for any of you."

"Then perhaps you have hired someone to locate Mr. Brashton?"

Even though I looked perfectly innocent with my hands folded in my denim lap and my feet barely touching the floor, Mr. Johnson was squirming in his seat. Guilt has that effect.

"We thought perhaps Reginald would contact us." He said this with a perfectly straight face, while tapping his pen nervously on his desk. "He was overdue for a vacation and requested several weeks off in July. It wasn't until he missed a court date that we realized he hadn't returned. It's quite possible he's met with a mishap and has been unavoidably detained."

A lawyer they didn't even miss. Our grandfather must have been seriously ill by the time Reggie Three took over his account. I couldn't picture Maximillian as the kind of man tolerant of imbeciles.

"When did he sell our house?" I asked, thinking as fast as I could.

Blackwell consulted his file. "The records show the estate was closed on July 10th."

"And Mr. Brashton left for vacation immediately afterward?"

He sat back in his chair and didn't consult his calendar.

"Approximately, I believe."

He knew where I was going with that, so I skipped to the good part. "You didn't realize your partner had a court date scheduled for July 11th for illegal sale of drugs, and that with a third conviction, he would have to do jail time and lose his license?"

Johnson almost ran his finger under his too-tight collar before diverting the gesture to smooth his tie. "I was unaware of that. I'm sure the charge is in error and will be cleared upon his return."

Right, and wild horses would fly. "What we would like to know is how your firm intends to deal with the disappearance of our funds," I responded in my most level voice, refraining from calling him liar. No anger here, nosirreebob. Just a purely casual question.

Johnson laughed and shot Nicholas one of those man-to-man looks. "The little lady doesn't mind saying what she thinks, does she? Refreshing."

Nick shot his cuffs, crossed his ankle over his knee, and leaned back in his chair, looking like the millionaire playboy he aspired to be. "The lady has been known to make bigger men than you cry. Chip off the old Maximillian block is our Ana."

I smiled, but I was looking down, and Johnson couldn't see my expression. Since the attorney obviously didn't think anyone in denim significant enough to demand an answer, I dropped a bombshell to end his complacency. "We thought it wise to engage a neutral party to discuss the liabilities and charges involved in embezzlement. I trust you and Mr. Oppenheimer can work together." I waited to see what the name of Nicholas's legal beagle would do.

Johnson's face fell four flights. So much for Botox. "Now, Miss Devlin, there is some possibility that..."

"We will have to read the will to understand the full extent of Grandfather's estate," I continued as if he hadn't spoken, "but the house and contents represent a staggeringly substantial sum. Grandfather had promised us the use of his home should we ever have need of it. And now this..." I couldn't put a name to the usurper without letting the imps of anger out of the cellar. I swept the envelope off the desk rather than mention Graham. "Someone else lives in the home Grandfather meant for us. Exactly how much money exchanged hands?"

Johnson harrumphed and fiddled with his pen. Nicholas and I waited. Silence has its own power.

"We don't know," he finally admitted. "The transaction was never recorded in the company's books. We are looking into it."

Oh, I could have a good time with that one. I love documents that begin with "Anastasia Devlin, party of the first part, hereby testifies..." and so forth.

Let Amadeus Graham try to throw us out. I'd slap him with a lawsuit so fast, his head would spin. Should he actually have a head to spin.

"But the deed and all transfers have been properly recorded," Johnson finished.

"How can that be?" I all but yelled as my little daydream exploded. "What about title searches and all the paperwork involved in real estate transfers? How can a crook claim our home?" I almost let my anguish show, and I hastily bit my tongue.

"Mr. Graham paid cash." Johnson's Botoxed eye twitched. "With no mortgage company involved, there was no need for more than a quitclaim deed signed by the executor. There is no question that Mr. Graham believed he was party to a fair market transaction which makes him the rightful owner under the law. The burden is on the victim of the theft, not an innocent party."

Yeah that advice and three bucks would buy a cup of Starbucks. I wasn't buying it. Nobody intending a legal transaction carries a few million in cash in his back pocket and settles for a quitclaim deed.

Show me the money, as they say in the movies.

Chapter Five

EG spies and Ana finds a butler and a mystery man or two

ILL FROM reading the online news stories about her father, EG poked around for a while on Ana's laptop, attempting to find the senator's address. She didn't often have access to a computer. Unlike her older half brother, Tudor, she didn't have an aptitude for breaking into the government-issued PCs that made up Magda's world, so she didn't have a lot of luck locating anything more than Tex's senate office.

She glared at a picture on the website of his ten-year-old legitimate daughter—*Eloise*—and slammed the laptop's lid. She needed a direction for her investigation.

She thought this whole set-up with the spook in the attic creepy. But Mallard wasn't what he seemed either, and her specialty was spying. Everyone thought she was weird because she knew things she shouldn't, but mostly, she knew them because she was very good at observation. And a cynic. Things almost always turned out for the worst, so it wasn't difficult to predict them.

Spying was an art form, and she'd learned from the experts. She wouldn't do anything so childish as to peer around corners. Ana used to hide in closets upon occasion, but then, Ana preferred living in the dark.

EG sauntered downstairs, located Mallard in the basement kitchen, and boldly walked in to inspect the refrigerator contents.

"Dinner will be at seven," he warned. "There are apples on the counter if you're hungry."

He wasn't doing anything more interesting than chopping onions. Closing the refrigerator door, EG started opening cabinets. The first one she opened hid a kitchen desk stuffed with bills. The electric bill still had her grandfather's name on it, she noticed, before Mallard nearly slammed her fingers closing the lid. The utilities had never been turned off, she'd wager. Magda had used that ploy before, to disguise their location.

As far as she could tell, Mallard wasn't hiding drugs or guns, but he shut the cabinets as fast as she opened them, so she couldn't study them for hiding places. She darted under his arm and grabbed crackers out of one he'd just closed before he could swing around and stop her.

Skipping out of reach, crackers in hand, she headed for the stairs to the front parlor. Mallard followed her up the stairs, grabbing the box from her grip. "We do not eat anywhere except the dining room."

"How about the kitchen?" she asked innocently while opening a closet door in the first floor foyer. Musty old winter coats greeted her with a stench of mothballs. She calculated the depth as the same as the stairs to the second floor. No hidden rooms here.

Just to make certain she wasn't missing anything, she shoved old wool out of her way and looked for a light switch. Mallard caught her shirt and tugged her out, slamming the door.

"Go to your room and play," he ordered stiffly.

EG flashed a wide grin of triumph. "Chess?"

"Certainly not. I have work to do."

Tough nut to crack, but she didn't give up easily. "Outside, then." She darted under his arm once more and ran for the back door. The CIA wouldn't approve her tactics, but there was more than one way to test a butler's mettle.

* * *

The house was ominously silent when Nick and I returned from the attorney's office. I was fond of silence, but silence in a house containing three people, one of them a capricious child who had earned the sobriquet of Evil Genius for good reason, incited my paranoia.

"Look to see if our bags are in the garbage," I muttered as Nicholas checked the front rooms and I aimed for the stairs.

"No signs of destruction on this floor," he called.

I knew he'd head down to the kitchen next. Men are bottomless pits. Although in Nick's case, he prefers tomato-basil ratatouille or some such concoction to burgers and fries.

EG's bedroom was open and empty. She'd dumped her clothes and books in the middle of the braided rug, apparently figuring it was easier to find them there—or that she'd have to pack them again shortly, which was a sad commentary on our lives. But she would never leave without her books, so she hadn't run to her father. Yet.

I found her in my bedroom-office, burning up my laptop keyboard. Now that I had Graham's Cobalt Whiz downstairs, I could move my aging Dell into her room when it arrived.

She was being entirely too obedient if she was actually doing as I'd told her. "Did you find your school records?" I asked.

EG cleared the screen before I reached the desk. Not a good sign. She pointed at the stack of paper on the printer. "There they are. All you have to do is notarize them and they'll pass. The medical ones don't need that much."

That EG had actually looked for her school records—or asked our geek brother Tudor to look for them—surprised hell out of me. I was about to question when the intercom intervened. "Miss Devlin, I trust you've located your missing funds and are prepared to move out."

Even deeply irritated, that voice had the mysterious ability to shiver my hormones into a mating dance. I was a sick, sick puppy if old men could turn me on like that.

I should have been collapsing in a puddle of weeping dismay at his admonition, except I knew my family well. I lifted an eyebrow in EG's direction. She looked guilty and called up one of my computer games. I didn't answer the intercom but waited expectantly.

"I might have made Mallard quit," she whispered when our landlord's sonorous silence spoke volumes. "I didn't mean to. He kept following me around, picking up everything I put down, and when he wouldn't let me get a snack from the kitchen—"

"She locked him out of the house so she could snoop through the kitchen," Graham's voice finished succinctly. "I like my dinner at regular hours. I cannot work my schedule around a change in routine."

I fixed EG with the evil eye I learned from my old ayah. She froze and awaited her fate.

"We will prepare your dinner and bring it up at seven as scheduled," I reassured the intercom. I glared at EG, who scooted from the chair and ran for Nicholas, our resident chef. "My sincere apologies for my sister's behavior. I assure you, she knows better. Once I find Mallard, I'll persuade him to return."

"I'm sure you can." Graham's voice was dry enough to reduce the Nile to sand. "You have a number of replies from your Asian friends. I congratulate you on the extensiveness of your network."

I couldn't tell if he was being sarcastic, but I *could* tell that he had been prying into the Cobalt Whiz. I had expected no less. Now that EG was gone, he spoke more freely. How did he know EG had left? Or was I imagining approval in his tone?

"Did you find anything useful in the translations?" The puzzle of Pao intrigued me. Of course, the more immediate puzzle of Amadeus Graham intrigued me more, but if he was prying in my computer, I couldn't very well snoop around looking him up.

"Sufficient to allow you to stay if you find Mallard." The intercom snapped into silence.

I needed to figure out how to work that intercom so I could disturb his complacency as he did mine. I had a mounting list of questions I'd like answered by Mr. Amadeus Graham—beginning with how he'd known this house was for sale and where he got the cash. If my calculations were correct, my grandfather died in mid-June. Graham had to have pulled together an enormous sum by early July for Reggie to have signed the deal and absconded.

But I wasn't ready to be thrown out for asking questions. I hate that homeless feeling.

I'd send Nick to look for the missing butler, except I couldn't cook and his Royal Heinousness expected dinner. I dashed down to the basement to find EG and Nick laughing in the kitchen. "Fix something for us as well as our lord and master while you're at it," I commanded as I entered.

Mallard's basement inner sanctum was quite impressive. The ceiling was low, but the cabinets were cherry at the top, with granite countertops below, over a pleasing blend of cherry and bleached maple—the kitchen probably cost more than the normal suburban ranch house.

And that wasn't including the stainless steel restaurant equipment. The stovetop alone could serve the entire New York City police department. Serious entertaining could be accomplished here. A pity Magda wasn't around.

"Salmon Florentine," Nick called, slicing a huge hunk of fish. "The freezer is enormous and packed to last out a war. Shall I send up some bruschetta to appease the hungry tiger?"

"Send the kid up with it. Maybe the tiger will bite off her head. I have to find Mallard or we'll all be out on our derrieres shortly."

"I'm not a servant..." EG started to protest. When we both glared at her, she got the message. "Check the Irish bar down the street. And I found my school records, didn't I? " She flounced out, her long black hair swinging down her back.

"Have you thought about sending her to charm school?" Nick called as I headed for the outside steps up to the yard.

I exited laughing. EG in charm school! I'd roll on the floor and kick my heels if I had time.

Not doubting EG's prediction, I took the kitchen door to explore the exterior possibilities of the house. The stairs from the basement emerged on a walled garden and small patio adorned with wrought iron furniture and a scattering of potted herbs. A suspicious pile of gray ash had grown cold in the center of the patio tiles.

The towering mansions on either side of the house shared a huge garden wall between yards. An ornamental cherry tree and a wisteria-covered pergola disguised the blank three-story brick wall across the back of the lot. I needed to check the next street to see what was behind it when I had a chance.

For now, I trailed down a pretty flagstone walk between our house and the one beside it, admiring the lattice of clematis and honeysuckle vine. Living in basements as I had, I'd never had a garden of my own, but I'd seen plenty over the years, and I always enjoyed them.

The various sections of historical D.C. are plotted on a hub-and-spoke design, if one ignores the major thoroughfares spiking the spokes. I simply followed the neighborhood street into the circle of businesses that congregated at the hub. It wasn't difficult to locate the bar. Or pub, as the sign called it. Even at this early hour the singing was raucous.

The painful rendition of "O Danny Boy" didn't halt at my entrance. Wednesday night, and they had the karaoke cranked up. If EG was right and Mallard was in here, I'd have to pour him out while he could still walk.

As I stood in the entrance, letting my eyes adjust to the dark paneled interior, silence fell like dominoes from table to table. Mallard's voice was quite clear over the last fading wail of folk song.

"I will not return until that evil child is gone," he declared loudly.

"Not evil child, evil genius," I said, approaching the table where Mallard held court. "Dealing with the precocious is difficult, I'll admit, but I thought you were man enough to handle her. She's only nine."

Ignoring my insult to his manhood, Mallard held his head of metal-gray hair high. "She set fire to my aprons and threatened to make a bonfire of the table linen," he protested with the proud indignation of two mugs of Guinness. "When I went out to extinguish the flames, she locked the door. I have never needed to carry keys in my own house."

"Our house," I corrected politely. "Grandfather left it to us. I daresay he expected you to continue looking after it for us after he was gone. Leaving would be a dereliction of duty."

Magda and my siblings had insulted enough servants over the years to start a colony on another planet. Once upon a time it had been my duty to deal with them. Some responded to monetary bribes. The better ones had pride and could be bought cheaply. I pegged Mallard as the proud type.

"I do not believe you are Mr. Maximillian's heirs," he replied. "He would not leave his precious possessions to heathens."

I crossed my hands in my skirt like a good penitent Catholic girl and dealt the fatal blow to his fantasy. "My name is Anastasia Devlin. Magda was eighteen years old and still living at home when she married my father and had me. Do you remember Brody Devlin? The diplomat?"

All eyes turned to Mallard, who seemed to wilt inside his starched collar. My father was once called the Mad Irishman. I won't go into his sanity, his politics, or the IRA—they're much too complex. Suffice it to say that any loyal Irish Catholic would lay down his life for Brody, if he wasn't already dead. Mad Irishmen don't lead long lives.

Maybe my father was the love of Magda's life, and she'd been searching for another like him ever since. If I were a romantic, I could believe this. Unfortunately, I wasn't.

"That evil child is no kin of his," Mallard complained, but he was standing up as he said it. If he was Irish, he was a Brody worshipper.

"True, but I'm here to testify that EG is Magda's daughter. And her son is currently preparing bruschetta and salmon in your kitchen."

"He's what?"

I'd never seen an old man move so fast. He held his alcohol well—like any good Irishman.

"Stay and have a brew, won't you?" one of Mallard's table companions called as the butler hastened away.

The day I lingered in a bar with a bunch of old—I squinted into the candlelight. The man lifting his mug in invitation wasn't old but a picture-perfect facsimile of Pierce Brosnan in his youth, except this man's black hair was curly, and he appeared a shade shorter. He still had the lovely bone structure and the crinkled-eye Irish smile that made women swoon.

I wasn't a virgin. And just because I was cynical and could defend myself didn't mean I had any masculine tendencies. I like a pretty man as much as any red-blooded woman. And this one was exceptionally pretty, with long lashes over cobalt blue eyes that would have been almost effeminate if it weren't for the broad shoulders and bulging biceps displayed beneath his silky knit pullover. I take it back, he was even better than the movie actor.

On my own, I might have considered his offer. But there wasn't any way I could afford to waste time on sex. And frankly, most men think I'm weird, so I figured this one had to be attracted to my father's name. Or Maximillian's millions.

"No, thank you," I answered politely. "Another time perhaps."

A rousing rendition of "Rose of Tralee" rang out as I fought the hindrance of my long denim skirt to catch up with Mallard. The pleasant baritone leading sounded very much like the movie star look-alike.

"I cannot promise to keep my sister in line." As an apology, that sucked, but I preferred the truth when available—made it easier to remember the lies. "She is exceedingly gifted, but I'm trying to help Mr. Graham. It's difficult to take care of both."

"Mr. Graham is not difficult," Mallard said stiffly. "He is a gentleman."

"Did Grandfather know him well?" Sucking up to servants often satisfies my curiosity.

"Mr. Maximillian seldom received visitors."

Which evaded the question. "What does Graham look like? Is he my grandfather's age?" If Graham looked anywhere near as good as his voice, I could be in serious trouble. I needed to find a gym and work off a few of these waltzing hormones before I did something foolish.

Mallard stalked along in silence. A couple of pints wouldn't faze anyone of his sturdy size. He should have gone into the bodyguard business.

"I was hired sight unseen," he eventually admitted.

I hooted with laughter. Graham had bought Mallard with the estate! He didn't know any more about our employer than I did. Or he was evading the question again. He scowled at me and walked faster.

"Whose idea was the intercom?" I asked as we approached the house.

"Your grandfather had a security system installed some years ago. Mr. Graham improved upon it. I believe much of it is wireless these days." He took the sidewalk path to the servant's entrance. He didn't seem surprised when I followed him down the stairs to the kitchen.

"You never saw him move in?" I persisted. "He just started giving orders?"

"I was interviewed by telephone. This is none of your business." He held the kitchen door open for me.

"He's usurping my family's home. It most certainly is my business." As I entered, I realized that swaying Mallard to our side could be a beneficial ploy in ousting the trespasser. How could a butler not resent an employer who had lived in the house for a month and never showed his face?

Curiouser and curiouser was our enigmatic host.

EG and Nicholas were slamming cabinets in search of who-knows-what when we entered. I left Nick and Mallard to consult while I marched EG upstairs at finger point.

"There's enough rare antique silver in here to pay for my college education at Harvard," EG remarked insouciantly as we reached the elegant dining room. "I could smuggle it out in my backpack, store it at the bus station, and we could live off a few teaspoons a week."

I rolled my eyes. Where did I start? Raising kids required a lot more than feeding them when they're hungry. "One, this is our house and we're not leaving." I stated my goal first, to impress her. "Two, you are putting schoolbooks in your backpack, not silver, and you're going nowhere near a bus station."

"That's three."

I continued. "Three, I wager Magda didn't teach you to steal from your hosts."

She grimaced but didn't argue the point. I just had to hope she hadn't made a habit of stealing from any of our various "Daddies." Powerful men tend to be vindictive when crossed.

"Four, this whole house is bugged, and he probably hears every word you say."

Her eyes grew huge at that. Ha! I knew something the genius didn't.

"And fifth, stealing is a crime, and you won't like jail." Belatedly, I added, "Besides, it's wrong to take from others."

"I was wondering when you would get to the morals clause," the candelabra in the dining room said. "You have a unique outlook on life."

It had been a long day, and I was well past my pleasant quotient. Resisting flinging the ornate candelabra out the leaded glass window was the most I could manage. "EG isn't stupid, just young. What's your excuse?"

"Not youth." The microphone clicked off.

I buried the candelabra beneath a ton of linen in the sideboard. I might admire Graham's technology and ingenuity in bugging the whole damned house, but I didn't have to put up with it.

"Did you deliver the bruschetta?" I whispered as I pulled out some china for our dinner and handed EG the silverware.

"He has a stand outside his door," she whispered back. "I left the tray on it."

"What else is up there?"

"I didn't look. I figured I'd better not make him any madder."

As I've said, she's not stupid. Just annoying. Guess I'd have to be the one to explore the top floor and find out more about our sexy-voiced, enterprising spider.

Chapter Six

Of terrorists and kings, and Ana dons a disguise

THERE'S something about midnight that gives cause for reflection, especially midnight in a creaky old mansion, knowing an eccentric spider haunted the top floor. I had to hope he wasn't venomous.

I ordered EG into bed at nine so I'd have a few hours to myself. She'd protested my checking on her, told me she didn't need a mother—she already had one. I knew better, but I didn't argue. I read somewhere that kids needed rules to feel secure, and I figured I needed a few to have peace. A bedtime ritual couldn't hurt either of us.

So she was tucked in with an old volume of the Encyclopedia Britannica, and I was sitting at the desk in my room, staring at a web site on Islamic fundamentalism that gave me creepy goose bumps. I wanted a mother to tuck me in for the night and tell me the world wouldn't blow up while I was asleep.

"They want to annihilate anyone who doesn't think as they do," I whispered, reading the translation that a Cambodian virtual assistant had sent.

"Doesn't everyone?" the intercom asked.

I jumped three feet and turned over the Aeron desk chair.

"Quit doing that," I told him, righting the chair. I wanted to put a face to that impassive voice, and then I wanted to punch it.

An instant message flashed across the screen. "Is this better?"

Amazingly, it wasn't. I needed a human voice right then. I hated admitting vulnerability, but at midnight, it seemed justified. "The instant message would have been a better way to call attention to yourself," I admitted grumpily—aloud. "But now that I know you're there, you may as well have your say."

"Nazis thought everyone should be like them." The intercom spoke again. "For centuries, African tribes killed other tribes who weren't like them, or shipped them out as slaves. They're still eradicating each other over there. Christianity attempted to wipe out Islam in the Crusades. The need to annihilate anyone different isn't limited to any particular race."

I didn't have a high level of tolerance for bigots—which probably made his point: I wouldn't mind annihilating the stupid. "People never learn," I admitted.

"Not until we learn to respect our differences and use them to work together to solve problems instead of waging war, but I'll spare you the lecture."

I admired his philosophy, but logically speaking, it was kind of hard to believe it was possible to "work together" with a stupid bigot. Wiping out bigots seemed more productive.

I scrolled through the translation of the web site of the fundamentalist organization that listed Pao's name as a fund-raiser. From where did he raise his funds? And for what purpose? Mosques or terrorism? "How do you expect me to find this guy? Go to Cambodia?" I asked. It wasn't as if I'd turned up an address for Pao's palace or hovel or even his elephant. I suspected guys like this traveled as much as Magda, for entirely different reasons.

Or maybe not so different. They were both running away.

"I have reason to believe Pao is in the D.C. area," Graham said, "raising funds for the Indonesian organization whose website you're looking at. Illegal funds, since they don't appear to be leaving the country by any legal means."

I'd ask him why in hell he didn't do his own research if he knew that much, but I suspected I wouldn't like the answer, and I certainly didn't want to lose the job.

"What are you, FBI?" I didn't like the idea of a spook in the attic, but it sure looked like I had one. In movies, spies got blown up—along with everyone around them. Maybe staying here wasn't such a cool idea after all.

But I knew a lot of CIA from hanging around embassies in my youth. They came in all colors and sizes, and except for those in war zones, none I knew had blown up lately.

"It's CIA that handles international security," he lectured, "and no, I'm not one of them."

I heard something in his inflection that whispered he might have been one of them, once upon a time, and I shivered. Our resident spook was inordinately chatty at midnight.

I tilted the Aeron chair back and put my feet up on the desk. "Pao owes you money?" I guessed. Remembering the accounting file, I opened it, but balance sheets were beyond me. I ran a search for Pao's name in the document, but it didn't appear. "Did he help you finance this house?" I asked, just to get a reaction.

"The house is mine." He sounded irritated at the suggestion.

At least I'd disturbed his dispassionate professorial attitude. Score one for me.

"Just locate Pao," he finished. "My purpose in finding him is not your concern."

"If I spend all my time locating your fugitive, I'll need more time to find my absconding lawyer." I tried negotiating, without mentioning my ulterior motive of Tex. "I'll need a month here instead of a week."

The following is not irrelevant information: It was hot up in my second floor bedroom, so I'd taken a shower, changed into shorts and halter top, and left my hair down to dry. When I leaned back in the chair, my hair fell free and swayed over the carpet. While I talked, I lifted one leg and admired the burgundy paint job I'd given my toenails. In the middle of my leg lift, the intercom went abruptly silent.

The sudden silence made me sit up and take a look around. I'd seen men swallow their tongues when Magda performed that leg lift exercise. I hadn't realized I'd imitated it until now.

Was there only one bug in here, or had he installed cameras, too? Did I dare go on a rampage in a home that wasn't my own? I scanned the room for hiding places. The painting of John Quincy Adams over the daybed had eyes that seemed to beam at me with disapproval.

Graham's silence could have been just annoyance at my presumption, but I tested my theory that Max's office held a concealed camera. I wiggled my toes at the painting. I had decent legs when I chose to flaunt them. I was thinking I should wear a pair of kick-ass heels to see if John Quincy would swallow his tongue.

An irritated message flashed across the screen. "Find him. We'll negotiate later."

"Fat chance," I told the intercom, but I already knew it was dead. Maybe I was developing EG's intuition, only mine applied to machines.

I hadn't proved a thing except Our Man Graham wanted Pao badly enough that he didn't throw me out on my shell-like ear.

Maybe I could find our missing lawyer, introduce him to Pao and Graham, and let them all blow each other up.

Entertaining ideas of Pao's nasty fundamentalist group exploding Brashton's yacht in mid-Caribbean, I threw a sheet over the painting.

Chapter Seven

Ana visits the home of US government and learns the ghost in the attic is real

EARLY Thursday morning, I carried my breakfast into the library where the Cobalt Whiz waited for me. I loved that computer, and wanted nothing more than to surf its waves to see how far it could take me, but I had clients waiting on projects, as well as a scoundrel lawyer and a mysterious Cambodian businessman to track down, so playing was way down my list of pursuits. The perfidious senator was also way down the list. I'm not a detective. I was hoping the police would solve the case before I had to get involved.

I'd sent inquiries to a few fellow virtual assistants in various locations in Southeast Asia to see if they could translate some of the websites I'd turned up. I couldn't do much about finding Pao until I had replies.

My old Dell had been delivered before I'd showered. I set it up in the library next to the Whiz and used it to follow up on my regular clients. I checked for a DSL line on the telephone and satisfied, dismantled the network connection and used the modem. Some of my clients value their privacy, so I took a lot of precautions. Unless Graham sneaked down here in the middle of the night, turned on the PC, figured out my password, and decoded the files, he was up a creek. Oh, and I changed my password daily and hid my hands while I typed it in.

Out of nagging curiosity, I dug out the old files in the Dell that I'd built for my missing Oracle client. I'd kind of enjoyed his wry observations and the erudite language of his messages. He typed everything without capitals, but otherwise his e-mails were far more grammatically correct and elaborate than the usual clipped messages of the Internet, as if he were old enough to remember what it was to write real snail mail. I'd pegged him as an elderly corporate mogul.

Although now that I perused his file, I could see that his interests were a little weird for the business world. Aside from the usual searches for ownership of various companies, I'd run searches on politicians, compiled campaign finance and elections laws for every state, and started researching the ownership of several textbook publishing companies at his behest.

I pulled up his last e-mail, the one with the text of *envelopes, poison, top hats, and pow.* It still didn't make any sense, although the pronunciation of "pow" was the same as "Pao." It was scary that "poison" was mentioned just before he disappeared. I rummaged some more, opening document after document. I had a niggling feeling at the back of my mind that there was something in here I ought to remember, but I didn't see any reason why it should be important—unless I wanted to believe the Oracle in the attic was my missing client. And I didn't. The writing style was completely different. They didn't even use the same type fonts from the little bit I'd seen of Graham's messages.

I sneezed and vowed to have Mallard vacuum every available surface in here. Old cat hair was the worst for allergies.

The library was wall-to-wall books except for the fireplace. There was a stylized two-hundred-year-old image of Washington D.C. hanging over the mantel, but no evil eyes watched me from it that I could detect. The PC's were parked on a mahogany library table wide enough to spread out half a dozen volumes around me and still leave room for a board meeting. There was a certain irony to placing computers in a room full of books—sort of like the Smithsonian hanging the Wright Brothers plane over a space shuttle.

I located a box of Kleenex in a drawer after another fit of sneezing. I'd never had pets growing up, but I'd run across enough cats to recognize the reaction.

Graham waited until I had finished with my clients and had powered up the Cobalt Whiz before he intruded.

"One of your correspondents sent an e-mail today giving us a new alias for Pao. Good job."

He'd forgotten to IM me first, but I'd been expecting him. I managed to stay in my chair this time, despite the dry compliment.

He went on as if I were a secretary taking dictation. "The name corresponds with a man currently contracting a low security assignment at the General Services Administration. I can arrange documentation and access for you by ten today."

I didn't ask why Graham couldn't go himself. I was beginning to suspect he was an invalid who couldn't leave the house.

I was a virtual assistant because I didn't *like* going out in the rat race. Obscurity is me. "It would be helpful if you could tell me *why* you want this guy and what Edu-Pub is," I growled back, doing my best to be professional.

"Because Edu-Pub may be part of an international cartel bent on taking over the world." The intercom clicked off after that little bombshell.

Swell, now I was working for a *paranoid* old guy. Which meant I'd better apply myself to his projects or he'd be calling me a spy and hiring the CIA to heave us out.

It was early yet. I'd just heard Nick and EG go upstairs after breakfast. While waiting for my documentation, I avoided thinking about tangling with the GSA by researching Edu-Pub. I checked every database available to me, and that's more than is available to the general public, but Edu-Pub was apparently privately owned. The secretary of state's office had a filing on their officers, but Pao wasn't listed. None of the other names rang my chimes, but I began a detailed search for each of them. They'd all used the same address as listed for the company on the Edu-Pub website, an address that appeared to be in a bad part of D.C., if Google Map was any indication. I went back to Pao's website. Sure enough, the donation address was for a post office box in the same zip code.

What any of it had to do with anything was beyond my understanding except under the theory that Pao might somehow be using Edu-Pub for money-laundering.

I sneezed a half dozen times, grabbed a handful of Kleenex, and at the sound of an odd creak, glanced up in time to see a long, furry black tail slipping out the partially open library door. Short hair, not long, but definitely cat—a large one. Where had he come from?

I emerged from the library in pursuit of the animal just as Nick and EG hit the foyer prepared to traipse off to the local school to get her registered with her manufactured records, then off to buy school clothes and paraphernalia.

"Where are you going wearing that?" Nick demanded at sight of me.

I thought I was dressed respectably in a black blazer over my black knit T-shirt and loose blue jeans, and I took umbrage at the criticism. "How professional do I have to be to sit in a library?" I decided not to mention the potential visit to government offices or he'd bodily cart me upstairs.

"You look like a woman imitating a man. Would it hurt to try something feminine?"

I'd learned long ago that the right clothes made me invisible, and that's the way I liked it. If I had to brave the real world today, I was wearing my armor. "I'm not taking fashion tips from a gay guy wearing an apricot ascot," I retorted.

He offered an inappropriate finger and shoved EG out the door.

I was tired of spinning wheels, especially in a room infected by a feline. I wanted Pao located *now*. As soon as EG was gone, I entered the library and started hitting all the buttons on the intercom. "Where is the documentation?" I demanded of the wretched machine.

The intercom sputtered to life with a definite ring of male annoyance. He didn't like it when I intruded on him as he did me. "Your identification papers are in the envelope on the table."

I wondered if one of the buttons I'd hit had set off some kind of alarm, and I grinned at the thought. Maybe the police would come screaming down the road any minute.

I glanced down the table and found a manila envelope where one hadn't been before. How had he done that? I'd just stepped out for a minute.

One more puzzle I'd have to figure out. Later.

I opened the manila envelope and studied the contents. By golly dadgum, he had a new copy of my passport—my old one had more stamps than the U.S. Post Office and screamed terrorist threat. I slid the ID into my jacket pocket and prayed it passed inspection. I was really going to have to research our landlord more.

I couldn't believe I was volunteering to meet a guy who sponsored inflammatory religious nonsense on the Internet, but the only other alternative was to believe the spook in the attic was tracking terrorists. That's not the job of private citizens. Given our missing millions, I was placing my wagers on financial hanky-panky. "Mallard has the address and instructions?"

"I've arranged an appointment through the security desk," the intercom continued. "You'll have to memorize your instructions. Mallard will burn them afterward."

Mallard would burn my instructions? Maybe Graham really was insane. Or a sarcastic bastard. I could relate to that.

The intercom blinked off. One of these days, I'd fling it out the window. If Oppenheimer came through, one of these days this house would be mine, and I would fling *Graham* out the window. It would be kind of peaceful having that top floor to myself.

But Nick's fancy lawyer wanted an enormous retainer to sue Brashton's firm, so we wouldn't be suing anyone soon. I was toying with plans to make the money, but there are only so many hours in the day.

Mallard waited at the front door with a sealed Priority Mail envelope in his hand.

"Isn't it a federal crime to use the U.S. mail for ulterior purposes?" I studied the envelope with suspicion. What if Graham was a terrorist and that thing contained a bomb? Wasn't that how innocent people got blown up—accepting packages from strangers?

"The envelopes are free and untraceable. There is nothing illegal in carrying one." Mallard had his nose up in the air as he shoved it at me.

"Mind if I look for myself?" I handled the sealed package with care, delicately sniffing the air for any scent of gunpowder.

"It is not to be tampered with," Mallard ordered sternly. "Here are your directions."

He held out a printed sheet of paper. I wanted to examine it, run it through a fingerprint test, and test for the type of printer, but of course, I wasn't a forensics expert and couldn't do any of those. Besides, Mallard wouldn't let it out of his grip.

The directions were so precise that they even told me what time the

Metro train ran that I needed to take. I had about five minutes to reach the station. Cursing Mallard for not letting the paper go, I memorized Pao's alias in the GSA: Ibrahim Nassar. Sounded like a New York cab driver.

"Graham said you're supposed to eat the directions when I'm done. And I should watch to see you do," I told Mallard after reading the message and losing the tug of war.

"You'll miss the train." Without blinking an eyelash, he stalked off.

Well, Graham better trust him, because I didn't. At least I now knew where to find the local train station.

I dashed down to the Metro, and leaped in before the doors closed.

As the train clattered down the track, I tore open the sealed envelope.

* * *

Growing up, I had roller skated in palaces and played hopscotch on the marble tiles of government offices around the world. The GSA might sound mighty and officious, but it was a boring office building and did not light my fires.

Even the contents of the package I'd rifled held no surprises or anything to fear. It merely contained copies of the Edu-Pub financial statements.

I stopped at the L'Enfant post office—conveniently located in the underground shopping center of the Metro station near the GSA. I picked up a new envelope and sealed the statements inside. Delighted by the shopping center, I made a few more hasty purchases before I emerged.

At the GSA office, I handed my new picture ID to umpteen thousand increasingly officious military guards, passed the metal detector and several IQ tests to receive a visitor's badge limiting my access to the reception desk specified in Graham's detailed instructions. My orders were to leave the package at the desk, ask to use the restroom, and listen at the door until I heard Pao/Nassar respond to his page. According to Graham's diagram, the restroom was just down the hall from Pao's office, and I should be able to glimpse him as he passed by.

This was the ideal set-up for a hermit like me who preferred no direct confrontation. Graham had me pinpointed to a T.

Which was why I didn't follow orders. I hate being categorized.

He'd given me too tight a schedule for any elaborate ruse, but I was creative. At the Metro center stores I'd purchased a pair of sunglasses, a sun hat, a man's white T-shirt, and bright red lipstick.

I pulled on the huge shirt to disguise my habitual black, tied the blazer arms around my waist, pinned my braid under the hat so it's color couldn't be seen, smeared on the cherry lipstick, and donned the dark glasses before entering the reception area. With my lack of height, I looked about three years older than EG. The security guards gave me curious looks when they checked the age on my ID and made me take off the glasses. With Magda's cheekbones and green cat eyes, my features are pretty identifiable, and they let me pass.

Returning the sunglasses to my nose, smacking a piece of chewing gum, I handed the envelope to the puzzled clerk at the front desk. "My dad said I'm to hand this directly to Mr. Nassar."

"All packages must go through security," the clerk intoned, as if the envelope hadn't just gone through more security than Winston Churchill had seen through the entire war.

But security had been in Graham's amazingly accurate instructions. No problem. I was supposed to simply agree, leave the envelope there, and go to the restroom.

Instead, I shrugged, said "Whatever," and glanced around the lobby while they ran the envelope through their bomb-sniffing routine in the back.

"I've paged Mr. Nassar," the clerk said, returning the envelope to me.

I could tell she was curious, but I just shrugged and continued smacking my gum, jiggling restlessly like any normal teenager with too much energy. I ought to have worn athletic shoes, but my sturdy sandals probably had the same effect. I didn't know what I was trying to prove anyway, other than my obnoxiousness.

A heavyset man trundled down the hall a moment later. He was wearing a businessman's gray suit and rumpled tie, but he in no way or form looked like the man in the photo. For one thing, he wasn't Oriental.

There is some truth to the insult when one race accuses the other of all looking alike. If we look only at dominant features—skin color, hair texture, eyes, height—then most people of one race do look essentially alike. But I had grown up in a world where I had to identify strangers of different races all the time if I wanted to find my nanny or the chauffeur or recognize the hotel clerk who promised me a lollipop. I knew how to look beyond the obvious.

The obvious here said WASP government official. Behind the bulbous nose and narrow eyes I saw a muscular physique that screamed security. I'm not sure at all that I was relieved to see a white Nazi instead of an Oriental one.

"Mr. Hagan?" the secretary said in surprise at his approach.

Hagan? What had happened to Nassar?

He gave her a look of annoyance that should have blasted her to kingdom come. When she didn't budge, he reached for my envelope. "Graham didn't have a daughter," he growled.

Daughter? *Didn't*? What kind of scam had the spook used to get me in here? And how much danger was I in of being thrown into an interrogation room, never to be seen again? If I screamed bloody murder, would all those officious military men run to my aid?

"Are you Mr. Nassar?" I asked suspiciously, holding back the useless envelope.

"Nassar doesn't work here anymore. And Graham's dead. Give me that envelope." He tore the packet from my hand.

Shit. Triple shit with raspberry ice cream on top. I needed to get the hell out of here, but running was way too suspicious. I stuck with the teenage disguise and shrugged. "My dad's not dead. Just deranged. Like, all he talks about is this pub that sounds like a school. You ever heard of an Edu-Pub? Think that's where teachers go to get drunk?"

The Hulk looked at me blankly. So much for that feeble effort. I wished I could think of an amazingly effective question to find out more from someone who apparently knew who Graham was, but I could manage fake teenager, not real spy.

I muttered the all-purpose teenage "whatever" again.

Glaring as if I were a mindless gnat and the secretary had been planted there just to keep him from swatting me, he scurried off with his prize.

"Is your father really Amadeus Graham?" the clerk whispered in a tone of near awe before I could slouch out.

I wasn't entirely certain what I had intended to accomplish by this meeting, but it had never entered my head that anyone would recognize Graham's name, or that it would even come up. Now *two* people recognized it. I lifted my naturally arched black eyebrows at the clerk and offered a grudging "yeah."

"I thought he was dead, too," she said, still in that note of awe. "Are you a stepdaughter? He actually remarried?"

In her attempt to pry info out of me, she was supplying me with way more than I'd known before. Instead of running like the wind, I nervously bounced up and down, unwrapping a piece of gum. "Yeah, sort of. Howd'ya know him?"

"Didn't you know he was once a presidential advisor?"

Shit, no. The man behind the voice was real. And important. Shivery scary. I poked the gum between my shiny red lips. "Nope. He's just there, like, you know?" In my opinion, the chick was way too interested.

"What's he doing now?" she whispered.

"My mom," I replied rudely. "What's it to you?"

She stiffened. "Well, give him my regards. Perhaps he'll be happy to know that the senator who had him fired has just been arrested for murder." She coldly swung to face her computer monitor and began typing.

Oh purgatory. The only senator I knew in danger of arrest was Tex. I couldn't imagine why the arrest would affect Graham, but I knew what it would do to EG.

I dumped my disguise in a restroom at the Metro, ran for a train going the opposite direction of the house in case anyone followed me, hopped off at a crowded station, and caught a taxi home.

I was shaking with delayed reaction by the time I got there.

Chapter Eight

Ana investigates a thief, finds his wife, a cat, and a gym; EG sends a message

APPARENTLY stupidity only affects me after it's over. I prayed Graham would return to his midnight routine so I had time to cool down and think over everything I'd just learned.

How would I tell EG about her father's arrest?

Could Graham have any inkling of what I'd learned about him?

Before I slipped into the safe domain of the library to ponder my thoughts, I checked on the whereabouts of the house's other inhabitants. Mallard was mangling chicken breasts with a hammer and deriving keen enjoyment from the blows. Not disturbing his depraved little world, I grabbed bread and jam from the pantry, then tiptoed up the stairs to check the bedrooms. I saw no sign that Nick and EG had returned from their school assignment.

I retreated to the library and made raspberry jam sandwiches. I wasn't certain if I was sorry or relieved that no one was available to tell my story to, but I hated to have EG hearing about Tex from the media.

I spent the afternoon on my private Dell, avoiding the Whiz and its invisible umbilical cord to the dragon in his lair while I verified all I'd learned today.

It took only a few keystrokes to find the news stories on Tex's arrest on suspicion of murder. They told me nothing new. Looked like I'd have to give Tex a higher priority, but not until I knew who was living in our attic.

If Amadeus Graham was known at the GSA, then he had to reside *someplace* online. I had already tested the usual places for birth certificates and property ownership and telephone numbers. The property evaluation office still showed the house in my grandfather's name, but that wasn't unusual. There really hadn't been enough time to record the deed.

I entered Graham's name into every search engine I could find. Any man whose name was known by the government ought to have files up the wazoo.

All I turned up was a Dr. Graham who lived in a town called Amadeus and a million and one references to the movie and the composer.

He'd erased himself. Not many people know how to do that. People who make up their identities prove their existence by deviously inserting their names on all the appropriate sites. I didn't know of anyone who could or would do the opposite, make themselves invisible, except

Graham. I even ran newspaper searches. Nothing. He'd removed the links. I needed to worm my way into the *Washingon-Post* archives, but bypassing search engines was time consuming, and I was afraid he'd catch me at it. I'd have to find a library.

Would he know what I'd done at the GSA? What I had found out about him? He seemed to know everything else. Right this minute I didn't know if I was more afraid of Graham or Pao.

According to the receptionist, the hormone-shivering voice in the attic had been married. He'd been fired by the government, on top levels if Tex had been involved. He existed. Or had the man upstairs usurped the name of the real Amadeus Graham—as he'd possibly usurped the moniker Oracle?

I suddenly found it more than coincidental and far into the realm of highly suspicious that the mystery man used the same screen name as my missing client. What did he know about my client? About me?

My client had been looking at textbook publishers. Graham had financial statements from a company that sounded as if it related to education. And *pub*lication, now that I thought about it. *Pao* sounded like pow. But none of that fit in with top hats and poison.

I needed to be checking on EG's father, but I had this gut awful feeling that investigating Graham would take me to Tex's arrest.

Frantically searching deeper, I kept sneezing. For some reason, an antihistamine run didn't rate high on my radar.

Now irritated as well as scared, I emptied the Kleenex box as I worked. I called up Senator Tex Hammond on-line and read the news clips, starting with the most recent. The man the real Amadeus Graham had every right to despise—EG's father—had been arrested for murder moments before I'd left for the GSA. I wouldn't put it past the spook to have arranged the timing.

It seemed the police had found evidence that the good senator was being blackmailed by Mindy Carstairs for past indiscretions, including accepting illegal campaign contributions.

If any of this was true, Tex was going down big time, even if he got off on the murder charge. Tex had been elected on the family-values and no-political-ties platform. Since Tex had been married for the last fifteen years to the daughter of his state's governor, EG's existence alone testified to Tex's lack of values. But that was politics. Everyone lied. None of it meant that liars were adulterers or murderers.

My concern was that our landlord may have had EG's father arrested on a trumped-up charge to get even with him.

With no other avenue left to investigate, I ran a search on Mindy Carstairs, the purported blackmailer, to see how Tex and Graham might fit into her background.

I had to wade through umpteen million news websites and scandal sheets before I hit anything real—a social page photo of Araminta "Mindy" Carstairs marrying *Reginald Brashton the Third*.

I slumped in my chair and stared at the grainy picture with a nasty taste crawling up my throat. Our missing lawyer was slightly taller than his bride, with a proud smirk above his crooked tie. They both looked very young. Mindy looked a little pale, a little dowdy—even in veil and white dress. Neither of them were beauties, but that was Nick talking inside my head.

I scrolled down to the wedding announcement with the names of Mindy's parents and copied it into a file. I didn't know if I was brave enough to confront grieving parents, but the connection between Graham and Tex and my family had now left scary and entered the Twilight Zone.

My first thought was that spouses, especially ex-spouses, were primary suspects in murders. And with Reggie's criminal record and lack of character, he ought to be right up there on the top of everyone's suspect list. Except Reggie had sold our house to Graham and left on "vacation" weeks before Mindy's death. He had an iron-clad alibi. Shit.

The niggling at the back of my mind made me open the old Oracle file again. I compiled years worth of documents into one, then ran a search for the words Mindy, Araminta, Carstairs, or Brashton.

I found one reference from nearly a year ago, an e-mail Oracle had forwarded to me from an A. Carstairs. She had forwarded a memo from a Bob *Hagan* on the education committee dismissing her concerns about the quality of textbooks produced by several publishers. Hagan had been the name of the man intercepting Graham's envelope. Coincidence? I thought not.

A. Carstairs' e-mail to my client Oracle was brief and a bit sarcastic, as if she knew Oracle well and their opinions on the memo's contents were similar. I hadn't paid much attention to it at the time since all Oracle asked me to do was track down the boards of directors of the various publishers listed in the memo. I figured he wanted to send them a scathing letter or two, and I had done as requested and forgotten about it.

Textbooks. *Envelopes, poison, top hats, and pow.* No textbooks there, but now I wondered who the hell *my* Oracle was, what happened to him, and if A. Carstairs was Mindy.

And if my Oracle knew Mindy, and Tex knew Mindy, and Graham bought my house from Mindy's ex, did Graham know Mindy? I was back full circle to Tex and Graham.

I sneezed again. It was impossible to think straight with my nose running down my throat. Ignoring my allergies, I started digging deeper into Senator Tex and preferably, his relationship to Graham and maybe

Mindy Carstairs.

By mid-afternoon I hadn't found anything pertinent, and I was turning over wastebaskets and shoving furniture from the wall, scouring the room for the wretched feline, without any more success than I was having researching our host. I was frustrated on so many levels that I could have punched walls. I couldn't clear my head to get any work done until I'd at least eliminated the cat problem.

I might not be a genius, but I was smarter than any damned cat. Applying the old brain, I sneaked into Mallard's pantry, located a can of tuna, and dumped the smelly stuff into a plastic bowl which I set near the sofa, leaving the library door partially open. Apparently, I had no problem confronting animals.

Now that I'd found a feasible solution to one of my many problems, I returned to work with a vengeance. Setting aside the Tex/Graham problem to clear my brain, I read through all the Pao and Edu-Pub files, organized the results, and almost had a pattern of action. I had no clue what to do if I caught him, but that minor complication could wait.

I turned my attention on Hagan, but GSA files aren't easily hacked. I had pegged him as security but I couldn't find him on any security lists. I did find a Bob Hagan listed as a minor lackey in the education division along with two gazillion other people.

I'd almost forgotten the tuna until I sneezed so hard I nearly dropped the wireless keyboard from my lap. Spotting the cat tail as it darted behind the sofa, I grabbed the sheet I'd left hanging over a chair, and lunged for the space where it had disappeared.

The cat darted out the far side—straight into the trash can I'd deliberately turned on its side in anticipation of this moment.

It hissed and yowled and had almost rolled the can around to escape when I emptied the can into the sheet. The blamed animal was huge, and holding onto it was a struggle. Sneezing so violently it was a wonder I could stand, I knotted the fancy Egyptian cotton around its hissing burden. I was annoyed enough to choose direct confrontation by returning both sheet and feline to their rightful owner. There wasn't any doubt in my mind who had chosen to run me out with the cat.

I was a mass of raging fury as I trudged up three flights of stairs, sneezing like a sitcom character, carrying a snarling sheet over my shoulder. Our host had insisted that he not be disturbed, and I had been prepared to respect his privacy despite my avid curiosity. But his damned snooping devices had invaded our space without apology. He'd possibly injured EG through her father. And now he was trying to kill me with cats. I not only wanted answers, I wanted justice.

The third floor hallway was heavily carpeted. The soles of my shoes sank inches into the plush silver wool. Closed doors greeted me on both sides of the hall. Apparently the stand EG had reported had been moved. I had no idea which one hid the recluse. Shit. If he really was one of my grandfather's doddering old cronies, I didn't want to stumble onto him in the shower and give him a heart attack. I just wanted to straighten out a few of the rules around here.

I should have been terrified, but stupidity leads to inexplicable courage at times. If Graham was a spook, I had no business tangling with him, but one thing I'd learned in therapy was to confront fear instead of repressing it. I preferred ignoring that advice when it came to myself, but my family is all I have. For them, I'd move the earth.

Goliath, meet David.

One would think the cat's owner would hear the yowling and come to its rescue, but I didn't hear a sound as I tip-toed down the hall. No music, no keyboard tapping, no shower, nothing.

I didn't think he ever left the house. I'd never seen or heard him on the stairs. If there was an elevator anywhere, I hadn't found it. Was it possible for a man to be that quiet? While sleeping, maybe.

Deciding if Graham was awake, he'd know I was there and be yelling at me by now, I reverted to form and gave up on the confrontation. I just wanted to be rid of the damned cat and get back to work. I opened the last door on the left side of the corridor, prepared to open the sheet, heave the cat in, and slam the door shut.

To my utter amazement, I walked into my version of fantasyland—a well-equipped gym. And not just one of those sissy "home gyms" with contraptions more complicated than an industrial automaker's but one with mats, bags, and barbells. My kind of place.

Releasing the cat into a room across the hall—an unused guest room from the looks of the dust—I sneaked back to the gym, closed the door, and leaned against it. Reverently, I gazed around at the beautifully equipped, fully modern work-out room. I really shouldn't.

I couldn't resist. It had been over a week since I'd had any outlet for my frustrations, and after the day I'd had, I was wound up tighter than a clock. Just one punch, maybe. Something to soothe the nerves, clear my head, and get me back to work.

I stepped up to the canvas heavy bag—high quality, with a pair of well-worn gloves hanging on a hook nearby. I couldn't imagine an old man wearing out bag gloves. After this morning, I might have to give up the reassuring image of our landlord as an old man.

My gut churned as I realized I'd relied heavily on my imagination and my memory of my grandfather to conjure up the occupant of this floor. Still, any *normal*, healthy male could not live as quietly as a ghost in the attic, even if the house had been sound-proofed. If I couldn't have my old man theory, I'd go with the invalid, especially if everyone thought

Graham was dead. Maybe the gym was therapy for crippling physical disabilities.

I tapped the heavy bag tentatively, just to see how much noise I'd make.

I don't recommend bare-knuckled punching, but it felt so good to slam my fist into the sand that I couldn't resist hitting it several more times. Then I gave it a good swift kick. I was getting rusty without my regular workouts.

My sneezing stopped, and my head was totally in the zone as I advanced from a few swift kicks to practicing my legwork. Kickboxing is an American combination of martial arts borrowed from Japan, China, and Korea. It's a competitive sport, but most women do it for exercise. I can always use exercise, but I'm in it for therapy.

And it worked great. Within an hour I was huffing and puffing and dripping with sweat despite the air conditioning. I ruined my T-shirt and wondered if Mallard did laundry. But the frustration was gone and my head was clear. Taking deep breaths to fill my lungs, I let myself out of the gym and stole back down the hall. Still not a peep from the spook.

I took a shower and put on fresh clothes and was in a much better frame of mind when I went back to work. At least, I was until Nick and EG returned. With their usual flair for the dramatic, they slammed open the library door, startling me from my inspection of the police department's crime scene notes. Don't ask me how I cracked their files, and no one will get hurt.

From the police files, I learned more about the life of a mid-level government hack than I ever wanted to know. Mindy Carstairs had been as much of a geek as I was, except her background was in history, and I was paid better.

I winced at the slamming door, hoping it hadn't woken Graham. If he was an invalid, I understood his need for silence.

"I gave them my school transcript, and they're still putting me in fourth grade!" EG wailed, throwing her bags on the library table. They had apparently spent a productive day at the mall with my credit card.

"She hasn't finished any grade she's entered." Nick sauntered in, dumping a file folder of smeary copies of school rules on the table and adding a few more shopping bags. "They're not taking my word for it that they should just hand her a diploma and be grateful." He didn't sound his normal cheerful self, which for Nick passes as irritation. The job of nanny really was beneath his skill level, and I'd sympathize, except I'd done it for years.

I flicked through the school rules folder, shaking my head at the errors in grammar and syntax and the appalling formatting. I didn't need to read any of it. I'd seen similar papers follow me home through all my years of desultory schooling. "It's all a game. You go, you mess with the teacher's head, they pass you up to the next grade. It won't hurt you."

"I won't go until you teach me self-defense." EG plopped down on the century-old office chair, probably adding three dozen cracks to the brittle leather.

"I'm not teaching you how to kick your classmates. Self-defense is for safety purposes only, not retaliation." I felt a tug of guilt at not mentioning the gym upstairs. I really ought to get permission before using it again. Besides, we had other issues confronting us. I had to break the news of her father's arrest, and this did not seem an auspicious moment.

"You haven't seen my classmates," she said gloomily.

"If the Neanderthals playing ball in the school yard tell us anything, she's probably right." Nick gracefully alighted in a wing chair with a copy of the classifieds he'd appropriated from the stack of newspaper he'd left on my desk. "It's an elementary school, but some of those guys looked sixteen."

"You promised me an alternative school," EG grumbled.

I understood EG's plight. That didn't mean I had a solution. "Look, it won't kill you to go until I've finished this job. Once we catch Brashton, you can attend any school you want."

"Show me the trick with the quarters."

"The quarters?" Nick raised his eyebrows over the newspaper and made a tsking noise. "What have you been teaching the dear sweet child?"

"The same trick you used to lay out bullies," I reminded him.

Nick had had it rougher than I in some of his Brit boarding schools. His prettiness was an obstacle at an early age. He was the one who had taught me the quarter trick. Some "daddy" or another had thought fighting back—even dirty—would make a man of him.

Nick and I had consequently spent our childhoods attempting to kill each other with ever more clever fighting techniques, until we'd reached a tacit agreement to kill others instead. Apparently our fights had made it into family legend if EG knew about our tactics.

"Fine," he agreed complacently, settling into the chair. "Time to pass on the family secrets. She's a girl. You do it."

"You're such a help. Thank you." I dragged myself away from the computer, which was all he'd wanted anyway—appreciation for dealing with school officialdom while I had presumably done no more than deliver a letter and play in the library.

I wasn't certain I was prepared to tell how I'd spent my day. I didn't want to leave our new home, and Nick was bound to insist on it if I told him my suspicions about our host possibly being a vengeful invalid.

"We'll go out back," I told the kid. "Just remember, if I catch you using these techniques for anything less than an attempt on your life, I'll not teach you anything else ever again."

"What if they make an attempt on my person?"

I looked at her scrawny frame as she dashed ahead of me. She was wearing shorts like mine, only her legs weren't much bigger than a toothpick. "Right, then. If they lay a harmful hand on you, whack 'em."

"What if they're hurting someone else?"

I could see this might take a left turn through ethics and straight toward the metaphysical. It's tough knowing when to use violence and when to refrain. That's why guns scared hell out of me. Running was always the best option, in my opinion. Explain that to a testosterone-fried male who believes he's bigger and better and should give back as good as he got. Or that he should get in the first shot. Competitive idiots. I hoped EG had more sense.

I swiped at the perspiration forming on my brow the second we walked out of the air conditioning into the sticky blanket of August humidity. Trying not to breathe in mosquitoes, I showed EG how to wrap her fist around a roll of quarters and use them to give her knuckles extra strength with an uppercut. Then I told her to deck the juniper while I sat on the back step trying not to melt.

When she'd got in her blows and looked winded but triumphant, I broke the news. "Did you hear about Tex's arrest?"

She jammed her puny fist into the tree branches enough to scratch her arm to the elbow. "He's scum anyway," she announced.

Technically, I agreed with that, but it hurt to hear it from a kid who idolized her father. "He's human," I suggested. "He's made mistakes. That doesn't mean he's a murderer."

She stubbornly refused to look at me. Maybe that was for the best. I didn't want to make promises I couldn't keep. That was Magda's territory. She would promise to bail Tex out, or break him out with helicopters, or something equally illegal, unjustified, or just plain insane. And she'd probably attempt it, too, until someone talked reason into her. That had been my job for the better part of twenty years. I didn't know who was doing it these days.

Instead of making promises, I showed EG a few more tricks she could use to keep the bullies at bay. She might look cool most of the time, but she had as much anger to let out as I did. Her frustration simply didn't have my repressed sexual bent. I wasn't a virgin by any means, but I'd been living like a saint for much too long.

By the time EG had grasped the basics of dirty fighting, she was looking more her smug self, and my clean cut-offs had grass stains on them. Dripping with sweat, we trudged in through the back hall to the delicious scent of chicken marsala from the basement kitchen. I could get used to living like this. My best meals lately had involved Chinese take-out. After all the unanticipated exercise, I was salivating.

We trotted downstairs, peeked in the kitchen, and discovered Nick glaring at the dumb waiter. I assumed it was used to serve the dining room, but it might also deliver to the third floor. There was no sign of Mallard or mouth-watering dinner.

"You're cooking?" I asked hopefully.

"He only prepared two servings," Nick said with disgust. "I utterly refuse to defrost good poultry in the microwave. Looks like stir fry for us."

Damn. My stomach had been prepared for a real dinner. I'd had enough stir fry to last me into hell. I'd had a rough day and would have enjoyed a pleasant time-out before returning to my frustrating work. I swallowed my disappointment. "How about pizza?" I suggested.

"If you mix the sauce while I mix the dough."

I'd been thinking in terms of ordering out, but if Nick was willing to make the real stuff, I wasn't arguing. Carbohydrates were my friends.

Which was how the kitchen became a war zone. Nick is a great cook, but he left a lot to be desired on the scullery maid side. And all I was interested in was eating and getting back to work. So in retaliation for being left off the guest list, we filled the sink with dirty pots and bowls and perhaps smeared a bit of sauce here and there. Flour littered floor and cabinets as we carried our dinner upstairs.

With the three of us settled at the formal dinner table, I savored the perfect combination of garlic, oregano, and tomato, with some delicious Italian sausage Nick had found in the freezer. "All right, here's the plan," I said. I'd had time to prioritize my to-do list and re-adjust my thinking while we'd prepared the pizzas.

I swallowed a little bit of heaven before returning to professional mode. "If you haven't run my credit card into overdrive," I lifted a questioning eyebrow at Nick, who shook his head, "we'll rent a car so you can drive out to the casino in the mountains tomorrow. If you can make enough to pay Oppenheimer's retainer, I think we need to go for a three-fold approach."

Nick's mathematical genius practically guaranteed he would win at any game that involved odds instead of chance.

"Oppenheimer will drag a lawsuit into eternity," EG predicted before I could tell them my plan to keep our house.

"Even I can figure that." Nick dismissed her pessimism. "He's just backup in case we can't find Reginald or bring his law firm to their knees some other way. Telling me if the casino has high-stakes Omaha would be more useful."

"I don't know card games." EG shrugged her skinny shoulders. "Can't predict what I don't know. Want to teach me to play?"

I rolled my eyes. "Excellent. I'll teach you to fight dirty and Nick can teach you to cheat at cards and you'll have a well-rounded education."

"Beats fourth grade."

I was a wee bit sensitive on the subject of education, and I wasn't taking any further sulking on the matter. I slapped down my tumbler of ice water and glared at her. "If you don't want an education, then I'll send you back to Magda, and I'll go back to Atlanta." With Tex in jail, that she certainly couldn't go to her father went unsaid. "With your genius, just studying history alone could put you into the class of people who can save the world. You have to learn from the mistakes of the past to change the future."

"I can read about the past without going to school," she pointed out.

"You can't interpret what you read until you hear it discussed by people who have experienced it," I retorted. "School, or Magda?"

She shoved pizza into her mouth and shut up.

I could be persuasive in my own way. I turned back to Nick who was jotting notes in his PDA. "Do you think you can walk away with enough cash to give Oppenheimer his fee?"

"Sure, as long as you don't need me to go back to that casino. I'll go on their banned list if I take it all in one day. What about Brashton? Won't we need funds to hunt him down?"

"Brashton is the sole owner of a corporation called IWM registered in Delaware." I summarized my research. "IWM lists assets of stocks, bonds, cash, a yacht, and property in St. Kitts. Guess whose assets they might be?"

"Our grandfather owned property in St. Kitts?" Nick looked fascinated.

EG gave him one of her evil looks. "Brashton bought the yacht and property with Grandfather's money," she concluded without me explaining, "so he could set up offshore accounts and run away."

I pinched the bridge of my nose and attempted to steer the discussion back to the point. "The yacht is named The Patsy. I'm tracking its course at the moment. I need to buy open-ended plane tickets to St. Kitts so I'm prepared when he finally lands there. That's pricey."

"Oppenheimer, option number one; Brashton, option number two." Nick was always good at math. "Your Cambodian is option number three? Do you really think you can find him? Or that our landlord will let us remain here if you do?"

If we were to help Senator Tex, it was more imperative than ever that we have a place to stay in D.C., and this house was our best alternative. I didn't mention my suspicions about the connection between Graham and

Tex aloud, given the electronics of the dining room. "I think I can find Pao." Amid all my other work, I'd been fleshing out the investigative scheme I'd been toying with. I might despise venturing into the real world, but I knew how. "I just don't know if I can find him before we can reach Brashton."

Nick and EG both sobered. Neither of them are dumb.

"If we don't find him by next Wednesday, the other options won't help us, will they?" Nick asked gloomily. "We'll be out on our ears long before Oppenheimer acts, and even if Brashton lands in St. Kitts tomorrow, it will take you the last few days of our stay to go down there, and you can't search for Pao at the same time."

We all stared at the sideboard where the candelabra still resided. Hidden behind the heavy English oak, it didn't make a sound.

"I'm not giving up this house," I said firmly into the silence. "This is our family home, and I'll do whatever it takes to keep it."

The candelabra didn't have to speak. I could hear the fury rushing through the third floor like a tornado. I hoped Mallard was listening, too. If he knew Magda at all, he knew it would take nothing short of murder to pry me out of here.

"Speaking of Magda..."

Which we weren't, but her presence hovered after my brash promise. I glared at Nick.

He shrugged. "She called my cell phone. Three times."

"Really?" I let ice drip from my voice.

He held up his hands to protest his innocence. "I didn't return the calls. You want to find out what she wants, you call her."

Nick might not be stupid, but he could be pretty dense. He knew Magda and I weren't on speaking terms. I'd e-mailed her notification of EG's safe arrival but had provided nothing more. This wasn't the first time we'd taken opposite sides over EG. The first time had been before she was born.

I scraped the chair aside and left them gobbling pizza. I had better things to do.

* * *

Verifying that Ana was still working in the library, EG slipped up the stairs to the laptop in her sister's bedroom.

She simply couldn't swallow the idea that her father was a murderer or that her mother might love a man capable of murder. Her parents were adults and did strange things, but violence wasn't smart, and they were. Smart men didn't risk everything to kill.

She scanned the latest newspaper articles and made a note of the time of the aide's death: between the hours of noon and three on Monday, three weeks ago.

She ran a search on her father's name, singling out any other names associated with him and running searches on them as well. If they had websites or e-mail addresses, she sent them messages using the screen name *EG9*. Few people knew of her existence. No one would recognize the screen name even if they did know of her.

She needed something general, something to raise curiosity without automatically raising suspicion. Something a guilty person was more likely to respond to than a friend.

She sent forty-six messages in all. Every one of them asked, *Where were you early Monday afternoon when a woman's life was taken and a man's reputation jeopardized? Do you have an alibi? And if you do, would you like to help save a friend?*

She was good at puzzles.

Chapter Nine

Visit Mindy's parents, talk to a hunky Irishman, win a fortune

"I DID NOT give you permission to use my personal exercise room."

I did not fall out of my chair at the disturbingly masculine voice intruding on my contemplation, despite the spike in my hormones at the possibility of a man in my bedroom. I had been expecting a rebuke ever since I retired to the laptop upstairs before midnight. This wasn't the scolding uppermost in my mind however.

Graham hadn't asked about Nassar, and I hadn't told him. I suspected that meant he knew everything that had happened at the GSA this morning. And made no comment? Was the good, bad, or just ugly?

I distracted my fears by wondering if he knew I was in my room because he really did have hidden devices—like cameras—that I needed to know about.

I leaned back in the Aeron chair and put my bare feet on the desk, prepared to take the gym argument to its limits. "Did I break anything?" I'm not about to apologize for invading *his* privacy under the circumstances.

"Do you think you could?" he asked dryly.

With a little imagination, this could be a cozily intimate conversation, the only intimacy I could handle since it involved no physical presence. "On a bad day, I can take the speed bag off the wall."

"No hostility there, right?"

I grinned at how quickly he caught on. "Among other things. How do you get your jollies?"

I practically heard him growl. "Leave the cat alone. Use the gym." He signed off.

Inexplicably hurt at this abrupt end to the evening conversation I'd come to anticipate, I waited to see if he'd return. What had I said wrong? I wanted to talk about Hagan. Even if I hadn't found the right man, I wanted to hear a little praise for my carrying out the assignment, or an argument against our staying, or a criticism of our plans for Brashton—anything but silence.

What on earth had come over me? I *lived* for silence. I thrived on isolation. I ought to have been delighted he'd offered the gym. I should have been powering full speed ahead into Pao's history, revved for the chase, not sitting there sulking because an intercom rejected me.

And that didn't even begin to cover my need to discuss the hostile relationship between our host and EG's father and how Graham came to usurp the name Oracle.

I was more interested in investigating Graham than a shadowy Cambodian or a philandering senator, but there were only so many hours in the day, and I had to prioritize. The sooner I found Pao and proved my worth, the faster I could get to Tex.

Calculating that Tex's attorneys would be doing the grunt work right now so I could steal data from them later, I turned my attention to Pao. If he was in this country, then he had to get money somewhere, if only to live on. If I believed the websites, he was raising funds to send to his radical organization. He had to be funneling them through a bank account or another organization unless he was carrying cash by the suitcase and sending it home by messenger.

I had only one starting place for finding him—the Edu-Pub warehouse address in the same zip code of the post office box where Pao's website directed donations. Graham had given me those financial statements from Edu-Pub for a reason. I'd already decided that if Pao was laundering his illegal funds through a textbook distributor, then I needed to locate their bank accounts. Finding those accounts was part of the overall desperate plan that I'd schemed these last nights. I'd spent hours designing and setting up a website, and I had a server lined up.

Calling up my server provider, I sent out the webpage I'd created for a fictitious school that would need textbooks very soon. I'd already created an identity for the owner of the school.

All I needed to do now was set up a shipping address, access Edu-Pub's website, and start ordering.

* * *

Saturday morning, Nicholas left for the casinos in search of our much-needed riches, and I dressed for a new encounter with Pao's shadowy empire of foreign economics, with a side trip of my own if I had the time. EG had promised to spend her day with my computer, and I showed her how to follow Brashton's erratic path as he partied his way toward St. Kitts. I knew she was capable of taking care of herself and that Graham and Mallard were nearby, spying on everything we did. I figured she was safe enough. I was none too certain about their safety if EG got bored, but I didn't have time for anticipating problems. I had enough on my plate.

I hit the Metro in search of a shipping address. A cheap one. I didn't want my textbook order delivered to our safe haven. UPS won't ship to a post office box. Fortunately for me, D.C. is a hub of storefronts willing to do whatever was necessary for a buck. I'd located a couple of likely places last night. It was just a matter of checking them out to see which ones would accept my deliveries and store them without too many questions.

I accomplished that much faster than I expected. Walking out of the small package delivery store, I took a deep breath and steeled myself for the really tough duty I'd set for myself. I wanted to talk to Mindy Carstairs' family.

I just didn't like coincidences. My old Oracle client was interested in textbooks. Mindy worked on a textbook committee, and my client may have known her. Graham wanted me to investigate a textbook warehouse. Mindy's ex had absconded with the money Graham had paid him for our house. It was all stacking up somehow, if only I could figure out why. Time was running out. I had to brace myself for personal confrontation instead of piecing puzzles.

I'd looked up the address of her parents on the computer, checked MapQuest and D.C.'s Metro website and concluded a taxi was the only way I'd get there after climbing off the last Metro stop. They lived across the river in Alexandria with the rich white-bread community, not far from Blackwell Johnson, our estate lawyer, who I'd also looked up just to see if I'd pinned him correctly.

I put on my preppy blazer after the taxi left me at the garden gate of a substantial brick house sitting on three acres of lawn. In this area, land was so expensive that each blade of grass represented a dollar bill. Why was Mindy Carstairs working a low-level government job and living in a tiny apartment in a crummy part of D.C. when all she had to do was go home to this?

Praying the answer wasn't Tex, I marched up the slate walk to the double teak doors of the fake colonial farmhouse and rang the bell. I could hear the first notes of "America the Beautiful" sing out. When a maid answered, I trotted out my rehearsed speech.

"I'm Ana Maximillian." I had decided my grandfather's name would get me further in this rarified atmosphere than Brody's. "I would like to speak with Mr. or Mrs. Carstairs."

The door swung open and the maid beckoned me in without question.

I tried to act insouciant as I crossed the wide pine floors and was offered a seat in a cushioned wicker chair in a sunny room at the rear of the house. In my journey over here, I had prepared an entire litany of reasons why I should be allowed to talk to Mindy's parents, and hadn't needed one of them. I wished I'd prepared more questions while I was at it.

A plump, harried woman with gray hair frizzy from the humidity, wearing a gardening smock over khaki shorts, hurried in through the back door with a trowel still in her hand. "Maximillian?" she queried before I could even stand up. "You're not Max's daughter."

Whomp, right upside the head. I was actually meeting someone who knew my grandfather. I tried not to swallow too hard as I extended my hand. "I'm his granddaughter."

She looked momentarily nonplused as she transferred the trowel to her left hand so she could shake mine. "I had no idea..." The thought trailed off as she gestured at the maid. "Betsy, bring us some iced tea, would you?" She collapsed in a wicker chair as I sat back down. "You must be Magda's oldest. How is she doing?" she asked politely.

I didn't mention I hadn't talked to Magda in five years. "Still world traveling, as usual." Should I ask how she knew my mother? That might raise more questions than I could answer.

"Well, I'm delighted to hear she's well. Max worried about her. How can I help you?"

I was so thrown off balance that I didn't know where to start. I had come here to find out about Mindy and Tex and Reggie, not my family. I was afraid the White Queen would start talking backward any minute.

My grandfather worried about Magda? Did he know what she'd been doing all these years? Had they communicated and never told us?

I had to jar my thoughts back to what I was doing here. Reginald Brashton Junior had been my grandfather's trusted lawyer, and Junior's son, Reggie, had married Mindy, so they all traveled in the same circles— as had Magda, before her escape. I knew this kind of closed society. I just wasn't used to paying attention to it.

"First, let me say how sorry I am for your loss." I knew the polite words, even if they were meaningless. I didn't know this woman or her daughter. I was a snoop. From the looks of the dark circles under Mrs. Carstairs eyes, she'd been suffering from sleepless nights. I ought to back right out of there. But I couldn't. She knew the connections I didn't. "I hate to intrude upon you in this manner, but my grandfather died so unexpectedly that I'm still trying to cope."

She nodded in understanding and seemed to relax as the maid brought us tall cold glasses of iced tea, accompanied by linen napkins to absorb the drips. "I hadn't given a thought to Max's family, dear. I'm so sorry. We haven't seen Magda in decades. You must be at a complete loss now that Reggie has pulled a disappearing act."

I tried not to shriek with joy at finally confirming some of my suppositions. Now, if only I could be certain Mindy had been the A. Carstairs who sent the memo to Oracle on textbooks— I needed more, but I had no idea where to begin. "The estate is in some confusion," I admitted slowly. "Did you know my grandfather well?"

She waved her hand. "He's been a recluse for years, but Max had a hand in every pie. Magda and I went to school together, so he's kept in touch. After Mindy divorced Reggie, he was kind enough to find her the job with Senator Hammond At the time, it was a blessing. It pulled her out of her depression. I still refuse to believe the senator had anything to do with her death. There was absolutely nothing going on between them.

I told the police that. The idea of thinking my daughter would blackmail a good man like that—" She shook her head.

I was amazed at the fountain of information—all because of the name I'd given. For EG's sake, I wanted to believe this nice lady. I still needed to steer the conversation to textbooks without sounding insane. "It's good to know my grandfather wasn't completely alone then. Mr. Johnson didn't seem to know him well."

She sipped her tea and settled in for a good gossip. "I don't know Black Johnson well. He lives for his work. His wife left him long ago, and his son refused to join the firm. Reggie hated Black, but now that we know what Reggie is, that stands in Black's favor, doesn't it?"

I could see that Mrs. Carstairs preferred speaking of the past to avoid the present, but I had to deal with the here and now. I squirmed on the comfortable flowered cushion and broached the only reason I had to be here. "I understand Mindy and Tex were working on some kind of textbook committee. I have a client who is interested in—"

She didn't even let me finish. She sat forward and gestured with her tea glass, sending water droplets flying. "Mindy was positively *obsessed* with textbooks! I told the police that. Who is your client? Perhaps he could talk to the police, explain what Mindy was doing. She had a history major, you know. She was simply outraged by the inferior quality of the information our children are exposed to these days."

She sat back and looked depressed again. "Although I can't imagine anyone killed her for complaining about books."

"No, ma'am, I shouldn't think so." I instinctively imitated her soft southern accent. I'd be drawling if I stayed much longer. "Did she ever mention a company called Edu-Pub?"

Mrs. Carstairs frowned and stared at her tea glass. "It sounds familiar, but I'll admit I really didn't listen to Mindy's diatribes. I was just thrilled to see her excited about something for a change. Reggie spent everything they owned and left her with mountains of debt. She wouldn't accept any help from us, and I know she was living in near poverty, but she was just like her old self again." Coming out of her reverie, she looked puzzled again. "How can I help you? If you're looking for Reggie, we don't have any idea where he is. I admit, I wish he was dead instead of Mindy. It just doesn't seem fair."

She was about to get weepy, and I stood up in a hurry. I didn't want to torture her anymore, and I wasn't a detective. I didn't know the questions to ask. "No, ma'am, it doesn't seem fair, but once I find him, I assure you, Mr. Brashton will wish he were dead. My grandfather didn't work all his life to let scum like that leave his affairs in such a tangle."

She rose with me, setting her glass aside. "If I can help you find Reggie, you just let me know, y'heah? I'd like to wring his neck for what he did to my daughter. I'm sorry to hear that he mistreated your grandfather. Max was a lifesaver. Mindy used to show him those textbooks she went on about, and he took more interest in them than we did, I'm afraid. He was even helping her investigate their publishers. I owe Max for being there for my little girl."

I would be sobbing right along with her if she kept this up. My grandfather was a good man, just as I remembered. That he was interested in textbooks along with half of D.C. just spun my head into new orbits. It was hard to imagine that many powerful people concerned about public education. I needed time to work that out. "I thank you for your time, Mrs. Carstairs. It's good to know someone thinks of my grandfather with goodwill." I edged toward the door with my brain whirring in so many directions that I might have ended up walking back to D.C. if I hadn't stumbled across the next question. "Would you happen to know Amadeus Graham? He bought my grandfather's house from Reggie."

Mrs. Carstairs looked dumfounded. "Amadeus? I'm quite certain I heard he died, dear. What has Reggie done now?"

With my guts twisting in tighter knots, I asked her to call a taxi.

* * *

I arrived at the house nervous, exhausted, and not in the humor to fight Mallard for the kitchen. He'd locked us out again after last night's pizza binge.

So I ambled down to the local pub to see what they had in the way of lunch. I needed time to sort my thoughts, and after the morning's extroverted excursion, my introverted nature needed to be alone to gather energy. I ordered their Irish stew and hoped for the best.

The pub was relatively empty in early afternoon. Some tourists carried on a murmured conversation at one of the window tables. A few locals talked quietly in the back booth. The place could grow on me—all that dark wood and quiet reminded me of a library.

My meal had just arrived when the curly-haired Pierce Brosnan walked in, and I forgot my need to be alone. I don't know how tall the actor is—I don't keep up with any news much less Hollywood news—but this guy had me beat by a good eight inches.

All right, so I may have had another eight inches in mind when he swaggered toward me. He had a stocky Irish build—square shoulders, square chin, and the biceps of a working man. Six-pack abs, I was willing to wager, admiring the way his black cotton shirt tightened as he slid onto the bench across from me.

"You came back." He looked inordinately pleased to see me.

My hormones did a little shimmy presaging an impromptu can-can.

"I didn't come back for you," I retorted.

"For Paddy's mouth-watering stew?" he suggested, his baby blues laughing.

Since the stew seemed to be made of last week's leftovers, he had me there. On some subconscious level, I'd been hoping to run into him again. I am capable of normal conversation when called upon, and the spook had left me hungry for company. Of course, if Amadeus Graham was dead, he really was a spook, wasn't he?

"Do they serve anything edible?" I tried the cornbread that had arrived with the stew. Dry.

"The beer and the hamburgers." He ordered both, then returned his movie star gaze to me. "Hi, I'm Sean O'Herlihy." He held out a calloused hand.

I didn't take it. I had cornbread in my right hand, and I took another nibble while I inspected him more thoroughly. The friendlier he was, the more suspicious I became. Paranoia wasn't a total waste of time. Sometimes people *are* out to get you.

"Hello, Sean. Come here often?" I didn't bother introducing myself.

"When I can." He dropped the handshake idea. "You're Ana, aren't you? Mallard's told us all about you."

Mallard knew damned well we'd inherited the house. His friends probably did, too. A working man could easily fool himself into seeing money written all over me.

"Discussing our situation must make for uproarious dinner conversation," I acknowledged coolly.

"Mallard carries loyalty to his employer to old-fashioned lengths." Unaffected by my coolness, Sean stretched his muscled arms along the back of the booth, providing good exposure for his sculpted chest. "He's having the devil of a time trying to decide if his loyalty is to Maximillian's heirs or the new owner. Quite a quandary, isn't it?"

Sean had the prettiest long lashes I'd ever seen on a man, even better than Nick's. I was striving not to fall for his muscled pose. "Mallard worked for my grandfather, not us. He's free to make his own choices." I hated having our private business the subject of barroom talk, but there was little I could do about it. I shrugged it off and tried not to choke on my drool.

He leaned forward in a confidential manner. "Mallard said Graham never leaves the third floor. Have you ever met him?"

Shoot, and I really liked this guy. He was good looking, friendly, Irish, and he seemed to be enjoying the view. I'm not hard to look at, but guys seldom get past the attitude. This one didn't seem fazed—for good reason. He was spying on Graham or whoever resided in our attic. I didn't rat on clients, even if they really weren't who they said they were.

"Nope, can't say I have." I dabbed my mouth with the linen napkin and opened my bill. Sticking a ten between the vinyl covers, I slid out of the booth. "Good to meet you, Sean. See you around."

I walked out, leaving him looking stunned. Guess not too many women ignored his pretty face, glib tongue, and six-pack abs.

Not too many women had Magda for a mother. I thanked the heavens for giving me a mother who had taught me all I needed to know about men. Magda was a piece of work, but her love affairs had taught me not to trust men who lie, cheat, or steal—which basically means there wasn't a man alive who could be trusted. Life was so much simpler once I accepted that premise.

When I got back to the house, I ran upstairs to change into cooler shorts and a crop-top. Either Mallard or the spook was energy conscious and kept the air-conditioning to a minimum. Or maybe this big old house didn't cool easily.

After the morning I'd had, I didn't know if it was the braids hurting my head or my thoughts. I couldn't take out my brain, so I unpinned the braids. I didn't bother brushing them out, which left my hair crinkly. It wasn't as if I cared how I looked.

I was already regretting not accepting Sean's masculine interest for some recreational sex, but my prickly exterior protects my equally prickly principles. All my life I'd watched Magda use people, especially men, and I simply couldn't treat others in ways I wouldn't want to be treated. The line gets pretty fine sometimes, so it's easier to just back off.

Remarkably enough, my life actually had meaning at the moment. Beyond EG's needs, Max and Mindy had come to life for me. They were real people, ones whose lives were cut off too short, and I had a driving need to know more about them.

I'd learned my grandfather was a man who moved in upper social circles and could find positions for friends in congressional offices. He was concerned about textbooks. And maybe he was concerned about Magda. Or had Mrs. Carstairs just been polite about that? It didn't matter, Max was now very real in my mind, and I ached to know him better.

But knowing more about my grandfather as family wasn't as important as knowing why Max had been helping Mindy investigate textbooks. I had to read the lawyers' files on Tex and see if they had run across this strange connection with books. Which oddly enough, led me back to Graham's pursuits of Pao at Edu-Pub, although I was still backing money-laundering as Pao's gambit.

During my research last night, I'd run across a fascinating website selling a newsletter of information on money-laundering. A credit card order later, I sat down to study my first issue of *Money Laundering Alert*. It was a real eye-opener. I might nab Pao *and* Reggie with this stuff. This was more fun than all my clients stacked together.

* * *

Hearing Ana downstairs, EG hastily closed up her e-mail account in the upstairs laptop and prayed her sister wouldn't notice it.

Quite a few of the e-mails she'd sent the other night had bounced back as no longer valid or not accepting e-mail from unknown screen names. She'd attempted to locate new addresses and tried several. Most of the e-mails that had gone through had been ignored.

One had been answered with an enigmatic *Who are you and why do you want to know?*

She'd checked, and that screen name belonged to a Robert Hagan who had given an award to Tex for his valuable work on some education committee.

Mindy Carstairs had worked as liaison from Tex's office with the same education committee. EG's instinct told her that her new correspondent had responded to her e-mail for a reason. Maybe he was Mindy's boyfriend, except boyfriends and family members weren't likely to believe Tex innocent and wouldn't be interested in helping him. Boyfriends and family members were the most likely murder suspects.

She started a research folder on a Robert Hall Hagan and hid it in Ana's computer files. If Ana didn't have time to help Tex, then EG would have to do it on her own.

* * *

Later that evening, after I'd sent EG off to bed, Nick appeared in the library where I was coloring in the details of my virtual school. Setting up credit cards for fictitious entities is more difficult these days, but the web is full of people willing to accept anything for a price.

With a dramatic flick of his wrist, Nick dropped a nice fat cashier's check across the table in front of me and announced, "I kept the change for spending money."

My eyes grew as round as the zeroes on the check. "I knew you were good, but this is outrageous," I said with sincere admiration, but I refrained from joyously hugging him. He wouldn't understand if I did. Sensing hesitation in his usual jovial attitude, I asked, "Did they ride you out of the casino on a spear?"

He made a graceful descent to the wing chair and examined his nails. "Not precisely, no. It was all very gentlemanly, even if Indians don't wear tuxes. I'm not welcome back, though. You had best make it last."

Nick hated to be seen as any less than a gentleman. He was embarrassed, and I hated that we'd used his talents for shady purposes. He was entitled to his own prickly principles. Just because we lived near Monaco for a year and gambling was the only education he found useful didn't mean he shouldn't move on.

And here I was, encouraging him. I grimaced and pushed the check around on the polished surface of the table with the tip of my finger.

"I thought you'd be ecstatic," he complained. Nick's far more sensitive than I am. Even though he appeared totally self-absorbed, he'd noticed my silence.

"I am ecstatic, about the money. I'm just worried about you. If we find our millions, what do you want to do with your share?"

His eyebrows rose, and he crossed his hands across his ascot. "It can't buy me love now, can it?"

I'm not good at emotional admissions. I would have liked to say he had my love, but I figured that wasn't what he had in mind. "What has love got Magda?" I asked instead. "Too many kids and no home. Why don't you think about the kind of jobs you like to do best?"

He quirked one eyebrow. "There are nasty words for people who get paid for that."

I ignored his sexual innuendo. "I guess we need to start a family bank account with this money. It more than covers Oppenheimer, the tab on my credit card, and tickets to St. Kitts."

"What will you do with Brashton if you find him?" Nick asked, shrugging off my awe.

"Hold him at gunpoint and force him to write out a check for the missing money?" Hell if I knew. Did criminal law extend to St. Kitts? I suspected it didn't or Brashton wouldn't have moved there. I'd already checked the dates—Reggie had sailed in mid-July. His ex-wife had died two weeks later. No wonder the police weren't asking about him. I couldn't find any record of Graham's purchase of the house, but my guess was that Reggie had sailed as soon as he had Graham's money in hand.

"A check won't get the house back," Nick intruded upon my thoughts.

As if I needed reminding. I wanted this house. I had no idea how many millions it had cost. Could we salvage enough of the stolen money to buy it back? With our background, obtaining a mortgage wasn't likely. "That's Oppenheimer's alley," I suggested. "Let's find Brashton first. We could start with filing a police report and asking how the law works."

We should have done that sooner, but we're kind of used to operating outside the law, for various reasons. It seldom occurred to us that the law might occasionally be on our side. Of course, one would expect Brashton's law firm to be hunting him down before we filed a crime report and sued, but I wasn't relying on that happening.

"Why don't I go down to St. Kitts and wait for Brashton," Nick suggested. "Maybe I can persuade him to sign over the stolen assets while we're waiting for the police to show up."

Nick can be very persuasive in his own way, but that didn't sound like much of a plan.

"Maybe all the police have to do is call their buddies down there to pick him up." I knew that was a crock, but I didn't want Nick abandoning me just yet. I was on a quest outside my realm of knowledge, and Nick was kind of like having a girlfriend I could talk to.

"I'll pack and be ready to fly down there at a moment's notice." With the stride of a confident man, Nick walked out.

To my utter delight, the spook did not come on at midnight to question my visit to the Carstairs. I must have exceeded the reach of a dead man's network.

* * *

I got up Sunday morning in a panic, wondering if I had until Wednesday to finalize my search for Pao or if we'd be out on our ears Tuesday evening.

I really needed to uncover our host's background. Maybe I could blackmail him into letting us stay. I needed a starting place. I hadn't had time to run a thorough title search on the house. There had to be papers somewhere.

Stepping out of my shower with my head crammed with paranoid thoughts, I hoped the mirror over the vanity didn't conceal any spying eyes.

For a Victorian, this old house had a surprising number of bathrooms. Mallard had one in his basement suite. There was a gaudy half-bath with the original gold faucets for guests just off the first floor foyer. My grandfather had a marble whirlpool and shower installed off the downstairs salon where he'd made his bed in his final years. I had no inkling of what was on the third floor besides the gym, but on the second, there seemed to be a full bath between every two rooms. Living in the occasional Third World country where we were lucky to have privies, a bath for each of us was untold luxury.

I usually took a day off on Sundays to pick up groceries and do house cleaning, but we had Mallard for that now, even if he wouldn't cook for us. I had way too many tasks piling up to take off much time. I was curious about how to detect bugs and wanted to check surveillance equipment websites. And I needed to see if any more information had come in on Tex's case.

Now that I had a delivery site, I could order textbooks, but I couldn't follow up on the trap for Pao until I had a real bank account. I wanted checks as well as credit cards to go into Edu-Pub's coffers so I could trace all available financial paths.

Sundays are a bad day to call the police about embezzlement, but I did it anyway. They took notes, answered my queries negatively, and gave me the overall impression that chasing runaway lawyers wasn't high on their to-do list unless I could prove Reggie had been in town when Mindy died. Otherwise, they had their hooks in Tex and considered their job done.

They gave me the phone number for the state bar to report the theft of Max's estate. I suggested they verify Reggie's alibi, but they got irritated when I told them how to do their job.

Maybe I should have tried the FBI. If I dug deep enough, Brashton was sure to be guilty of something the feds might be interested in. Or the IRS, for certain. But I suspected retrieving our money and politely returning it to us wouldn't be the priority of either. It was a criminal shame that this country was more interested in protecting crooks than victims, but I was used to looking out for myself.

Despite the pressure, I took a few hours off that afternoon so we could play tourist with EG. The kid deserved an outing before school started. She'd read everything she could get her hands on about her father's arrest and probably researched more online, but she'd been amazingly quiet about it. That should have worried me, but I already had enough fears without adding more. I wanted to pretend we were all normal for a few hours.

The cordoning off of Congressional Hill for Homeland security purposes set my paranoid hackles on edge, but EG pretended she wasn't interested in the Capitol Building. We dragged her into the Smithsonian instead, and the dinosaurs finally caught her attention. She had an armful of books and was chattering like a normal kid by the time we returned home.

Mallard had apparently returned during our absence. He greeted us at the door with his usual disapproving expression. "We dine at regular hours in this house. Dinner was at seven. It is after eight."

As if we'd known he intended to feed us. "Just stick it in the fridge." I breezed past him carrying sacks of posters I'd bought with malice aforethought. I dumped them across the horsehair sofa in the parlor so I could sort through them. "We'll eat it for lunch tomorrow. We had chili dogs on the mall."

"Garlic." Nick sniffed the aroma drifting through the house. "Italian?" he asked, dropping his arm over Mallard's shoulders. "Lead on, my good man. I can always sample your fare."

I didn't think that was the response Mallard expected, but if he thought scolding us would put us in our places, he didn't know Magda as well as I thought. Chips off the old princess, all of us. Insults, threats, and innuendo flit right past us and out the door.

EG dropped her haul in the middle of the genuine antique Persian carpet in the front room and sat down to choose her evening's reading material. Between Nick's magazines, my posters, and all our combined shopping—including a giant dragon kite—the formal front room looked like a nest inhabited by eccentric magpies.

Mallard stiffened at the disaster area the formal room had transformed into within minutes of our arrival, but Nick dragged him past the doorway, chatting of an Italian bistro he'd eaten at in some byway in San Remo.

Gazing at the colorful scene, I experienced an unusual swell of happiness at this normal family Sunday evening in a normal family home. I scratched behind the ear of a bronze spaniel andiron, and just let the moment happen. Home. Amazing concept. Maybe I'd try it this time.

"There are three messages for you," the lamp intoned, interrupting my pleasant reverie. "In the future, I would rather you not give out this number."

Properly shot down and dropped back to earth, I didn't bother explaining I didn't know the number to give it out. I knew of only two people who might track it down: our mother and Blackwell Johnson, the lawyer. I didn't think either would call on a Sunday to tell us we were good little kiddies. If the number remained unchanged since my grandfather's death—and how the spook might manage that led down any number of interesting trails—I assumed Magda would call it because it was in her address book.

I picked up a Don Quixote poster and headed for the library. Given my suspicion of our landlord's prying habits, covering up spybots with the mad Spaniard seemed perfectly logical to me.

EG gaped as I strode blithely past without picking up the phone. "Aren't you going to ask who called?"

"I don't recommend it."

I left her to run after Nick. Let him deal with Magda if he wished.

If the Princess intended to come after EG, I thought grimly, she'd damned well better do it now—before I got used to having a family again.

Chapter Ten

EG skips school and Ana owns stock

ON MONDAY, Nick and I walked EG to the nearby elementary school. I'd persuaded her to wear her long hair in pigtails by telling her she needed a disguise. She'd even allowed me to trim her bangs, although I'd done a ragged job of it. Wearing her uniform and backpack, she almost blended in with the other kids streaming down the sidewalk and leaping out of school buses.

Unfortunately, Nick and I were more noticeable, so people still stared. Nick was heading to the bank to deposit his weekend winnings, then over to Oppenheimer's with his retainer, so he wore a dashing sport coat of raw silk with a lovely burnt orange ascot and cream silk slacks. The exotic threads around a D.C. public school caused quite a stir.

I was on my way downtown to set up a bank account for my fictitious firm, so I'd spruced up my ankle length denim dress with a sequined t-shirt, but the thick braids around my head attracted attention. I didn't think they were worse than the blue hair and spiky cuts on the kids, but I never had a mob mentality—my downfall, so to speak. No one could claim Magda had raised clones.

EG growled at a chubby kid who pointed at us, then kicked the shin of a black kid who laughed out loud—not an auspicious start.

I grabbed her jumper strap and leaned over to whisper in her ear. "Smile, say nice things, and maybe they'll return the favor. *Try*, will you? The whole family may depend on your genius one day, and if you have no education, you'll fail."

Horrid thing to say to a normal nine-year-old, but EG wasn't normal. She straightened her slouch and looked me in the eye. "Then go away. You don't need to walk me in."

It was like sending a babe off to her first day of kindergarten. There were tears in my eyes as EG marched bravely up the front steps all alone—the new kid in town. I knew what she was in for, and I prayed I'd done the right thing.

"Being a kid is lousy," Nick grumbled, as tense and worried as I was.

"We'll hire a tutor when we're rich," I assured him.

That possibility relieved both our guilts sufficiently to allow us to walk away.

* * *

Settling into the disgusting little contraptions that pass for desks in public schools, EG sat through all the boring rituals of opening day. She wasn't familiar with the paperwork going around, but some kids had folders of it that had apparently been incorrectly completed and the teacher had to fill out. Half the class had to hunt down immunization records and needed reminders. The record-keeping grew tedious.

Giving up on the formalities, she helped herself to a social studies textbook from a shelf and began reading.

She'd learned American history on a high school level from books her government tutors had provided. She winced at this book's outright propaganda on the negative effect of conservation on natural resources and the economy, then frowned as she tried to balance what she thought she knew about global warming against the book's text. She wanted to ask questions, but the teacher finished homeroom duties and had moved on to dividing the class into reading groups.

EG scanned the book handed to her, sighed, and rolled her eyes. When called upon to read aloud to test her skill, she recited the entire last page from memory and began reciting Hamlet's soliloquy for amusement. The teacher told her to sit down.

She did and immediately fell into the social studies book again. Engrossed in making her own calculations, she didn't hear the teacher ask her to join her designated group.

A ruler whacked the plastic desktop. She looked up at the teacher with curiosity while all the kids in class laughed and stared.

"Just because you've had the privileged education others haven't, doesn't mean you can't sit with the rest of us, Miss Max*million*." That's how she pronounced it—without the "i" and the emphasis on *million*.

She might as well have said "Set your rich lily white ass in that chair over there." The effect was the same. Everyone turned and stared.

Bravely ignoring the mocking smiles on the faces of her classmates, EG marched over to her *reading group*, clutching the social studies book to her chest. She would put up with this for a while because Ana asked her to and because she desperately wanted Ana to help her father.

The reply she'd sent to Mr. Hagan at the education office had bounced. Until she came up with a better plan, she'd have to rely on her sister.

But if any of these laughing bullies got in her face, she had a roll of quarters that would knock the smirk from their teeth.

* * *

With EG safe in class, I spent the morning arranging a bank account for my fictitious school and obtaining real paper checks to pay for the textbooks I ordered. I knew this was a long-term option and not likely to find my guy by Wednesday, but by this time I was curious enough to follow up on my own—especially if it had involved my grandfather.

The process of tracing the checks and credit card deposits from EduPub was a distant chance at best, but it was all I had. Pao had no social security or visa number and his name didn't turn up on any D.C. payroll tax rolls. He was obviously living in a cash-only underground or under an alias.

Returning home, I changed into shorts, rummaged in Mallard's amazing pantry for peanut butter and crackers, then settled into my desk chair in front of the Whiz to see what news had turned up on Tex. Flexing my fingers, I fed in my password and downloaded new messages.

"Precisely what did you think you were doing this morning, Miss Devlin?" the intercom asked just as I was really getting organized.

Now that I was in front of the computer, I didn't want to talk. It wasn't midnight, and I didn't like being dissed. "What I'm paid to do," I responded, keying in a reply to an inquiry.

"You are paid to traipse all over town looking like an escapee from a space opera?"

He'd noticed my braids. I should preen. "Don't question my methods, and I won't question yours," I replied—without preening. Just because the man had noticed my hair didn't detract from the fact that he spied on me. That he knew what I looked like and I'd never seen him *proved* he had a camera somewhere. I thought I'd covered up his spying devices with Don Quixote. "I don't have time to waste on useless interrogations. Did you want something?"

The intercom was silent, but I knew he was still there, trying to figure out how to respond to my rudeness. I get that reaction a lot.

"I prefer that you remain at your desk where you belong unless told otherwise."

Oh, that took the cake. I flung back in the over-sized chair and sent the intercom a glare so sizzling that the wires should have fried. "Welcome to the twenty-first century. Women have equal rights these days."

"I had wondered if you knew which century you were in."

If that was a reference to my aging jumper or my Birkenstocks, I could appreciate his humor. That didn't mean I had to respond to it. "I repeat, did you want something?"

"I do *not* want you risking your life in pursuit of Pao. He is extremely dangerous."

I didn't want to know that. A Cambodian businessman seemed harmless to me. One who might be funneling funds to radical fundamentalists on the other side of the world is iffy, but believe me—and I've had a lot of experience on the international scene—this kind of thing happens all the time. For all I knew, Pao was building a temple to himself over there.

"You have someone else who can set up the trap?" I asked in my most sarcastic tone.

I thought he might growl, but he apparently controlled his temper far better than I did.

"Your brother comes to mind."

"You didn't hire Nick. You hired me. Nick is out looking for a job so we have money to go elsewhere after you throw us out."

I wouldn't beg. I desperately wanted him to say we could stay as long as we needed, but vulnerability ain't me.

"Who will look after the child in his absence if you are otherwise occupied?" he asked in an ominous tone that should have warned me what was coming.

"EG is in school. I'll be here when she comes home. What do you care as long as I'm getting the job done?"

"Your sister is not in school."

He clicked off, leaving me open-mouthed. I figured he did that on purpose to get in the last word. It's a guy thing.

To hell with Pao. I had to know where EG was.

I rolled back the chair and ran up to EG's room. Her school backpack was there, but she wasn't. I checked all the other rooms upstairs, and she wasn't in them either. I wasn't about to attempt the third floor until forced.

Libraries were EG's usual haunt, but she wasn't in the one downstairs because that's where I'd been. I tried not to panic, but when fear kicked in, I could be quite imaginative. I thought of her traipsing the streets of D.C. looking for the prison where they'd taken her dad. Or hiding under the desk of some police detective telling him how to do his job. They'd be locking her up in foster care if I didn't find her. Once social services got their hooks in a kid like EG, they'd never give her back. In fact, they'd probably run us out of town.

Out of obvious places to look and growing more scared by the minute, I ran down and started a systematic search of the first floor. I scoured Grandfather's old room and double-checked the library and parlor and the closet under the stairs. I ran down to the basement, but the kitchen was locked, so I couldn't find Mallard for questioning. Running out of rooms, my heart pounding so hard I needed fresh air to breathe, I ran up the outside stairs to check the back yard.

I almost stumbled over EG sitting on the cool cellar steps leading up to the tiled patio. Long hair hiding her thin face, she was bent over some project at her feet. As I watched, Mallard came through a gate hidden behind the canopy of wisteria vine in the back corner of the yard. He was pushing a wheelbarrow.

They both noticed me at once. EG eyed me warily and said nothing.

Mallard rolled the wheelbarrow of dirt onto the patio, dusted off his grimy hands, and nodded. "Good day, Miss Devlin. I must start on dinner."

He stepped around EG and attempted to brush past me, but I climbed up a step and leaned my shoulder against the stair wall, blocking his escape. "You could have told me she was here so I didn't spend the last half hour scared out of my mind."

"I have no idea what you're talking about," Mallard said in that aloof British tone of his. "Miss Elizabeth is potting herbs. I'm sure there is nothing to fear in that activity."

It occurred to me that Mallard didn't know EG's last name. Not that EG carried Tex's since he and Magda were having an affair and not a marriage, but for the first time I realized no one but Nick and I knew her father was a United States senator in jail for murder. Unless Graham did. He knew everything. A virtual oracle was that man, or so he obviously thought.

"Miss Elizabeth is supposed to be in school," I snapped.

EG had been watching for my reaction. Now she turned her head and stared into the yard as if I wasn't there. We needed to talk, but that required privacy.

"Well, she isn't in school." Mallard looked me in the eye. "If you wish dinner, I suggest you let me pass."

"Does this mean you're feeding us tonight? Or do we have to break in and fix it ourselves again?"

He shuddered and visibly blanched. "Under no circumstances are you to ever touch the kitchen again."

"Even if all we want is a cracker?" EG asked, showing interest in the conversation now that it had turned away from her.

"Perhaps for a cracker, if you ask permission," Mallard agreed stiffly.

Knowing where this led, I didn't step aside but let Mallard suffer a while longer.

"What about a banana?" EG asked innocently. "If I'm studying and need a banana, can I get that?" She observed Mallard through a curtain of straight inky hair.

"Ring for it," Mallard replied crisply. "Now, if you will excuse me?"

I stepped aside as EG was asking, "What about a glass of warm milk before I go to bed? Should I ring for that?"

Mallard escaped without answering. EG stood up to follow, but I blocked the stairs.

I consulted my watch. "School isn't out yet. What are you doing home?"

"Mallard needed herbs potted. It's a botany lesson."

"Then tell me what chemical components plants consist of."

"Green things," she said defiantly. "Chlorophyll."

She pulled that out of her encyclopedic memory. She could probably pull out more, and I wouldn't know if she was right or wrong. I just knew she needed a real education and not the fake home school thing she gets from books. Nick and I weren't teachers, and books lie. She had to learn the people skills to question and know where to go to find answers.

"Why did you skip out?" I demanded.

"Because it was *dumb*," she shouted, on the verge of tears. "I just asked how we could say our form of government represents everyone like the book says when everyone knows over half our population is female and minorities, but our government is ninety-percent white male! She sent me to the principal for disobedience when I told her the book was wrong."

"And you walked out instead." I knew the feeling. I just didn't know how to counteract it. Brains disturbed the flow in classrooms geared for the average mentality.

Besides, I knew there were two sides to every story. I wouldn't be one of those parents who blamed the schools for everything. As proud as I was of my kid sister, I knew EG applied her intelligence like a weapon, diverting any form of interaction straight to hell. Maybe textbooks lied, but arguing with the teacher didn't fix the problem.

"Look, I know it's hard, but couldn't you just sit there and play dumb until I figure out what to do next? Graham yelled at me for not being here to know you skipped. How can I leave the house and find Pao if I'm worrying about you loose in the streets?"

"I'll sit in the library all day and Mallard can verify I'm there. I promise, I won't get in your way. Or better yet," she said eagerly, "I can go out with you."

She was breaking my heart, and I couldn't do anything about it. I wanted to tell her that's fine, we'd just muddle through until Magda arrived. But I didn't want our mother swooping down and hauling EG off to a desert harem or whatever. And the best way to hold our mother off was to show that I was raising EG responsibly.

I could probably even fight Magda in the courts for custodianship if I could show I had a home—which Magda didn't—and that I was providing EG's education—which Magda did but in unconventional, non-court-approved ways.

Of course, if I couldn't keep EG in school, I wasn't any better than Magda.

"We'll talk about this later," I admonished, chickening out. Nick was a people person. Maybe he'd have some suggestions. "I've got to get back to work."

"Can I help you work?"

I heard the plea and my heart desperately wanted to answer it, but I'd spent years getting my head together and was terrified of dividing and parceling out myself as I had before. It's far easier to obsess over my work than over a life in which I had no control.

"Give me a report on the herbs you're potting." Then, sad to say, I walked off. Let's face it. When up against an unfamiliar situation, we all react as we've been brought up. It takes an extra effort to stop and say *wait a minute, how can I do this better?* I didn't have time for that effort, or so I told myself.

EG poked her fingers into the newly potted herbs and didn't watch me go.

* * *

"Blackwell Johnson for you, Miss Devlin," the intercom announced coolly as I sat at the library table with the Whiz whizzing across the Internet. "Line one."

Mallard was the intercom voice, not Graham. Interesting. I studied the blinking lights on the fancy telephone until I had them figured out, then poked the button for line one. "Ana Devlin here." Did this mean it had been Johnson and not Magda who had called last night after all?

"Miss Devlin. I'm just calling to see if all is well with you. We are untangling some of your grandfather's accounts and have located some of his investments. Not many, I fear."

"Glad to hear you're looking out for us, Mr. Johnson. Shall I send Nick over to sign anything?"

"That won't be necessary. I'll send you a report and you can decide your preferences. Mostly it's stock in a small textbook company. How are you and Mr. Graham getting along?"

Textbook company? Was all this foofaraw with Mindy because Max wanted to buy cheap stock? "My grandfather owned stock in a textbook company?" I asked before answering his query. "Which one?"

I could almost see the lawyer frowning over the phone. "Something called Education-Pub, I believe. I don't have the file in front of me. Not a major investment by any means."

Edu-Pub. Max had helped Mindy investigate textbook companies, and then he had bought stock in one? But it wasn't publicly traded.

Blackwell didn't give me time to ponder all the paths this opened up. "I understand there is some question about Mr. Graham's connections to the senator who has been arrested for murder. Are you certain you are safe there?"

His phony concern shot the lid right off of my suspicion-ometer. "I have yet to meet Mr. Graham," I answered with an air of carelessness. "For all I know, he's not here at all. What do you know about him?"

"Not a thing, Miss Devlin," the lawyer said smoothly. "Not a thing. Then you have no reporters at your door asking about Senator Hammond? That's a relief."

"I'll be certain to call you if one shows up. I have no fondness for reporters."

If I was the imaginative sort, I'd believe I felt his relief as he said his farewells.

Shouldn't Johnson be more afraid of our pit-bull lawyer and the police right now instead of worrying about Graham and Tex? What on earth was he up to?

I pulled out my old Oracle file and ran a search for my grandfather's and Blackwell Johnson's names. And didn't find either.

* * *

Nick showed up after EG went to bed. From the disgruntled look on his handsome puss, his day hadn't been any better than mine.

"Oppenheimer refused the case?" I asked immediately.

"Men like that don't refuse money." He dropped into the wing chair, crossed his knees, and made a tent of his fingers over them. "He's filing charges against Brashton's law firm and recommends that we hire an unsavory agency he knows to go to St. Kitts and haul him back."

I frowned. "He wants more money to hire this suspicious outfit."

Nick shrugged. "It takes money to make money."

"I don't like lawyers who think they're above the law."

Nick brightened, and I could see he'd feared he'd have to card-count. My heart was getting a hefty workout today. Add new principle: Don't make Nick gamble.

I explained to him about EG's skipping school and added, "What we really need is tuition at some fancy school, not dubious lawyers." I'd been stewing over this all evening, but I didn't know how to go about finding a school that would take her.

"That's been taken care of," the intercom announced.

Nick sat up straight, and I glared at the intrusion on our private conversation. The spook had no right listening in on us. I had half a mind to go upstairs and hunt him down and rip off his head, but he spoke again before I could put my rage into action.

"There is a private school at the next Metro stop from here. A friend of mine is on the board. I've arranged for Elizabeth to be enrolled on a scholarship basis. She will need to report tomorrow to present her credentials."

A big gaping hole opened in my midsection. I didn't want this stranger dealing with my family. That's my job.

But he'd found a school now instead of later. EG would be on top of the world.

"We don't take hand-outs," I informed him. I wanted to ask where the hell we were supposed to live if EG went to school here and he threw us out, but I was holding my breath.

"And I'm not giving any," the voice replied. "If she can do the work, she has the slot. Send your brother to St. Kitts while you finish your work here. You don't have to do everything yourself." The intercom light snapped off.

I didn't have to do everything myself? Now there's a concept. I stared at Nick, who stared back. I'd always done everything myself. There'd never been anyone else to do it.

Until the spook had taken us in. I rejected that notion instantly.

"I can truss up Brashton as well as any unsavory detective agency can," Nick announced. "I even know how to sail his yacht. Just let me know when he arrives on the island."

And I could see his determination. Here was something he really wanted to do, and I'd have to let him do it. Which meant...

I'd have to let Graham send EG to school. It could be weeks before Brashton decided it was safe to reach St. Kitts.

Did this mean we could stay until I found Pao? If everyone else got what they wanted, couldn't I have my wish, too?

Chapter Eleven

Ana discovers the Oracle's secrets and heads for political trouble

I LIKED being alone, I told myself as I returned to the computer after Nick left. I would hate traveling to St. Kitts. The thought of trussing up Brashton and hauling him back here might give me a vicarious thrill, but logically, the hassle wasn't my thing. Nick was as capable of handling—or mishandling—the capture as I was. Besides, he could sail and I couldn't.

I hated the idea of Nick becoming involved in something that sounded vaguely nefarious, even if it was necessary, but he was a grownup. The money and the choice was his.

Instead, I concentrated on resenting the spook's interference in our affairs. EG was too young to make her own decisions. That was my domain. What if I didn't want EG going to a private school? What right did Graham have to talk to people about us? To make arrangements without asking permission?

We didn't have to send her.

She wouldn't stay in the public school.

Conceding defeat ungraciously, I switched to the news site for the latest on Senator Tex—his lawyers had scheduled a bond hearing for him in the morning. Jolly good for him. Maybe once he was out I should just go over there and ask him if he was a murderer because he had a daughter who wanted to know.

As I glared restlessly at the computer screen, wondering how to investigate murder, an e-mail with an attachment from an unknown sender popped up in my mailbox. I abhor spam, but I can't delete all unknown senders since I can't possibly memorize the continually changing addresses of all my correspondents.

I ran it through my aggressive virus check then downloaded it.

The file opened in Adobe Acrobat, and an analysis of Edu-Pub's financial statement appeared before my wondering eyes.

* * *

After a frustrating evening reading unfathomable accounting gobbledy-gook, I got up Tuesday morning wondering if our clothes would be on the street the minute we left the house. The fear of homelessness had haunted me all my life. I had to confront Graham in his lair sometime soon. Like today.

Graham had full access to the accounting analysis I'd studied last night. If he had any comment on it, I hadn't heard. My correspondent's accountant had commented that Edu-Pub seemed to carry an inordinate amount of cash in an industry that relied heavily on accounts receivable and inventory, but that didn't *prove* they were funneling illegal cash.

Just because Pao's website address was in the same zone as Edu-Pub didn't mean he deposited his donations in any account but his own. I'd already sent a check to the website but it hadn't cleared yet. One must presume innocence until proven guilty.

I had to talk to Graham.

Even contemplating bearding the lion in his den didn't induce the same anxiety as telling EG she could go to private school, or worrying about Nick departing for St. Kitts to capture a crook. Maybe Magda was right. Maybe it was better to keep them all at home where they couldn't get into trouble.

Not that this philosophy worked, mind you. We were all fine upstanding examples of how we could get into trouble anywhere we went. And "home" to Magda was anywhere she or her friends happened to be.

Frighteningly enough, I was beginning to grasp my mother's twisted logic. The kids were safe with people who understood them—their family.

By the time I vacillated between dress and jeans, neither of them precisely the elegant ensemble I imagined private school mothers wore, and descended to the dining room, Nick had already informed EG of her new position. EG didn't do excited well, but she did suspicion excellently.

"Why is he doing this?" she demanded when I entered.

The candelabra had reappeared on the table, but our host didn't deign to reply. Maybe he slept in the mornings after battling the Forces of Evil all night.

I poured fresh-squeezed orange juice from the pitcher on the buffet. Apparently we were back in Mallard's good graces. "If you don't know, how would I?" I countered.

That momentarily shut her up, and I contemplated letting silence reign. If I didn't offer anything, she couldn't argue, right?

"I don't have to wear a uniform, do I?"

Okay, so she didn't know the answer to everything. Makes one wonder how she knew the answer to things we hadn't asked, but I wasn't ready to blow my mind pondering the mysteries of the universe. "We won't know until we go over there."

A neat file of school applications and scholarship recommendations waited by my plate. How the devil did the spook do that? He'd had less than twenty-four hours to produce material that would take weeks of normal filing and approving. Perhaps he was even better at forgery than we were. I prayed the school believed them, if so. I'd hate to get EG's hopes up only to have her ridiculed and bounced out. Nick and I had developed armored shields taking chances that way, but considering our eccentric lifestyles as the result, it would be nice if EG didn't have to.

"I'll take her over, if you like," Nick offered, eyeing my denim jumper with distaste. "But if I'm not going to St. Kitts yet, I need to go job hunting, and you'll have to pick her up. I've talked to a few people, and there should be plenty of openings around Dupont Circle. Not lucrative, but sales positions never are."

I'd like to see what kind of frou-frou establishment we were sending EG to, but I felt guilty about neglecting my assignment after Graham's gracious gesture—or controlling presumption, depending on how I looked at it. If Nick was willing, we might as well work this parenting thing together, at least until Tex was proven innocent. Or otherwise.

"All right, if you'll see EG settled into school, I'll check what came in overnight."

I hesitated, waiting for the candelabra to object. I wasn't certain whether to be relieved or disappointed when it remained silent. It was oddly comforting to have an omnipotent figure watching over us. Not to mention unsettling.

* * *

I was torn in so many ways that it was difficult for me to focus. I had to find Brashton and our money. My week to find Pao ended tonight. I ought to be looking for a place to rent. And then there was Senator Tex rotting in jail, where I'd personally like to leave him if it hadn't been for EG and my nagging conscience. I really ought to be investigating Blackwell Johnson now that he'd floated onto my radar screen, but there's only so much a girl can do.

I picked up my e-mail and let my various problems knot my stomach until I could figure out which to work on first.

The correspondent who had given us the Nassar alias for Pao claimed Pao had used the name Nassar while traveling in Jakarta. The picture on the passport she had copied looked identical to the one Graham had given me when I first started on this hunt. Sal was a friend of mine from the government school I'd attended the year we stayed in Jordan. She moved in diplomatic circles these days and was stationed in Jakarta. I trusted her sources.

I located the GSA files Graham had apparently lifted to find Nassar's name and photo ID. There was no mention of his leaving the GSA, as I'd been told, but the file could be old.

I assumed Pao had somehow obtained Nassar's passport and pasted his photo into it. The details of height and eye coloring and so forth were close enough to pass. So, did Pao obtain the passport fraudulently from Nassar, and that was the reason Nassar had been fired? And where did Hagan fit into the scenario? I'd already checked, and knew Hagan's wasn't a highly secure government position. Could Pao access government records, or could Hagan be his inside accomplice?

And could Pao be using Nassar's identity to establish the financial funnel to Jakarta that I couldn't seem to find?

Before digging deeper into this possibility, I scanned down the list of messages until I hit an encrypted subject header. *Shit.*

I recognized the sender. We virtual assistants work in an invisible world behind public events and had to be careful of our identities or any information we divulged. If we were to rely on each other for research, we needed some confidence that our sources were genuine. I'd attended a conference or two, met a few people I trusted, and we occasionally shared tidbits about the people for whom we worked.

Shana worked in a federal government office in Atlanta, and I had used my international connections to do her a few favors over the past year. After moving to D.C., I'd sent her a carefully worded message telling her with whom I was working, and asking her to do a little poking around.

Apparently whatever she'd discovered required the use of the encryption software we'd both been experimenting with. I don't think she was sending me Leno jokes.

I knew Graham had access to this mailbox. He was probably staring at his screen, waiting impatiently for me to decode the message. Whether he knew it was about him might be questionable since even I didn't know it for certain. But I wasn't about to take a chance.

I transferred the message into my thumb drive and tucked it into my pocket. I left the Whiz searching and downloading some sites recommended by another e-mail and slipped out the front door. Even Mallard didn't know I was gone.

My thumb drive, or portable drive, whatever you want to call it, is a heavy-duty five gig and carried my essential software. I could plug it into any machine with a USB port and an operating system newer than '95, and be up and running. I hurried as fast as my sandals would carry me to the Kinko's down the street.

I waited impatiently for an acne-pocked nerd downloading porno to vacate the public computer. He hunched over the keyboard as I tapped my shoe and watched over his shoulder. When he turned around to scowl at me, he got a panicky expression on his face and hurriedly departed. As already established, I'm not large enough to scare a rabbit. I was wearing my usual braids and a generic jumper. I didn't think I looked fierce, but maybe militant enough to cause alarm in a sex fiend.

I sat down, plugged the thumb drive into the port, opened my encryption software, entered the e-mail with our code, and read Shana's note.

Amadeus Graham, age 35, law degree, Harvard University; PhD in political science, Princeton; associate chair in Fletcher School of Diplomacy, Tufts University; political advisor for Department of Defense; married; widowed on 9/11; dismissed from post for health reasons in 2002 after public disagreement with vice president and Secretary of Defense. No current info in our files. This the guy?

I was still reeling over *age 35*. He did all that and became such a recluse at thirty-five that people thought he was dead? This did not compute. Nothing about Amadeus Graham computed. He should have been in every search engine around the world with those kinds of credentials. I was right. He'd erased himself. Or someone had done it for him.

Widowed on 9/11. Wounded, too, maybe? Was that the health reason that had made him an invalid? If so, the guy had suffered more trauma in his lifetime than I had. He was a regular Icarus, soaring to the sun in his chariot of gold and getting his wings singed so badly he'd crashed to the ground, never to rise again.

I was almost feeling sorry for the bastard, except he had my grandfather's house and I didn't. Where did Senator Tex factor in? Had he complained to the Secretary of Defense about some transgression resulting in the public firing? I knew enough about politics to know there was always a private story behind the public one.

And what about Mindy Carstairs? There wasn't much of an age difference between Mindy and Graham. They both had worked in government. Mindy's mother had known of Graham, even if she thought he was dead. This was getting way too complicated.

While I was there, I scanned the other e-mails I'd copied into the drive. Working with Graham looking over my shoulder all the time was a trifle unnerving. I wanted to enjoy my momentary freedom. I was thinking of stopping at Starbucks—until I opened a file containing the list of investors in Edu-Pub. It was a privately held company registered in Delaware, so it had taken some major networking for one of my friends to track down a list of owners.

EG's father was on the board of directors.

My mouth went dry as I stared at the computer screen. I could feel people hovering, waiting for me to end my time online, but I couldn't tear my gaze away from the monitor. That old black paranoia welled.

Was Graham hunting down Pao to get at EG's father? If so, would he go so far as to frame Tex for murder?

Or should it be the other way around? Maybe Tex really was guilty of murder or was involved in Pao's money-laundering and deserved to be in jail and Graham was proving it.

I had some difficulty picturing conservative Tex as a supporter of radical Islamic groups in Indonesia, but his relationship to Edu-Pub wasn't promising. Edu-Pub's amazing cash flow could very well be my key to Pao's ability to live in D.C. without any seeming source of income.

I hastily printed out the list, shut down my program, retrieved my thumb drive, and strode out onto the blistering sidewalks of a D.C. August morning. Would it be possible to talk with the senator about Pao? It didn't seem very likely if he was still behind bars. I had never tried to talk my way into a prison and hadn't the slightest idea how to go about it, even if I knew where they locked up senators.

Did I want to let Tex know I was on his trail if there was any possibility that he really was the bad guy? I didn't perceive anyone associating with Pao as a saint. Radical Islamic fundraisers might not come under the heading of *bad guys* in my lexicon, but money-laundering did, if that's how Pao was hiding his donations.

Not that I thought Graham was any saint either. I was beginning to wonder if he wasn't even more paranoid than I was. But unlike EG's father, Graham had made it a point to find EG a good school. That put him in my corner. For now.

I had less than twenty-four hours to find Pao or confront Graham and tell him I needed more time. I wanted to be in a position to go to Graham, say here's Pao's address, and ask for another assignment so we could stay in the house.

I scanned the list of Edu-Pub owners looking for other names that might ring a bell and found several interesting facts. First, a Bob Hagan was on the list—coincidence?

I shouldn't have been surprised, but the second name I recognized was Reginald Brashton Junior. What were the chances that Reggie III— he who now sailed to St. Kitts on our stolen money—had inherited his father's shares of Edu-Pub?

Third was interesting in what *wasn't* there. I didn't find my grandfather's name. Had Johnson lied about our inheriting the stock? Or had Reggie done some fancy transferring of his shares? To what purpose?

The fourth and final fact was the most shocking: Senator Paul Rose, the current administration's favorite for his party's nomination for president owned a large percentage. Even living behind the blinders of my basement world, I recognized his name.

Wow. Gripping the paper so hard it wrinkled, I stared blankly up the street lined with imposing edifices containing embassies and religious foundations and other power centers. How did I proceed? Brashton Two was dead. The Third was in the Caribbean. And it might be easier to reach Tex in jail than a candidate for president. How likely was a man of the stature of Paul Rose to even know who Pao was?

What the heck was Graham chasing? He'd said an international cartel bent on taking over the world. I hadn't believed him, but it was starting to sound as if the picture could be a lot bigger than I'd thought. Why did it all keep coming back to textbooks and how could I find out?

The old lizard brain kicked in—*fundraisers know fundraisers*. Rose would have a huge fundraising campaign headquarters in D.C. If Senator Rose was on the board of Edu-Pub, what were the chances the firm was one of Rose's contributors? Pretty damned good if my understanding of politics had any foundation at all, and I was schooled at the knees of the best.

I didn't want to go back to the house until I had something more concrete than a piece of paper, but computers are my right hand. I couldn't work without one.

I returned to Kinko's. The public ones were full. Totally focused on my goal, aware my time was running out, I simply walked behind the counter, appropriated an unmanned PC, called up the Internet, and looked up Rose's campaign headquarters in the white pages. Then I called up a map of the location and had it printing before anyone thought to question me. I am so much part of a computer that I looked as if I belonged there, I suppose.

Ripping the map from the printer, I apologized, offered to pay them for the use, and walked out without anyone calling the cops.

I was developing a healthy respect for the Metro. Although I'd learned how to drive in deserts and jungles, I'd never owned a car and had never wasted time with a driver's license. The Metro relieved me of the hassle of car ownership and traffic, and I could be an environmental paragon in EG's eyes.

Rose's campaign headquarters were a bit of a disappointment though. Plastered with red, white, and blue posters, stickers, and buttons, staffed by volunteers, it only needed a Sousa band to be a political version of Chuck E Cheese's rah-rah carnival. Some of the geeks behind the desks didn't even need funky costumes to complete the image.

My eyes widened as I realized I fit right in. I had some vague notion that political campaigns operated on the bronzed and beautiful, but those were the people in the front lines. Back here on Ground Zero were the outcasts, the bitter, and the idealists who earnestly thought that seeing their candidate nominated was of earth-shaking relevance. Geeks, like me.

I could have told them that if Senator Rose disappeared tomorrow, there were a dozen more wealthy snake-oil salesmen to take his place, but I resisted. I merely watched for one of the geeks to leave his desk to get coffee. Then I appropriated his PC. Since the computer was already on, I didn't need a password to call up Windows Explorer—the campaign was obviously using old computers with ancient versions of Windows, but I know my way around them all.

Within minutes I was perusing Rose's complicated list of campaign contributors. I didn't fool myself into believing it contained all of them, but it would contain enough hard money to cover up the soft, and Edu-Pub was legitimately allowed to contribute a certain dollar amount. I e-mailed the list to myself and was busily accumulating names and addresses to be used immediately when the geek returned to his desk.

"Hey, what are you doing?" he cried with amazing originality. "Who are you?"

Looking up, I saw him turn to shout to a bulky guy who would make three of me. Desperation called up a Magda-ism. "Why hello there, big boy, how did I miss you when I came in?" I purred deep in my throat, twirling a loose strand of hair and rising to step between him and the thousand-pound gorilla.

To give the guy credit, he didn't look old enough to legally drink alcohol, and his nondescript dishwater-blond hair was already receding. He blinked at me from behind a pair of lenses that would have done an old-fashioned Coke bottle proud. And I was channeling Magda, the vamp. He didn't stand a chance. It didn't matter if I was short and wore braids. I was female. I had always thought it unfair to take advantage of that fact, but experience will tell, and Magda was my teacher.

His Adam's apple bobbed up and down as I stepped further away from his desk. I wished I was wearing shorts instead of the ankle-length jumper, but it didn't seem to matter that I could wiggle only a bare ankle in funky sandals. He stopped shouting.

"Paul will be delighted to hear he has such diligent workers," I cooed. "It's people like you who make his efforts worthwhile. Thank you." Still channeling Magda for all I was worth, I patted his cheek and sashayed past.

I could never have pulled this off with anyone possessing a modicum of self-confidence, but I knew geekdom well. I'd lived there for many, many years. I was older now, with years of therapy behind me.

I strode out as if I were five-ten and wearing French heels.

No gorilla came roaring after me.

Chapter Twelve

Ana accomplishes her task, blows up a building, and meets an Oracle

MY MAGDA persona evaporated, and I morphed back to a nonentity by the time I turned the corner at the Metro station. Since it was nearing noon, the crowd was hustling. People would walk right over me if I didn't slide between them in my haste.

Every single, solitary officer and board member of Edu-Pub had contributed to Rose's campaign. The file had neatly marked their addresses and even the address of the contribution from Edu-Pub. All perfectly above board and prepared for public examination. I couldn't imagine Graham investigating Edu-Pub because of a politician. Of course, I couldn't imagine a high-ranking politician having anything to do with a company that harbored a fanatic like Pao, so obviously my imagination lacked creativity.

According to Google, the address on the donations for Edu-Pub's headquarters was in a sleazy warehouse district—not precisely the classy company one would expect to support senators. Or that would have senators on their board.

I had no idea what I was doing or how I would do it, but I hopped the first train heading southeast while I pondered. As blind as I might be about politics, even I knew the sky was the limit when it came to cash and campaign funds. I had assumed the large amounts of unexplained cash in Edu-Pub's accounting statements were illegal contributions to Pao's cause, but what if Pao wasn't the only one laundering cash?

The opportunities for blackmail and fraud were rife. And if Mindy Carstairs had been investigating textbook companies, she might have been in a position to know all about it. Tex was dead meat if the cops found out. If we really owned stock in the place as Johnson claimed, I wanted it sold immediately.

I got off at the Metro stop closest to the Edu-Pub warehouse and looked around warily. With my white skin, I'd stick out like jam on rye. I'd been in far worse parts of the world than the slums of D.C., but American thieves are bigger and have more powerful weapons. I could eliminate a knife fairly easily, but kickboxing didn't work on AK-47s. I wasn't channeling Magda anymore. I was channeling an idiot.

But I couldn't go back to the house empty-handed. I wanted visible proof that I had Pao nailed so I could ask for another assignment and an extension of our stay. We could have Brashton within a week. Once we had our money, anything was possible. The dream of owning Grandfather's mansion shimmered like a beacon of temptation—or like

Circe on a pile of rocks.

I needed camouflage. I located a Goodwill on the corner and my eyes lit up. Just call me an urban cockroach. If I can find my way around the dusty alleys of Marrakesh, I can survive in the modern streets of D.C. It just takes a modicum of common sense.

I couldn't change the color of my skin, but I could look less like a victim. If I were as tall as my sister Patra, I'd head for a police or military supply store. But no one would believe a five-two cop. I'm not proud. I'd shopped Goodwill before. If this one was similar to the others, they'd have what I needed.

I lucked out. I found a khaki long-sleeved shirt with *Dave* on the pocket name tag. It was too big, naturally, but the bulk added to my figure. For ten bucks I bought the shirt, a cap to pull over my eyes, khaki pants, and a belt to hold the mess together, plus cool metal-toed shoes. I tucked my trusty sandals and jumper into my shoulder bag, slung it around me like a backpack, and covered my braid with the cap. I looked dumb, but not out of place where I was going.

Walking the blocks to the derelict industrial center where Edu-Pub was headquartered, I saw no one suspicious on the steamy street, and no one gave me a second glance.

It was rather liberating retreating to invisibility. I was free to roam where I pleased. This couldn't be said of many of the other countries where I'd lived growing up. If the good ol' US of A had problems, I wasn't complaining. I knew the alternative.

I hurried down cracked and filthy sidewalks with my head down, my billed cap pulled over my eyes. I knew the city dweller defense mechanisms well. Brisk, purposeful tread, and I was outta there. I succeeded in reaching my destination without interference.

Instead of going in the front, I circled behind the warehouses to check out the rear. I needed some way of circumventing any clerk at the front desk.

I didn't know how a crap joint like this could be the corporate headquarters of anything except Flyspecks Anonymous, but I'd seen a million dollars of hashish thrown in a broken basket in the back of a Bedouin tent before. Poverty is the best disguise for wealth.

The industrial center didn't even have a Dumpster. I encountered nothing more dangerous than broken glass, cracked blacktop with weeds growing through it, discarded rags that might once have been clothing, and accumulated trash. I counted doors until I guessed the peeling orange one belonged to Edu-Pub. There weren't any delivery hours posted.

I still had no idea what I would say: *Hi, I've come to pick up my textbook order?*

Spurred by my earlier success of rifling computers, I had some foggy notion of locating more open computer files if I could get inside. Was stealing information from unlocked computers illegal? I didn't have a clue and didn't want to press my burgeoning integrity with questions I wasn't prepared to answer.

I know next to nothing about security systems, although that was a topic I was hot to research. I studied the door and walls and saw nothing resembling wires or cameras. Maybe if I tried to open the door, an alarm would sound, causing much confusion, and I could run around front and slip in there unnoticed?

Well, nothing ventured, nothing gained. Using a Kleenex from my pocket, I reached for the dented aluminum knob.

The door swung open soundlessly.

Maybe I should have checked the front. Maybe the place was empty. *Stupid, Ana, stupid.*

Figuring this was my first attempt at real-world spying, and that I was entitled to be dumb, I stepped inside the dark interior. The air-conditioning didn't appear to be working, so the atmosphere inside was thick and hot, but not as bad as it would be later in the day. This back room was undoubtedly an office.

The light from the open door was sufficient to reveal that the filing cabinets had been ransacked. Papers from the desk drifted across the floor with a meager draft from an inner door leading into the warehouse. The Edu-Pub staff had absconded, leaving everything behind. Why?

The question alone should have terrified me into backing out. Instead, the empty office gave me confidence that I could work undisturbed. All I needed was an address. And maybe a peek at their textbooks, for the sake of curiosity.

I rifled through the filing cabinet first. Drawers of orders from schools across the country. Invoices of textbooks shipped. Correspondence that would put a dead man to sleep. If there had been anything in here to link Edu-Pub with Pao and the Cambodian websites, they had taken it. I slipped an order list of current publications into my bag.

My check for textbooks mailed to this address had yet to clear the bank. Who had the deposits?

I hadn't bothered with the computer first because I figured if they'd left it behind, it was worthless. To my utter amazement, I accessed Windows without a password. Who in hell abandoned operating computer equipment? That was damned eerie, and if I stopped to think about it, I'd scare myself.

Instead, I plugged in my thumb drive. I had a random password program in it, but someone didn't much care if the computer was accessed. It must have no essential information.

But what I found tickled me into grinning hugely. Within seconds, I had discovered the cable system was still on-line, and I'd forwarded the list of contract employees to my own e-mail address, and stored a few stray items that might be useful. Since no one had arrived to stop me, I figured I could explore some more.

I followed the flow of air through a cheap wooden door into the warehouse. Dusky light filtered through the filth of the high windows. Metal shelves lined with neat stacks of textbooks filled the enormous space. To my inexperienced eyes, it looked like a perfectly legitimate publishing company warehouse.

I was walking up and down the aisles, picking up textbooks to check copyright pages, wondering how one got a job writing this gibberish, when I heard a noise in the front office—the area I hadn't checked. I froze.

At the approach of murmured male voices, I moved as quietly as I could toward the shoddy door I'd entered through—the only one I'd seen in the warehouse. I'd been living in my insular world too long. I knew better than to enter a building without planning an escape route.

I had mental pictures of me stepping into the back office just as men in black entered through the swinging doors from the front and Pao sauntered in the back.

I'd almost reached the warehouse door when my toe caught in the hem of my overlong khaki uniform. I stumbled, grabbed a shelf, and a stack of books tilted and slid to the concrete floor before I could catch them.

A voice shouted.

Oh, shit. I gave up silence in favor of speed. Still holding one of the textbooks I'd grabbed, I sprinted out of the warehouse, aiming for the open door to the alley.

Bursting past the filing cabinets, I came eyeball to eyeball with a brown teenager no taller than me. He shouted something incomprehensible to his companion in the front room and grabbed my arm.

I'm not much on being manhandled, or kidhandled. And the pungent smell of gasoline shot off my internal alarms. Not stopping to contemplate whether the kid was a Cambodian relative of Pao's or just the usual run-of-the-mill gang arsonist, I acted on automatic. I whacked his wrist with a swift down-chop of the book in my hand and kicked his shins with my metal-toed shoe. I'd learned from kickboxing that the pain from a kick to the shins can cripple.

He released me with a wail of agony. I skirted around him, leaped over the desk, and fled out the back door.

I was half way down the block and running for home when I crashed full-length into a black suit stepping out of a doorway in front of me.

High on adrenaline, I raised my knee so fast he had to spin me around before I emasculated him. And I didn't even know the guy.

"Crap," he shouted, grabbing my waist from behind. "What the hell are you doing down here?"

That was all I heard before I jammed my elbow backward. I aimed for the solar plexus, hit abs of steel, and almost shattered my funny bone. I wasn't laughing.

Releasing my waist, the goon grabbed my braid, wrapped it in his fist, and held me far enough way to keep my deadly elbows out of his midsection. "I'm one of the good guys, dammit," he said as I flailed with arms and legs.

If I'd had a knife, I would have sliced off my braid to get away. As it was, I twisted in his grip, ignoring the pain of pulled hair to get in a good side kick to his kneecap and a karate chop at his jugular. He grabbed my arm before I connected.

Grabbing an arm like that is strictly amateur stuff. Any professional would have thrown him half way across the street for a sorry-ass move like that. I'm a lightweight, but with the right leverage, even I could have humiliated him by flinging him over my shoulder and into tomorrow.

The explosion half a block away was the only thing that saved him.

The blast rocked the street, and we both dived for the shelter of a storefront doorway. Bricks, glass, and flying pieces of concrete whipped through the air in a tornado of dust and textbook pages. I heard shouts in the distance and hoped the stupid kids had escaped. Silly of me, but I didn't want body parts raining down with the other debris.

Now I knew why they'd left the computer and everything behind. They'd planned on destroying the evidence.

* * *

"You can't sit there with your head between your knees forever," Nick said in a harsh whisper while black police shoes worked around me.

"I can if it means they won't question me because they're afraid I'll barf all over their shiny shoes," I retaliated, but he was right.

Black suit had disappeared into the woodwork with the first sirens. And I'd immediately gone into adaptive mode. Just replaying that moment when the guy in a black suit had asked what was I doing there—as if he knew who I was—had practically stopped my heart.

I'd frantically called Nick's cell phone, then blended with the scenery until he arrived. Honest citizen that I was, I'd felt compelled to stay as a witness.

"Is your sister feeling better yet?" a bluff police sergeant asked impatiently. "We really need to ask her a few questions."

"I'm better, thank you." I held out my hand to Nick who hauled me up from the concrete block I'd been sitting on. I was totally freaked by the smoking remains further up the street, but I'd had time to give thanks that no one would be able to find my fingerprints inside. They'd be lucky to find an entire finger. The street was littered with textbook ashes.

The book I'd stolen was now in my essential bag. I wasn't good citizen enough to tell the cops that. I was too shaken to think clearly enough to explain it away.

"We verified the address you gave us, Miss Devlin. You want to tell me what the hell someone who lives up your way was doing down here?" The sergeant was black and probably royally ticked to have to deal with an uptown white girl. I couldn't blame him.

Nicholas started to step protectively in front of me, but I squeezed his hand. I'd had time to think this out, and he hadn't. "I'm a virtual assistant," I told him, wishing I could channel Magda again but still too shaken for sexy. Besides, geekdom seemed the best tactic here. "I can provide credentials, if you like. I was working on a story for one of my clients on textbook companies."

The policeman towered a foot over me and was probably glaring down at my shiny braids with disbelief. I'd changed my disguise before the cops arrived so I didn't look too insane, but I wasn't certain my jumper over the khaki shirt was an improvement. The trousers had joined the textbook in my bag. I hoped I looked appropriately humble and scared.

"Your *client* sent you down here?" the good sergeant asked.

That could be a problem. He'd be asking for the name of my client to see if he had any relation to the explosion. I shook my head and turned an innocent stare up to the cop's disbelieving expression. "I'm very methodical when doing a random sampling. I printed out all the textbook firms in the country, cut the names into individual strips, and dropped them into a hat. I chose five to investigate personally, and this was one of them." I had actually used this method in a random sample for a legitimate client, so I figured it would sound convincing.

"Miss Devlin, are you all right?"

The voice was warm, concerned, and familiar. Surprised, I glanced past Nicholas. A lean-hipped, blue-jeaned hunk wearing a construction foreman's hard hat is difficult to miss. Even in this unusual environment, I recognized him instantly. The surprise and concern on Sean's handsome face warmed the cockles of my heart. For a gaze like that, I might even figure out what cockles were and if I had a heart.

"Mr. O'Herlihy," I said, carrying out my current role of modest little sister and research nerd. "What are you doing here?" I turned to the two men with me. "Sean O'Herlihy, an acquaintance of mine. My brother,

Nicholas, and Sergeant Jones."

I could sense all three men sizing each other up. I wanted to kick Nick because he had no business looking at Sean as if he were both dessert and enemy, but my knees were still shaking.

"I'm working on a parking lot job behind here." Sean removed his hat and his blue eyes twinkled. "I thought the blast had made me crazy as well as deaf when I heard your voice."

He lied. He'd grabbed that hat from a work crew, I'd bet bottom dollar on it. I could see it in the curve of his lips. My money was on Black Suit arranging for O'Herlihy's arrival. Suspicion was always my first reaction, but I had too many things happening to keep tabs on a glib Irish liar. "That could very well be, Mr. O'Herlihy." I'd just agreed he could be crazy, and his lips twitched upward. He caught on quick. "I appreciate your concern."

"This is a police investigation. Unless you're her lawyer, I'll have to ask you to leave," the sergeant said gruffly.

"My crew works a street over, Sergeant. We didn't see anything except the blast, but if we can be of help, you let us know." Sean tipped his hat to his forehead and sauntered off.

"My, my," Nicholas murmured admiringly, watching him go. "I had no idea you'd been so busy, Ana girl."

I didn't elbow him as he deserved. Everything was in the focus, and getting out of here was my objective. I'd already wasted enough time being honest and upright and waiting for the police instead of running like hell as I should have.

I tucked my hand around Nick's elbow and blinked like a doofus at the poor policeman.

I had already told him about the arsonists, but I could only describe one of them. I really had no further reason to linger except my shaking knees, and Nick's arrival had solved that. "May I go now, sir?"

"We may have a few more questions for you later. Do you have a work number?"

"Just Nick's cell phone. Our landlord's number is unlisted," I said listlessly, trying to look suitably pale and limp. Since my natural color is vampire white, that wasn't difficult.

Nick got the message. Patting my hand, he straightened into his officious best. "The heat and shock are kicking in, I fear. I need to take her home. I'll see that she gets any message."

Another cop was shouting something indecipherable, and distracted, the sergeant nodded and let us escape. It was fairly obvious we weren't viable suspects, and we had the potential to become real flakes. Letting us out of his hair was a sensible decision for a cop without enough time or manpower.

"Who was that movie star hard body?" Nick demanded as he practically dragged me up the street to a busier corner where taxis might be managed. Nick had his dignity and wasn't much taken with subways or buses.

"You don't ask me what I was doing here or any of those sensible things that a normal brother would ask?" I was being rhetorical. I wanted an answer to his question, too. Who the hell was Sean O'Herlihy and what was he doing there?

"Nothing you do is ever accidental," Nick grumbled, "and I figured I'd have to shake you if you actually told me the truth. You could have been killed."

Nick sounded abnormally stiff as he thumbed down a taxi. I think I may have scared him. I wanted to reassure him that the risk had been worth it.

I took a deep breath of exhaust-fumed air and rolled my shoulders to relax. It was hard to feel triumphant when my only source of evidence had gone to that great book burning in the sky. "I have Pao's address."

I'd won. I'd completed my assignment. I wanted lights to flash and bells to ring.

A bus belched diesel instead.

Pao's address had been in the Edu-Pub computer as one of their commissioned textbook salesmen. I had evidence to connect the Islamic fundraiser with a very suspicious company with large amounts of cash and a board of directors made up of politicians.

I could now confront Graham in triumph, but I was too drained to celebrate.

A taxi rolled up, and Nick knew better than to question me in front of strangers. Damned good thing, too. The back of my neck prickled, and I had the uneasy feeling Black Suit was just around the corner. I entered the air-conditioned taxi with more than one reason to sigh in relief.

I looked over my shoulder as we drove away, and caught a glimpse of black slipping into a doorway. Nary a street crew of hard hats was to be seen.

After Nick was reassured I hadn't knocked any brains out and that I really had the address Graham wanted, we rode back to the house in hopeful silence.

I prayed my snooping hadn't set off this dangerous turn of events. Given how ineffectual I'd been so far, I didn't let my conscience blame me for long. I had the confrontation ahead to terrify me more.

I had learned that Amadeus Graham was a man with the power to eradicate his very public identity, or with an enemy powerful enough to eradicate it for him. This was not the kind of man I wanted around. Magda was the power magnet, not me. I'd seen enough over the years to know that power ultimately corrupts. It's impossible to play God without tempting the Devil.

Play God. Exactly what Graham was doing, if my suspicions were confirmed.

I shivered. Maybe I shouldn't give Graham the information he wanted.

I am not a coward. I am perfectly willing to fight if threatened. Admittedly, I'm more willing to walk away than face conflict, but I had no excuse for not meeting Graham face to face. I wished I was built like an Amazon. The world would be a simpler place if I could just intimidate people into listening.

"I'm not letting you go up there alone." Nick intruded on my reverie as the taxi halted outside grandfather's mansion, and I stared up at the turrets.

For reasons I couldn't explain, I didn't want Nick with me when I faced our nemesis. "He's more likely to talk to me than to a posse. You're woman enough to know what I mean."

Nick groaned at that adage and steered me toward the front door. "And you're mental enough not to need back-up," he growled.

"What's he going to do, shoot me? It would bloody the historic carpets," I scoffed. "The best he can do is throw us out of the house, and that's going to happen by morning regardless." It wasn't as if Graham had promised we could stay if I proved myself. That was just my dearest hope. "Go interrogate Mallard as to the best housing alternatives in the area. And one of us needs to pick EG up by four."

Leaving Nick to hunt down Mallard, I ran upstairs to my room, and took a quick shower. I plaited my wet hair in neat braids that I wound around my head. Then I rummaged in the file drawers for my business-like blazer to go over a clean, ankle-length jumper. A non-combative Quaker stared back at me from the bathroom mirror. This was the person I was striving to become: quiet, unassuming, gracious, secure with herself. Princess Leia in civvies.

In reality, I was a raging inferno with lava for blood. People did not blow up warehouses to disguise money-laundering. Politicians did not own textbook companies run by terrorists. Graham was investigating something far more complex than a religious fanatic.

One side of me *hated* violence, despised politics, and wanted no part of whatever he was up to. On the other hand, my Irish temper wanted to blow up something to make myself heard.

Kickboxing, karate, and dirty fighting wouldn't get me through this next scene. I had to face Graham and communicate rationally.

By now, Graham ought to be waiting for me. He had to have figured out that the encrypted message was about him. He knew I'd left the house and returned primed for bear. He probably even knew about the explosion. I didn't know if he knew I'd been down there, but if he was half the spook I thought he was, he knew I wasn't at my computer.

He probably had motion sensors on the stairs to tell him when I headed up. The minute I put my foot on the first step, I couldn't turn back or I'd be a coward in his eyes and my own.

I climbed the stairs slowly, trying to think through the pounding of my anxiety. I was about to meet the monster who had stolen our house. That was enough to up my blood pressure.

I heard the low hum of machines when I reached the top of the stairs. I hadn't heard them the last time I was up here. Gazing down the corridor of doors on either side of the stairway, I realized one had been left open. He was expecting me, all right. He didn't want me flinging open all the other doors to see what was behind them. That made me feel a little better. He knew what I was capable of.

My denim hem brushed the thick carpet as I approached the opening. I folded my hands and politely stopped in the doorway, nervously pretending I was the civilized businesswoman I'd seen in the mirror.

The room was dark, lit only by the light of the computer screens circling the walls. In a quick survey, I recognized monitors focused on the various entrances and halls of the house as well as ones playing all the major news websites. Some screens had indecipherable words flowing across them. There were too many to take in all at once. Just the confirmation that the house was riddled with video cameras should steam me. Instead, guilt drew my eyes to the screen with Shana's message on it—decoded.

He knew I knew who he was. He was going to kill me.

If this was really Amadeus Graham, he was a man whose life had been shattered. That didn't make him a good man or a bad one. I suspected it had made him a dangerous one, and I'd been messing around where he didn't want me.

My eyes were adapting to the dimness. I could see Graham's silhouette facing a large flat-screen monitor in the back of the room. He hadn't even turned around. He was sitting in a chair with a high back, and all I could see was the breadth of his shoulders extending beyond the narrow chair, his head held straight as he examined a document on an upper screen. It's difficult to judge height from a distance and more so when the object isn't standing. But from here, his silhouette looked like Christopher Reeve, Superman, and my idiot libido went into overdrive.

I had the inexplicable, insane urge to saunter closer, to tease his hair or tickle his chin, to jar him as much as he did me. I wanted a real personal exchange instead of a mechanical one. This was a man with intelligence to match mine, and he was looking damned attractive from here. Or maybe I just had a wounded hero complex.

But my innate defense system screamed warnings, and I played cool. I remained in the doorway.

"That modest pose doesn't fool me in the least."

He had a deep voice that rumbled my lower parts like heavy bass. Devoid of human emotion, it still struck me in my soft places. I didn't know how he could see me with his back turned. For all I knew, he had a camera on the door and watched me on a monitor.

"I wear it to fool myself," I said in the same clipped, professional tones he used, strolling closer and surreptitiously examining the monitors. The eerie gray light created only shadows.

"You took unnecessary, dangerous risks this morning," he intoned, rolling his chair from one monitor to another, still not looking at me. "I warned you not to go out on your own."

So, he knew. Either Sean or Black Suit was a spy.

He rolled about in a desk chair, not a wheelchair, but I suspected he didn't rise and confront me because he couldn't. The Christopher Reeve image took on new meaning—what if he was paralyzed?

The new monitor flicked on with the addresses I'd e-mailed from Edu-Pub. It was more than annoying that he knew everything as soon as I did, but at least he hadn't bellyached about my wasting time researching him. Yet.

"Did you take unnecessary risks to end up in that chair?" I retaliated. I could have smacked myself after I said it. What the hell did I care whether or not he was crippled or how he'd got there? All I wanted was to show I'd accomplished my task and ask to keep my home.

"My job is about risk. Yours isn't." He scrolled through the list on the monitor without giving me any indication how I should take this. Did I assume he worried about my safety? When was the last time anyone had cared about my wellbeing?

So much for my bad attempt to get personal. I was operating in a total vacuum and losing touch with reality if I thought Graham had any interest in me. "Textbooks are a risk?" I asked, keeping up the sarcastic front that served me well.

"They weren't until now," he muttered, sounding a little less like himself. "Edu-Pub was just a loose string I needed yanked. I didn't expect you to unravel a hornet's nest."

"You had me investigating loose strings?" I resisted the urge to swat him over the head.

"How was I supposed to know you had such a talent for trouble?"

I didn't bother with an obviously rhetorical question. "That list you're looking at contains Pao's address," I pointed out with pride. "I've accomplished my task. What will you do with the information?" I was trusting that he wouldn't use it to murder Pao. That would certainly cure my crush on the pleasant fantasy who called himself *Oracle*.

He didn't look up as he scrolled through the list of Edu-Pub contractors to Pao's name. "I can neutralize people without need of violence," he replied, as if reading my mind.

I believed him. Maybe I just *wanted* to believe him, but instinct told me he could have me disappear and no one would question. Not totally reassuring, but enough to make me feel easier about dead bodies.

"This address is not viable. Neither is the social security number," he continued without an ounce of inflection either way.

The little bit of confidence I'd built up evaporated like helium from a leaky balloon. I didn't need this mechanical ass. I could live anywhere.

EG couldn't.

"I'm close," I argued. "I could probably find him today, but it's difficult to concentrate with homelessness looming. If we have to leave, I need to hunt for a place to stay. It's pointless to continue searching for Pao without the promise of reward."

"It irritates you to fail," he said with certainty.

"I'm not accustomed to it," I agreed.

"I set you up for failure."

Well, duh. I stalked for the door, wrapping my fingers in a fist to keep from bashing him with a heavy object. Defeat tasted bitter. "Thank you so much for that," I threw over my shoulder. "I'm sure the humility will do me good. Pao doesn't exist then?"

"Of course he exists. He's attending a fundraiser for Senator Rose on Friday. If you'd read all your mail instead of running off like a wild hare, you'd know that."

Professional. I must remain implacable like a good virtual assistant. I must not kick him into next week. I halted in the doorway and looked back. "You aren't suggesting that I attend?"

"No. I'm suggesting that you find out how he's traveling so I can have him followed."

I opened my mouth to tell him that was impossible, then promptly shut it again. There were a thousand and one things I could have asked, but there was only one I must have answered now. "Does this mean we're staying?"

"You've earned a chance to stay until Brashton lands in St. Kitts and your brother nabs him, but only if I can trust you to keep anything you think you know about me quiet." His voice remained perfunctory, but I heard the implied threat. I'd wondered when he'd mention the encrypted message.

He turned, and just for a moment, our eyes met. My fingers locked around the door jamb, preventing my knees from collapsing under me.

His face was in shadow, but his eyes were dark and glittering and shot arrows straight through my heart.

"I know nothing about you," I felt called upon to mention.

"Exactly," he intoned with what almost passed for warmth. "And let's keep it that way. You may go now."

I stumbled from the room, reeling from the myriad questions I didn't have the courage to ask. We still had a home—with a man who put new meaning to the term *evil genius*.

Chapter Thirteen

Ana goes to private school

WE HAD a home.

I must be doing something right spun dizzyingly through my head. I knew I was good at my work, but no one with credentials as impressive as Graham's had ever approved of me, in however remote a fashion. He'd called me a *wild hare*, but I knew the difference between being called camel spit and a hare. I'd been called the former by some of Magda's acquaintances who hadn't respected my talents any more than they'd valued EG's. Graham trusted my work, and I *liked* being trusted. By a sexy spook.

I staggered a little under the release of the heavy burden I'd been carrying.

Maybe I needed to find a new therapist.

That I didn't know what the hell Amadeus Graham was up to ought to have been my biggest concern, but I was a selfish beast. I appreciated being appreciated. Let Pao worry about Graham. At the moment, the man who owned this house was my best pal.

Apparently, I had decided that a guy who looked like Superman couldn't be a murderer. I probably needed to find Sean and have hot doggie sex to clear that idiocy out of my head, but it was hard to determine if it was sex or the house that had me blind.

My opinion of Super Spook would change quickly enough once I figured out where he had all the cameras hidden, but I wanted to float on the cloud of success for a little while. It had been a difficult day, and I needed the reward.

Nick was pacing in the library, impatiently awaiting the outcome of our meeting. I daresay the stunned look on my face was priceless, but he merely raised his eyebrow.

"Bad address, good information," I replied to the implied question. "We're staying until we nab Brashton. I need food." I plopped down in my chair and fired up the Whiz.

"Write me a letter and tell me all about it. You can eat it later. You have to pick up EG. I have a job interview." Nick strode off, apparently more irritated at my lack of communication than happy about my good news. I wanted to be a good sister, and Nick was my best friend, but I was stoked and already absorbed in my mission. We could chat later.

Wild dreams of becoming Graham's permanent assistant and never having to leave danced through my head as my fingers flew across the keyboard. I refused to consider the possibility that Sexy Man might be a terrorist, although nutcase was still a possibility.

If we could just stay until we could buy the house back or Oppenheimer sued and got it back for us...

Graham wouldn't be a happy camper about that one. Best not broadcast that hope too loudly. For all I knew, he could pick up brain waves. I needed to start hunting for his cameras.

All right, back to square one. I wasn't giving up on finding an address. "Not viable" meant many things. I wasn't taking Graham's word for it. I made up a hokey advertisement for computer repairs, and using the phony school for a return address, sent it to Pao's supposedly non-viable address with *Address service requested* on the envelope. I did the same with Edu-Pub's address.

Next, I found the e-mail from a D.C. virtual assistant who had located Pao's name after running a search on her boss's upcoming guest lists. Clever of her. Fundraisers had to attend fundraisers. There he was, Sak Thai Pao, businessman, no address. They had to have his address to send an invitation, didn't they? I sent a return mail asking for details. My network of VAs was gratifyingly effective.

I really wanted to dig deeper into Edu-Pub's finances and owners, but first things first. I began a search of taxi and limo services for Friday evening. It was possible Pao might drive himself, but D.C. traffic was appalling and parking limited. Smart money was on paid transportation.

Patience is a virtue in my business. With a list of phone numbers in hand, I began calling every transportation company in town.

Within the hour, I was firmly down from Cloud Nine. Transportation companies took confidentiality to heart. What did they think I would do, blow up the limo?

Only the large companies had online reservations I could hack into. I was down to asking my network for help again and had to wait for answers. I'd already seen enough violence today, so I wasn't eager to take on Senator Tex as my next assignment. Blood sugar running low, I slumped in my chair and contemplated my navel.

I was working for a frightening man who thought he was a god, who was manipulating our lives and probably others, and who seemed to know more about us than we did.

The man had understood my love of computers enough to bless me with the Cobalt Whiz. He'd understood my psyche enough to give me the kind of difficult task that would most appeal to me. And he'd known my pride would force me to turn myself inside out accomplishing it. He'd set me up for failure and *admitted* it.

He'd known where EG was when I didn't and provided a solution to her problem before I could. He'd offered to let us stay in his home until we found our money. I desperately wanted him to be my grandfather.

That's about as stupid as it gets. And also a sad case of denial. I didn't want Sexy Man to be my grandfather. I wanted him to be available, like Sean. Crippled Psyche, meet Crippled Superman, and make the world go 'round. Right, like that was gonna happen.

It was time to check out the school he'd arranged for EG. For all I knew, it was a school for budding spies. Nick might be smart and charming, but there wasn't a suspicious bone in his body. He would only notice what the students wore.

Confronting school administrations wasn't one of my specialties, except on a combative basis. Or a punitive one. But I needed to get out of the house, and EG ought to have an escort home. I'd already removed the blazer in the barely air-conditioned heat of the old house. Wearing my unfashionable jumper and sandals, I caught the Metro to EG's private school.

The building was all brick and encompassed a city block from the looks of it. I didn't see any kids cavorting on the strip of green lawn revealed through the iron gates.

I showed my passport to the guard at the door and marched into the school office as if I had a clue to what I was doing.

I'd never seen a school office like this one. No modern metal desks, cardboard partitions, and cluttered stacks of paper here. The outer office was carpeted and draped, the furnishings were mahogany, and the wallpaper had been chosen by an interior decorator to elegantly complement the school colors of silver and blue. If any records existed, they were computerized or neatly filed in cabinets behind closet doors because even filing cabinets weren't visible.

"May I help you?" the young, very blond secretary inquired. Apparently trained in all the right schools, she held her curiosity well.

"I am Anastasia Devlin. I wish to speak with the school administration about my sister, Elizabeth Maximillian. I'm her guardian."

"Of course, Miss Devlin. I will see if Mr. Appleby is available." Not a blink of an eyelash at my long skirt and tight braids. She probably couldn't see my scruffy sandals.

I checked out all the official-looking accreditation awards on the walls, memorizing them for further study later. Why wasn't I as paranoid about Graham as I was about everyone else?

Because he had a voice like thunder-laced whiskey, and I wanted to believe he was looking after us. I hadn't wasted all those years of therapy. I just didn't often find them useful.

Mr. Appleby, to my disappointment, looked like every school official I'd ever seen—stout, balding, rumpled suit, the works. His eyebrows were gray and bushy, his thinning hair had been silvered and trimmed by an expert, and the suit probably cost three fortunes, but eggheads are undisguisable.

"How lovely to meet you, Miss Devlin. I spoke with your brother this morning. Wonderful gentleman."

He held out his hand for me to shake, but I walked past him into his office and took a seat. He followed, leaving the office door slightly parted.

"I am E..." I halted before using EG's nickname. She deserved to start fresh in this imposing school. "...Elizabeth's guardian and responsible for her education. We appreciate the opportunity offered by the scholarship. Her previous education has been private and advanced."

"Of course, Mr. Graham explained this to us. It is sometimes difficult for a privately tutored child to be assimilated into the general population..."

I heard and understood the hesitation in his voice. EG had already brought attention to herself. "Elizabeth is a genius with an extensive education in international affairs. She does not think on the same planes as most children. She needs advanced instruction to keep her active mind occupied."

"Yes, yes, I see that now. Excellent. Perhaps we could give her a few tests..." Appleby ruminated, tapping his fingers against his flabby jaw. "I'm glad we had this little talk Ms. Devlin. I had assumed... But one should never assume."

He'd assumed EG had been trained by real teachers from government schools who taught one and one were two, not a teacher who had taught her that if you catch the midnight train to Marrakesh you can sleep for the price of a train ticket and save the cost of a hotel.

"We've just moved into the community," I informed him. "I will give you our phone numbers as soon as they're available. In the meantime, if we could correspond by e-mail, I would appreciate it if you would keep in close contact until Elizabeth has found her place here."

He rifled through the folder on his desk. "Mr. Graham has given us his private numbers. Will those be sufficient currently?"

"Of course." The bastard. He would know everything EG was doing before we did. We had to find our millions and establish our own lines of communication.

A creepy crawly feeling hit me as a new thought occurred. What if Graham had arranged for Reginald the Thief to elude the cops in exchange for our house? Maybe there were no millions. Just the house and Reggie's yacht. We would never be able to buy it back.

On that unhappy thought, I left the school office with a schedule in my hand to canvas classrooms. Checking out the politely behaved students sitting at their desks, I grimaced.

I had no particular love of fashion, but I was aware of the difference between Wal-Mart cotton and Saks silk. The sturdy outfit we had sent EG to school in today was somewhere in between, but pathetically inadequate in comparison to the designer outfits holding up desks in this place. No jeans and T-shirts here, nosirree. I saw *six*-year-olds with shoes, purses, and cell phones all matched and costing more than I earned in a year.

Just the concept of a six-year-old with a purse and cell phone gave me a headache. We would have to go wardrobe shopping.

I checked the class schedule. I was under the impression that normal fourth graders do not change classes, but this school had specialty teachers for everything. EG was in her last class of the day, social studies.

Wondering what kind of *social studies* one taught fourth graders, I slipped down the hallway, trying to appear unobtrusive. The occasional drone of voices emanated from partially opened doors.

I recognized EG's voice before I located the classroom.

"The modern concept of democracy cannot sustain itself without the benefit of an educated voting class. By reducing public schools to wastelands of ignorance, the government has effectively emasculated the constitution, thereby guaranteeing an aristocracy of the wealthy and privately educated."

Well done, young grasshopper, I murmured to myself. I was impressed with the quality of a classroom discussing such pertinent topics. I was less impressed with EG spouting Magda dogma, but occasionally, our mother had her head screwed on right.

"Miss Maximillian, that is not a definition of democracy. You will sit down and write 'I will not spread communist propaganda in this classroom' one hundred times."

Ouch. I tensed and waited for the explosion.

When EG didn't come barreling out, I was really worried. A quiet EG is a dangerous one. She'd bombed her kindergarten class just before Magda sent her to me a few years ago. Admittedly, it hadn't been more than a smoke bomb, but they'd been in Saudi Arabia at the time. They had to evacuate the school, and the U.S. Army had parked outside for a month afterward.

I peeked through the opening of the partially ajar door. She was sitting in the front of the room, dutifully scribbling her sentences across a notebook page. Or writing something anyway. I doubted if it was the prescribed sentence. She's never that obedient.

The other kids were sniggering and shooting her curious looks, but that's nothing unusual. I studied the lot of them. She was the shortest one in there, but there were as many international students as blond-haired all-American sorts, so she didn't look particularly exotic. Just small and alone.

I tip-toed down the hall and waited on a bench outside. The smoggy city air suited me more than the rarified oxygen inside. This mothering business was extremely difficult. As a kid growing up, I figured all a mother needed to do was keep food on the table and a roof over our heads. That's certainly the most Magda had ever done. I'd been the one to clean dirty noses, give baths, and get them into bed, like an unpaid nursemaid.

I'd listened to their tales of woe, but being as helpless as my younger siblings, I'd shrugged off their whining. Life is tough. You learn. That had been my motto.

I wasn't certain that motto was adequate any longer. I had resources now, and I wanted EG to be *happy*. Foolish of me, I suppose, given her predilection for pessimism, but I felt responsible for making her happy. I would have to talk to her teachers. Shit.

It occurred to me that Appleby hadn't agreed to test EG because I'd come in to see him. He'd agreed because he didn't want to lose Graham's favor. How could an invisible man wield power and influence? He'd been in the president's cabinet. In what capacity? In this town, only a man who held the president's ear would be seen as truly influential, but Mrs. Carstairs had thought him *dead*.

I really needed to ask more questions, but I'd been trained to keep eyes and ears open, not my mouth. And now I was obligated to the man.

A bell rang and kids came tumbling out the front doors while I was lost in plotting. I drew curious stares, but the kids had other things on their mind, like TV and food and the limos waiting for them. EG dragged out at the tail end. Head down, scuffling her shoes, she didn't even see me until I stepped in front of her. She scowled when she recognized my sandals.

"I don't need an escort," she growled.

With EG, it was best to ignore the protests. I was beginning to realize she didn't always mean them any more than I did. I started down the sidewalk. "Did you have to stay after class?"

"The history teacher is ancient," she complained. "I bet she belonged to the John Birch Society."

I screwed up my brow and tried to recollect who in heck John Birch was. A lot of my education was in foreign schools. I could tell you the monetary differences between rubles, shekels, and drachmas, but I have no memory of any Birch.

It didn't matter. She was on a rant.

"Not one of those mindless clones cares that their gas-guzzling vehicles are destroying the environment and eating up the world's oil reserves. They think Americans are better than anyone and deserve to have whatever they want, whenever they can take it, and that Europeans are just sore losers."

Well, yeah, that's been the attitude as long as I can remember it. Didn't they write a book about it ages ago? *The Ugly American*, I think. Got my nose rubbed in that one. I wrapped an arm around her shoulders. "Fourth graders don't generally know a great deal," I assured her.

"I'm talking about the teachers," she said with scorn, picking up speed as we headed down to the Metro. "Even the textbooks are as dumb as the ones in public school. They don't mention that Nazis tried to eradicate an entire race of people in World War Two. They're so politically correct that they don't mention most of the wars in history were caused by *religion*."

None of her fellow students followed us down to the subway. A lot of them watched us from the windows of their limos though.

I had a nasty twist in the pit of my stomach that said a wealthy private school might not be the place for a socialistic atheist like EG.

Was I doing the wrong thing, just like Magda? Nick had hated some of the schools he'd been locked up in. How did I know when a kid was just complaining and when she was right?

I had wanted a decent education so badly I had sneaked out of the house to sit in schools in which I wasn't enrolled. I had even sat in the back of large university classes to learn about subjects no one had taught me. Was I putting my needs and wants on EG's shoulders?

Maybe I should just slither back into my dark basement hole and not come out again. What made me think I could be a responsible parent?

As we climbed out of the Metro and walked down the busy city street toward the substantial mansion grandfather had left us, I felt the same tug of heartstrings I'd suffered the first day we'd arrived. I drew strength from the elegant brick turrets and towering roofline.

This was home. This was ours. Regardless of the errors I made, we were going to make it together, come hell or high water.

I squeezed EG's shoulders. "Nick and I will stay on top of things at the school. Someday, you'll teach those kids to think for themselves. Just remember that, and keep your mouth shut until then. You'll be fine."

She stared at me incredulously, then pulled a piece of paper from her backpack. "That's good, because my homeroom teacher has signed you up to blow balloons for the school festival Friday night. They're raising funds for new draperies for the auditorium."

Oh yeah, that's gonna work. I'd wear my best capris and Grateful Dead T-shirt. Maybe the balloons would be black, and I'd feel right at home. I'm gonna be *so* good at this parenting business.

Friday night was the night Pao was appearing at the fundraiser, and if I needed any more convincing, the thought of balloons did it—I'd rather follow Pao home than go anywhere near a private school festival run by smug, overeducated yuppies. Fine example for EG I made.

Chapter Fourteen

Celebration time

NICK met us at the front door and gestured for us to turn around and walk back to the street. He had returned from job hunting, evidently to see how EG had fared.

EG tried to push into the house, but I understood—he didn't want our resident spy listening. I caught her shoulder and spun her around. "Party time," I declared.

That caught her attention. "Whose birthday is it?"

I will give Magda credit for one thing. She knew how to throw a party. She did her level best to throw the most spectacular birthday parties she could manage in whatever godforsaken hole we were in at the time. And when we were living lavishly, the parties knew no limit.

I couldn't hope to match that, but this wasn't a birthday either. "I've decided to create a new tradition," I declared, marching down the street in the direction of a small Italian ice cream stand I'd noticed in my trips to the Metro. "We party every time we want to celebrate."

"Sounds good to me," Nick said cheerfully, reducing his long stride to meet our smaller ones, his earlier resentment apparently appeased. "What, exactly, are we celebrating?"

"I'm celebrating finding Pao and our extended stay in our new home."

Nick agreeably whooped in mock exuberation. He hadn't been willing to celebrate my triumph earlier. Something was up.

EG slanted a suspicious look at me. "The Spook says we can stay? We must have something he wants."

"Yeah, me," I agreed, breaking out in a smile that probably shocked anyone who knew me. I shoved open the door to the gelato parlor.

"Or both of us," Nicholas countered in a tone more worried than proud.

We stopped a few yards short of the counter. "He wants you to gamble?" I asked first.

Nick shook his blond head and tightened his tie. For the first time, I noticed he was wearing a normal business suit. He would blend right into the crowd over at the GSA.

"They let Senator Tex out on bail this afternoon," he said.

That couldn't be the announcement he'd intended to make, but before he could continue, EG let out a whoop of delight. "He's innocent! They'll see."

Seeing that look on her face was worth celebrating, but I wasn't getting the connection here. "And?" I prodded.

"I thought we might learn a little something about Tex if we got closer to him," Nicholas admitted with a hint of sheepishness.

"You're helping my father?" EG's eyes went round in astonishment. "You mean it?"

With mixed emotions, I watched the two of them. Nick had looks and dignity and that lofty British accent, but he wasn't much of a father figure. Still, EG was looking at him as if he'd just created the world. She needed people in her life she could trust and rely on.

I waited to see what Nick didn't want Graham to find out.

"I've been seeing someone on the senator's staff. He mentioned an opening, and let's face it," Nick shrugged, "there aren't too many people applying for Tex's staff. I got the job."

EG and I shouted war whoops and whopped him on the back until he flushed. Graham was bound to find that out if he didn't already know it, but it was good news anyway.

"They said I was highly qualified for diplomatic circles," he said, as if we were doubting his abilities.

"Except for the homosexuality thing," I pointed out, not that I was doubting his diplomacy. "Don't they frown on hiring politically incorrect people who are easily blackmailed?" I proceeded to the gelato counter and ordered the raspberry. I didn't want to discourage Nick's initiative, but diplomatic circles were where we'd grown up, and no one had ever said Nick belonged there despite all his spit and polish.

"It doesn't matter at staff level. Besides, it's not as if I'm trying to hide anything—except from Tex." Grinning, Nick ordered blackberry and mint together, with chocolate sprinkles on top. "We're celebrating, remember? Let's not be stingy about it."

Encouraged by Nick's selection, EG ordered a vanilla and strawberry striped concoction that couldn't possibly be as good as gelato, then ordered chocolate and whipped cream on top of it. The proprietor, obviously no purist, beamed in delight.

While we ate our ices out of Graham's hearing, I explained everything I had learned today, carefully eliminating any mention of exploding buildings for EG's sake. We raised our cones in toast to our extended stay in our new home, and then Nick regaled us with tales of interviewing for Tex's office. EG wasn't quite as forthcoming about her school day, but she did manage to admit that it wasn't dumb.

"School clothes!" I remembered aloud. "You need matching cell phones and backpacks."

I barely noticed clothes, but technology fascinated me. Some of those backpacks had been quite a striking design, all aluminum, with wheels that looked as if they'd carry a pup tent.

"Our sister needs educating," Nick confided to EG. "Now that we've ruined your dinner, I think celebrating ought to include clothes. Come on, let's go."

Jumping up as happily as any nine-year-old, EG ran for the front door. I did not follow.

"Take my credit card, and I'll return to work." I probably sounded a little stiff. I'm not of much use on a shopping expedition, but I'd kind of been enjoying our mutual celebration. I didn't want it to break up so quickly, even if I had been the one to mention shopping. I hadn't meant right now.

EG returned to glare at me. "Are you going to fill balloons on Friday looking like that?" she demanded, and I knew I was outvoted.

I know how to say *shit* in every language from Afghani to Zulu. I put my expertise to the test as they dragged me into a taxi to the mall. The Pakistani driver threw me an alarmed look when I reached his part of the alphabet.

The first shop we encountered was a hair salon adorned in shopping bags of pink tissue paper. I shivered in horror as Nick stopped at the door. The salon stank of chemical scents that didn't induce me to come within thirty yards of it. "Don't even think about it," I warned him.

He looked at my heavy braids, sighed as if he'd just lost his best friend, and gallantly trudged on.

"Bookstore!" EG cried, grabbing Nick's hand and trying to tug him inside.

I was already half way there when he marched determinedly past the entrance. "Nope. Books are for every day. Clothes are for celebrating. EG needs clothes."

"Tyrant," I muttered, but he was right. If she was going to fit into school, she had to dress appropriately. Maybe then she wouldn't turn out like me. I'm not saying normality is the only way to go. I just wanted her to have choices.

EG obediently headed for a Kids Gap store. Nick tapped her on the shoulder and shook his head. She gaped, looked at me, and marched ever onward.

I had a sinking feeling I wasn't going to like this.

With the look of a man marching off to war, Nick steered us into Nordstroms.

I knew palaces existed. I'd been inside several. I preferred all that marble on Roman palazzos where it belonged, though. I tried not to gape and blink like a rube as the glaring lights and glass and perfume hit me all at once. I started backing toward the entrance, but Nick caught my elbow and dragged me onward.

"Lands End," I muttered. "I can handle catalogs. I don't need this." I needed an oxygen mask to get past the perfume counter. I flinched as a skeletal model in filmy black aimed a sprayer at me. They may as well have taken me into Dark World and introduced me to vampires.

Nick made some magic sign with his hand, and she backed off, confirming my evil fantasy. "You want to deal with EG's school?" he demanded, striding determinedly toward a display of misshapen manikins wearing enough wool for several sheep. "You want to cow lawyers like Oppenheimer and Johnson? You want the Spook to treat you with respect?"

"Respect?" I stumbled and came to a halt in front of row upon row of pastel suits. "You want me to gag here or wait until I try something on?"

"Right. Mata Hari it is, then." He dragged me deeper into the store, up and down escalators and through glittering rows of glass cases until I wasn't certain if we were still on earth or had reached another planet. EG peeled off at a manikin modeling kids clothes. He'd corrupted her to the point she could shop for *herself*. I was horrified.

He finally found a sea of denim and leather, and I relaxed. Black. I like black. I'm too short to look good in jeans, but denim has a certain earthy appeal. I looked for a new jumper. Nick shoved a black knit dress in front of me. I couldn't even figure out how to put it on, much less when I should wear it. The skirt looked as if it had been split up to the crotch.

"I am not Magda," I informed him, locating a garment rack of corduroy. It might have been August in D.C., but it was winter in Nordstroms.

"You are the heir to millions. Act like it." He started grabbing things from the racks that I wouldn't touch with surgical gloves.

I ignored Nick to poke through the racks of clothes I could relate to. I'll never look like a model. I prefer invisibility. I found a sale rack of long beige cotton summer dresses and contemplated those. For EG, I might manage beige and sleeveless. For one night, maybe.

Nick rolled his eyes and dragged me toward the dressing room. "You have cheekbones to die for, legs that could drive a man mad, a figure that can wear anything, and you *are not wearing one of those shapeless pillowcases.*"

Nick never talked to me like that. I was so shocked that I let him shove me toward the dressing rooms where a saleslady was waiting with his selections. Before I knew what hit me, I was stuck in a mirrored closet with clothes that would make me look like a dwarf Magda clone, while a genial goblin outside kept asking if she could bring me anything else. This wasn't quite as bad as exploding warehouses, but it was close enough to scare me.

This was celebrating? What? A millennium of female oppression?

I was having flashbacks to Magda's magical closet. Now there was a closet a kid could get lost in and never be found. I know, I'd done it. My therapists licked their chops over my childhood adoration of dark, safe closets.

I poked through the selection with the distaste with which one treats raw meat. I tried to think in terms of EG's school gig, even if chances were good that I wasn't attending. The faster I bought something, the faster I could escape was the theory I was operating on. I kind of liked the embroidered black halter and capris outfit, but the halter was some slippery substance that molded to me like a second skin, and the pants were a clingy knit that had to be dry-cleaned. And neither were suitable for the sister of a genius attending a snobby private school.

Gingerly, I pulled out a black and white floaty thing. It had *flounces* on the hem and layers of gauze. Was Nick out of his mind? It was a damned good thing for him that clerks didn't see him as female enough to come back here or I'd strangle him.

But unless I wanted to wear the red, three-button suit with knee length straight skirt, I saw nothing else suitable. The floaty thing had no sleeves and a flimsy halter neckline. I had this sudden image of me wearing it in front of one Graham's cameras, and I smirked.

I tried it on. Personally, I thought it looked like a Gateway computer logo on silk, which gave me a certain fondness for it. The skirt had several layers that fell at different lengths and at weird angles so I wouldn't blame anyone for mistaking me for a black-and-white fairy, although wings might be required. It was freakish, and so was I. Why not?

I carried out the one dress and shoved it at the hovering clerk. "I'll take this one."

"Did the others fit?" Nick asked, inspecting a little black dress that he would never fit into.

"I like this one," I said stubbornly. "Let's go find EG."

Nick winked at the saleslady. "Get the others. She'll take them, and this, too." He threw the tiny little dress across the counter. "Direct us to the shoe department, please."

* * *

"It's my credit card." I was still furious as we carried sacks full of ridiculously expensive clothing out of the mall and waited for our taxi at nine that night. "I'll never wear this stuff in ten million years. I don't even have a *closet*."

"If you wouldn't insist on living in an office, you'd have a closet. I'll hire someone to move in a wardrobe."

"We don't have that right," I argued. "We could be living in the street next week."

"Did I, or did I not, win enough for us to live on comfortably for the next year if we so decided?" he asked loftily, helping EG to climb into the taxi beside me. He took the front seat where I couldn't punch him.

"We need that money to bring Brashton back. I'll return all this tomorrow."

"Then I'll have to return mine," EG said equitably. "If you can't keep your celebration clothes, neither can I. It's not as if I want to look like a Barbie doll anyway."

That shut me up. She'd actually bought clothes that weren't all black for a change. Admittedly, they tended toward the punk rocker image and not Barbie, but she looked cute in red leather, especially with all that black hair hanging over the matching jacket. Nick had even persuaded her to buy a beret.

"We're corrupting her." I collapsed against the back seat, too exhausted to argue more. We'd held a celebratory feast in the food court and shopped until we dropped. Admittedly, it had been kind of fun sampling all the atrocious fast foods we hadn't known growing up. Who knew pizza came with pineapple on it? And they could have closed down the Brookstone store with me in it, and I would have died happy.

"It was fun," EG agreed, saying aloud what I'd been thinking. "I like this celebration thing. We should do it more often."

We'd made her happy. It felt good to feel good. I caved. "We'll celebrate with fireworks when we get our house back, and buy the gelato stand with our millions."

It felt fantastic to have family to share the good feelings with.

My mind traveled to the wounded widower sitting alone in his dusty attic with only computer screens for company. I knew better than to feel sorry for him, but the image haunted me anyway.

Chapter Fifteen

Ana converses with Graham and Blackwell, visits the school, and meets Tex

LIKE everything else in this world, celebrations have their upsides and downsides. Sitting in the library on Wednesday morning with EG off to school and Nick off to his new job in Tex's office, I had plenty of silence in which to ruminate. I was wearing my new dry-clean-only stretch capris with my old Grateful Dead T-shirt. The combination eased my conscience and soothed my soul. I tried waving my ankles to see if I could make Graham gasp, but Don Quixote still covered the painting I figured hid the camera. Maybe uncovering it would ease my moroseness.

It was all very well to celebrate. It was quite another to wake up next morning and realize one must still locate a possible terrorist and a murderer along with a larcenous lawyer—while living in a house with a spy. My Atlanta basement was starting to look appealing again.

My correspondent had forwarded the addresses to Friday night's guest list, but Pao's invitation had gone to the Cambodian embassy.

It would be really convenient if I could combine the burning of Edu-Pub and the murder of Tex's assistant by implicating Pao in both. I was all for efficiency, and the combination and timing was suspicious.

I clicked through my e-mails to see if anyone had found a means of getting me into the passenger lists of local limo and taxi rentals. I didn't hold out much hope for that one. For all I knew, Pao was riding with the ambassador from Cambodia. Graham was giving me another irrelevant assignment he figured I'd fail. I was determined to stuff it up his nose.

My checks to both Edu-Pub and Pao's foundation had cleared my fake school bank account. I went online to read the photo image of the back of the check. *Bingo!* As I'd suspected, they shared the same bank account. Money laundering, here we come.

Then I ran through the list of Rose's campaign contributors. Every right-wing, liberal-bashing religious conservative in the country had contributed. Surely the good senator didn't know Edu-Pub funneled their cash into the same account with Pao's fanatical Islamic fundamentalist group, but he was on the *board* for crying out loud! He ought to know.

The my-God-is-better-than-your-God mentality always fascinated me. I briefly considered creating mockups of Rose's fundraising invitations and sending them to the guys over in Indonesia, but even if they all showed up and sat down and talked it out with Rose's right-wing guests, it was a waste of time unless terror and mayhem were my goal.

I wasn't that bored.

Why would an Islamic Pao contribute to a Christian Rose? Why would Rose be on the board of Edu-Pub? To heck with oil and water. The pair were more like fertilizer and fuel oil. And why did I think Tex played into this scenario?

Out of frustration, I ran a thorough search on Tex.

Married the governor's daughter fifteen years ago while a member of the Texas House of Representatives. Ran for U.S. House of Representatives ten years ago and lost. My interest picked up when I ran across a newspaper article from that year. The governor's daughter went home to papa after that debacle. Tex had a sore loser for a wife.

But the president at the time was another good ol' Texas boy, and he appointed Tex ambassador to Spain. I didn't have to count backward far to remember where Magda was living that year. EG was born in Barcelona.

That was the year I'd walked out on Magda and my siblings. I stared at the monitor and wished my head were a computer so I could compute all the probabilities and improbabilities.

"I thought you were researching limos," a dry voice commented from the intercom.

"I thought you only chatted at midnight," I countered with irritation at the interruption. "Up early this morning, are we?"

He ignored the repartee. "If you cannot complete your task, then you are of no further use to me. You may begin searching for other accommodations."

I was just annoyed enough to think *Stick it up your ass, spyboy,* but not stupid enough to say it. "A—I have applied all available resources to the search and I'm waiting for the results. B—the only other direct method involves disguising myself as a taxi driver and infiltrating their offices, and I figure you'll yell at me if I do. C—This is only Wednesday and you gave me until Friday. D—there are other means of achieving your goal besides the transportation route."

"And I'll have you tied and gagged if you choose those." The voice never lost its dry inflection. "You will not go to the fundraiser. You will attend Elizabeth's school festivity Friday night. You have been investigating Mindy Carstairs. Mind explaining why?"

That stopped me in my tracks. I'd tried to keep my Tex and Mindy research to my old Dell so the snoop wouldn't notice, but I couldn't resist using the Whiz's marvelous spy network to crack police files. Graham didn't ask about Tex. He asked about Mindy.

Mindy Carstairs' family knew Graham. Did he know her?

"I have a personal interest in the case," I said warily.

No response. It was as if God waited for me to continue.

I leaned back and put my bare feet on the desk and tried to choose what I would reveal. I wasn't used to telling others what I was doing or why, but a second opinion might be useful. "She was Reginald's wife, and now she's dead."

"You know where Brashton is. You don't need a dead ex-wife for that."

He had me there. I contemplated stonewalling, but my curiosity is a dangerous thing. I wanted to see just how much Graham knew and how much I could rely on him. "A client of mine knew her," I acknowledged cautiously. I didn't see reason to reveal EG's parentage.

"And?" he broke his silence long enough to ask.

I'd finally hooked his interest. I wiggled my bare toes and threw a verbal dart. "I don't know my client's name, but he used the screen name Oracle, and he disappeared mysteriously."

Dead silence. I knew the intercom was still on. Was Graham staring into one of his monitors at the contents of my computer? Or watching me wiggle my toes?

"I am not the only one who chooses to use ironic screen names," he responded coolly, catching my drift. "Your Oracle mentioned Mindy Carstairs? In what capacity?"

Ironic, was it? My moniker was Tweety Bird. Did he consider that ironic, too? "I'll share if you share," I answered wickedly. "Did you know my client?"

"How should I know?" He sounded a bit testy at being challenged. "Show me your client's file, and I'll tell you."

"No, you won't. Tell me why you want Pao, and I'll tell you what I've discovered about Mindy. My client's file is confidential."

"You have no legal obligation to a client. You aren't a lawyer."

"I have a moral obligation. If I went around talking about my clients, how could you trust me to keep quiet about you?"

"Touché," he admitted grudgingly.

"Who are you really after, Pao, or Tex?" I demanded, determined to get satisfaction out of this circular non-conversation.

"I am after the truth. How about you?"

The intercom went dead. I toyed with the thought of pounding all the buttons and yelling until I caught his attention. But despite all appearances to the contrary, I am not unintelligent and I am capable of deeper thought than raspberry jam. What truth should I be after?

That question nagged at the back of my mind the rest of the morning as I worked, but it was about as answerable as *what was there before the universe*? One of these days when I had the leisure time again—and it appeared that wouldn't happen with family around—I might ponder the truth about my grandfather and the reason Magda had left him. But more immediate matters had to be addressed first.

I cursed as the library telephone rang. I punched the most insistently flashing button and replied, "Ana here."

"Miss Devlin." No question, just statement. I recognized the flat style of Blackwell Johnson—soon-to-be-bankrupt lawyer, if I had my way.

"Yes," I agreed without smiling, trying to think of how many ways he could screw us with this phone call.

"I had not realized you intended to permanently move into your grandfather's house."

Well, duh. "It's our house," I replied, striving for sweet but managing curt at best. The hesitation on the other end of the line probably indicated surprise and curiosity, but I didn't intend to help him out.

"Mr. Graham sold it to you?"

I tried not to laugh. "Not yet."

"As your grandfather's attorney, I must advise you that staying there could be prejudicial to your case. You really should return home and let the matter be settled in court."

Ha. Showed how much he knew. As if we had homes to return to. But now he had me wondering why he wanted us out of the way.

"Mr. Oppenheimer has advised us that possession is nine-tenths of the law." So, I lied. Oppenheimer just kept his hand out to have his palm greased. "We have reached a suitable agreement with Mr. Graham for the interim."

"I see. That is unwise. Even should we locate the funds, we could not return them to you while you are occupying the disputed property."

"You haven't even sent us the stock you mentioned last time. Have you located more funds?" I asked with interest.

"We are prepared to make a settlement on you until our partner returns and clears up matters. Your continued possession of the property complicates matters."

That was so much bull— He must think I was some kind of simpleton who'd slept through the last century. "We don't want or *need* a settlement, Mr. Johnson. We want Max's entire estate, intact, as he left it to us. But thank you for your thoughtfulness." I hung up. My supply of patience had reached its end.

I was being high-handed by throwing away the offer of money, but in the totality of the universe, money was irrelevant. I wanted this house *and* the money.

More angry than frustrated now, I returned to my research.

I had two bulging computer files on Tex and Paul Rose before the morning ended. Both belonged to the same political party. Both had Texas and presidential connections. Neither file turned up Magda, but I *knew* she was in Tex's background. It would be interesting to know if she was in Rose's.

Both of their wives served on several civic committees together. Both men served on the board for Edu-Pub, but there was no indication that they actually knew Pao, who was supposedly nothing more than a salesman on the company books—with Cambodian embassy connections.

Pao was on Rose's guest list for Friday night because that's where one put campaign contributors. None of this led to anything seditious, dangerous, or radical in any way beyond the usual *money follows money*.

I'm not prone to headaches, but this knotty problem could induce one.

I took it up to the gym.

I'm not much good at analyzing myself. I leave that to the shrinks. I just knew I needed a physical outlet to a lot of emotions and frustrations or I would explode. Graham had told me to use the gym. He'd offered it as apology for the cat, and the cat hadn't been around lately, but that wasn't any reason I shouldn't take advantage of the offer.

I changed into shorts and sighed with relief the instant the gym door closed behind me. I could be myself here.

A brand new pair of red leather bag gloves hung beside the battered ones, welcoming me.

Despite the immediate surge of delight at the unexpected gift, I hesitated over reaching for them, searching for motivation. Deciding it was simply Graham's way of stopping me from using his gloves, I slid my fingers in, wrapped the wrist supports, and went to work.

I pounded the shit out of the bag, limbered up my legs with half an hour of kickboxing, and cooled down with some basic crunches and push-ups. The gloves were ideal for my routine.

I heard no complaint from the spook. Feeling decidedly better, I traipsed down the stairs to my shower. I didn't actually whistle with happiness, but I'm sure I would have if the burdens of the world weren't already coming back to haunt me.

After my shower, I donned the clingy capris and halter top and hoped Graham was watching his damned cameras as I bounced down the stairs to the kitchen. I didn't even bother putting my hair in braids but let it dry out naturally, in a heavy river over my shoulders and down my back. I might never be Magda, but I was still female, and my libido needed feeding as much as my stomach. If the only sexual satisfaction I could achieve was causing a mercenary cripple to have a coronary, I'd take it.

Feeling cocky in my spiffy new clothes, I contemplated taking a pub break to see if the mysterious Sean would show up, but the pub food wasn't nearly as appealing as Mallard's. Besides, I preferred the spy I knew to one who hadn't thought to give me a great pair of gloves. I definitely had a lot of Magda in me.

Mallard raised his graying eyebrows when I entered the kitchen, but I ignored any implied criticism to rummage through his immense refrigerator. I'd given up keeping track of when we were in his good graces. If the kitchen door was unlocked, I figured I had a chance at food.

"There is crab salad in the blue container, and sun-dried tomato bread in the bread drawer," he said crisply, while sautéing something that smelled scrumptious.

Remembering my intention of befriending Mallard to pump him for information, I obediently found the crab salad. I've eaten fried ants upon occasion. It's well proven I'll eat anything. What I don't do well is conversation, but I could give it a try.

"How long did you work with my grandfather?" I asked, innocently enough, as I spread the salad over a slice of bread.

"Long enough," he said severely.

That wasn't promising. I sniffed the air appreciatively. "That smells delicious. I don't suppose it's soup?"

"Certainly not. It's ninety degrees outside."

I rolled my eyes and tasted the sandwich. "This is yummy. Where did you learn to cook?" I reached for the bottled water in the refrigerator.

"I don't believe that's on your need-to-know list."

Ah, military background. Interesting what one can learn even when the other party is uncooperative. "Did you know my father?"

"Of course."

So maybe I needed to pave the road of friendship a little more if I wanted to pry useful information out of him. I chugged the water, then wiped my mouth with the back of my hand.

Mallard shot me a severe look. "Your mother should have taught you better manners."

I belatedly searched the drawers for napkins. "She did. I even know which fork to use and when." I defended her automatically. "But I'm not entertaining ambassadors at the moment."

"Mallard was once chief military attaché to an ambassador," the Kitchen Aid mixer intoned in a familiar mechanical voice. "I'd advise you to treat him accordingly and practice your interrogative skills elsewhere."

Leaning my bare back against the granite counter, I spotted the interior speaker behind the mixer. Even odds there was a camera in here as well.

I threw back my head to drink more water from the bottle, well aware that the motion lifted my breasts in the wired halter. The intercom shut up. I kept my grin to myself. Being introverted means I find prolonged social interaction exhausting. It doesn't mean I'm shy.

Setting the bottle down, I politely dabbed my mouth with a linen napkin I'd retrieved from a drawer beneath the mixer. "I apologize for my rudeness, Mallard. Working for a mechanical tyrant is hardship enough. Shall I treat you to a pint at the pub to make amends?"

The insult was a mere cover for my implied threat to take this conversation where Graham couldn't go. If he knew about Sean—and he certainly knew everything else—maybe my threat was also an awkward attempt to stir jealousy. Who knew? I'm a mass of contradictions.

I thought Mallard almost smiled, but he turned away to chop an onion. "That won't be necessary, Miss Devlin. I thank you for the offer, though."

"Besides, Miss Devlin has other duties. If you are quite done delaying my lunch, I believe you have a phone call to answer."

"A phone call? Me?" Panicked, I reeled through all the possibilities—Magda, the lawyer, Nicholas—

"The school, Miss Devlin. It seems your sister has a genius for disturbing the inmates. Line one." The intercom clicked off.

Mallard pointed at the sleek console phone on the built-in desk, and I dived for it. "Anastasia Devlin here," I said crisply into the receiver even though my heart threatened to leap from my chest.

"There has been an unpleasant incident, Miss Devlin. We are asking parents of the students involved to stop by the office to discuss it immediately."

"What happened?" I demanded. "Was anyone hurt?"

"No one went to the hospital," Mr. Appleby stated as wryly as Graham at his best. "But we believe it best if the students in question return home for the day."

Oh, shit. I glanced at the clock. It was going on one. Fine. She wouldn't be missing a lot of classes. "I'll be right over." I didn't waste time in niceties. I hung up.

Mallard looked concerned. "Is Miss Elizabeth all right?"

"Until I get my hands on her. Thanks for lunch." I dashed out, grabbed my purse, and almost made it to the front door before a disapproving cough from the intercom caught me.

"You might consider a more suitable costume under the circumstances."

If I ever found those damned cameras, they were history. Grudgingly, I dashed up the stairs, comforting myself with a litany of curses and a cloud of resentment.

I reached for my denim jumper in the top file drawer, but the Gateway silk dangled on a hanger on the back of the door. It was ninety degrees out, and an evil imp asked, *Why not?*

Nicholas had even forced me to buy the appropriate underwear. I couldn't decide if I liked having a brother who knew more about women's support garments than I did, but it was convenient. I actually looked like I had breasts in this scrap of material.

Accepting Appleby's assurances that EG wasn't in need of immediate medical treatment, I took the time to wrap my hair in a hasty twist, secured it with a few pins, and located the flimsy heels Nick had insisted I buy. I even slashed on lipstick. No one could convince me I had Magda's impact, but I probably looked normal enough to fight the Establishment on their terms.

Amazingly, the intercom in the foyer said nothing as I dashed past it this time. Worse, I found myself hoping Graham had noticed my get-up. So much for feeling feminine and sexy. I began to feel like an idiot.

A taxi waited outside. I blessed Mallard and jumped in rather than examine my descent into Magda country. The school wasn't far, but I paid the driver well for his patience in waiting for my transformation.

I flashed my ID at the guard in the front of the school. Self-conscious, I had a feeling he was looking at my half-exposed chest, but he checked his guest list and ushered me in.

The frou-frou outfit made me more nervous than secure. My heels clicked against the tile, keeping pace with my pounding heart. I was terrified I'd blow this parenting thing.

I pushed open the door to Appleby's reception room. Ignoring the startled look of the secretary, I crossed right past to the interior office from which issued tearful and angry voices. None of them were EG's.

Until I entered.

"Holey moley," she murmured, staring at me as if she hadn't seen me buying this dress just yesterday.

The other occupants of the room seemed equally incapable of expressing an intelligent word, giving me time to assess the situation. The principal rose to his feet and stared at my entrance. Or my well-haltered chest. Two students unknown to me hovered together on the opposite side of the room. I turned to study the parent sitting in the corner.

I nearly dropped my teeth when I recognized the tall, stern-jawed man in an expensively tailored suit.

Senator Tex.

Chapter Sixteen

Confrontation with Tex and Elsie, Nick gets tickets to party, Ana gets threatened

TEX STARED back at me in equal disbelief. Unlike Appleby, he did not stand up. Two demerits for lack of manners. Maybe jail time had made him rusty. I am not impressed by powerful political figures, and having everyone gawking at me didn't improve my humor.

Once Tex recovered from his astonishment, the suspected murderer of Mindy Carstairs looked angry, tired, and more human than in his campaign ads. He still didn't win my sympathy.

Dismissing the flustered and stuttering principal as irrelevant, I turned my attention to the two unfamiliar occupants of the room. The bloody nose of the tall blond boy spoke volumes. The demure miss with *Tommy Hilfiger* emblazoned in pink silk across her scrawny chest bore a striking resemblance to the square-jawed man belatedly rising from his chair in the corner, shoving his pepper-and-salt hair off his forehead.

Tex still looked stunned. I'm arrogant in many ways, but I certainly didn't think it was my great beauty and shocking figure that had thrown him off balance. We'd bumped into each other briefly in Barcelona, but that was ten years ago, and I'd hid behind bangs and teenage attitude back then. Besides, he hadn't spent a lot of time looking at me with Magda around. Still, good old Tex might be putting two and two together. As Nicholas had said, I do bear some resemblance to my mother, particularly in revealing silk.

It didn't take a genius to read the whole scenario in EG's smug expression. I held out my hand. "Give me the quarters."

Silently, she fished them from the pocket of the blazer she had to have worn deliberately to carry the roll.

"Miss Devlin, I don't think—" Appleby began.

"Fine. Don't think. Tell me exactly what happened." I knew how to be officious on the phone or computer. I'd never tried it in person, but if I'm listening to Nick these days—I'm an heiress. Why not act like it? I certainly had an excellent example to ape.

The principal blinked as if he'd just seen a mouse roar. On his feet now, Tex stepped into the breach. "Yoah daughter called mah Elsie a crass, hypocritical waste of humanity. While Ah admire her vocabulary, a child ought to learn respect and obedience first."

My daughter, my ass! I'd get my revenge for that later. I stayed focused. "That's your opinion, not mine," I replied with the ferocity of a lioness protecting her cub, ruining the image by turning the same ferocity on EG. "You insulted one classmate and hit another. I assume you have a good explanation?"

She shrugged and looked defiant, but I knew my sister. For the first time in her life, she was in the presence of her father, a man she admired above all others. A man whose attention she craved more than air. She would act on her version of a code of honor in front of him, but that didn't mean she hadn't instigated the incident to get his attention in the first place. My heart might go out to her, but she's too bright for these games.

I pinned my gaze on the boy with the bloody nose. I had to remember these were elementary school kids. Both Elsie and the boy were a head taller than EG, and probably a year or two older. That didn't induce me to sympathize with them either.

"Why did she feel compelled to hit you?" I asked.

The boy squirmed in his pretty white Nikes. "I pushed her," he muttered. "She was calling Elsie names."

I sensed Tex taking a step forward, but I cut him off at the pass. I doubted if he knew anything about school bullies, but I could have written a book. And I wasn't talking about Bloody-Nose Guy either. Still, I avoided looking at the prissy missy in pink. "You pushed Elizabeth?" I arched my eyebrows articulately. "She's nine and you are how old?"

"Miss Devlin, I'm the authority here. We can discuss this separately with Brian's—"

"No." I shot Appleby a steely gaze that was pure Magda. "I want the story from the source, not wrapped in bubble wrap and ribbons."

"Mah daughter has nevah caused a hint of trouble in her life." Apparently recovering from the shock of my entrance, Tex attempted to regain the floor. "You cain't talk to her and Brian as if they're convicted criminals."

I gave him a ruby smile of evil sweetness. "Elsie has never encountered someone willing to stand up to her bullying is my wager. But let's not choose sides until we have all the facts, all right, Senator?"

No introductions had been made. He couldn't know for certain who I was, especially if he thought I was EG's *mother*. I ought to rip his throat out for that alone. Not even recognizing his own daughter was a crime so high on my hostility meter that I didn't dare touch it.

I returned to interrogating the pretty pair trying to look innocent. I knew EG was capable of terrorizing the entire school if she desired. The fact that she'd chosen the senator's daughter did not bode well. But I figured it took all three to create a brawl.

"Would one of you care to explain why Elizabeth felt compelled to hurl insults?" I continued my questioning. "It's not something she does without reason."

"Elsie didn't do anything," Blond Boy said defensively, while Elsie just looked as defiant as EG. A certain similarity in sisterhood was arising.

I nodded understandingly. "I see. Elsie can't speak. How distressing. Does she stutter?"

Behind me, EG sniggered, and Tex started to roar. I swung around and pinned him with a glare. "Unless you've cut her tongue out, let the child speak for herself."

I don't believe Tex was accustomed to being spoken to in quite that manner—unless Magda had done so. I think he got the message. He shut up.

"I do not stutter. I merely asked if she was taking the subway again today." Elsie finally spoke up, apparently to prove she didn't stutter.

"Ah, I see, and this is where she called you a crass, hypocritical waste of humanity?"

"No, first EG called us nattering nabobs of conspicuous consumption when Elsie asked what kind of limo EG's father had," Brian offered helpfully.

Interesting that Elizabeth Georgiana was already reduced to EG. So much for my trying to give her a new image. Like, a new name would change the image of any child calling another a nabob? But I could see where this was going. It was my turn to spin a smug smile on good ol' Tex. He didn't flinch, so I guess he just didn't quite get it yet. It was time he did.

Throwing caution to the wind, I turned back to the clueless Brian. "EG's dad has the same limo as Elsie's dad does. I assume some label was applied to one who rides subways?" I arched my eyebrow inquiringly.

"She does not have the same limo as my dad does!" Elsie replied furiously. "My dad is the only dad with a Pierce-Arrow. It's the only one in the whole city. And *she's* just a smarmy little upstart who doesn't belong with the rest of us. She doesn't even have a *cell phone*."

"*Smarmy upstart*. My, the vocabulary does seem to come naturally, doesn't it, Senator? Right along with respect and obedience?" I turned to Tex. "Shall I continue the interrogation to see if this gets any sweeter?"

Tex ignored me to glare at the principal. "Applebay..." I swear, that's how he pronounced it. "Ah won't have mah daughter corrupted by creatures of this ilk. Ah was told this heah is a refined establishment, and the students are properly vetted before admittance. Ah'll not pay the outrageous tuition for mah daughter to be insulted in this mannah."

Appleby looked as if he'd like to slide under his desk and hide until this was over. He started turning purple, so I generously came to his rescue. "Senator, I will not resort to the name-calling of a child. If you would like Elizabeth's credentials, the school has them on file. If you would like her ancestry examined, I will be happy to call her mother.

Magda can be here tomorrow, if she must. Would you like that?"

I was being so upright and polite, I didn't even give him my evil smile. I just waited for the name to register.

It did. There for a minute, I thought he might choke on his tongue. He looked from me to EG, and a slow flush crept up his starched shirt collar. Tex was slow, but not totally dumb. I think maybe he finally grasped the significance of EG's dad having the same limo as Elsie's.

I'd just insulted and indirectly blackmailed a man accused of murdering his aide for lesser crimes. Not the smartest move of my career, but I was flying high on fury and adrenaline and couldn't kick the nattering out of his nabobs in front of others.

"Ah'm sure that won't be necessary," he said in a strangled voice. "Applebay can arrange to have the children kept to different classrooms. If you will speak to your..."

"Sister," I completed for him.

He sighed, then shook his head. "Of course. Your sister. Ah will speak with Elsie. Ah'm sure we can overcome this minor outburst, and everyone can return to bidness."

"Thank you, Senator. Mr. Appleby, I'll take Elizabeth home with me now. I expect better precautions will be taken in the future to prevent brawls in the hallways, and I assume your classes will teach courtesy and respect for individual differences. Come along, EG. I need to explain the facts of life to you *again*."

I didn't turn to see if she stuck her tongue out at anyone. I would have stuck out mine, but EG's more mature than I was at that age. She obediently hopped up from her chair and trotted out after me as if she didn't have a care in the world.

As if her father hadn't just pretended he wasn't her father.

* * *

EG knew what she had to do now.

Peering around the corner to be certain neither Nick or Ana was nearby, she slipped down the hall to Ana's laptop. She had a textbook in hand to show she was doing homework should anyone ask.

Piling a stack of pillows in the office chair, she settled in front of the computer and called up the e-mail program she'd used the other night. She'd thought and thought about this. She hated doing anything dumb, but today's episode required action.

She'd watched her father watching Ana this afternoon. In that halter dress, Ana had looked an awful lot like a shorter version of Magda, except for the hair color of course, and there had been something in Tex's eyes that said he'd been remembering the past. What would happen if Magda and Tex got together again?

If her father would only confide in her, EG knew she could help him solve the problem with the police. Magda knew lots of important people. Maybe she could help. Between them, they'd prove he'd been framed. And then maybe he'd notice her existence.

She knew better than to say that to her mother. She was playing with fire to even contemplate this. She was counting on Ana to save her if her plan blew up in her face. Ana might hide in dark rooms, but she could be counted on to fly out on her broom and whisk trouble in the face when forced. EG hated forcing Ana into action, but today had been enlightening, and despite the humiliation, almost as entertaining as the Italian nanny episode.

Carefully, she composed her e-mail to her mother. *We have moved into Grandfather's house. I am going to a private school. They use the same dumb books as the public school, only with fancier covers. My social studies book says world economy depends on oil, and that oil companies protect the environment better than alternative fuels. How feeble is that?*

Magda thought that oil, next to money, was the root of all evil.

Then, to add fuel to the flames, she fired off a note to Magda's maid, EG's best friend in the household. *I met my father and his legitimate daughter today. I beat up her boyfriend.*

Smiling, EG hit the *Send* button, then settled down to compose another e-mail to Robert Hagan. Her last reply had bounced, but she'd discovered a new e-mail address for him in the directory for the GSA. She didn't know why someone who worked with education had a GSA address, but she was just learning about American government.

She thought it quite interesting that the committee Hagan chaired recommended schoolbooks to the public school system. Perhaps he should be advised that he was recommending erroneous propaganda. Or would he already know that?

For the first time, EG wished she had a PhD to put after her name as she compiled a detailed memo of the errors she'd located so far in her books. Wanting to be as correct as an adult, she jumped down from her chair and went looking for her encyclopedia.

Maybe if she did this well enough, Hagan would wish to talk to her, and then she could question him about her dad. Nick and Ana didn't seem to be making any progress on the investigation, so she'd have to speed them along.

* * *

"That's two schools in three days, Nick. We can't pull her out because of a minor altercation with a snot." I spun around in the library chair and contemplated the Don Quixote poster I suspected covered a camera. I thought my head might explode from thinking so hard. Perhaps I ought to remove the poster so Graham could get the explosion on tape.

I had a scary thought. "Did you run into the good Senator on your first day of work? Can he recognize you?"

Sprawling his long legs across the wine and navy Oriental carpet, crossing his hands across his flat abdomen, Nick looked half asleep, but he didn't fool me.

"I was in school in England that time Magda was in Spain, if you'll remember," he said. "I don't think he knows the name of his assistants except as 'hey, son.' But he should have recognized you the instant you walked in."

Remembering how Tex had stared, I shrugged. "He sees a lot of people in his work, and it's been ten years. He thought I was EG's *mother*. It took him a little while to place me."

"So now he knows you know about his little peccadillo. You could blackmail him into tomorrow by threatening to tell his wife. You'd really hang the guillotine over his head if you threatened to tell the press. He'd be justified in wanting you murdered. I think you and EG ought to retire to some obscure hotel in Kansas while I run down to St. Kitts."

"Excellent idea," the intercom said mechanically, but I still heard the malicious intent behind the interruption.

I glared at the black box. "I *am* allowed to have a few hours of personal time, aren't I? Even slaves are given a night's rest."

"Balancing what you have accomplished professionally today against the hours spent on personal activities, it seems to me that you're taking a holiday. Have you located Pao's limo service yet?"

"He's not using any of the usual ones, all right?"

Nick crossed his ankles and looked on with interest as I argued with a box.

I called up my document file on the Whiz. "There is my list of contacts. I am now working my way through the independent drivers, but most of them won't reveal the names of their clients. I can't blame them. I have tried saying Mr. Pao would like to cancel his reservation, but so far, no one has heard of him. Most of them have sensibly asked for the pickup address, which I obviously cannot provide, although I've used the address from the warehouse and the Cambodian embassy as well. If you can do this any better, why do you need me?"

"Excellent question, Miss Devlin. I have been asking myself the same thing." The intercom clicked off.

"Go ahead, get your kicks by having the last word," I muttered. I hated failure, and I hated disappointing someone who'd trusted my talents, but it looked like I was racking up big goose eggs all across the board.

"He wants us out of here," Nicholas reminded me.

I looked around at the library lined with volumes I might never have time to peruse. I caressed the Cobalt Whiz with longing and contemplated the ornate plaster on the ceiling. I had a sense of connection here that I felt nowhere else. D.C. was a sprawling city with a nasty reputation, but this house belonged to us. A home was worth fighting for.

"We'll have to take EG to school and pick her up every day," I decided. "I can't believe Tex would attack his own daughter, but I'll feel better keeping an eye on her."

"He has enough problems without bringing Magda flying back here. I think she's safe enough. And we can take care of ourselves. Here, I brought you a present." Nick slipped a couple of large cards from his inside coat pocket and threw them on the desk.

They were engraved invitations to Senator Paul Rose's fundraising reception on Friday night. I admired them with trepidation—and pride at Nick's resourcefulness. Then I covered them with a legal pad so a camera couldn't see them. "You're a good man, Charlie Brown. Forged?" I mouthed, hoping Graham couldn't read lips if there were more cameras in here.

Nick nodded. "Tex had a handful of them. Computers can imitate anything." He looked inordinately pleased with himself. "You can wear your little black dress."

I greeted that observation with a few appropriate phrases. "Just because I went out once looking like Model Number Nine—"

"Quit pretending you're not female. You look like Magda," Nick reminded me. "That's why Tex believed you without question. Use what you have instead of hiding it."

As much as I'd like to believe I could slay dragons with a seductive flash of my Irish green eyes, I looked down at my B-cup chest and snorted. "Right. Half a cantaloupe on each side ought to do the trick, but I think hiding it is the better way to go."

"It's all in how you wear it, mushroom. You have better ideas on how to locate your suspect?" He shot the intercom a look that dared it to interrupt. We held our breaths, hoping Graham wasn't listening or wasn't following our guarded conversation.

"I can keep working on the connections between Edu-Pub, Pao, and the good senators," I finally said when the intercom didn't scream. "Maybe Pao helped them with fundraising in the Islamic community, and they agreed to serve on the board of directors without knowing more."

"And maybe they're all thieves looking for a cover-up. You're not going to find out with a computer," Nick scoffed, rising from the chair.

"You need jewelry to go with that dress."

He was referring to the reception that Graham didn't want me to attend. I circled my fingers on the legal pad covering the invitations and bit my tongue. I wanted to nail Pao. Nick had given me the means.

He sauntered out, completely confident of his social skills and certain we'd locate Pao in a crush of wealthy humanity. I'd rather turn myself into a valet and watch everyone entering the party. I'd had enough of Magda for a lifetime without imitating her.

I turned back to my computer just in time to see an instant message to Tweety Bird flash across my screen. *I've traced your e-mail address, Miss Devlin. Stay out of what you don't understand, or someone will get hurt.*

I spent the rest of the evening frantically attempting to hack into the server of the return address displayed, with no success.

How could anyone except my clients know my private screen name?

Chapter Seventeen

Magda arrives

THE DOORBELL rang at midnight.

I was up in my room, but I wasn't sleeping. I had given up tracing the threatening instant message for the moment. If it was Graham's idea of a joke, it was a tasteless one, but I preferred to think of it as a bad joke rather than the alternative of Pao or Senator Tex attempting to intimidate me. I didn't know enough to be a threat to anyone. I was more worried that I was actually starting to understand the man in the attic. His intelligence and cynicism fascinated me. All right, he provoked my nosy curiosity, as well. I'm a sucker for a puzzle.

I was deep into looking for some connection between all my favorite people—Graham, Tex, Rose, Pao, and Magda—when the doorbell startled me into next week.

I knocked my wireless mouse off the desk and cursed. My heart started pounding as if I'd taken bad acid. Midnight was not the time for doorbells to ring.

I leaned over the wide desk and tried looking out my window, but a tall holly blocked the view of the front door. I caught the taillights of a cab pulling away from the curb.

D.C. is busy at night, but generally not with the kind of respectable street life inhabiting Manhattan. The mansion didn't overlook any theaters or nightclubs or fancy restaurants. The rich ambassadors and foreign despots living in the surrounding museums didn't walk the streets but glided silently past in limos with tinted windows. The debonair hip hoppers standing beneath the imitation gas lamps at the circle weren't exchanging business cards.

At times like this, I almost appreciated Graham's security system. As the doorbell rang more insistently, floodlights illuminated all corners of the house and half the street. I still couldn't see the door. I couldn't hear the mechanical intercom from here, either, but I didn't doubt its operation. It was Graham's favorite time to chat.

If he was having visitors, I wanted to see them. I had changed back to black capris and halter earlier. I was barefoot. I could be stealthy.

I slipped from my office-bedroom and down the hall to the stairway. I knew just the right corner for hiding in to look over the banister without being seen. I had the eerie feeling I had done this before, more than once.

Any memory of childhood incidents dissipated as soon as the door opened and the visitor entered—Magda.

Graham must have released the lock electronically. She walked in alone, as if she belonged here. Wearing her blond hair up in a sophisticated French twist, she entered wearing form-fitting jeans and a casual open-necked polo shirt with the collar turned up. I figured the shirt was knitted with genuine gold and the black jeans had been tailored expressly to fit. The colorfully painted gold slides on her feet probably cost a few hundred all by themselves. My bet was that she wore over half a grand to appear casual. Her lovers tend to be generous.

She tugged a wheeled Vuitton overnight case over the threshold, but I knew somewhere there were a dozen matching bags waiting to be delivered if she decided to stay. My heart sank to my unpolished toes.

"My old room?" she called gaily, evidently conversing with the intercom she must have known was there.

"Perhaps your daughter should decide that," Graham's mechanical voice said with the dryness that meant he saw me.

Shit. I hope I haunted his dreams the way he haunted my life. He knew Magda and knew she was my mother?

Stepping from the shadows, I started down the stairs. "I have no idea which is your old room." I tried to sound welcoming, but it was hard. We hadn't spoken for years. I've always loved my mother, but in a distant, bewildered sort of way.

"Anastasia, dearest! It's so good to see you again." She approached the stairs in a cloud of Opium perfume. "Thank you for looking after EG until I could get here. Honestly, she's even worse than you were at that age."

No doubt. EG had a few more IQ points.

She spoke to me as if I were still a child, and we'd seen each other just yesterday. She's my mother. She had that right. But counseling had taught me that I didn't have to let her control my image of myself.

Reminding myself that I was not her live-in help any longer, I didn't stop at the bottom of the stairs but started down the hallway to grandfather's remodeled parlor. "The guest room is this way. You'll appreciate the whirlpool after your trip."

No hugs, no kisses. As earlier noted, we weren't a touchy-feely family. If I was to believe her fairy tales, my grandmother must have died when Magda was quite young. Perhaps a lack of love and affection had made her what she is today. And the rest of us what we are. Magda didn't dispense affection without an audience.

"In the parlor?" she protested, following me. "Are all the other rooms taken?"

"Musty," I said gruffly. "We weren't expecting company."

I didn't expect her to explain her arrival, but I suppose I was an eternal optimist and waited for an explanation anyway. Trying to figure out Magda had been my goal throughout childhood, and the main reason

I learned to research. When no explanation was forthcoming, I didn't bother clarifying that we were trespassing on Graham's limited goodwill. I could blame lack of communication for our family dysfunction, but it was only a symptom of the real problem—we were all as competitive as hell and liked to always be one up on each other. I tried not do that to the kids, but with Magda, it's an irresistible challenge.

"I must say, I'm amazed that Amadeus is living here. Whatever possessed him to move into D.C.? I thought him more the Alexandria type." She swept into the parlor cum bedroom and glanced around with approval.

I, on the other hand, stood there like a dork in shock. See? See how she always pulls the rabbit out of the hat?

"You know Graham?" I hated asking but couldn't help myself.

Her long-lashed cat eyes narrowed. "Of course. Didn't he tell you?"

I didn't want to hear about it if Graham was another of Magda's lovers. That would be a crushing blow I didn't want to take. I shrugged, leaned against the door jamb, and tried to look disinterested. "We don't talk much."

"You mean, he doesn't talk much. Never did. Strange, even as a child, obsessed with electronic devices. Well, no matter. I'm here now. We can catch up on old times. Is Nicholas still here? We can have a lovely family breakfast together."

Once upon a time my heart would have swelled with joy at the thought of our fairy tale princess mother condescending to arise early enough to breakfast with us like normal mothers did. But she kept midnight hours and needed her beauty sleep. I no longer begrudged Magda her lifestyle, but I no longer believed every word she said either.

"EG has to be at school by eight. We eat at seven. I'll leave you to get your rest so we can talk in the morning then. Good-night." I turned around to walk out.

"Ana," she called quietly before I could escape.

I turned, and just for a very brief moment, I saw her without the shield of glamor. She wasn't fifty yet. She still had the fine skin of a child. The striking gold of her hair complemented the cream of her complexion. Fine lines at her eyes said she hadn't resorted to plastic surgery. She still had a figure to die for, even after all the kids she'd carried. But for that very brief moment, the corners of her mouth sagged, and she looked like a lonely woman.

So I waited to hear what she had to say.

At my hesitation, she smiled, the glamor returned, and she was the Magda I remembered. "You look stunning in that outfit. Your grandfather would be very proud of you."

"My grandfather died two months ago. None of us knew to attend his funeral. I don't think he would be proud at all."

She stiffened and tucked a long spiral of blond hair back into its pin while looking in the mirror rather than at me. "My father liked being judge and jury and lord of all he surveyed. He was a good man, and his intentions were of the best, but he had difficulty accepting that the opinions of others mattered or that the ends don't justify the means."

Talk about the pot calling the kettle black! Sounded to me as if Magda was a chip off the old block. But I obediently held my sharp tongue and waited for her to continue.

"I think, towards the end," she added, "he may have finally come to understand he might be wrong, but it was too late."

I waited, hoping for explanations. Again. Silly of me. "Too late for what?" I asked.

Magda smiled. "Never mind. This house brings back memories, and I'm in danger of sounding maudlin. Good-night, dear."

She'd upstaged me again. If Grandfather was anything like Magda, I could understand why the two of them couldn't live in the same house. They'd have to live separate lives just to keep from killing each other—just as I'd had to move out to keep from strangling my mother. How did one fight environment and heredity to change the way a family interacts?

I returned upstairs, half expecting Graham to lodge a protest the instant I opened my door. Instead, the intercom remained blessedly silent. Or maybe not so blessedly. I could have used a little human contact right now. But I didn't want to wake EG or Nick, and Graham wasn't really human now, was he?

Maybe that was the best way for my family to get along—by mechanical means. A virtual family. I'd ask my therapist about that the next time I hired one.

* * *

I saw no reason to compete with Magda on any level. Thursday morning, I wore my usual black cotton capris and T-shirt, tugged my hair into a single thick braid, and strode down to breakfast doing my best to feel as if I was in control of my little part of the planet. I am, after all, the best virtual assistant in the world, and I could leave on my own anytime I liked.

The trouble was that I had begun to enjoy having Nick and EG to talk to—and even Graham, however frustrating he might be. I could return to my basement mole hole, but I wasn't certain that I wanted to anymore.

That was too frightening to think about, so I didn't. That's how one survives, not stressing over things one can't control.

Evidently forewarned by Graham, Mallard had set an extra place at the breakfast table. He even hovered anxiously in the doorway, looking up the instant I entered the room. If he was disappointed that it was only me, I couldn't tell from his wooden expression. He held out my chair for me as he never did before and whipped out a linen napkin to lay over my knees.

"He's been doing that ever since we came down," Nick said, reaching for the jam. "I think he's sailed around the bend."

EG gave him a lofty look. "Magda arrived last night."

Nick almost choked on his toast. I stirred my tea and let him choke. Magda could change the atmosphere of an entire palace simply by her presence. Mallard was already showing the effect, and one will note, our mother had not yet put in an appearance.

"This doesn't change anything," I said for EG's benefit. "If you want to stay with me, you can, as long as you understand that I expect you to go to school. Your choice."

She nodded and tried to look blasé, but I liked to think she relaxed a little.

"I'll escort her to school," Nick offered. "It's on my way to work anyway."

"Then I can wait for her after school," I agreed.

"My father wouldn't hurt me," EG said defensively, knowing what we were talking about. "He just didn't know who I was. He was protecting Elsie. That's what fathers do."

I tried not to roll my eyes too obviously. "Fathers are men, and men are capable of anything. Remember that, and you'll be fine."

"And by *anything*, I assume you mean world peace as well as war." Magda swept into the room in a cloud of Opium shower soap and lotion. She wouldn't be so crass as to wear perfume in the morning.

Nicholas rose as he'd been taught to do at an early age. Always more comfortable with men, Magda pecked him on the jaw. "Nicholas, dearest, why aren't you in Hollywood by now?"

She wasn't wearing casual this morning. She was dressed to thrill in a red silk dress that clung to every voluptuous inch of her figure before flaring into a flirty ruffled hem. A bolero jacket embroidered in small black beads made a poor attempt to hide her cleavage. Untouched by gray, her shiny blonde hair was stacked in an elaborate coiffure I thought only possible with a master stylist.

Without waiting for Nick's reply to her flattery, she turned to smile at Mallard, who stood at stiff attention behind the chair he held out for her. "Mallard, you haven't changed a bit!"

He reddened, but I caught the shadow of a smile on his lips. I wanted to sulk because he never smiled at me, but then, I hadn't given him reason to do so. Therapists had told me that my desire not to compete with my mother came from fear of failure. They're probably right.

"Elizabeth, how lovely you look, dear!" She flashed a ruby red smile at EG who merely sent her a glower.

Dear EG, we're alike in so many ways. "She chose the clothes herself," I said, easing the tension with EG's non-answer. "She has your flair for fashion. And Nick's," I added at his cough. "The school we've found seems to be an excellent one." *Line drawn, battlefield readied.*

Magda smiled prettily at Mallard as he leaned over her shoulder to pour her tea. From the advantage of distance and experience, I could tell she was merely using the delay as a means of rallying her forces. I had hoped to have our millions before she showed up so I'd be in a position strong enough to fight for EG.

"D.C. is such a dreary place," Magda said with a jaded air, waving her rings in the sunlight from the leaded glass window. "I cannot imagine why anyone would wish to live here when there are so many more suitable climes. The humidity alone is enough to make one gasp." *Cannons in place. Fire one.*

"D.C. has some of the best educational facilities in the world," I asserted. *Return fire.* "The museums alone provide a lifetime of learning. Life is not just about the best sunny beach in spring."

"Life is about living, dear. Education is pleasant if it helps one to live well, but mostly it clutters the mind with irrelevant information that gets in the way of actually doing anything."

Magda truly believes this with all her heart and soul. She was not being facetious or argumentative. We'd had this discussion many times over the years so there was no point in taking it further.

"Nevertheless, the law in this country requires that a child have an education. Until she does, she's not in a position to decide whether or not it is beneficial. EG's mind is large enough to encompass a great deal of information before it becomes cluttered."

It was as if ten years had dropped away, and we were right back where we once were, arguing over my desire to go to college. Nick and EG faded into the woodwork. This wasn't their argument and never had been.

Nick's father had paid for his schooling. I assumed any money from EG's father paid for more education than I'd received. My father was dead, and we'd lived out of suitcases when I was little. My irregular primary education hadn't been strong enough to produce scholarships. Or even a formal high school degree. I'd taken the GED when I'd returned to the States.

"Daddy's in trouble." EG dropped that tidbit like a bombshell to smash the pattern of our argument to smithereens. She hadn't been around ten years ago to do that.

Magda smiled brightly and reached across the table to pat EG's hand.

"He'll be just fine, dear. He has a raft of lawyers who will prove he's innocent. There isn't a thing you can do to help him. You can come home with me where you don't have to listen to all the silliness."

"No." EG shoved back her chair and stalked out of the dining room, her long hair swaying across her Ralph Lauren polo.

I had no idea if this was the usual pattern between EG and Magda, but our mother showed no sign that the abrupt departure disturbed her. She merely slid a sliver of jam over her toast.

"Guess I'd better be going, too. Don't want to be late." Taking a last quick sip of his coffee, Nick pushed away from the table. "Good to see you again, Mother. Hope you're staying for a while. See you later."

Nick knew how to say all the polite meaningless phrases that smoothed over the fact that chances were very good Magda would be gone by evening. Etiquette and small talk wove a silken cocoon to conceal the emptiness of our conversation. Growing up fatherless, we all wanted more of Magda than she was capable of giving. We each dealt with it in our own ways.

I dealt with it by escaping, if only to an apple tree in the backyard. Or more likely, the camel's shed. But I'd established a beachhead in this house. This was my home, and I didn't intend to leave unless caught in something fatal like a riptide. I sipped my tea and waited.

Magda inclined her head in acknowledgement of my refusal to escape like the others. "It's time I told you why I left D.C., dear."

I almost spluttered tea out my nose.

Chapter Eighteen

Magda and Sean talk; Ana learns who Oracle is and falls in love with a dangerous car

MALLARD had disappeared into the recesses of the kitchen after greeting Magda, but he suddenly appeared in the doorway now. Had Graham warned him of what she was about to say? I was suspicious of everyone, including my mother, but I'd still like to hear her excuse for abandoning Maximillian and the home and security he had offered us.

"Mallard, go away, please. This is private." She didn't even have to turn to know he was behind her. She winked at me. "This house has always had ears."

"Wireless communication has made it more so. Perhaps you would prefer to wait until we go elsewhere?" I asked politely, although I silently gnashed my teeth in frustration.

"Oh, Graham knows everything. Daddy always wanted a son, and events provided him with one. Isn't that so, Amadeus?"

The candelabra didn't reply.

My head was already spinning in shock, and she hadn't even begun. Graham had the grandfather who should have been mine? "Graham knew Max?" I asked, as if my temper hadn't reached 212 Fahrenheit and my brain wasn't flashing lights like a berserk computer.

"Of course, dear. My father liked playing puppetmeister. He mentored any number of protégés who have had their hands in lots of sticky little plots." Still no comment from the candelabra. "I assume Max kept Graham too busy to kill himself after his wife died, but you'd best ask Graham that, dear."

"But they knew each other before 9/11?" I asked, proud of my nonchalance.

Hands wrapped around the fragile teacup, Magda tilted it back and forth as if trying to read the tea leaves. "Long before. Graham may have been Max's last protégé. Your father was possibly his first. Brody was a bit of a firebrand, though."

From my understanding of my father, he was a lot more than a firebrand. He was a raging, fiery orator with a voice and way with words that could sway multitudes. The Irish government had thought to neutralize his message by sending him here, sensibly not creating a martyr by killing him.

I believe one source I'd read said he succeeded in raising more money for the IRA in one year than the renegades had seen in all their history. A brilliant man, my father, but he lacked common sense.

"Your father was assassinated. Did you know that?"

"I assumed as much," I acknowledged, wishing for something stronger than Darjeeling to get me through this. Where was she heading with this?

"Max took Brody under his wing when he first arrived here. I was about eighteen. At the time, Max had plans for me to marry an Ivy League man and rule over Washington, preferably as First Lady. If he'd wanted me to be president, things might have turned out differently."

I had to smile into my teacup at that. That was pure Magda and the reason I loved her despite all evidence otherwise. She was a strong-minded woman who never let anyone or anything put her down. That made for tempestuous relationships, but she could handle them.

I was the one who couldn't. "You would never have been able to compromise enough to pull a political party together behind your campaign."

She shrugged. "One doesn't understand that at eighteen. I only knew I hated Vassar, had no desire to wear gray suits, and that Brody Devlin was the most gorgeous man I'd ever seen. The more Daddy disparaged him as husband material, the more I defended him. When you came along, I married him. Daddy almost killed us both."

I didn't think I liked the way this was heading. "I remember my grandfather as a loving man who bounced me on his knee."

"Oh, Max adored you. You could barely talk when I got in an argument with him and called him an oracle of Mammon. From that day forward, you called him Oracle. He loved it."

Magda didn't even notice that I almost fell out of my seat. The cogs in my head were whirring so erratically that I barely caught her next words.

"You were the apple of his eye, the next brilliant generation of Maximillian who would take over the world since I was such a severe disappointment." Magda nibbled at her toast as if she wasn't answering all the questions I'd begged for her to answer over the years.

"Did he stay in touch with you? Ever ask after us?" I asked, trying not to put too much of my hope into the question.

Magda waved her hand dismissively. "Of course he did. If he'd had some way of pulling our strings, he would have. Be grateful I kept you out of his hands, but be assured he knew everything we did."

I was still digesting the "oracle" bit and flying high on mixed hope and despair and didn't want to hear the downside of her tale. *I might have been communicating with my grandfather before his death.* If so, he really had cared. He'd help me get my fledgling business off the ground. I wanted him to be a superhero. Or had he been manipulating me? "Let me keep thinking of him like a helpful old man, all right? Sometimes, the fairy tales are better."

Magda eyed me through witchy green eyes and disregarded my plea. "Like me, Brody wouldn't let Max pull his strings. To acquire the weapons he needed, Brody became embroiled with several terrorist groups. There will always be people who think they know what is best for others, and the destruction of authority is their goal. It's kind of like marriage in a way."

She'd had me hooked until she hit me with that comparison. My tea went down the wrong way and I choked. "Marriage?" I spluttered, dabbing at my mouth with a napkin.

"Girls spend their youth dreaming of the prince who will sweep them off their feet and the wonderful wedding where they'll be queen for a day. They never think about waking up the day after the wedding to a man with a stubbly beard and body odor and a world where they have to get up and fry the bacon."

I spluttered some more, but that was muffled laughter. Magda had certainly arranged it so I never suffered from marriage delusions. She smiled approvingly and waited for me to recover.

By the time I'd washed my coughs down with water, I had grasped her meaning. "Terrorists only dream of the destruction of authority and haven't planned the morning after. Got it. Men are always big on competition and lacking in detail."

"Or vision. I loved your father, but he loved getting his way more than he loved us."

"I don't want to hear about it," I insisted, although that was half a lie. I was desperate to hear about my father, but not through the filter of my mother's vivid imagination. "Tell me more about Max."

Magda waved a dismissive hand. "Daddy was Old World. Brody was New. Your father had the brains to overthrow the government, but not the vision to see that terrorists create anarchy, not equality. Your grandfather wasn't involved in Brody's assassination." She drained her teacup and gazed ruefully at the dregs. "I was."

"You killed my father?" I shouted, despite my best struggle to avoid conflict. I preferred thinking that Brody had been the love of her life, and she'd run off because she couldn't live without him. Even a hard case like me can have a few romantic fantasies.

"And Graham's father," she added reflectively. "They were in it together."

"Magda, crawl back to your sheik's tent," the candelabra said with distinct disgruntlement. "You'd think you would have outgrown the drama queen tendencies by now."

"Oh shut up, Day. You were eight years old and more annoying than EG when it happened. What do you know?"

Day? Ama*deus*. Deus. Day. God. I shook my head and staggered up from the table. I didn't want to hear any more of this. This is the reason I preferred my insular world. The big wide one that my mother, and apparently Graham, inhabited was much too scary. Or—as Graham insinuated—my mother was spinning fairy tales again. Magda did have a tendency to overdramatize. Her tales often made Grimm's look like children's books. Could she have made up the part about my calling Max Oracle? Shouldn't I remember it?

I didn't remember my father's death.

"How do you think Max spent all these years since you left?" the candelabra scolded as I walked out.

"I gave him lots of little Maximillians to follow in his footsteps, didn't I?" Magda responded in her usual insensible fashion.

One can see why I learned to avoid asking questions and relied on documentation for my answers. Asking questions of Magda was akin to banging my head against a brick wall because it felt so good when I stopped.

I wanted to return and shout, "Every time I thought those kids were old enough to take care of each other so I could leave, *you had another one!* And that was for Max's benefit?" But I'd resolved that argument before EG was born, and obviously, it hadn't got me far.

Sick to my stomach, I retreated to the Cobalt Whiz and called up the website of Pao's fundamentalist organization. What in *hell* made people think they knew it all?

I didn't know it all. Neither did Graham or my mother. No one way was ever the right way for everyone or there would be no individuality. I wanted no part of their quarrel. I had a job to do, and that's all I would do.

Ignoring my own argument, I shut down the Pao file and opened my Oracle file. Could these messages really have come from my grandfather?

A tear wet my cheek as I read the courtly, old-fashioned phrases. My grandfather. All these years we'd forgotten about him, but he hadn't forgotten us. Regardless of what Magda claimed, I believed he loved us enough to watch over us. I wanted to put my head down on the table and sob.

Except *envelopes-poison-tophat-pow* suddenly took on new and alarming meaning.

* * *

I spent the morning hunting for an apartment. I would get the hell out of Dodge entirely, but I'd come to the interesting conclusion that my mother had never returned to D.C. because she had been afraid of being arrested. If I lived here, she wouldn't push her luck by visiting often.

I'd probably continue going after Reggie and our money so my siblings would be able to find their own way as I had. But I didn't want any part of Graham or Magda or my grandfather and the manipulative world they lived in. I didn't like the pieces of the puzzle that were falling into place. I was circling the wagons to protect my family first.

After working through my Oracle file, I was positive my disappearing client had been my grandfather. Now that I had my mother's clue, I could look at the other evidence as more than coincidence. The dates matched. Mindy and textbooks matched.

If "pow" translated as "Pao," I wanted EG out of that house where Max might have been killed. *Poison* his note had read.

I was devastated in so many ways that I was amazed I was still functioning. I'd been working with my *grandfather*. He'd reached out to me in the last years of his life. Why hadn't he identified himself? I would have come running if he'd only asked.

Tears running down my cheeks as they had half the morning while I worked, I rubbed briskly at them and strode down the street keeping an eye out for For Rent signs.

To hell with Pao. With murder and Graham and the treacherous Reggie, I had far more on my plate than I could possibly solve. So I stayed with what I could do—find a home for EG.

I stopped at the pub for lunch and to peruse the classifieds. And maybe I stopped there in hopes of a human connection to slow my gyrating thoughts. Not that I believed Sean O'Herlihy was just a common working class man interested in me as a woman, because I didn't believe that for a second. But he at least came attached to a male body and not a candelabra.

He didn't disappoint. It took a while for my hamburger to arrive. When it did, it came accompanied by Sean wearing a hardhat and looking like every woman's wet dream.

He slid into the booth across from me. "We meet again. Blown up any more buildings?" He threw the hat on the bench beside him, revealing a head of thick black curls damp with sweat.

"Did it ever occur to you that Brody was a terrorist?" I muttered through my hamburger.

I had grown up with the idea that my father was a hero, killed in the line of duty, so to speak. I knew tens of thousands of Irishmen idolized him. And like EG, I'd preferred the fairy tale and hadn't thought beyond childish hero-worship.

Sean raised his eyebrows and signaled the bartender before turning the full blaze of his blue eyes on me. "People are only terrorists if they work for the enemy. If they're on our side, they're heroes."

"And here I thought I was cynical." But I suppose he spoke the truth.

We always like to think our country is right, and we're marching off to a just war, but then so did the Crusaders and the Nazis and all the other men who marched off to war.

"Women always think the world's problems can be solved by talking," he scoffed. "Very few men are granted the gift of gab. Your father was one of the few. He accomplished a great deal of good in his time."

"By talking." I didn't see the point here.

"By talking," he agreed, "and amassing arms to defend himself should the talking fall through, as it often does when injustice prevails and frustration builds."

"Because men are assholes who'd rather blow each other up instead of compromise." I tore off a bite of hamburger. I'd lost my father and my grandfather and possibly the home that should have been mine because of violence. The world wasn't pretty.

"Well, you can take your mother's methods, if you prefer. Women can accomplish a lot behind the scenes."

My head jerked up. He knew my mother, too? "Ummhmmm," I murmured through my mouthful. Anything else would have been blasphemous.

"Don't sound so doubtful. World peace isn't achieved by armies. It's the people behind the scenes talking reason to people of power who are the unsung heroes."

I was milkshake to his straw. He was sucking me in, and I couldn't resist. Magda blew up her husband to achieve peace, and in her own strange way was now doing so by vamping men in power? Yeah, I could just about buy that. My mother was that warped. "Right, and you're CIA and know that for a fact," I said with as much scorn as my milkshake spine could manage.

I'm an introvert. I don't ask questions willingly. But I listen. And put things together. And irritate the answers out of people. Sean wasn't falling for the ploy, though. He continued on his own wavelength—which seemed designed to teach me my history but was just making me wonder more about his.

"In a way, your father and Pao had similar goals, just different religions. They represent fundamentalist minorities attempting to force their governments to recognize their beliefs."

"Which is why this country keeps religion out of government," I said caustically. "Don't tell me Magda blew Brody up over religion. She doesn't have any."

Sean snorted. "Brody was still idealistic enough to have principles. He uncovered a dangerous cell of black-market dealers and had turned them in to the authorities. *They* killed him, not your mother, although she may have said something when she shouldn't that revealed his identity to the wrong people."

And carried the guilt with her into exile. Or to chase his assassins? She was capable of both. "So you're saying there are millions of people who believe Pao is a hero, like Brody."

He shrugged. "No one achieves that kind of power on their own. It's like money. They buy and trade with others who have it." His beer arrived, and he sat back to swig it.

"Like Paul Rose," I guessed, hoping to keep him talking.

"All politicians buy and trade power. As long as we expect them to buy their seats through campaign contributions, our government is owned by the wealthy and powerful."

Sean knew about Pao and Rose. He was either in cahoots with Graham, or a spy for the feds, and I wanted no part of his political propaganda. But as mentioned, curiosity was my besetting sin. "Was the Edu-Pub arson to cover up money laundering?" I asked flat out.

"My guess is that someone was getting too close to whatever was happening in there," he agreed with a pointed look at me.

I hadn't been close to anything except that damned building, and if he couldn't give me any better than that, then he didn't know more either. Big pictures were as fuzzy as hell. Until men started seeing the crisp details of little pictures, they'd never get it. Someone had almost killed me. That was as crisp as it got.

"Why are you telling me this?" I already understood he wouldn't answer questions that weren't on his agenda. He was just too pretty to dismiss though. Sean gave me some inkling of what Magda must have felt when she met my father, only I was far older and wiser than she had been at the time.

"My father admired yours," Sean admitted. "I was brought up on tales of his heroism. I don't want Brody's daughter hurt. There's a reason your grandfather didn't invite you or your siblings to stay with him."

"Graham." I suspected with Sean, it all came back to Graham. And now I had a better understanding of why. Graham knew Max. And Max may have been murdered. I wanted to believe Graham was there to revenge his death, but I'm an optimist when it comes to my home.

"You're quick," Sean said with admiration. "You're your father's daughter, without a doubt."

"No, I'm not, not in the way you mean." I stood up and left a ten on the table. "I believe in live and let live. My father believed in killing."

"Don't go," he protested. "I've given you the wrong impression. Stay and let me buy you a beer."

Despite his political agenda, I was beginning to like Sean a little too much. Therapeutic sex with a stranger was one thing, but getting involved was quite another. Magda used men, not me. "I don't like beer, and you gave me exactly the right impression. See you around."

I had second and third thoughts about leaving, but I had to pick EG up at school, and I certainly didn't need a Brody admirer messing with my libido. If there were conspiracies lurking beneath the grime of D.C.'s political world, I didn't need to hear about them. If my best client was actually Max, protecting me by keeping me happily employed and out of D.C., I'd be wise to trust his judgment. It was time to pull back. Graham could find Pao on his own. Sean could spy on Graham some other way. Magda could go back where she belonged. Civilization had survived without me this long. I'm sure it could struggle on another few thousand years.

If the house was dangerous, Graham could have it. My one and only goal had just become keeping EG safe and happy.

* * *

A mile-long, shiny champagne-colored car with a fortune's worth of nickel-plated grill waited at the front of the school when I arrived by Metro. The sleek machine so obviously belonged in a museum that it could only be the infamous Pierce-Arrow.

Normally, I am not an obnoxious person. I treasure my invisibility. If I had a religion, I would choose Quaker. But that was me. And that car was for EG. Maybe we couldn't have Max's house, but EG ought to have a limo and a rich dad, just like her sister.

I looked up at the tier of steps from the school, heard the bell ring, and with a smirk, leaned against the waxed fender, crossed my arms, and waited.

It had been a rough day, and I got my jollies where I could find them. I mean, how many times can a girl hear her mother say she killed her father? Not killed, assassinated. Add that to the prior night's threatening message, Sean's knowledge of Pao, and my new fear about Max's death, and my sense of humor needed something outrageous as a restorative.

The chauffeur climbed out of the driver's seat. "Don't lean on the car," he said coldly.

I cast him a provocative smile. "The Senator won't mind. My sister and Elsie go to school together. We could use a ride home."

The driver was an old black guy with tight grizzled curls and a proud carriage that said he'd worked for the senator for a long time and held some degree of authority. Heck, for all I knew, he was a bodyguard. I was feeling just reckless enough not to care.

"Don't lean on the car," he repeated stonily.

"How will I make an impression if I don't lean on the car?" I asked with honesty. "If I stand next to it, I'll look like I'm asking for a ride. And

I'm not."

"You just did," he said with blinding logic.

"Nope. I demanded it. As if I owned this car. It puts the Phaeton I used to ride in to shame."

"You rode a Phaeton? Where?"

Men are so easy. "Manchester, England." That was the truth, too. At least, I think it was a Phaeton. We didn't stay there long, and I was pretty young. I'd heard of the Phaeton anyway.

"Why are you talking to *her,* Boy?" Darling Elsie ran down the walk in a twirl of pink skirts and hand-painted plastic sandals.

"*Boy?*" I asked, lifting my eyebrows at the chauffeur.

The creases in his black face deepened as he smiled. "For Boise. I'm from Idaho. My mama never thought about nicknames."

I grinned. Keeping an eye out for EG in the throng of chattering students, I faced down the little pink cow. "This is a free country, darling. Mr. Boise may speak with anyone he likes."

"Well, he can't like you. My mama says I'm not to talk to cheap tramps."

Elsie was starting to look as much like a cow as her name suggested. Who named their kids after cows in the first place? I needed to meet this poor kid's mother. But not today. I'd had enough for today.

"What about expensive tramps?" I asked, taking up EG's ploy. It seemed to work pretty well on fifth-graders. Elsie looked confounded.

Fortunately for Elsie, EG strode down the stairs about then, her eyes wide in inquiry. She wasn't slumped over and dragging her feet as she had been the other day. Maybe she'd had a better day than I had.

"Hey, kid. Mr. Boise said he'll take us home. Hop in." One of the things I don't lack is leadership qualities. I come from a long line of people who took command. I'd been trying not to imitate my ancestors, but what the heck.

Not cracking a smile, the chauffeur opened the door and gestured the kids into the back. I opened the front door and made myself at home in the passenger seat. The tan leather fit like a kid glove, the gold-plated fixtures gleamed like new, and a white rose adorned the interior vase. Mr. Boise kept his car sharp.

"Have you worked for the senator for long?" I inquired after the driver pulled away from the school. Maybe if I forgot Max and Graham and Pao, I could concentrate on Tex. Not likely, but it was a better diversion than thinking *envelopes-poison* and tearing up like a girl.

"I've worked for the senator almost ten years," Boise replied without inflection as he scanned the busy street.

We were stopped at a red light, so he really didn't need to concentrate on traffic. I wondered what he was watching for. Had the senator, perchance, received threatening messages recently? Maybe nasty e-mails were making the rounds. Had I endangered EG by putting her in her father's car? Or had my normal paranoia escalated with recent events?

I saw nothing more out the windshield than the usual steamy D.C. streets, hordes of tourists with maps in front of their faces, and locals hurrying for their favorite mode of transportation. People did not linger on hot sidewalks in the smoggy glare of the sun.

The light changed and we rolled away from the intersection. I tried not to sigh in relief. "Ten years? Before or after he came back from Spain?" I asked, not at all innocently. The senator hadn't been a senator when he returned from Spain, but a recalled ambassador. Why would he need a chauffeur? Or a bodyguard, if that's what Boise was?

"After," Boise replied curtly, obviously with no intention of explaining. His mouth suddenly tightened into a grim line. I glanced out the windshield just before I heard a squeal of brakes and watched a black Lincoln with tinted windows pull across the narrow street we'd turned down.

A hail of gunfire rattled the street signs.

Without a word, Boise swung the long hood of the lovely car into a narrow alley, hit the gas, and ramming garbage cans, spewing trash left and right, accelerated through a dead end beneath a railroad bridge.

Chapter Nineteen

Ana's wild ride; Tex talks; Graham admits to knowing Max

FINGERNAILS digging into the leather seat, I didn't say another word as Boise whipped past concrete barriers, bounced through potholes, and raced up gravel construction ramps to a main highway. Maybe I'd been a little young to recognize the expertise of some of the drivers who had chauffeured Magda around, but I was old enough now to fully grasp Boise's ability. To pull this off, he had to have memorized escape routes all over the city.

The burning question was—*Why?*

I didn't ask it as we sped down the interstate. I didn't inquire when he pulled off the highway into a residential area of Georgetown. Elsie was weeping uncontrollably. EG was white-faced and tense, but a quick glance told me she wasn't injured. I wasn't even certain if the gunmen had succeeded in pocking the pretty car with bullet holes or if they'd just beaten up stop signs. My brain had quit functioning with the first shots.

"Wait here," Boise ordered as he whipped into a private drive and switched off the ignition.

He had my respect. I waited, shivering with shock, still not quite believing real men had shot real bullets at us. After the morning I'd had, I should have, but I'd been thinking Magda's world didn't apply to me. We watched silently as Boise helped Elsie out of the car and led her into the house.

Seeing this scene through EG's eyes, I could feel my own heart breaking as the pampered daughter received the attention that EG never would. So much for respect. I threw open the door and climbed into the back seat with my sister.

As mentioned, we weren't much on hugging, but when I put an arm around her shoulder, she fell against me and shuddered with silent sobs. She was so damned *small* and helpless.

I rocked her and tried to pretend she was merely venting fear after a terrifying incident, but I knew she was the same seething mass of emotions as I was. I didn't know how to make her world right. Kicking someone wouldn't help, and neither would crying along with her.

When the man responsible for this volcanic pressure appeared in company with Boise, I almost blew the lid off the car. I sat EG upright, leaped out, and rammed my fist against the roof of the Pierce-Arrow. I pack a punch powerful enough to dent it, but I wasn't looking at the car.

"What the hell are you involved in that requires assassination attempts?" I yelled, not very sensibly. I do better with physical reactions than verbal.

"Ah have enemies," Tex said calmly, although he looked almost as pale as EG beneath his tan. "Get back in the car. We'll take you home."

"This car is a moving target! Thank you, but I think we'll take the Metro." I waited for EG to climb out, but she was gazing hungrily at the man who had ignored her all her life.

His hokey drawl slipped into clipped, curt tones. "Did you think I would endanger my daughter? This car has been armored against attack, as my enemies now know. Get in. Your mother has already been notified, and she's waiting for you."

Oh shit. I was already plotting my return to Atlanta when I climbed in on one side of EG while Tex climbed in on the other. I am lousy at this parenting thing. Neither Tex nor Magda would have bullied their way into a car that was a moving target for killers.

Generally, people didn't shoot at me. If they shot at Tex often enough to require an armored car, then I needed to get my head straight. EG didn't belong with him either.

"Ah have found an excellent school for the gifted in Switzerland," Tex said stiffly as Boise backed the car out of the drive. "Your mother says she will be residing in Switzerland shortly. We think it best if Elizabeth returns with her."

That would certainly take care of flying bullets. It also meant Magda and Tex were currently speaking to each other. Oh, to be a fly on the wall...

EG slid her small hand behind the bulging backpack on the seat between us. She looked tiny next to Tex's imposingly broad figure. He wasn't looking at her. I wanted to punch him just for that. I reached behind her backpack and pressed her fingers into mine. The connection helped me regain some form of control.

"You and Magda think a Swiss school is best for yourselves. I don't suppose it occurred to you to ask what EG thinks is best for her?" I asked calmly.

He finally turned to glare at me, but EG was between us. His gaze inadvertently fell on her. She was sitting stiffly, staring straight ahead as Boise navigated D.C. streets to return us home. Tex's tight-lipped expression softened as he studied this daughter he didn't know, and again, for just a moment, I almost liked him. That feeling seldom lasted, and he didn't disappoint now.

He shook his head. "You have seen the danger of remaining here. This is a very bad time to be exposed to D.C."

"Why is that?" I demanded. "What have you done that requires bodyguards?"

His suave expression froze. "That is not your concern."

EG squeezed my hand, reminding me that going ballistic wouldn't get my questions answered. I needed to put my nonexistent social skills together with my brains. I needed to be Magda. Scowling, I kept my voice patient. "It's my concern when my sister gets shot at. Can I expect the school to be fired upon next?"

"Not if she's in Switzerland," he replied stiffly.

I really needed to kick him into next week. Not having the leverage for that, I tried a verbal slap. "Is that because the gang behind Edu-Pub doesn't have henchmen in Switzerland?"

His shocked silence told me more than he realized. Tex knew about Edu-Pub.

"You're worse than Magda," he finally said, with not a little horror.

First I'd heard of it, but I shrugged off the news. "If you'd learn who your friends are and who they aren't, you'd be a happier man."

Back on ground he understood, Tex chuckled grimly. "Read Machiavelli and tell me that again. A man in power has no friends."

"I've read Machiavelli. I've already figured you've sold your soul to the devil, probably when you were in Spain." I was guessing wildly here, calling on basic instincts learned at my mother's knee. "Your new friends got you elected, helped you out. They scratched your back, you scratched theirs, yadda yadda. But now they want something you aren't prepared to give, so they're warning you off by crippling your ability to act. How hot am I?"

"I don't even know you," he said crankily. "Talk to your mother. She probably knows more than I do."

We were approaching the house. I didn't have much time left for answers. "Magda has the sense to pretend she's powerless. No one's gunning for her."

"Well, they ought to be." Tex glared as the car rolled to a stop. "And if you've guessed that much, you're smart enough to realize EG is safer in Switzerland."

I felt as if every occupant of the car froze in anticipation of my reply, especially EG.

Tex was offering to pay for the expensive schooling her genius required. Magda was offering to move closer to the school so she could provide a home. They were giving me the opportunity to walk away not only with a clear conscience, but nobly, to protect my sister.

EG desperately wanted to be wanted, and she hung onto every word.

To my eternal shock, I heard myself reply, "Security comes with a home and a family. If EG is tired of being tossed from nanny to school and back, I'll dare what you won't. She will always have a home with me if she wants. It's her choice."

Considering the glance EG shot me, I had just been elevated to sainthood. I was officially as crazy as the rest of my family.

"We're her parents. Ah don't think you have the right to offer that choice," Tex replied stiffly as the car idled.

"Are you going to stand in front of a court and admit you are her father if I choose to fight you on this?" I asked, hiding my evil smirk.

That silenced him. He glanced down at EG. She crossed her arms and refused to look at him. Tex wasn't a persuasive politician for nothing. He tried again, talking to EG and ignoring the fly in his ointment. "You'll like this school. I'll teach you to ski in the Alps."

Dirty pool. EG's eyes lit like emerald fires. She gazed up at him with all of a child's eagerness for love. But then her genius radar kicked in, and she saw the emptiness behind the promise. "You won't win the next election," she informed him coolly.

I love EG. She knows how to go straight to the heart. I have no idea if she was prognosticating or simply telling him that he'd lose if he recognized her, and I didn't care. Tex's appalled expression was worth all the fury and fear I'd suffered this past hour.

I figured we might as well blow up our bridges while we were at it. I climbed out to let EG run into the house, and then I leaned back in. "By the way, just as a matter of courtesy, did you know that Edu-Pub not only funnels cash into Paul Rose's campaign, but it is quite likely laundering money for a radical Indonesian religious organization as well? You might wish to question your definition of terrorists."

I slammed the Pierce-Arrow's door and followed EG inside without looking back. I had a funny feeling I'd just declared war.

"Where's Magda?" I demanded of Mallard the instant we entered the house.

EG had run past Mallard and up the stairs without a word. I daresay both of us were still wide-eyed in shock. But a slow-burning anger had replaced my fear. I didn't think it was a coincidence that the senator's car had been shot at on the same day as Magda had arrived home. It was quite possible the men behind the shots knew Magda's interfering ways too well.

"She is with Mr. Graham," he said stiffly. "They are not to be disturbed." He blocked my path to the stairs.

Oh yeah, that was gonna work well. In my checkered past I'd learned one or two tricks to slip past intrepid guardians. I had an entertaining array to choose from, but I was furious and I wanted it fast. Out of respect for Mallard, I didn't use my kickboxing moves. I played on his weakness instead. I bent over at the waist and moaned as if I was dying.

The instant Mallard stepped uncertainly toward me, I dodged past him, still bent double so he couldn't get a good grasp on me. I was up the stairs faster than he could follow.

Graham must have been keeping his eye on the monitors. Magda was already on her way down the attic stairs before I reached them. I cast a glance above. Graham's door was closed.

"I'm damned tired of being kept in the dark like a two-year old!" I shouted. Okay, I had a tantrum like a two-year old. But if that was the only level we could meet on, I used it. "I want explanations."

"Of what, dear?" Magda asked coolly, treading down the stairs as if she were in a ballroom. She had to be aware Graham was watching.

"Why did Tex leave Spain and hire bodyguards? Why is he being framed for murder? Who is shooting at him?" I thought I heard EG's door open, but she was smarter than me and ought to hear these answers, too.

"I think those questions ought to be directed at Tex, don't you? Is EG packing her bags? I can take her with me."

EG's door slammed and the key turned in its lock.

Magda and I had a face off. She narrowed her eyes and waited for me to tell EG to pack. I crossed my arms and smiled.

"I'm not two, remember?" I said more quietly this time. "She wants a home, not a boarding school. She wants family, not servants. Did Graham invite you to stay?"

Magda sighed and brushed past me, aiming for the guest room. "Ana, you are intelligent enough to understand that there are some things you're better off not knowing."

"So we should all remain homeless, ignorant, and unhappy? Sorry. I'm not buying that any longer." I followed her down the hall to Max's room. Mallard was nowhere in sight.

"No, I don't want that either," she said with a sigh, allowing me in and closing the door. "If you could take EG back to Atlanta with you, stay out of DC and politics, you might have a chance at what you want."

It was one crossroad after another today. I was in danger of getting lost in the maze of choices. "If that's what EG wants, I might consider it," I said carefully, not really meaning it but willing to consider a compromise. "But Max meant for us to have this house. He wouldn't have left it to us if he thought we would stay away." I didn't know where that thought had come from when I'd been planning on moving out, but I liked the sound of it.

She folded up the last of the clothing on the made-up bed and placed it neatly into her carry-on. Magda was nothing if not an expert suitcase packer, but in this case, she was stalling. I'd finally stymied my mother in an argument.

"Max knew it wasn't safe here for you, not while he was still playing games. Perhaps he thought he would clear the playing field before he died. But the field isn't clear. It's not safe, and Graham owns the house."

She slammed the suitcase closed. "You've been here a week, and you're already in danger."

She looked up and glared at me. Magda didn't do glares unless she was out of ammunition. I refused to cringe.

"Graham should never have let you inside this house," she said furiously.

Ah, now we were getting somewhere. "Was it you or Graham who arranged to have Reggie abscond with our money?" I asked.

"If I'd known Reggie's father was dead, *I* would have arranged it, although I'd certainly not let the little snot escape justice. Reggie got in over his little cokehead, and Graham grabbed the house before Reggie sold it elsewhere. Graham is another reason you need to leave. He's worse than Max."

Magda was finally talking to me as if I might be a grown-up. I had a dozen more questions and a few comments of my own buzzing around in my head—including wondering if Max might have wanted us to finish the job he'd left undone—when the gold-filigree dresser mirror chose to intrude.

"That's a matter of opinion, Magda," it said in a deep, recognizable voice. "This house is far safer than many other places I can name."

My eyebrows shot to my hairline. Graham was *defending* us?

"Graham is worse than Max and Brody together," Magda warned. "Go back to your basement, take EG if you must. But forget the family business. You'll be much happier."

The family business? And what, precisely, was that?

She swept out without explaining, calling up the stairs as she headed toward the door. "EG, darling, my limo awaits. I'll send tickets so Ana can accompany you to Switzerland, if you like. Give me a kiss?"

Silence greeted her. Her smile looked almost sad as she turned it in my direction. "I know you have to be a princess of your own story someday, but be a better one than I am."

With Mallard holding the door for her, she gracefully swayed out on three-inch heels. Mallard picked up her suitcase and followed. Someday, I would really like to understand what made Magda tick.

In the meantime, I had to vent my confusion before I could proceed to the next step of whatever I'd just committed myself to.

The door to Graham's office was closed as I charged up to the third floor. I wanted to barge in and spew more questions, but I wasn't operating on rational. I aimed for the gym.

I sneezed as I traversed the hallway and glared at the room where I'd last seen the cat. He hadn't trespassed on my territory lately, so I couldn't complain when I trespassed on his. I escaped through the door into the gym.

Tears mingled with the sweat running down my face by the time I unleashed all my conflicting emotions into the bags and collapsed on the mat to do a few cooling-down exercises. My mother might have caused my father's death. My grandfather had mentored Graham instead of his grandchildren. My grandfather might have been poisoned. EG had nearly been killed today because of my obnoxiousness. And I had just pretended I would make a better parent than Magda. It had been a very bad day.

"Now that you've got that out of your system, shower, and get in here. We need to talk."

The words echoed from the track lighting on the ceiling. I lay there glaring at them, wondering which one hid the camera. It was a damned good thing I wasn't a killer like my mother, or I'd have targeted my first victim.

But I needed to talk, and EG and Mallard didn't offer the kind of conversation I wanted.

I showered and retreated to my dowdy denim dress for the interview. Graham knew Magda. He wouldn't be impressed by my feeble attempts to vamp him. Besides, I needed the comfort of familiarity. I braided my wet hair and returned upstairs.

As before, the computer room door was open, and the only light inside came from the monitors on the walls. I sneezed the instant I entered the room.

"There are pills you can take for allergies," he said from his chair in front of a screen depicting the Lincoln crossing the intersection in front of the Pierce-Arrow.

I didn't know if he was watching CNN or had a personal connection with a satellite. He was far more than a news junkie, and I had the sudden sensible desire to get the hell out of there. But rage and my libido overruled sense, and his preference for dark caves provided a bond of sorts. I shouldn't hate him just because he knew Magda, and it would be very shallow of me to be jealous of his relationship with Max.

The screen flashed a license tag. "The Lincoln belongs to a professional hit man," he continued in the same mechanical voice as the intercom produced. "If he'd wanted any of you dead, you wouldn't be here now. It was a warning, probably to the senator."

"*Probably.*" I latched on to the one word of doubt in his token reassurance. In the dim light, I located the cat—in Graham's lap. He was stroking its back as he turned to a different screen, and for a moment, I wished I was the cat. I wanted someone to hold and stroke me and tell me everything would be all right. "I don't want EG to come that close to *probably* again."

"Then keep her away from the senator," he said. "The man is under pressure, and you and your sister are not helping matters. You chose the wrong time to descend on D.C."

That was the second time today I'd been told that. I casually eyed the nearest wall in search of a light switch. No healthy man in his thirties could spend his life haunting this modern version of a wizard's cave. Was he so badly scarred as well as crippled that he hid in this dimness? I wanted to put an end to any illusions I might be harboring.

I couldn't find the switch, so I chose to push his buttons instead. "You remember my telling you about the client called Oracle who knew Mindy?"

I'm not certain why this, of all the questions I could have asked, came out first, but I was desperate to have my theory confirmed or denied. I couldn't bear the idea that my client might have been murdered, much less how I'd feel if that client turned out to be my grandfather. I was trying to be objective here. And failing badly.

He keyed in a few letters and produced the police reports on Mindy that I'd already read. "Yes," he said mechanically, not chastising me this time for keeping my client file secret. "I can find no reference to Oracle in her files."

"You call yourself Oracle," I pointed out. "You knew her."

"Only as the name of a neighbor," he declared. "Alexandria is a small town. I have never corresponded with Mindy Carstairs. I can assure you that I was not your client."

"Mindy knew Max. Could Max have been my client?"

He wasn't a restless man. He obviously possessed more patience and determination than a saint if he could sit confined in these rooms all day doing nothing but monitoring computer screens. But something in his stillness told me I had him riveted. He said nothing.

"I lost my client the same week that Max died."

I thought, there for a minute, that Graham might turn around. His fingers clenched his chair arms rather than clicking relentlessly across his keyboards. "Your client, the one you called Oracle," he stated to confirm what I'd said.

"Exactly." I waited, but he still wasn't admitting anything. It was up to me to open communication by giving him a piece of my private files. "His last e-mail to me said *envelope-poison-tophat-pow*, spelled p-o-w."

I watched as Graham rubbed his hand over his face in a gesture that might have been despair. Or frustration. Or sorrow. I didn't know him well enough to interpret and was filtering his reaction through my own.

"Max was always a double-dealer," he muttered, seemingly to himself. "He should have sent that message to me." Reluctantly, he admitted, "I took Max's screen name after he died." He sounded more human than he'd ever done. "And if that was his last message to you, I've changed my mind. I think you'd better leave immediately. This house is no longer safe."

"We're not leaving," I said. I knew I was contradicting my earlier desire to get the hell out. I turn contrary when threatened. "You knew Max well enough to know his screen name. You must have known grandfather left the house to us. He was trying to *warn* me. He had to know I'd follow through once I found out. Did you know about the warrant for Reggie's arrest and bribe him to sell so he could get out of town?" This was only one of many conclusions to which my paranoia had led me.

"You have a suspicious mind worthy of your mother," he said dismissively. "Under law, the house is mine. The subject at hand is that D.C. has become too dangerous. There are elements at work here that you know nothing about. I'm taking you off Pao's case. There is still time to enroll your sister in a good school I know about in St. Louis."

"No." I surprised myself with that reply, so I hoped it shocked Graham equally. He didn't give any indication, if so. He merely fiddled with something on the keyboard and changed the image on several screens. One now showed the corner of a keyboard and small fingers typing away at it.

It was my laptop, in my bedroom. I'd hung a Grateful Dead poster over John Quincy but evidently hadn't covered the entire camera lens.

"You rat," I muttered. "Is this how you get your jollies? Want me to hire a stripper for you so you can really have something to look at?"

"It's a security measure. I turn the screen off when you leave the desk," he said without an ounce of shame. "Among other things, your sister is e-mailing the day's events to your mother's personal maid. The CIA pays Emily to keep track of Magda."

"Who the hell are you?" I asked, aggravated out of my introversion long enough to question. "Or better yet, who do you think you are? Batman?"

His chuckle broke the cloud of gloom. He had a deep rich chuckle that rumbled my gonads in ways I didn't wish to acknowledge. Even beating the tar out of a hard bag hadn't lowered my libido. This man had once been *hot*. I knew it with all the feminine instincts in me. And I hated knowing it. I wanted to call him murderer and have him hanged. But I knew he wasn't. I was starting to suspect he was as angry and confused as I was, which made him just a trifle more human than I was prepared to deal with.

"Batman's technology was highly overrated," he scoffed. "A bat signal in the sky? Just a little obvious. It doesn't matter who I am. Your grandfather trusted me to look out for you, and that's what I'm trying to do. I should never have let you stay."

Just knowing Max had told him to look after us recklessly raised my spirits. "Then why did Grandfather leave the house to us if he didn't want us here? Do you really think I'll take your word that D.C. is dangerous for us? For all I know, *you* shot at the car."

"I could have," he agreed. "And that's one of the reasons you need to leave. I'd rather not waste time trying to keep track of all of you should I need to take action." Stroking the cat, he finally turned to face me.

I narrowed my eyes and stared, trying to catch a glimpse of the man silhouetted against the monitors. The eerie light only revealed broad shoulders against a tall chair and long fingers gently stroking an immense cat. I imagined a square jaw and broad cheekbones in the dark shadow that was his head, where the light illumined the gleam of thick glossy black hair.

I had to get out of there before I started inventing my own fairy tales. "Well then, don't shoot at things, and the problem is solved. We're not leaving." That sounded like a good parting line, so I started for the door before his attention gave me wrong ideas.

"I'll help you get your money back."

It would have been nice to get in the last word for a change, but my inexperience at socializing didn't stand a chance against his manipulative skills. I waited for the stick that always followed a carrot.

"For EG's sake, go to St. Louis. I'll hire someone to catch Brashton when he reaches St. Kitts. You won't need to sue. I can get the money back without the law."

It was very tempting. If I was inclined to trust, I'd be halfway out the door in my eagerness to escape guns and terrorists. But my life with Magda had taught me not to believe strange men offering candy.

"*I'll* get our money back, and then I'll hire a lawyer to prove you stole this house from us. We're not leaving."

By the time I'd stalked down to my room, I was so suspicious, I had to wonder if I hadn't just been manipulated by a master into doing exactly what he wanted me to do.

Graham's chocolate-y chuckle would haunt my dreams for weeks.

* * *

I took down the Dead poster and the painting of John Quincy in my bedroom, located the camera behind them, and contemplated ripping it out of the wall. But I admire the resourcefulness of technology. The camera might come in handy someday. Instead, I taped the lens with duct tape I filched from the Ali Baba cave that Mallard called a pantry, returned the painting to the wall, and hung the Dead over it for good measure.

I tracked EG down in her lair and searched beneath all her artwork while she watched me with boredom.

"I could have told you there aren't any cameras in here," she said when I came up empty-handed. "The room is in a tower, and the wiring is too difficult except in the closet on the wall between this room and the next."

She shouldn't know these things. But if we were to stay in D.C., she needed to be as prepared as a Medici in Renaissance Italy. Better. The Medicis didn't have AK-47s.

"Did you know Emily is being paid to spy on Magda?" I asked. It would be nice if just once I could know something she didn't.

"Someone is always spying on Magda. She likes knowing who it is so she can feed them information." EG shrugged. "Emily supports her family on the bribes she receives, so I give her what news I can."

I rolled my eyes to the ceiling. If Graham heard that, he'd be convulsed with laughter about now. Here I'd thought I was paranoid, when it turned out I wasn't paranoid enough.

"If you know so much, then what the hell is Magda doing that people spy on her?"

"Makes people suspicious," she said with a shrug.

How could I reply to that? She was right. Even I was suspicious, and she was my mother. "You told Emily where we were and that's how Magda found us!" This was what happened when I let cuckoos in my nest. I needed another round with the punching bag.

"Unlike you, I have no need to hide from her." Without confirming or denying, she flipped over on her belly and returned to reading her encyclopedia.

Nah, she didn't need to hide; she'd just run away because she felt like it. I had EG's number now. I had decided on a course, and I was bound and determined to follow it. If EG was attempting to annoy me just to test my limits, she was losing. If I was staying, she was staying. I just needed to find a way to eradicate the nest of vipers threatening our home.

I traipsed down the hall to my laptop and began researching schools for the gifted—and I started with D.C. My grandfather hadn't left the house to Graham. He'd left it to *us*.

Chapter Twenty

EG finds yet another school, and textbook publishers are connected

IF EG WASN'T safe attending a school with Tex's daughter, she deserved an alternative, a school for free-thinking geniuses. Surely if Graham could find her one in St. Louis, I could find her one in D.C.

Ensconced in my bedroom-office with the laptop and my list of private schools, I heard Nick return home and go to his room. Engrossed in reading the material on schools, I nearly bit my pencil in two a little while later at the sound of a dinner gong and Mallard calling us down to dinner. Had Magda returned that he had actually fixed dinner for us?

Still holding the information I'd printed out, I opened my door to glance down the hall. EG and Nick stuck their heads out of their respective rooms at the same time. As the echoes of Mallard's gong died into silence, we stared at each other. Then, with all the savoir faire of an experienced theater troop, we shrugged and emerged from our rooms to play this new act.

I wore my denim. EG and Nick were in school and office attire. We weren't precisely dressed for a formal dinner, but we'd not been offered formal invitations either. We were hungry, and food was food.

Magda wasn't there, but Mallard had set the table as if she were.

After a day like this one, food was more than food. Sitting down to a linen-covered table, flickering candles, polished silver, and the welcome faces of family, I finally understood that a meal was a celebration and sharing of survival and togetherness, and not just about food.

We all looked slightly shell-shocked at this scene resembling a normal family dinner. Naturally, it didn't take long for us to revert to form.

Nick beamed in delight at discovering the Salad Nicoise waiting at our places, and fired the first round with his usual charming obnoxiousness. "Forget buying the house with our millions," he declared, savoring the perfectly dressed vegetables. "Let's buy Mallard."

I waited for the candelabra to choke or otherwise object, but it merely gleamed in polished splendor. If Mallard was listening behind the door, he didn't give any sign of it. Briefly, we had the stage to ourselves.

"Did you hear about the attack on Hammond's car this afternoon?" Nick inquired next, as if imparting a piece of fresh gossip.

Before I could explain, EG complacently intervened. "We were there. You should have seen Boise take that ramp at ninety."

Nick choked and spit beans across the tablecloth. "You were there? In the *car*?"

I knew EG well enough to see the pride behind her devious smugness.

I didn't interfere in her little show. Yet.

"My dad brought us home afterwards. He talked to Magda," she announced proudly.

As Nick applied his napkin to his mouth and stared wide-eyed at our evil sister, I diverted the impending shouting match by invoking a more peaceful subject.

I set the papers I'd just printed out on the table. "Family discussion," I announced.

EG squirmed. Still appalled, Nick gave me the same evil eye he'd given EG, as if I had anything to do with shootings and Boise and EG. He wanted explanations.

Individuals all, we tended to act separately without consultation. We weren't a family that normally discussed things together, but I was trying my best—probably because the responsibility of raising EG all on my own terrified me. But I sure the hell didn't have the skills to discuss Tex and Magda, so I moved on.

"EG has been offered the opportunity of a school for the gifted in Switzerland," I said in my best professorial tone. "I see no reason why we can't find a school of equal value in D.C., as long as she refrains from riding in the senator's car."

EG poked at her salad, but she was listening. I'd debated the wisdom of having her stay here if men were taking potshots at her father, but Magda's life wasn't any safer, and no one except family knew Tex's relationship to EG. Unless I wanted to believe Graham was a murderer, I couldn't believe we were a danger to anyone. I pushed the papers toward her.

"I think I've found the perfect school. We can think about it. Take a look around. Decide what we want. And if you're interested, they offer testing for entrance."

"Testing, that's all?" she asked in suspicion, eyeing the papers. "They don't want school records all the way back to grandfather's university and references from the pope?"

"Nope. Pass the test, they put you in classes according to your abilities. It's not a fancy place," I warned. "It's in an old house run by some parents who were looking for alternatives for their kids. The student population is limited."

"In this neighborhood?" Nick asked. He looked interested. "How much will it cost?"

"It's not far from here. They offer scholarships. We'll work it out." I hoped. Graham had twisted arms last time. I'd never done anything official in my life. I figured it was time to start learning how.

"I want to see their textbooks," EG grumbled. "I'm not reading another one that blames environmentalists for sagging economies."

"Housing could be problematic," Nick warned, ignoring EG's complaint and watching the candelabra as warily as I did. "Are you sure we should stay in D.C.?" He directed that question at me and not EG.

"Look at you." I gestured at his elegant silk tie and suit. "You're in your element here. You were born to diplomatic circles, not slot machines. Do you have to ask?" Max had meant for us to have a house for a reason—because we belonged here. I might not be the best leadership material, but I was buying the family fairy tale for my siblings.

Awakened to a world outside her own, EG looked as shocked as Nick, but awareness dawned slowly as they thought about it. Nick straightened his tie. EG studied him as if he were an interesting insect.

"Tex won't like it," she finally decided. "He'll find out and fire Nick."

"Before or after Tex loses the election or goes to jail?" I scoffed, dismissing her prognostications as cynicism and not knowledge. "We're not counting on anyone but ourselves. If Tex goes down, Nick has the credentials to apply elsewhere. And if Tex loses the election, maybe he'll have more time for you. We'll take opportunity where we find it."

Mallard arrived with a steaming serving dish that he set with much ceremony in the center of the table. He didn't serve us individually as if this were a formal occasion, but his attitude gave him away.

"Magda left, remember?" I reminded him. "We're still here. We're still slobs. And we're still annoying."

He gazed soulfully over my head. "You brought Miss Maximillian home. Your grandfather would want the occasion appropriately marked."

Ignoring the pomposity, Nick lifted the lid and sighed in gratification. "Beef Stroganov. Mallard, you're a genius. I say we always mark occasions with Beef Stroganov."

"Mallard stays here," the candelabra intoned in warning, intruding upon our fantasies. The implication was clear—we did not.

Nick and EG and I exchanged glances. We knew our chances of winning this battle were slim. But this was our moment, and we wouldn't let Graham ruin it.

We stood as one. Nick lifted the elaborate candelabra. I blew out the candles. And EG opened the sideboard door. With the offensive apparatus deposited inside, Mallard slammed the door on it.

* * *

There were worse ways to end a miserable day than with Beef Stroganov and Death by Chocolate. Deciding life outside my tiny cave had a roller coaster quality that I might learn to handle, I tucked EG into bed at nine. We didn't exchange sentimental sophistries or discuss what was left unsaid. EG knew she had a home with me if she wanted it.

Examining that fragile bond would only lead to questions neither of us were prepared to answer. I wasn't prepared to be a mother, but I could learn anything once I put my mind to it. And EG knew it.

Nick had gone out for the evening. Even if by some miracle we acquired the mansion, I didn't expect him to live here. He needed his friends and his privacy. Unlike me, he probably had a sex life, and EG probably shouldn't be subjected to evidence of it.

Leaving her room, I passed Mallard on the landing carrying stationery boxes up the stairs. Or boxes of envelopes? The brand label on them was from an office supply store that delivered.

I had better things to worry about. Maybe Graham was starting a letter writing campaign. I hurried downstairs to the Whiz to see if miracles had happened in my absence.

None of my e-mail revealed Pao's whereabouts. For all I knew, Pao lived within walking distance of the reception. The transportation path of investigation was a dead-end. This was Thursday night. The reception was tomorrow. I was reaching desperation.

EG's school expected me to blow up balloons for their festival, and Graham had insisted I attend, forbidding me to go to the reception. Did that mean he thought I should look after EG rather than earn my keep?

"Anastasia."

The pen I'd been using to take notes flew out of my hand and off the table. Blinking, I glanced around. I must have dozed off to be so startled.

Fully awake and irritated now, I attacked the intercom with my heavy notebook, pounding it as if it were a terminally annoying insect. The box let out an ear-piercing squall that would raise the dead if we lived in a cemetery. Fortunately for me, we didn't.

"That was unnecessary." The mechanical voice had a cranky note to it now. "I merely wished you to take a look at the textbooks I left for you."

Rubbing my eyes, I checked the massive library table. I hadn't bothered turning on any lights, so the table was cast in shadow from the light of the monitor. At the far end was a stack of EG's textbooks.

I was too sleepy to be smart-assed. I simply retrieved the books and flipped through them. "Boring," I concluded. "Two American history books, one social studies, and a rather oppressive tome on civics that looks way too advanced for a fourth grader."

Neither of us mentioned Max or Mindy or their fascination with textbooks. The thread dangled there temptingly.

"Your sister is reading the Encyclopedia Britannica from 1956. None of those volumes you hold compare in quality or depth, as she has told you *ad nauseum*. If you will open your eyes, you will see that she is right about the tampering with history and the slanted contents of the text. The books constitute extreme right wing propaganda. Check the copyright pages."

I switched on an antique gooseneck desk lamp and scanned the pages. Two of the books had the same New York publisher, the other two had different ones. I shrugged. "Three different publishers. They were all copyrighted last year. Pablum for the masses. So, what else is new?"

"If you knew history as well as your sister, you would understand how the masses can be manipulated through propaganda—although we call it marketing or 'spinning' these days. I would like you to research the publishers."

"Now?" I grimaced. "You're about to throw me out because I haven't found Pao, and you want to make certain I don't have time to find him?"

"Check the publishers."

I was too tired to go up three flights of stairs to fling a book at his head. Handicapped or not, the man's social skills needed more improvement than mine.

Before I could beat the intercom into submission, Graham quietly added, "I gave you a very minor thread to investigate, and you may have unraveled the entire cloth. Don't quit now." The intercom clicked off.

I stared at it for a full minute before deciding I'd dozed off and dreamed. But just in case the compliment was real, I studied my assignment.

In comparison to privately-held companies like Edu-Pub, researching big honking corporate publishers is no big deal. The SEC requires all publicly-held companies to file forms and statements and they're all on-line somewhere. I'd already compiled a textbook publisher file for my Oracle client—Max. I pulled up his documents and tried not to choke on shock. Max had asked for information on these same publishers before he'd died. Max and Mindy had been studying textbooks, and both had died. Envelopes, poison, tophat, pow— *envelopes*. Graham was investigating envelopes—and poison. And now, textbooks.

Heart pounding, not wanting to consider that my grandfather had been poisoned over *textbooks*, I flipped through the screens of SEC reports I had gathered and located the board of directors for each of the publishers. Most of the directors had addresses and names I didn't recognize. Directors weren't necessarily major stockholders, but the likelihood was high.

Under the assumption that Graham wasn't leading me astray and this had something to do with our search, I compared the board list to that of Edu-Pub's, but nothing leaped out at me. I Googled the unfamiliar names of the individual directors to see what turned up.

By the time I'd sorted and filed the results, I had a pattern, and my throat was closing up in fear. Had this been what my grandfather was working on when he died?

I opened an Excel file, set up headers for the three New York publishing companies plus another for Edu-Pub, and started inputting names from each set of directors under the headers.

By the time I was done, I had a chart for a dozen directors for each company, and every frigging one of them were interrelated—a dozen men ran all three textbook publishers and Edu-Pub was their distributor.

"Holy shit," I muttered, trying to calculate the scope of this discovery as I stared at the worksheet.

"Not precisely the adjective I would choose," said the intercom. I assumed Graham was looking at the material I'd just compiled.

"You want to tell me what this is all about?" I wanted to demand it in a belligerent voice, but I was too overwhelmed. I'm a detail person and not good at big pictures. I just knew this one smelled.

"Read your history. I'll order a few books on Nazis and propaganda. Start with the monopolies of the early twentieth century. But use the Britannica and not those textbooks."

Oh yeah, I'd fit reading an encyclopedia right into my schedule. "Why don't I start with Livy in the original Latin?" I asked sarcastically. "If you're so smart, why didn't Max tell you what he was looking for?"

"He did. I didn't listen." He clicked off, but I still heard the regret in his voice.

I gazed at the stack of thick tomes, sighed, and dragged them upstairs to bed with me. Might as well give up both sex and sleep.

* * *

I sneezed loud enough to set off earthquake alarms in southern California. A hard object covering my face slid sideways and hit the rug with a thud. I'd fallen asleep on my daybed with a book on my nose.

Sneezing again, I blinked blearily and tried to read the mantel clock. Two inquisitive amber eyes stared back at me from the desk.

I sneezed. I screamed. I jumped up and sent the cat soaring for the file cabinet. The cat's leap dislodged my purse, propelling it to the floor in a cascade of notebooks, an assortment of pens, batteries, subway tokens, and the miscellaneous detritus that gathers in the bottoms of bags.

"Most women carry lipstick and a comb," a deliciously masculine voice announced in the privacy of my chamber. Hearing a man in my room sent shivers down my spine, but recognizing the sexy voice, I knew they weren't shivers of fear. I'd been dreaming about him again.

I glared at the early morning emptiness of my bedroom. Someone must have removed the duct tape from the camera lens. I was going to kill Graham. Or Mallard.

Fortunately for everyone, I'd fallen asleep still clothed, so murder dropped down my priority list. I jumped up, ripped the poster and painting off the wall, and sure enough, the lens was untaped. I shook my fist at the lens. "You will not drive me out of this house!" I declared rashly in my sleep-deprived fog.

"As events yesterday should have warned, D.C. is a dangerous place. Security measures are necessary. Your sister has just e-mailed your mother that she is staying here. Expect rash consequences." I heard the distinct click of the intercom switching off.

Rash consequences, I muttered, kicking the fallen encyclopedia and searching for the cat that had scurried from the cabinet during my diatribe. *I'll show him rash consequences.*

I wanted Graham to come down here and fight it out like a man. But with the bed in the room, I probably didn't have kickboxing in mind. Damned good thing he stayed upstairs.

Locating the shiny amber eyes beneath my desk, unwilling to lift the furry creature, I opened my bedroom door—how in hell had he come in if the door was closed? *Shit.* Now I'd have to start hunting for secret passages.

Leaving the door open, I stalked down the hall to EG's room. Of course, she wasn't there. Since I slept with the laptop, the available computers were downstairs in the library.

Uncaring that my braid had come unraveled and my jumper had a slept-in look, I stalked downstairs. The library lights were out, but in the gray light of dawn I could tell my old Dell was playing a screen saver instead of resting in sleep mode as it should have been if someone hadn't been playing with it recently. What else had EG been up to while I was sleeping? And was I really prepared to put up with her dangerous mischief for another nine years or so?

That was one too many questions for this hour of the morning after too little sleep.

"There's a reason I didn't talk to Magda for years!" I shouted, hoping EG could hear me.

I wasn't in a mood for playing hide-and-seek. EG was probably already in the kitchen with Mallard, stealing breakfast. I stomped back up the stairs and took a shower. Besides, I had no clue what to say to her. She had every right to communicate with her mother.

Fortunately for the cat, it had taken the opportunity of my absence to disappear. I'm sure cats are loveable creatures, and once upon a time I would have loved to have had a pet, but this just wasn't going to happen now. I had enough to do without looking for allergy pills so I could take on another irritant in my life. I might be a doormat for my family, but not for animals.

I'd located Mallard's laundry but hadn't got around to doing any wash, so I was down to a choice between jeans and shorts, neither a personal favorite. August hadn't gone away and the air conditioning hadn't improved, so I opted for black shorts, and with a hint of Magda, a red halter-strapped pullover. Leaving my hair down to dry, I ran downstairs to catch Nick and EG before they left.

They both appeared more than usually gloomy. "What now?" I poured a glass of orange juice from the sideboard and didn't bother sitting down. Although from the looks on their faces, I probably should have.

Nick pointed at the front page of the *Post*. As far as I could tell, we didn't get the newspaper, so he must have stolen it from the neighbor's doorstep.

"If you'd pay attention to the news once in a while, you might learn something."

I was getting just a bit tired of people telling me I was ignorant. My little world didn't require the depressing news of the day—or of the past—to function. I had started reading the textbooks last night—in defiance of Graham's edict—but reading how Rothschilds and Vanderbilts had built their fortunes on skill and ambition, then had given their wealth to charity, hadn't been fun or informative. I might not know history, but I know the rich. They build their wealth on the backs of labor and don't give their wealth to charity without getting something in return, so there was more to the story than the books were telling, which was why I'd picked up the encyclopedia. I'd fallen asleep before I grasped the big picture.

Briefly, I wondered what Graham had wanted me to see in the encyclopedia, but I had more immediate concerns. The *Post* headline read: D.A. TO PRESENT CHARGES AGAINST SENATOR HAMMOND TO GRAND JURY.

Scanning the article, I sipped my juice the wrong way and choked. The police had found a notebook in Mindy's handwriting briefly outlining a connection between Tex, Edu-Pub, and the textbook recommendations of some obscure education committee for public schools that Mindy Carstairs was working with on Tex's behalf.

The police, in their obviousness, seemed to think Tex was involved in a little profiteering.

Just wait until they found out about Pao and money-laundering.

Chapter Twenty-one

Tex faces resignation; Ana investigates Hagan and shoes

FOR EG'S SAKE, I was almost willing to believe the beleaguered senator was innocent. I felt sorry for his wife and his kid. But mostly I wondered what the hell Tex had to do with Pao, because I knew damned well that Graham wasn't chasing the little scum because he thought it would keep me busy and out of trouble. Not any more, at least.

I had issues with the man who had uncovered the camera in my room and returned the candelabra to the table. I whacked the silver with my knife. "You knew Max was looking for Pao, didn't you?" I yelled at the silent base. "You're as clueless as I am about why, aren't you?"

The candelabra didn't answer. Wise decision. I hadn't broken the news about Max possibly being murdered to anyone else yet.

I hadn't found Pao, hadn't solved anything, and now EG's dad was going down. It was Friday, and I'd blown my little piece of the game, along with the chance to win a mansion and a family for EG. I was a loser. My propped-up image of myself as a do-gooder collapsed.

"CNN says they're calling for him to resign," EG said gloomily, picking at her granola and ignoring my outbreak.

I scowled. "CNN? I didn't even know we had a television."

Nick made a rude noise. "Would you watch one if we did? I saw it last night and EG picked it up online. Pay attention, Ana. There's a big world out there, and we're part of it."

I leveled my scowl on EG. "You're the one e-mailing Magda and stirring up a hornet's nest. Serves you right if she comes sweeping in here to whisk you away to Switzerland."

"I hid my passport. She can't take me anywhere," EG said haughtily. "I'm not a child, you know."

Yeah, I knew. She only looked like one. And sometimes, she acted like one. Like now. "Graham duplicated my passport. What do you think Magda is capable of?"

"He duplicated your passport?" Nick asked in awe. "That requires..."

"Keeping your mouth shut," the candelabra said.

"Someone had a busy night," I retorted, referring to the candelabra and the untaped camera. "Do we need to lock Mallard in his room?"

Ignoring me, Graham continued, "You have failed to locate Pao. The offer of a school for the gifted in St. Louis is still open. I strongly suggest that you take it. Nicholas can go to St. Kitts. You have no further need of these premises. I expect you to be gone by evening."

Silence fell like a pall over the coffin of our dreams.

There it was, the eviction notice I'd feared from the first. What had happened since last night when Graham seemed to admire my research? I'd thought we were coming to some understanding, that maybe he needed me. How could he have become such a vital part of my life that I would actually miss the bastard and his insults, the challenge of getting to know him?

We would be out on the street again like the strangers we'd been when we first arrived.

Despite all my brave attitudes, I knew Graham had the right to call the police and have us physically removed. I suspected he would be a little more subtle than that. He'd just have Mallard pack our things and heave them into the street while we were out. Or if he was being really polite, he'd put them on a bus to St. Louis and hand us the tickets.

Nick's mouth formed into a stubborn set I'd not seen there before. EG shoved her cereal bowl away and stood up, apparently ready to pack and leave. That's what she'd done all her life.

My little dream of a safe haven was crumbling fast.

"I have a friend with a spare room," Nick said carefully. "I'll go to St. Kitts when you're ready, but I'm not leaving D.C."

I nodded agreement with that wise decision, unable to speak just yet. I didn't cry, but something uncomfortable stuck in my throat. I shook my head at EG when she gave me an inquiring glance.

"I'll walk you to school," was all I said.

Taking a muffin from the sideboard, I checked my e-mail while I waited for EG to brush her teeth and pack her backpack. I had no more promising leads on transportation companies. I knew I wouldn't find Pao that way. I suspected Graham had set me on another wild goose chase so I'd fail. I never knew when to trust the spook. Connecting the ownership of textbook publishers didn't prove Edu-Pub laundered cash for terrorists or politicians, or that Tex had been framed or Max and Mindy murdered for investigating them. I was convinced Pao was the key.

The only thing I knew for certain was that I wasn't letting Graham have my house if I could prevent it, and if I had to move out, I would only be nastier about acquiring it again.

I debated going up to the attic and confronting my nemesis in person, but I didn't see the point. I'd named the game, and even though I felt I was close, I'd lost. I had only one option left—the forged invitations for the reception.

Hearing EG plodding down the stairs, I went out in the foyer to meet her. The waxed hardwood floors gleamed in the sunlight from the leaded-glass transom. The antique side table sported a fresh arrangement of yellow sweetheart roses that Nick had probably brought home. The gloomy oil painting of some long dead ancestor even seemed welcoming.

I didn't want to give any of this up. I knew in my heart that grandfather had meant for us to have it. If Max and my Oracle were one and the same, he'd been taking care of me for years. I wanted to cry.

"Blackwell Johnson on line one," the intercom announced. Mallard's voice, not Graham's.

I didn't have time for lying lawyers. EG arrived to stand beside me. "Tell him I'll get back to him later." I opened the door and we walked out silently. At least EG wasn't a whiner. I gave her credit for that.

"We're not done yet," I told her. "I won't make promises I can't keep. If our bags are on the step when we get home, I'll find another place for us. I meant it about finding you an alternative school."

"I told Magda I was staying," she said gloomily.

"Yeah, and Graham yelled at me for it." How much did I tell her about our mother? Magda wasn't a beautiful airhead but a dangerous unknown in our equation. "You'd better tell me where your passport is so we aren't thrown out without it."

"It's not in the house. I can get it."

I saw a certain resemblance to Nick in the grim set of her mouth. For all I knew, mine had the same tight lines. We'd started on this adventure as something of a lark, but it had become a lot more in this last week and a half.

I tugged her hair affectionately as we squeezed into the crowded Metro. "If you planted it in Mallard's herb pots, I hope you wrapped it in plastic."

She offered a half-hearted grin. We understood each other. We might want to murder each other upon occasion, but we were sisters. Murderous urges came with the territory.

We said nothing on the subway ride. By the time we reached our destination, I had worked up a lot of fears and was having doubts about letting EG out of my sight. But the security guards at the gates reassured me as we walked up to the school.

"You still think my dad is innocent?" she asked quietly before we reached the entrance.

"Most probably," I agreed. "A man like Tex is capable of questionable acts to get what he wants. I think he may have been trying to escape a bad situation and someone framed him. I can't imagine him as a murderer, not any more than we could do something like that."

She nodded, knowing the gray areas our family often trod. "That's what I thought. I won't mind living in a small apartment."

She walked down the hall, leaving me shell-shocked. EG wasn't much inclined to express herself, but I think she'd just said she wanted to stay with me even if we lost the house.

I was the best virtual assistant in the world, and I couldn't find one lousy scumsucker so my sister had some hope of acquiring a home and a father. Damn, that made me feel like camel spit.

* * *

I wasn't in the mood for apartment hunting. Since textbooks were on my mind, I decided to find out more about the educational committee Mindy and my grandfather and possibly Tex had been investigating. And I didn't want to be near Graham while I did it.

I grabbed the Metro to L'Enfant Plaza instead of returning to the house. It's almost impossible to find a public telephone now that everyone possesses a cell, but there was a hotel in the station, and I looked like a tourist. I sauntered in to make use of the public phones.

I didn't know the number for Tex's office, but I knew Nick's cell number. Fortunately for me, he actually answered it. "Where is Tex today?" I demanded without preamble.

"What are you up to?" he asked in a very un-Nickly way.

I wasn't certain I liked what D.C. and power status was doing to my normally easygoing brother. Or maybe my paranoia was contagious. "I thought I'd have a word with the dear, sweet man before we leave."

"Balderdash." Only Nick could get away with a word like that. "Besides, he's in meetings all day. He's with his lawyers now."

"Then perhaps I should stop over at his house and have a conversation with his wife. She belongs to that family values group, doesn't she?" I asked as sweetly as I knew how, although two men and a teenager lingering near the phones hurried away when they caught my expression.

"For pity's sake, Ana, leave her alone. Go look for an apartment. You can't push everyone into doing what you want. We'll have money before long. Everything will be fine."

"Nick, you're sweet, but a moron. All right, give me whatever you can find about that educational committee Mindy Carstairs was working on."

"If you're actually planning on helping the senator, then I can fax you the info, but you'll have to twist the fax number from our resident spider."

"I'm not going anywhere near that man or I'm likely to get arrested. Send it to my e-mail address, and I'll pick it up at an internet café."

We reached an agreement, and I headed for the desk to ask for the nearest computer. The hotel had computer services, but funny thing, they didn't lend them to non-guests. With directions in hand, I stopped in the restroom of the hotel's convention center to powder my nose. Say what you will about big American hotels, but they're a class service for the homeless.

I got some cash out of my account from the hotel ATM, sauntered over to the internet café, fed my money to the clerk, and accessed my website. One Christmas a client had sent me an impressive leather Daytimer. I pulled it out now, using it to jot down the info Nick sent on Mindy's contacts and duties. Then I looked up the directions to the office housing the educational committee. It was in the same complex as the GSA, just down the road.

Hotel gift shops are dreadful places to buy clothes unless one threw money around like chicken feed, but I refused to return to the mansion, and I needed something besides shorts and a halter to visit the stifling corridors of authority.

Vowing to charge Tex for expenses, I bought a long rayon skirt in a swirl of bright colors and topped it with a hideously expensive silk sleeveless pullover in black. I might have been forced to crawl out of my cave, but I can still do eccentric. Besides, they didn't have denim.

I tucked my black bag under my arm—out of reach of purse snatchers—and walked over to the education building. Knowing I was walking into the annex where Mindy Carstairs was last seen, I used a modicum of caution for a change.

I politely informed everyone who asked that I was Ana Maximillian from Senator Hammond's office. I convinced the appointment clerk that someone must have screwed up because I'd had this appointment for weeks. I held up my passport ID with my finger casually blocking *Devlin* and had her check for appointments in the name of Mindy Carstairs. I made a show of annoyance that the appointment hadn't been changed to my name and the right date after Mindy's death. The clerk bought it.

I referred them to Nick's new business cell phone if anyone inquired. I love having connections in the right places. I don't love government offices, but their one advantage is that the right hand seldom knows what the left hand is doing. Despite all the new security restrictions, we still had a government of the people, for the people, and people were seldom predictable or reliable. With my ID and a big smile, I worked my way right up to the authority overseeing the education committee. Mindy had been the liaison between Tex's office and the committee, and according to the police reports, security had seen her here just before lunch. She'd made a call from the lobby, then hadn't showed up for her appointment later.

"Miss Maximillian, how may I help you?" the boss man over the committee asked with a pompous, busy air intended to tell me I wasn't welcome.

This would be a lot easier if I were a cop or a PI and could ask for what I wanted. But I was raised a diplomatic corps brat and knew the jargon and the procedures well enough. I don't recommend trying this at home.

I pulled out my Mont Blanc fountain pen—purchased on E-bay—and my freebie Daytimer, flipped a few pages, and read the notes I'd taken from Nick and added a few of my own. "Mindy Carstairs was working on the textbook recommendations for the committee. The senator's office doesn't have that report in our files. Could you please provide us with a copy?"

He made a note on a legal pad. "Anything else?"

No chitchat about *how's the senator doing* and *we're so sorry about Miss Carstairs* and *anything we can do to help*. Bastard. But I knew the system. One sided with the survivors to avoid going down with the ship.

He obviously hadn't read this morning's papers or he'd be a little more suspicious of my request. That he wasn't in the least interested crossed him off my suspect list. Or else it crossed out the report as a motive. Admittedly, I was chasing up a pretty thin tree.

I had read the police files on the case. I had a good memory. As long as I had Mr. Boss Man listening, I pretended to read the details from my notebook. "Ms. Carstairs had an appointment with Mr. Hagan that she didn't keep." Because she'd been murdered, but that went without saying. "I would like to speak with him, if I might. There are several matters that need clarification."

Like the full name and address of the man Hagan claimed to have been meeting at the time of Mindy's death. The police had verified the alibi, but I, being of suspicious nature, didn't take any one person's word for it. I wanted his parking ticket or subway pass or other proof that both men didn't lie. I was ripe for a conspiracy theory.

If I had investigated the annoying man who'd told me to go home when I'd been looking for Nassar, I would have had a dossier on him by now. But I hadn't got his full name, and there'd been a few dozen with the name Hagan in the huge files of the GSA, and I'd had other things on my mind. Now, the circles were tightening.

Boss Man talked to his secretary, then glanced impatiently at his watch.

Now see, if I were a violent kickass kinda person, I'd have whacked him. A woman had died, an important man was about to go down for it, and all this pig cared about was his golf date. As taught, I swallowed my bile by smiling. "Thank you for your time. If your secretary could prepare those papers before I leave, I won't have to waste any more of the taxpayers' money by returning." I swished out as if I were the boss and he was the toady.

His secretary wasn't particularly happy with me either, but I could understand that. I was adding to her overworked and underpaid burden. I called up my Magda charm and complimented her shoes. They looked shiny, so I figured they were new.

"Oh, I just bought them this weekend." She held out a pink pointed toe that matched her Pepto-Bismol suit. "They hurt like the devil but they were on sale."

I swallowed the caustic remark leaping to my tongue. It burned going down and I nearly choked, but this was for EG. I would behave until I exploded. "You're fortunate you can wear those. I have bunions and can barely tolerate shoes. Mindy used to have the most fantastic heels." I knew this from the police file. One of the detectives on the case had been female and couldn't resist commenting on the Manolo Blaniks, which started the blackmailing mistress rumors. In the normal run of things, aides couldn't afford five-hundred dollar shoes, especially if they refused help from their parents.

"Oh, Mindy found the most gorgeous shoes at the consignment shop down the street. She always scheduled her meetings here around mid-day so she could shop at lunch." She handed me the papers I'd requested hot off the copy machine. "Her death was quite a shock to us."

"As it was to us all," I murmured politely. "I simply don't understand her fascination with textbook publishers. She was obsessed." That came straight from her mother.

The secretary raised her eyebrows conspiratorially, glanced over her shoulder to her boss's closed door, then leaned across the desk to whisper to me. "She told me the committee was recommending textbooks that all came from the same publishing houses, and congressmen own those publishers. She thought it was scandalous and believed kickbacks might be involved. Of course, she was a liberal. I don't know why she was working for Senator Hammond."

"Because she was good at her job," I said curtly. And she must have been to have learned what it took me several hours to dig out, and only then after Graham had told me to. It had taken the cops weeks to discover it, and they were laying the blame on the wrong person. "I would think the police would be harassing *all* the congressmen instead of just Senator Hammond."

"About textbooks?" the secretary inquired incredulously. "No one cares about textbooks. The committee makes recommendations on the basis of content and cost. Owning stock in those companies is smart business. Why would the police care?"

The little bit I'd read about monopolies in the Britannica before I fell asleep popped into mind, but I said nothing. Buying up the competition was only American business savvy, after all.

The Britannica, unlike the textbooks extolling the virtues of Vanderbilts, had mentioned poor wages and bad job conditions as a result of monopolies like the textbook cartel. But if I were to believe the *textbooks*, the men who became rich off the profits of monopolies generously distributed their wealth to charity—the charities of their choice, of course. That way, they got to reward the people who supported them while ripping off the people who didn't. I was beginning to see the light, but it was dim. Where did Pao fit in?

"Thank you so much." I rifled through the papers and looked enlightened, although the documents appeared to be a perfectly innocuous list of recommended books for different grade levels and not a scathing diatribe naming names as I'd hoped. I didn't think Mindy had been murdered for this. "If you could direct me to Mr. Hagan's office?"

Following the secretary's directions and entering the next office, my antipathy for the head of the education committee skyrocketed. I recognized him, but he didn't seem to recognize me without my teenage disguise. Unlike his boss, Hagan rose from his desk, greeted me with a smile, and limped forward to hold out his hand for me to shake. I studied him now as I hadn't earlier. I figured him at fifty, with the vaguely athletic figure of someone who had once taken pride in his physique but no longer had the time to care. His graying hair didn't have the silver style job of Blackwell Johnson, and his shapeless suit screamed off-the-rack. His disguise was as invisible as mine. He could be anything from government hack to CIA.

"What can I do to help Senator Hammond's office?" As an underling, he didn't have a private office but offered me a chair in his cubicle.

"We merely needed to ascertain where Ms. Carstairs left off with her committee work and what we need to do to pick up the reins again." I pulled out my Daytimer and posed my pen.

"Actually, Ms. Carstairs had made an appointment so she might tender her resignation," he said smoothly. "It was just a formality. Her work here was done. I believe she meant to hand over her final report."

That's what he'd told the cops, too. If there ever was a final report, it wasn't in the material Nick had e-mailed from Tex's office, and the list of textbooks the secretary had given me didn't qualify. I'd have to ask Nick if the police had given back her computer yet.

"How odd." I frowned and wiggled my pen. "No one at the office was aware of that. Her files were in order, and aside from the notes the police took, I haven't seen a final report."

He relaxed infinitesimally. Martial arts had given me a few years training in studying an opponent's reflexes. He'd been tense, ready to take me on. Now he wasn't. The report was the key. Or my paranoia had gone into overtime.

"Perhaps she had it with her when she died," he said sympathetically. "The police don't always tell us everything. I'm sorry I can't help you."

On my own, I might have accepted his blatant dismissal, but my family's safety came first. Stomach clenching, I sat tight and forced more questions to my reluctant tongue. "The police said you were in a meeting at the time Ms. Carstairs was to deliver the report. Was the meeting supposed to have included her?"

His cheerful charm disappeared into a frown, but his mouth straightened as he found a way around whatever obstacle I'd inadvertently formed.

"When Ms. Carstairs failed to appear, I met with a textbook salesman who arrived unexpectedly. The meeting had no relation of any concern to Senator Hammond's office."

Textbook salesman.

I rose, desperate to get away before I really exploded.

Hagan thought he'd neatly evaded a government lackey, I could tell by the satisfied expression in his eye. He knew the police didn't have Mindy's report, the report that would have made his committee look very ugly—the report I suspected Mindy had been working on. Had her report included the connections between the *textbook salesman* and Hagan and whatever hanky-panky was happening over at Edu-Pub?

"I thank you for your time," I murmured without inflection, backing out. "Perhaps our computer gurus can locate the file in her hard drive."

That was cruel. Hagan's face sagged to his desk as I turned and walked out. I hope that gave him a few sleepless nights.

I had an urgent need to call Nick and ask him about Mindy's computer, but there weren't any public phones here. If there had been a cell phone office nearby, I would have bought a blamed phone right then. I don't like constant contact with people, but I could see that if family became a part of my life, I'd need it.

Outside, I debated heading in the direction of the Smithsonian in search of a public phone or in search of the consignment shop with hopes of finding a phone in the process. I chose the shop and found it before the phone. Hidden from the blazing concrete of blocks of government offices in a shadowy nook beneath one of the many walls, the shop clearly bought and sold office wear to low paid government employees on a budget. The pinstriped suits—male and female—in the display window were a giveaway.

I checked my watch. I'd have to hurry if I wanted to meet EG at school. Surely there would be a phone over by the school where I could call Nick.

Operating on a desire to nail the killer of a woman with enough courage to go after an unscrupulous textbook monopoly, I entered the shop and located the shoe department.

The lone clerk headed my way when I lifted a pair of Ferragamo's. "May I help you?"

"Mindy told me this was the best place to buy shoes," I murmured sorrowfully. "We were supposed to meet here the day she died."

The young woman looked disturbed. "I'm so sorry. Is that why she was in here that day? The police never came to see me, so I didn't know."

Bells of triumph clamored in my head. You'd think the female detective who'd commented on the Blahniks would have known to talk to secretaries and shop clerks, but maybe she only did forensics or something. I knew nothing about police procedures. I didn't even watch TV to catch CSI. So, yeah, maybe I was ignorant.

"I was delayed," I said, trying to look distressed. "Who knows? If I'd been here, she might never have been killed." I set the open-toed shoe down. "Wrong size."

"Oh, I thought she died that night, not after she'd been in here at noon. How *awful*." She looked thoroughly shocked. "I should read the papers more, but I have a three-year-old. There aren't enough hours in the day." She lifted a similar pair of heels. "What size do you wear?"

"Six." I took the pair she handed me and checked the designer. No one I knew. "I hear you on the toddler. Kids are so time-consuming." Setting down her choice, I picked up a blue high-heeled slide that would look good with denim. "Mindy never returned to the office after lunch. They didn't find her until evening, but the police think she died in mid-afternoon. I always wondered if she went to lunch with someone else."

"Oh, maybe with the gentleman she ran into outside!" Remembering, the clerk looked wide-eyed. "They seemed to know each other. He was kind of old, but I just thought he was one of the people she worked with. She seemed to know him and the Asian gentleman with him."

I almost dropped the shoe at this piece of knowledge I hadn't found in the police reports. D.C. police were *way* too overworked if they hadn't uncovered this. I managed to hold the shoe out to indicate I wished to buy the pair. "That was probably Mr. Hagan," I said casually, using the first name coming to mind. "I don't know the Asian gentleman though."

"Is Mr. Hagan a big fellow with gray hair and a limp?" She took the pair back to the cash register, not noticing the shock I must have broadcast at hearing my casual reference confirmed.

"That's him," I managed to say without stuttering. Hagan had met Mindy *outside* the office. In the company of an "Asian" fellow. Evidence, I needed *evidence*.

"That's all right then, if she knew him," the clerk said casually. "I was afraid I'd have to call the police or something, and I so hate to have that kind of publicity. I can't believe the senator did it, though. He seems such a nice family man."

"What about the Asian fellow?" I suggested as if this were a good mystery story we were gossiping about. "Are you sure she knew him?"

Her head came up and her eyes grew wide. "You think? He wasn't much bigger than you, and let's face it, Mindy was pretty hefty."

"Martial arts," I suggested. "Maybe you'll get a reward if you call the police."

I paid for my shoes and left her thinking about it. My heart was pounding too wildly for my brain to register anything more than picking up EG and hiding out until I could put all this together.

Chapter Twenty-two

EG calls a bomb scare and gets kidnapped

WHILE THE other students diligently worked on their internet assignment, EG set her instant messaging system up to see if Tudor was online. Her older half brother lived in England. He never slept and seldom went to class. After a brief exchange of messages, she sent him the school busy-work and settled down to more important fare.

Why had Mr. Hagan blown her off? She thought her e-mail on the textbook situation had been maturely discussed. He could have at least sent a polite thank you. What she really wanted was an interview with him, though. Of course, if he had nothing to do with textbooks, he'd probably just passed on her information. This detective business was tougher than she'd realized.

If she was as good with computers as Tudor, she could send e-mail that would sound like it came from her father's Senate office, but she wasn't that good. So she set up an account called "interested citizen" and e-mailed Mr. Hagan from there. She just needed answers to some questions, like how well did he know Tex, but she wouldn't tell him that in an e-mail. Maybe if she asked for the name of someone who dealt with textbooks, she could persuade him to call. She gave him Nick's cell phone number and e-mailed Nick at Tex's office with her questions. Nick wouldn't give her a hard time. He might not do it, though, so she had to think of something else.

She had considered accepting Magda's offer of a school in Switzerland. It had been tempting thinking of Tex teaching her to ski if he got out of this mess. But she didn't want to learn to ski. What she *really* wanted was for Tex and Magda to get back together again. It might be impossible, but she didn't see any harm in creating the opportunity. She'd like to see that little cow Elise on the outside looking in for a change.

She just had to help Ana and Nick find the real murderer, then arrange it to look as if Magda had done it so Tex would be grateful. That was the ideal solution. She'd accept variations.

"Whatcha doin'?" The bespectacled kid next to her leaned around the cubicle to stare at her computer screen.

EG reduced the window so he couldn't read it and opened a website that looked remotely like something she ought to be studying. "Working," she replied dulcetly. No more getting called to the office for her. Not yet anyway.

"I'm bored," her new-found friend complained. "Want to see some excitement?"

With a little more interest, EG looked up. "What kind of excitement?"

He grinned and shoved his glasses up his nose. "It's Friday. Let's get out of school early. I'm going on the web to my father's account and e-mail a bomb threat to Apple-bum."

"Your father will be blamed," she pointed out, although a new idea had bloomed at the thought of getting out before Ana arrived. All those security guards at the door were a serious obstacle to her freedom.

"Nah. My father works for Paul Rose. They'll say his account was hacked. He has a big party tonight, so he won't even know if I get home late."

"Bomb threats are pretty crude. I'll think of a better way next time," she said as indifferently as she could while her idea blossomed and grew.

"There's an arcade on the next street. I'll meet you there after the alarm goes off." Removing his glasses and rubbing his nose, he returned to typing at his keyboard.

Thoroughly amused that it wasn't her mischief about to empty the school, EG returned to her messaging. If the threat went through in time, she might have a chance to catch the Metro to Tex's office. If she could just talk with her dad alone for a few minutes...

Efficiently, she sent messages to both Tex's home and office addresses asking for a minute of his time.

* * *

I climbed off the Metro at the station nearest EG's school, my head spinning with all the things I needed to do to nail Mindy's murderer. I was trying hard not to believe the same person may have murdered Max, but the textbook connection looked grim.

The facts as I knew them sounded bad but led nowhere: (1) A number of senators and corporate moguls owned Edu-Pub and had a stranglehold on the textbook publishing industry. (2) A woman who had discovered that association had died, and so had a man who had tried to help her. (3) One of the senators in a position to expose the monopoly was now being threatened with jail or worse. This sounded uglier than a drug cartel with just as little evidence to nail anyone.

I had no proof that Hagan and Pao had been the men who had met Mindy a few hours before she died, but the description was close enough to suggest the meeting wasn't coincidence.

I prayed the shop clerk called the police as I suggested. Investigating suspects was their job. All a virtual assistant like me could do was to research and provide leads. Just leaving the confines of my computer was way above my pay grade.

The police knew about Tex's connection with Edu-Pub, but they wouldn't know the bigger association with the publishers yet. I bet Hagan did. I didn't fully grasp that as a motive for murder, though. I needed the advance report Mindy must have sent to the committee chairman, the one making Hagan so nervous. I was afraid the police would have her computer, or if there really was something in that report, the villains would have wiped it. But I had to call Nick and meet him at Tex's office to see if the report was around somewhere.

First, I had to pick up EG. I worried whether to take her back to the mansion or to Tex's office. I hadn't made a decision either way when I shoved off the crowded Metro at EG's stop only to land in an even thicker throng of disgruntled passengers and police. The cops shouted commands at commuters trying to leave the cars, but we weren't listening. There were more of us than them, and the men in blue finally gave way to let us pass, hurrying those departing toward the exit and ushering the rest into the waiting train whether they wanted to go or not.

They were clearing the station.

My heart lodged in my throat and stayed there as the mob carried me up the stairs to the street.

Police were cordoning off the entrance, preventing commuters from going down. Even as our trainload emptied into the street, they shut down the station and began backing people off the main thoroughfare and down a side one.

The normally busy four-lane highway at the Metro exit looked like a parking lot. Trucks, buses, taxis, limos, all idled or had their engines off. One carload of teenagers had turned up their CD player, and the teens were boogying in between a bus and a BMW. Other drivers responded less coolly, cursing and honking in a foolish attempt to reach their destination, which they couldn't because of a barricade several blocks away—in the direction of the school.

Barricades on busy streets meant danger.

I'd learned the uselessness of panic at an early age. Instead, my adrenaline pumps, I get angry, and I get obnoxious, but I do not have hysterics. Or so I told myself as I shoved my way through the crowd with both elbows. I bit a jerk wearing a muscle T-shirt who tried to push me back. Just because I'm small doesn't mean I'm not mean, especially when it comes to my family. All thoughts of murderers and Tex dissipated with my need to find EG, *right now*.

I clawed my way to the front of the crowd and saw with relief that the students from the school were arranged in an orderly fashion behind the barricade under the supervision of the teachers. I wouldn't have to maim anyone after all.

I zoomed in on Appleby. "What's happening?" I demanded as I

stepped on the toe of the teacher to whom he was talking so she had to shift out of my way.

Recognizing me, he frowned and scanned the crowd. "Standard procedure for a bomb threat. We usually don't have them until spring when the students are restless and want to go home early. Given the political situation lately, we thought it ought to be taken seriously."

I'd recently seen a warehouse blow up under the hands of a couple of teenagers and a can of gas, probably combined with a little fertilizer. I didn't think this crowd was back nearly far enough if there was a bomb in the school. "I'm taking EG home with me. Where is she?"

I'd been scanning the crowd, too. And not seeing her. She's small, but she's usually right in the thick of things. I'd break her neck if she'd chosen this moment to skip. I'd have to go back to the house to find her, and without the Metro, it could take me who knew how long to get there. I didn't have that kind of time.

"I'm sure she's here somewhere. The teachers are supposed to stay with the group they led out. I don't suppose you know her schedule?" He seemed to be worriedly taking a head count of his teachers.

I checked my watch. School should be out now. "Her last class was social studies."

He nodded. "Miss Millard. Over there." He nodded at a tall, gray-haired woman who towered over everyone. She had her hand on the head of one child and was keeping an eagle eye on the others. I still didn't see EG, but I could assume she'd ducked down to tie her shoe or something. There were a lot of adults who could block my view. I had to push closer.

I tried to be more polite in my assault now that I knew EG should be safe. I mumbled *pardons* and *excuse me's* as I worked my way down the side street. I was aware of policemen standing behind the barricades, keeping traffic and crowds back, but my gaze focused entirely on the well-dressed children with the tall teacher.

This was one of the many, many reasons I left Magda and my siblings ten years ago. It's impossible to keep up with a tribe of intelligent, curious kids on *safe* streets. In some of the places we lived, I existed in a state of constant terror that I would lose one of them. I'd had some foolish hope that my departure would prompt Magda to take them out of harm's way.

No one ever said I was the family's brightest light.

My heart cracked and fell apart in fear as I saw Nick shoving through the crowd from the opposite direction. His expression was so grim and un-Nick-like that I knew the news was bad before I reached him.

I reached the teacher first. "Miss Millard, I'm Elizabeth Maximillian's sister. Where is she?"

The teacher looked around wildly. "She was here when we came out. I made certain she was with me when we left because she's so small, and I didn't want to lose her."

Her lips moved, and I could see her rapidly counting heads as Nick approached from her opposite side, waving a cell phone in my direction.

"They've kidnapped Eezhee," he shouted over the low roar of the crowd. "They called me at the office. Graham wants to talk to you."

I tried not to trip over any munchkins as I dived past their heads to grab the phone from his hand. "Who has her?" I shouted into the phone.

"Since they request your passports, three plane tickets to London, and Max's millions, I might assume it's Magda," Graham's dry voice said into my ear.

"No!" I screamed at him. "Magda is nuts, but she'd never do that to me." That was a head trip I'd analyze later, but not now.

This time, he sounded a little less unruffled. "Whoever it is wants you to take the items to the reception this evening where you'll be given further instructions. I'll be more than happy to provide the plane tickets."

His black humor didn't amuse me. I clung to Nick's arm and kept a constant scan of the crowd, hoping I'd see EG reading a book in a doorway. "Whoever it is had a means of inciting a riot to get at her. Can you call your school connections and find out more?"

"*Riot?*"

I might not panic, but Graham's alarm nearly sent me over the edge. I'd known something he didn't, and he didn't like it. I could hear him clacking at his keyboard, fiddling with his computers. It took him a few minutes to catch up with the news. I winced at his sharp whistle.

"Bomb threat," I explained, assuming he was seeing the crowd. "They've shut down the streets and the Metro, and the bomb squad is inside scouring the school."

His silence was thunderous. I remembered why I admired him from the first—his expressive silences. Other men cursed and shouted and lost control. Graham shut up and acted. I clenched my teeth to keep them from chattering. It must have been a hundred and ten in the shade, and I was shivering. His silence had that kind of power.

"I'm buying three plane tickets and sending you to the airport. Get back here, collect your passports, and I'll have a limo waiting." He hung up.

I needed to find EG, and *he hung up on me.*

I started to heave the damned phone into the street, but Nick caught my arm and jerked his baby out of my hands.

"What?" he yelled. His designer silk tie was crooked, and his perfect blond hair had fallen into his wild eyes. EG would be impressed.

Hit by a tidal wave of terror, I bit back a lump in my throat and tried not to wonder where EG might be right now. EG was quite capable of staging a kidnapping to get her own way, but I didn't think she'd willingly put me through hell any more than Magda would.

"Graham wants to put us on a plane to London and get us out of his hair. Or out of D.C." I wasn't trusting him to find EG on his own. A sudden, horrible thought struck me.

"Call Graham back," I shouted over the honking, tugging Nick down the nearest side street. The traffic was still thick, but the crowd of onlookers dwindled as we moved farther away. "Tell him Bob Hagan on the education committee and someone of Asian origin who might be Pao may have had a motive to murder Mindy Carstairs."

I hated getting past my mental block to this next step, but if Mindy had something worth killing for, and she'd told it to Max... "Tell him—" *Oh shit*. Another piece of the puzzle almost fit. "Maybe *Reggie* had something to do with Max's death. He needed the money, he was desperate to escape jail time. He knew both Max and Mindy and now he's gone with our millions."

I should have been communicating with Graham all along. Paranoia made a lonely hunter, and a useless one. "If the Edu-Pub gang wants to get rid of Tex..." I'd thought Hagan was my best suspect in Mindy's death. Did he know Reggie?

Reggie was gone before Mindy died. Had Max's lawyer known EG was Tex's child? Could he have told Hagan? What was the connection I was missing?

Nick was looking at me as if I were crazed, but he was hitting a button on the phone to redial the last number. I only prayed Graham didn't have some kind of weird phone transmission that would divert the call elsewhere. I still didn't know his number.

"I had e-mail from EG earlier today giving me questions to ask someone from the education committee." Nick frowned at his cell, hit a button to clear the screen and tried again.

"To ask Hagan?" Terror took root deep in my heart.

"I don't know. As best as I can tell, she sent a message complaining about the quality of school textbooks and asking someone to call me."

"Why in the name of heaven would she do that?" I think I screamed. It was hard to tell above the noise and confusion, but screaming seemed the best reaction to knowing my sister had e-mailed the office of a potential murderer. "Did anyone else see her message? Does anyone else in Tex's office know who she is?"

Nick screwed up his forehead in thought. "Can't say. We share each other's stuff all the time. I could have been overheard talking to her."

Of course, given the immensity of the GSA, it was unlikely a single complaint would reach Hagan anytime in the near future, if ever. Unless he was looking for it. Unless he already knew about her... Had he known about me? Had he sent the threatening message? How could he know about us? Except through Reggie. And Reggie was gone. How could there be any connection between Hagan and Reggie?

Blackwell Johnson. Blackwell knew Reggie, knew we owned stock in Edu-Pub. My brain was on the verge of frying. None of this formed clear-cut connections.

Nick looked relieved as the cell apparently worked this time. I scanned the street while he waited for someone to answer.

"Tell Graham to locate Mindy's hard drive," I ordered, "and retrieve her last report to the committee. The police probably won't make anything out of it, but Graham will. See if he can find any connection between Hagan and Reggie or Blackwell Johnson."

"The spook in the attic works for the police?" Nick asked incredulously while holding the phone to his ear.

As if I knew. "No. But he'll know where that hard drive is, I'd bet my million on it. And even if the police have it, I'm betting he can get it. I'm going after EG." Insane, but I'd decided to trust Graham. I ought to be accusing him of EG's disappearance, but I still had the urge to rely on him—just as I was counting on my family.

Spotting my opportunity, without waiting for Nick to protest, I dashed into the street and hopped into a cab stuck in traffic on the cross street.

"Ain't going anywhere in this, lady," the driver said laconically.

"A Chinese bicycle cab could. Bump that car in front of you. He has a whole car length he can move up." I locked the car door while Nick pounded on the window. I leaned over and locked the front door, too.

With a wild man pounding on his windows, the cabbie obligingly nudged the bumper of the SUV in front, waking the other driver up. We got a middle finger salute for our efforts, but the SUV rolled forward.

"Wiggle into the turn lane at the intersection. Traffic's blocked coming out so you can make the turn against the light."

"You're crazy lady," he said in disbelief, but he nudged his way into the empty turn lane. Nick shook his fist at us, but I knew he wouldn't attempt to follow. He was shouting into his cell phone—I hoped at Graham. Between the two of them, they'd find that hard drive. I prayed it had the answers because I didn't.

Horns blew and drivers shook their fists, but we wiggled into the jammed intersection, forcing cars on both sides to ease back or forward. People ought to know better than to pull into intersections when traffic was stopped. Following our example, several cars began the wriggle-push or made U-turns into any open lanes available.

The driver wiped his brow as we made the left turn onto the open street. "Where we goin', lady?"

"Georgetown, to the home of Senator Tex Hammond." I gave him the address I'd memorized the day we'd rode with Boise. If Tex was a murderer, then there was one cabbie in town who could pin him to my cold dead corpse.

Amazingly, I was dressed for a visit to Georgetown. I was still wearing my expensive hotel clothes. If I kept this up, I would really turn into Magda. EG wouldn't recognize me. But Tex would.

I couldn't believe Tex was behind this. It didn't make sense. Except, even if EG e-mailed Hagan, a stranger like that wouldn't know who she was or how to get at her. As far as I was aware, Tex was the only person outside of family who knew EG was his daughter and went to this school. I had to eliminate the obvious before I could move on to the seriously weird.

I couldn't do what the kidnapper wanted. Only EG knew where her passport was. Blackwell knew I didn't have Max's millions. Who would think I did? Sean. I had no idea where to find the Irishman.

The cabbie kept a news station on the radio, but the school was being treated as a routine bomb scare and a traffic hazard to re-route around. I dug my fingers into the soft leather of my purse and stared at the scenery flashing by as we progressed out of the traffic onto the open highway.

My thoughts skittered from *Pride goeth before destruction* to a silent prayer to a Being I wasn't certain existed. My ignorance of religion probably surpassed my ignorance of history, but I'd read the Bible. It had more conflict in it than a good thriller. That wasn't conducive to calming thoughts right now.

And I needed to be calm. Wild-eyed madwomen generally did not make it past security in the homes of government officials.

The cab's CB spluttered, and the driver switched the news off to listen. Looking startled, he picked up a phone receiver and handed it over the seat to me. "They want to talk to a short woman with a long black braid. Reckon that's you."

I knew of only one person in the world who not only knew how to find me, but could persuade a cab company to locate the exact car and hand over a company phone to a passenger. I wasn't in a humor to be yelled at again, but just in case he'd heard something from EG, I took the receiver and snarled. "This had better be to tell me you know where she is," I said before Graham could get out a word.

"You don't have any idea what you're getting into," he said calmly, but in my terror, I heard a note of tension. "The envelopes in Max's office tested for poison. I'm looking for their delivery driver now. Get back here and let's work this out together."

My grandfather had been murdered. Like my father. Like EG? I hit full scale hysteria.

"That would have worked half an hour ago—before you hung up. Now you can listen to me," I screamed. "Hagan and a man who looks like Pao met Mindy the day she died. May I remind you that Mindy was Reggie's ex. Reggie was Max's lawyer and executor. Max had him buy shares in Edu-Pub, so Reggie had to know the other investors to buy private shares. Robert Hagan on the textbook committee owned shares and Mindy knew him, so what are the chances that Reggie did?

"Reggie was desperate for money to leave town to beat his third-time's-the-charm drug charges," I continued as quickly as I could. "If either Max or Mindy mentioned their textbook inquiries to Reggie, he may have told Hagan. Hagan could have panicked and paid him to poison Max. Or blackmailed him. Either way, Reggie would have his hands on millions once Max was dead. Motive and opportunity. Talk to Blackwell Johnson. And find Mindy's damned computer and Hagan." Without waiting for response, I handed the phone to the driver, ignoring the shout of outrage that could be heard over the engine's roar.

I no longer cared what Graham thought or what he wanted or what in hell he was involved in. Max was dead. Despite all his electronic wizardry, Graham hadn't prevented it. I wanted my sister back before she was dead, too, if I had to bulldoze my way through Washington to do it. If I was really, really lucky, I'd only have to bulldoze my way through Tex.

As the cab pulled up to the house, I took a deep breath and counted out my money. I should have taken more out of the ATM, but there was enough for a good tip. I'd probably have to walk back downtown though.

The cabbie looked at me with a cross between awe and suspicion as I handed him my cash. "You ain't a terrorist or nothin', are you?"

"I am woman, hear me roar," I said sweetly, opening the door.

Men never quite grasp that pint-sized females dressed in swishy long skirts can have the power of forty-megaton bombs when their fuse was lit.

And I was beyond furious. And scared. Bad combination.

I punched the button on the security gate and dared anyone to deny me entrance.

Chapter Twenty-three

Ana visits Tex's wife and goes home with Sean

AFTER MY experience with Graham and his wizardry, I fully expected to get a mechanical voice demanding my name, rank, and social security number when I buzzed Tex's house. Instead, the wrought iron gate swung open without a protest.

The taxi had lingered while the driver presumably counted his money. As I stepped into the entry garden, he started up his engine and eased away. My last chance to turn back had gone.

Houses in Georgetown are prohibitively expensive, but not necessarily large. Minutes from the airport, White House, and Embassy Row, Georgetown is all about location. The yuppies favor the old Federal-style houses. I didn't get the attraction. The buildings are old, narrow, and built one on top of the other. Admittedly, they're dreamily historic in old brick, with carved wooden shutters and architectural details new houses cannot compete against, but they needed their guts ripped out to be livable.

A climbing rose spilled heavy perfume over the high white picket fence that guarded this particular row of houses. Red geraniums and asparagus ferns overflowed the flower boxes on the upper story windows. Far from being intimidating, the senator's house looked like the ideal home for EG. I'd been fooling myself to think I could provide anything so welcoming.

Which meant I was probably fooling myself to even consider Tex had kidnapped his own daughter to get her out of his life. I might dislike the man and everything he stood for, but that didn't mean he was a murderer or a kidnapper. One irritating illegitimate daughter exposed to the press hardly compared to murder charges.

I was trying desperately not to worry about Hagan or Pao having EG.

I rapped the brass knocker, and a maid dressed in a black uniform with a white apron answered the door. "I'm Anastasia Devlin, here to see the Senator and Mrs. Hammond," I said in my best British boarding school voice. I'd lasted about six months in that school, until Magda's affair ended and we moved again.

The maid bobbed her head as if an unexpected visitor wasn't an unusual occurrence. "Wait here, please." She shut the door in my face.

So, this wasn't Victorian society, and one didn't trust strangers into the guest parlor. I could understand that. I was just too angry to like it. I tested the brass knob. It was unlocked. I swung the door open and let myself in.

Wide oak planks varnished in their original golden color gleamed down a straight hallway leading to a brick-floored kitchen or sunroom at the rear. A circular oak staircase led to the upper stories. To my right was an elegantly furnished parlor with precisely mismatched furniture and drapery patterns that indicated an accomplished interior designer at work. The terra cotta of the walls worked with the terra cotta in the antique Oriental carpet to pull together the collection of golds and browns.

I tried to tell myself that EG would hate a formal place like this, but EG had grown up as I had and could live in the street if necessary. She'd make her own space in no time.

I heard low voices upstairs, classical music playing in a distant room, and the clatter of pots in the kitchen. If EG was here, she was being very quiet. I supposed they could truss her up and stash her in a closet, but I just didn't see it happening. I hadn't thought about asking Nick which airport we were supposed to go to. Not that I could search any of them without bloodhounds and a police force and maybe Homeland Security.

Why the devil would a kidnapper want us to attend the reception tonight?

A woman I assumed to be the senator's wife descended the stairs with the grace of someone who has been trained from birth to walk with just that kind of Miss America poise. Or maybe women like her were born with poise. Not a hair was out of place in her short bouffant coiffure. Her navy suit and white silk blouse appeared as if they'd been tailored specifically for her slender middle-aged figure. She trailed manicured fingers down the curved bannister as if unaware of its presence. She didn't hurry or even frown after she discovered a stranger had let herself into the house.

I wondered if she was made of plastic—Middle-Aged Barbie.

"Anastasia Devlin?" she inquired with an accent as polished and sophisticated as the Queen of England's.

I had no idea what I would say to this woman. I had no real reason to dislike her. I didn't know her. It wasn't her fault that Tex was a philandering meathead. I tilted my head in acknowledgment and tried to channel Magda, but Magda wouldn't have been insane enough to come here. I'm the one with anger management problems.

"Mrs. Hammond?" I inquired in return, trying to sound civilized and not a frightened nervous wreck. When she did not deny the charge, I continued. "My sister Elizabeth is in school with Elsie. She was kidnapped during the bomb scare. I trust Elsie is safe?"

I thought I saw a flicker of something behind the woman's face-lift, but she didn't express any emotion in her voice.

"Elsie had a dental appointment this afternoon. She's with our driver.

Why would you come here to inquire?"

I thought that more than a little convenient, but I didn't express my opinion. Yet. "Because Elsie and Elizabeth have exchanged more than antipathy for one another, and Senator Hammond has threatened my sister with expulsion. The kidnapper is requesting that she be put on a plane back to her mother." I was beginning to feel like a fool even suggesting such a thing.

Mrs. Hammond had reached the bottom of the stairs by now. She stood only a few inches taller than me, but I had to stand as straight as she did to prove it. I looked her in the eyes without flinching, aware of the dishevelment of my braid and the lack of sophistication of my long skirt and short top. I met a speculative look there, but she'd been trained to hide the emotions that flared in my eyes on the slightest provocation.

"Are you suggesting my husband is a kidnapper?" She gazed at me with carefully manufactured distaste. She must practice that look in the mirror. I suppose that's necessary when one's husband is accused of murder.

"I'm suggesting there is no other reason for anyone to kidnap my sister much less wish her on a plane to London. If not your husband, then someone of his acquaintance. You might ask the senator why he would go to these lengths. I'm simply here to let him know that Elizabeth isn't going anywhere without her passport, and I don't know where it is. If he'll have his henchmen set her at the nearest Metro station, she's quite capable of finding her own way home."

Would Tex think we had Max's millions? I refrained from mentioning them now.

I caught the tightening of the muscle at her jaw and the flare of something more than cool dismissal in her eyes, but I'd said my piece. I didn't see a chance of this proud woman aiding my cause, but I bet Tex had a chunk of his ear chewed off by nightfall. That's all I could do.

"I will certainly pass on your message, Miss Devlin," she replied.

"Thank you. You might also mention that I think I know who murdered Mindy Carstairs and why, and if EG doesn't return home safely, the senator can fry without my help."

So, I had my family's taste for the dramatic after all. I blamed genetics and too many years of Magda's company for the exorbitant falsehood. I swung on my sandal and stalked out, my braid swaying over the black silk on my back. If I really wanted to be Magda, I'd have my hair lopped to bounce over my shoulders in a thick waterfall of waves, but I leave the work of styling all that hair to shampoo models.

Mrs. Hammond softly closed the door behind me.

Well, shit, now what did I do?

All the rage and terror rushed out of me, leaving me feeling like a miserable dishrag. Where did I go next? I didn't want to stop and have to think about all the horrible places EG could be stashed right now. I wanted to keep on believing Tex had her.

Worst of all, I had to admit that Magda had kept EG safe for nine years, and I couldn't keep her safe for two weeks.

An old convertible MG rattled to a halt between a fire hydrant and someone's driveway, but it wasn't a Pierce Arrow. Digging into my purse for my address book, I didn't pay it any attention. I'm sure the sports car was someone's pride and joy, and it was a cute baby blue, but I had more important things on my mind.

"Ana!"

My head jerked up, adrenaline energizing me again. I glanced around, but I didn't recognize anyone I knew—until I glanced at the MG's driver.

Sean O'Herlihy.

This was beyond coincidence. I stepped off the curb and grabbed the passenger door rather than reach in and strangle the truth from him. His black curls were tousled with the wind from his driving. His blue eyes gleamed with mischief. And he flashed a toothy smile that would have made millions on film.

"Do I have a tracking device implanted?" I demanded. "And don't give me that crap about working around the corner again." I wanted to add him to my suspect list, but I could find nothing to connect him to anything except me.

He smiled even more broadly and pushed the door handle to let me in. "I don't think you precisely made it a secret as to where you were going. Need a ride?"

I had made it a secret, actually. I hadn't even told Nick where I was headed. But it didn't take too many light bulbs for Nick or Graham to figure it out. They were the only ones who knew about EG—I thought. For all I knew, I could be standing in the company of a kidnapper.

"I don't carry a gun," I informed him coldly. "I have no way of guaranteeing that you'll take me where I want to go. So I'll find my own transportation, thank you."

"Your brother said you have only a few hours to get ready for the reception. Rush hour traffic has already started. You'll be lucky to have time to dry all that pretty hair."

He'd noticed my hair. Intellectually, I wasn't impressed, but my neglected feminine ego got its thrills where it could.

Nick had told him to where to find me. I'd introduced Sean to Nick at the Edu-Pub warehouse, and of course the nosy Irishman had made it his business to get to know my brother.

I was trusting that was because Sean was after Graham. It wasn't as if I had a lot of alternatives. Figuring I could escape a convertible in rush hour gridlock, I reluctantly accepted a seat. For the hell of it, I asked, "What can you tell me about my sister's disappearance?"

He pulled the low-slung car back into the flow of vehicles down the narrow residential street. It didn't seem at all odd to discuss EG's kidnapping with a perfect stranger. Obviously, he knew more about me than vice versa. Had my life not been so crazed this past week, I would have had him investigated down to his toenails.

"The police found no bombs," he said, revealing he knew what I was talking about. "Traffic is back to normal. EG hasn't been heard from. Your brother is burning up phone lines trying to reach your mother. All is as sane in the Maximillian world as it ever is."

"Who *are* you?" I asked tiredly.

"You wouldn't believe me no matter what I said," he pointed out.

Which was the truth, although I didn't know how he knew it. "Make up something I can believe then." I desperately wanted a friend on my side right now. I might be an isolationist out of habit, but I'd take every bit of help I could get right now.

"I'm a journalist. I don't live too far from you. I know Mallard. It isn't too strange that I'd be curious, is it?"

"You're very good at making things up, thank you." I leaned my head against the seat and let the hot rush of air blow over me. Sean might be the sexiest man alive, but right now, my hormones were dormant and my mind was rushing ahead of traffic. He could have been a cab driver for all I cared. My paranoia was too overworked for more.

"Marjorie Hammond is a piece of work, isn't she?" he asked, whipping up the ramp to the highway.

I turned my head to admire his profile. Tanned and gorgeous, he drove with one hand on the wheel and the other on the stick shift as if he'd just driven out of some fifties movie. I wanted him to be the cavalry rushing to my rescue, but for whatever reason, I trusted Graham more. It was definitely time to have my head examined again.

"She's no different than any of the other political wives I've known."

"Then you don't know them well." He dodged in and out of inbound traffic as if the highway were a Nascar track and not a parking lot. "You might spend more time learning and less time judging."

Shades of Graham. Now I had James Bond preaching at me. I turned my gaze back to the road, then closed my eyes as a semi loomed in the windshield. "All I want is to be left alone to do my work." I couldn't tell him that I'd had some strange prayer that Marjorie Hammond might be a motherly woman who would welcome EG with open arms. That was stupid even for me. Besides, he knew nothing of EG's parentage.

How many people did? I wondered. Would someone be trying to get at Tex through EG? That didn't make any better sense than anything else. I couldn't believe anyone would kill Mindy Carstairs over textbooks. How could I begin to fathom the minds of someone who would poison an invalid or kidnap a kid?

Max had been poisoned. My grandfather had been murdered. The news was just starting to sink home. My emotions had been unused for so long that they needed time to connect.

EG could be murdered like Max. What in hell kind of world was this?

"You have tremendous potential that could be put to good use helping others."

I heard disapproval instead of laughter in Sean's voice. Well, so much for cavalry. At least he was diverting me from hysteria. He was telling me the same thing I'd told EG, but she was the genius, not me. "I can't even take care of my own sister," I told him coldly. "I can't imagine how I could help others, or why I would want to. What are you, a preacher?"

He was silent for so long that I almost opened my eyes to see if he was still there.

"I believe our purpose in life is to make the world a better place," he finally responded. "And those with the most abilities should make the biggest difference."

I couldn't argue with that. Well, I could, but my mind wasn't there yet. It was on EG, wondering if she was afraid, or hungry, or plotting to burn down her hiding place.

"Fine. I'll improve the quality of my clientele," I muttered. "Right after I get EG home."

I shouldn't have opened my eyes.

Sean shifted gears, crossed three lanes, and reached the off ramp in a blare of furious honking. "Your father wouldn't approve of that attitude."

Frozen to the leather seat, I clenched my fingers into fists. "My father was a violent terrorist. Should I take up arms and follow his path?"

"Brody was not a terrorist. He was practical. He forged peace agreements, persuaded terrorists to lay down arms, and when his enemies rose against him, he arranged weapons for those who needed them for self-defense. He saw that the fight was equal instead of slaughter."

And he got himself killed for it. "Fine," I snarled. "We should all vote with guns. That will make the world a better place. Tell me where my sister is, and maybe I'll even listen."

"Women," he snorted with disgust. "You're all alike. You can't see the big picture. All you're interested in is papering the walls of your own safe homes."

Considering the cement walls of my basement, I could have laughed, but I wasn't in the mood for it. "If we all stayed home and papered our walls, we wouldn't need guns, would we?"

"And no one would have food either. C'mon, Ana, wake up to what's happening around us. You could make a difference. Go to that reception tonight and keep your eyes and ears open. Men like looking at you. All you have to do is flutter your lashes, and they'll tell you their darkest secrets."

I did laugh then. The image of me fluttering lashes was roll-on-the-floor material. "Thank you. I needed that. Do you think Tex would tell me where EG is if I fluttered my lashes?" I didn't tell him that I'd damned well go to that reception and twist heads until I found EG. Why did everyone—except Graham—want me to go to the reception anyway?

"I'll look for EG, if you'll go in there and persuade Paul Rose and Hammond to talk to me about the monopoly in the textbook publishing industry," Sean replied to my idiocy.

I sat up straight so fast that I nearly rammed my head into the windshield when he pulled the car to a shuddering halt in front of the mansion.

"How do you know about Paul Rose and textbooks?" I demanded.

He smiled that breathtaking smile of his and reached over to push a strand of hair loosened by the wind behind my ear, brushing my cheek as he did so. "I'm a reporter, remember? The investigative sort. And you're a perfect candidate for my partner. We could make beautiful stories together."

Chapter Twenty-four

Preparing for a reception

SITTING beside me in his miniscule MG, Sean O'Herlihy made me hot and cold at the same time. He was too damned close.

I avoided studying the tan column of his throat against the casual open neck of his shirt, and I refused to test the faint traces of beard stubble on his jaw the same way he'd touched my cheek. I am very good at solitude, but I was starting not to like it when it meant turning away this kind of temptation.

Realizing he was callously pumping me for information while my sister was in danger froze my hots quickly.

"You should be a fantasy writer," I replied, climbing out of the MG without his help. "I'll find Tex and torture him until he tells me where to find EG. I'll hand him over to you then, if that makes you feel better."

"You have to learn to trust someone, sometime, Ana. See you later." He departed in a noisy roar of engine and tire.

Depleted, I pushed the entry bell. Mallard wouldn't leave his front door unlocked as Tex's maid had. The door swung open on its mechanical wheel.

I didn't know what I expected when I returned. My bags on the doorstep, I guess. I could hope for the quiet of my office so I could plot my next action, but I didn't expect it.

Instead, I was greeted by Mallard carrying an hors d'oeuvres tray and wearing what appeared to be gray livery and a worried frown. Nick was already halfway down the stairs and shouting at me to get my rear in gear. He had on tuxedo pants with a cummerbund but his white silk shirt was open to his waist. It's a pity he's not only gay, but my half brother. I'd trust his blond charm and genuine panic to Sean's dark Irish poise any day.

"Grab some food and get up here," Nick shouted. "If we're there early enough, maybe we can have Eezhee on her way to Switzerland tonight."

"You're dreaming right? Or did you hit up a bank for the millions? I need to check my mailbox." I scarfed up a handful of toasty things with mushrooms and sun-dried tomatoes on them. I'm sure they tasted delicious, but I wasn't noticing. My mind was far from my taste buds.

I aimed for the library. Nick raced the rest of the way down and glared at me in frustration as I woke up the Whiz and opened my mailbox.

The kidnapper had a different screen name from the yahoo who'd warned me off before Magda arrived—"Big Brother." Very funny. The subject header simply said "EG." The mail server was Yahoo, which hosted ten bloody million accounts, including fronts for a lot of other servers. Like the earlier threat, this one would be impossible to trace without involving federal agents and a week's time. I opened the message.

For your own safety, bring your passports and London plane tickets to the Rose reception this evening. A cashier's check for a million will suffice.

A polite kidnapper—with an offshore bank account. Reggie? Insane but not impossible.

"Why the reception?" I asked aloud.

"Where's the least likely place for a kidnapper?" Graham's dry voice asked from the intercom. "The security will be tight. You won't be able to carry in weapons. I have notified the authorities and purchased three plane tickets to London from Reagan International. Pack your bags and your passports and Mallard will place them in the car."

"And you'll send the authorities to raid the reception?" I demanded, wondering if Graham hadn't chosen this route to drive us out, but I heard concern in his voice, or maybe I was imagining it. I didn't know whether to thank him or yell at him. "I'm not willing to take that chance. Besides, I don't have EG's passport, and we're not going anywhere." I'd made that decision long before I knew my grandfather had been murdered. Did he really think I'd turn my back and walk away from that news?

I didn't hang around waiting for his reply. "Which dress?" I asked Nick as I hurried past him for the stairs.

"I have it laid out," he said in relief now that I'd ignored Graham. "After you shower, let me put up your hair. We're running out of time and you can't go wearing that braid. If nothing else, it's a disadvantage in a fight." He hurried behind me, still working the studs into his shirt. "Do we want to go separately or should I stick by your side? The message didn't say anything about going alone."

"They obviously know us well enough to know we belong together. It won't fool them if we arrive separately." How many people knew we belonged together? Graham. Magda. Sean. Had Tex figured it out? The school officials at the public school and the private school knew. *Shit.* A few inquiries, and the whole world could know.

I'd seen the guest list. Thinking of all the powerful figures attending the reception, I shivered. Any of them could have made inquiries once I'd revealed my name to all and sundry. I thought I'd been clever concealing my real name, but *Maximillian* is as obvious as *Devlin* and could lead right to EG—especially if the murderer knew Max. I groaned at the thought.

How many damned people knew about the textbook cartel? The cops knew about Edu-Pub, but chances were they hadn't made the other connections. Hagan had to know, but mid-level government employees couldn't afford the reception ticket. Sean would be there. And Tex. His other buddies on Edu-Pub's board? How many others?

"Did you find Mindy's hard drive?" I asked before I dashed into the shower.

"We've secured the drive," the bronze statue appearing suspiciously akin to Rodin's *Striding Man* said from a niche in the hallway.

"Did you find the report?" I asked.

"Ms. Carstairs had a history major," the statue testified. "She reported the committee's history textbook recommendations as seriously flawed. She listed the more egregious errors in content and was so outraged that she took it upon herself to investigate the origins of the publishers and the textbook writers. The report is an incendiary diatribe on the waste of government funds for inferior quality materials and right wing propaganda, and a condemnation of profiteering by an illegal consortium of members of congress, including the senator. I fear Ms. Carstairs held the foolish belief that government employees still possess First Amendment rights."

I stared at the statue in bewilderment. Maybe Graham really was insane. "You're saying the government took her out for exercising freedom of speech?"

"There are zealots in every fold," he said complacently.

I wanted to pick up the statue and fling it. He was certifiable. But then, what about a kidnapper who called himself *Big Brother*? That wasn't precisely sane. It wasn't as if civilization operated on sanity. I'd lived in the big world. Private passions and greed got things done faster than logic and common sense. I didn't want to consider whose private passion might be creating inferior history textbooks. If there was profit to be had in it, someone would do it.

"I told Hagan on the textbook committee that we had that report," I said aloud. Why in hell was I talking to a statue? *Because I was beginning to rely on Superman.* "If he's in any way responsible for Mindy's or Max's murder, could he be behind EG's disappearance?"

The statue didn't reply. I figured that was ominous, and panic reared its ugly head. I didn't have time to go upstairs and throw rocks at Graham's computers until I had an answer.

Nick looked as if he would burst with questions, but I waved him on and hit the shower. It had been a miserably long hot day. It would be much simpler if I could cleanse my mind as easily as the rest of me.

Focus, I told myself as I stood in the lukewarm rain of the shower. If EG was in the hands of strangers, she would irritate them into killing her if we didn't find her quickly. I didn't want to think Hagan or Pao or any of the other potential baddies had her, but I had to think of the worst and work from there.

I toweled off in the shower and stepped out to an array of perfume products Nick had left for my perusal. *Why the hell not?* I'd prefer an armored tank and cannon, but if perfume and cosmetics were the way the game was played in D.C., I'd play them to the hilt.

Wrapped in the towel, I dabbed perfume on all my pulse points and for good measure added matching lotion all over. I knew how to do this stuff. I'd spent twenty years watching Magda, after all. Ammunition comes in all flavors.

Nick had laid out the gauzy silk fairy dress with the layered skirts and tiny little strapped heels. I wasn't feeling like a dainty fairy. I wanted AK-47s on both hips. I examined the other outfits, seeking an alternative.

I yanked the little black dress off its hanger. Slinky tight and mid-thigh, this number would have eyes rolling in their sockets. I liked that idea. If I had to make a fashion statement, it would be along the lines of *Don't mess with me, Bob.*

Nick knocked and shoved his way in while I was smoothing knee-high black leather boots over my calves. I thought he'd have a stroke right then, but I ignored the steam emerging from his ears. These boots had been my choice off the sale table at Nordstroms. No flimsy little strappy heels for me, nosirree. The metal-tipped spikes on these babies sent serious dominatrix messages. I was beginning to see the advantages of good foot gear over sandals.

"Want me to find my whip?" Nick asked with a deadliness that matched Graham's.

"A spiked collar would work." Boots on, I reached to fasten diamond studs in the three holes on my left lobe. Magda had insisted I have my ears pierced when I was thirteen. I'd topped her act by letting the right lobe close up and adding holes to the left whenever I was feeling disagreeable. I normally kept plain studs in them just to keep them open. Tonight, I was going past disagreeable and aiming for mean. "I think leaving the hair down works, don't you?"

"I'll drag you out by the length of it," he growled. "Are you planning on terrifying them into handing over EG?"

"Magda seduces her enemies," the intercom intruded. "So naturally Anastasia terrifies them. But if you won't listen to my advice about the airport, at least admit that heels are useless for martial arts and wearing the hair down gives an advantage to your opponent in a bare knuckle fight. If you must insist on endangering your life, have the sense to take all precautions."

I ripped the poster and painting off the wall, flung them on the bed, and took the spike heel of Nick's shoe choice to the camera and pounded the lens into metal mush.

Perhaps it was my imagination, but I thought I heard an explosive thump of something hard being flung upstairs. I wanted to believe I'd given the spook something serious to think about, but I had probably just pissed him off. I often have that effect.

I presented my back to Nick. "Zip it up."

He did—without argument. Sometimes, it's necessary to make a statement graphically.

Once my temper had settled enough so I could sit still, I let Nick perform his magic. He wrapped huge strands of my hair onto some kind of round platform, pinned it securely, worked other strands loose and twirled them into dangly waves with a curling iron. I didn't spend any time admiring the sexy image he created. I tugged at the hairpiece thing to make certain no one could drag me around by it, and satisfied, I let Nick wrap my throat in a black velvet choker with a silver and onyx stud on it. Creative. I liked it.

I glanced at the clock on the mantel—quarter 'til seven. The reception started at seven.

Nick opened the door and held out his arm for me. I lingered to admire his attire. If Sean was the Pierce Brosnan James Bond, then Nick was the Roger Moore version. I patted his red silk pocket handkerchief. "You look like an ambassador. I'll try not to ruin your career."

"I remember now why I didn't go into the diplomatic corps," he replied, dragging me down the hall. "I have too much imagination."

I would have laughed, but I was too scared. I stopped at the top of the stairs, spun around until I found the most likely location for a camera in the carved cornice, planted my hands on my hips, and glared. "If we somehow end up at the airport instead of the reception, I will personally return and set fire to the place with you in it."

"Magda should have spanked you more often," was all the reply I got.

I still had the hysterical need to laugh. It wasn't as if we had a lot of choices at this juncture. Graham might buy plane tickets, but he wasn't handing over a million dollars.

I had a dainty handbag containing as many dirty tricks as I could think of and boots that would put a hole through metal, and I still didn't know the enemy. I'm a virtual assistant. I haven't trained for cops and robbers or spooks and haunts. I shivered in my spike-heels.

Mallard opened the door and bowed us out, then donned a gray chauffeur's cap and followed us. A silver-gray Phaeton waited illegally in the street, with half a dozen cars angrily hitting their horns as they maneuvered around it.

"Excellent means of catching a cab," I said brightly, heading down the walk toward one stuck in the traffic jam behind the enormous car. "You're a genius, Mallard."

Torn between the gleaming magnificence of a chauffeured Phaeton and a dirty yellow cab bearing his dominatrix sister, Nick wavered. It was his choice, but I wasn't taking any chances on ending up at the airport. I didn't need his help. I'd managed on my own for years.

Nick's long legs carried him down the street to the cab before it pulled into traffic. I tried not to show my relief as he opened the door and slammed in.

"When will you learn to trust?" he growled.

"When Mallard works for us and not Graham," I countered.

The Phaeton rolled out behind the cab. I couldn't imagine Mallard following an indistinguishable yellow cab if we wanted to elude him, but he knew where we were going. I didn't mind having him along for backup.

"Did you locate Magda?" I asked quietly. For all I knew, cab drivers reported directly to Graham. Or to kidnappers. My paranoia had reached whole new levels.

"Patra said she talked to her in Switzerland last week, which doesn't help. I couldn't reach Tudor at school."

Tudor is sixteen. The last I'd seen of him, he'd been a red-headed imp, but the latest reports indicated he'd probably corrupt the internet and reduce technology to the Dark Ages unless someone gave him something better to do. I knew networking, but he'd grown up with computers. His skills involved programming and hardware, far outmatching anything I could do, so I had no intention of being the nanny who kept his active mind occupied.

Not being able to reach Tudor was a given, but he always knew where everyone else was.

"I don't know where Magda is working these days," Nick continued. "I left a message on her voice and e-mail but she hasn't replied."

I nodded. That was typical Magda behavior and nothing suspicious. As long as all her chicks were well and accounted for, she let others tend them while she went about her business. I knew from personal experience the communication gap between the time a chick needed her, and her receiving the message and acting on it. The gap had been dangerously long upon occasion, or immediate on others.

If Nick told her EG had been kidnapped, she'd be on the next space ship from Mars if she had to, but first she had to pick up her damned voice mail. I never questioned my mother's love for her children—just her priorities and parenting skills.

"All right. Then we'll look for Tex first." There had been a time when I had meant to use this reception to follow Pao, but right now, if I found him, I'd lock him up with Tex until I had questions answered. I just wish I had more suspects so I could lock them all up in one place.

"What are you going to say to Tex if you find him—'hand over my sister'? That could be embarrassing given that we have no reason to believe he's behind EG's disappearance." Nick brushed a lock of hair from his forehead and anxiously regarded the traffic jam in front of the reception hall. "What was that business about Max being murdered?"

"Graham says envelopes from Max's office contained poison." It's a damned good thing I don't do snail mail because I was the one using Max's office these days.

I was trying really hard not to think about my grandfather because tears kept forming behind my eyes, and I just didn't have time to cry. "I think Max was working with Mindy. Someone must have interfered with the envelopes before they were delivered."

"Reggie?" Nick asked instantly. "So he could get his hands on the money?"

"And maybe because someone asked him to," I agreed with a sigh of defeat. "Or blackmailed him into it."

"Magda isn't behind this, is she?" he asked gloomily.

"I'm thinking not. She's more devious. Maybe we should split up when we get there. I'll stand around as bait, waiting for the kidnapper to approach. You hide and follow them."

"You don't have EG's passport or the money," he pointed out.

"I'll tell them they're at the airport with the tickets. It's not as if we could get paper tickets at this late date." I was thinking aloud just to keep from imagining all the bad things that could happen—like what if they really didn't care about tickets at the airport because they intended to kill us.

"This isn't going to work, is it?" Nick asked glumly, apparently following a similar train of thought.

"It would if I could make sense of it, but I can't. I assume that's what they're counting on. We'll just have to wing it. It's better than doing nothing."

The traffic around the reception hall had come to a standstill. If we'd been in the Phaeton, the police would have ushered us into the lane that had been cleared for guests. The cabbie tried to argue his way in, but I saw no reason to make life difficult for the men in blue. We paid the driver and walked through the gates, flourishing our fake invites.

How had the kidnapper known we could get in? Or had they counted on us arranging invitations along with passports and tickets? They knew us damned well, if so.

Or they knew Graham. That possibility knotted my insides.

Maybe the kidnappers had counted on us getting invites by making a huge contribution to Rose's campaign fund with our supposed millions. I'd flashed my passport all over D.C. in this past week and a half, and called myself Maximillian today. It wouldn't take much to discover I was one of the heirs to my grandfather's fortune—especially in Reggie's circles. Money would get us invitations to anywhere.

I knew presidential campaigns used a lot of dirty tricks, but kidnapping a kid to obtain campaign contributions would set new lows. I couldn't find any logic in kidnapping EG at all—unless someone was after us *and* the money, and we were walking right into the trap.

I walked up the drive in my aggressive thigh-length mini-dress and do-me boots, trembling in fear. I deserved an Oscar.

If the kidnappers murdered Max, surely they knew Reggie had our money. Maybe Graham murdered Max and he was going to bump us off tonight and let Tex take the blame. Apparently, I could be real imaginative when I put my mind to it.

Men in pin-striped suits climbed out of limos with women in designer gowns. It wasn't a white-tie affair, but men like Nick in tuxes are never out of place. Women in killer boots were totally wrong—unless they stood five-nine and sported silicon boobs. We've already established that's not me. I dressed myself in attitude.

The security staff at the door studied me with suspicion but my dress didn't leave room for so much as a splinter much less a weapon. They searched my purse and took my pepper spray, but left my roll of quarters, keys, and pick-handled comb. Silly men.

I saw Pao the instant we pushed our way past the reception line to the punch bowls.

Chapter Twenty-five

Ana questions Blackwell and finds a closet

"JUST STAY right there and behave yourself, Elizabeth, and I'll bring Senator Hammond to you as soon as he arrives."

EG nibbled an apple from her backpack and tried to look as if she believed the suave old guy in a suit as he departed.

She'd been dumb. She hadn't done anything this dumb since she was five and smoke-bombed kindergarten.

The door closed and the lock clicked behind her kidnapper. Dropping her innocent pose, EG narrowed her eyes and scanned the unadorned bedroom. They'd walked past caterers and harried office workers and men in suits to get here, so this must be a fairly public place. She hoped no one moved the book she'd dropped on the table when she realized her driver hadn't taken her to Tex's office as expected.

Silver Hair had told her that Tex was working on the reception, but he'd been so nervous he hadn't even noticed when she'd dropped the book. Her suspicions had kicked in by then, and she figured she ought to leave a clue for Ana—just in case.

The guy in the limo at the school had said he was one of Tex's aides. And she'd believed him. That's how desperate she had been. Magda would kill her, if Ana didn't first. They'd been taught from birth to ID strangers, but she hadn't thought anyone in D.C. knew who she was except her family. The stranger had known she belonged to Tex. Only her family knew that.

She checked the window. It looked down on a parking lot filled with work vans. The historic old home had looked impressive from the front, but it was obvious it was more office building than residence. She was on the third floor and too far left of the portico to climb out.

There were people down there. Maybe they could hear her. She tried opening the small attic window but it was painted shut. She could try breaking it, but she doubted anyone would hear her from up here. The workers below were all yelling into cell phones or at each other and racing back and forth into the kitchen.

Maybe she was panicking over nothing. Maybe Tex really did know she was here. It seemed a very odd place to stash a kidnap victim. Maybe Tex was using her to bring Magda back to town. She didn't think she'd told anyone but her father that she'd be out of school early. How else would they have known to come get her?

Except the limo hadn't picked up Elsie. And it hadn't been Boise with the Pierce-Arrow. She'd been dumb. She'd climbed into a car with a stranger just because he'd known who she was and who her father was.

Thinking hard, she patted the wall behind the bed, hoping for a hidden door. How had the guy in the suit known about her father unless he was actually from her father?

The e-mail to Tex's office. She'd thought Tex would be the only one to see it. She really was losing it. School must have rotted her brain. Someone else in Tex's office had seen her message, someone who meant to hurt him?

Her brain was revving into gear now and not liking what it thought. EG patted the wall faster, checked the baseboards, and scanned the floor and ceiling.

Finding nothing, she started looking for something with which to break glass.

* * *

"Circulate," I murmured to Nick as we pushed toward the buffet where I'd seen Pao. "Find Tex."

Oddly calm now that the enemy was in sight, I knew what I had to do. Pao had made it to my short list of potential kidnappers. Apparently, I was about to flaunt my recent discovery that I was no longer the normal one in the family.

Nick hadn't spent the last week and a half focused on Pao. He didn't see what I saw or know what I knew. He simply looked confused.

"I thought I was playing backup," he protested. "Tex will be in a smoke-filled room somewhere. Are you staying here alone until I find him? That's risky."

"I'm in a roomful of people guarded by the Secret Service. I'll grab plates for both of us at the buffet."

Poor Nick still suffered under the illusion that I was the geeky sister who hid in basements. Okay, maybe I still was. But he hadn't been with me when a warehouse blew up, or when I confronted Hagan and Tex's wife. I had wells of stupidity I hadn't plumbed yet. A double-pronged approach to my paranoia seemed like the perfect answer.

Nick gave my outfit a doubtful look, shrugged, and sauntered off, probably relieved to be rid of the embarrassment of my sartorially-impaired company.

Keeping an eye on Pao, I picked up a plate and randomly selected munchies that didn't require much attention. Flowery radishes and curled celery might look cute, but I've had years of experience at buffet tables. Raw veggies were nasty without dip, and dip looked bad dripping off my limited cleavage. Anything piled in three layers was even worse to manipulate, particularly with wine in hand. I wasn't born with the coordination of a juggler or the slight-of-hand of a magician. I claimed food I didn't have to watch. Caviar on crackers works.

I studied the men to whom Pao spoke. I hadn't spent much time pondering photographs of newsworthy figures, but I recognized a congressman here and there, and several of our distinguished representatives stopped to shake his hand. Pao might have shadowy connections, but in this million-dollar crowd, they knew a foreign attaché and fundraiser when they saw one.

I hadn't been around Magda or her diplomatic cronies in ten years, but I recognized several of them circulating through the room. Other than adding a few pounds and a few more gray hairs, they hadn't changed much. I had to wonder what they were doing here, if Magda might have sent them. I didn't walk up and ask, especially if they spoke to Pao. None of them were high enough up the food chain to be important as far as I was aware.

I knew which of Magda's circle were CIA, of course. Everyone did. They rotated regularly, but then, so did Magda. If my old friends noticed me, they didn't let on. Amazing how small government circles are. I hadn't thought I'd know anyone here, but many of these people could know about EG. And possibly her relation to Tex. Now I had to wonder if I was surrounded by friends or enemies. Goose flesh crawled up my bare arms.

Nibbling a lovely piece of French cheese and sipping a glass of white wine, I stayed out of Pao's line of sight and kept my ears open.

It's odd how the mind takes unexpected leaps and bounds when pressured. All the tiny cells of information from the past week and a half had suddenly coalesced into an amorphous pattern that didn't quite make sense yet but was starting to take shape.

I noticed the candidate of the hour holding court in a far corner. Pao didn't go near him, but men who stopped to speak to Rose spoke with each other, and the same men often spoke to Pao. I couldn't follow the network without knowing all the players, but it was obvious Pao was far more than a textbook salesman or a hotheaded Indonesian radical.

I circled closer. My boot heels added three inches to my height, and my stacked hair probably added another couple. For someone with social anxieties, I was pretty conspicuous. People looked at me. Only those people who got in my way got noticed in return though. I politely rebuffed a suit high on arrogance and another high on reefers. Drunks tend to be more tenacious, but then, my stilettos were metal. I felt no remorse for their cries of pain. I dodged their spilled drinks with finesse. I might look the part of Magda, but I am *so* not into this scene.

Because events had unfolded unpleasantly since my meeting with Hagan that afternoon, I kept an eye out for him, but it was EG's textbook that I spotted first.

I almost spilled my wine trying to reach it. I stepped on toes, elbowed stout bellies, and almost kicked a waiter. He dodged out of my way to avoid mutilation.

Just as I reached the table in the corner, I realized if the bad guys were watching, they knew they had me, but I didn't care. Setting my plate down, I flipped open the history text. Obviously, there were hundreds of thousands of these books out there, unless most of them had blown up with the warehouse. But there was no good reason for one to be here.

EG's name was boldly scribbled inside. Most nine-year-olds were just learning script writing. EG practiced calligraphy. It was hers.

Did that mean she was here? *In this house?* Or was this some demented means of identifying me? If I'd come as my usual invisible self, that was a wise approach. I was likely the only person in the entire room who would inspect a textbook, so it was a certain means of recognition—to people who knew me. I didn't want to believe kidnappers were that smart.

I preferred to think EG had left the book to show she'd been here. I was counting on her being alive and well and wearing her thinking cap.

I was torn between waiting here for Nick and Tex or ripping the house apart brick by brick. It was an old Greek Revival mansion I assumed some organization had purchased for these kinds of functions. I would more likely intrude on offices than bedrooms if I conducted a systematic search. How long would it take to locate Tex?

If I could find EG first, we could avoid a messy scene where we accused Tex and everyone associated with him of kidnapping. Even I really didn't believe Tex was guilty.

If the kidnapper had left this here intentionally, why hadn't the moron left instructions? Was I supposed to stand here eagerly clutching the book until the kidnapper arrived? Or parade through the reception waving the text in my hand until someone recognized me?

And if EG had left it here, it had to be a cry for help.

I hated playing twenty questions. I preferred action. With malice aforethought, I set down the book and aimed a full-blown Magda smile at the first man who looked my way.

* * *

Working my lip-sticked smile, I explored the ground floor rooms under the escort of any available male willing to risk embarrassment at being found where we didn't belong. Men have their purposes—like following any female with hips that swing so women don't appear alone and helpless. I wasn't stupid enough to wander off by myself to get bonked over the head by kidnappers. I know self-defense, and the first rule says *don't be stupid*.

Once I decided that EG wasn't downstairs, I lost the escorts. My next gambit included scouting closets. I'd learned that ploy in the numerous habitats Magda had dumped us in. Closet hiding didn't work well if I was hindered by drooling Neanderthals who thought uninhabited spaces were meant for things other than I had in mind—unless the Neanderthal was Sean. But he had conveniently not appeared yet.

Having found the right closet, I was back in the main room by eight. Either Nick couldn't find Tex, or he was waiting somewhere for the senator to show up. Neither of them was present. Pao was still holding court in one corner. The kidnappers hadn't attempted to contact me.

Rather than dither anxiously, I staked out all my suspects.

I shouldn't have been surprised to see Blackwell Johnson present, but I was. He looked older and grayer than I remembered. Maybe the threat of our lawsuit had finally made our plight real. Maybe the call I'd ignored this morning was an apology.

Give the man a chance. I needed information, and I didn't care who provided it. "Good evening, Mr. Johnson." I appeared at his side, startling him into tomorrow from the looks of it. "Don't you think your money would be better spent in refilling our bank account than on candidates who don't stand a chance of winning?"

He jerked nervously at my first words and glared anywhere but at me as I continued. "You sound just like your grandfather," he said dismissively.

"That's promising. Perhaps when I have his millions, I can turn them into billions. In the meantime, have you determined who blackmailed Reggie into absconding with our funds?"

That really shook him. I finally had his attention. I beamed sweetness and light. I don't think he believed the innocent look anymore.

"What are you talking about?" he demanded.

What could he do if I made up tales? Have me arrested for storytelling? I really had learned more from Magda than I'd thought. Spinning out the few facts I had, I tried to sound knowledgeable. "Reggie was about to do time for his third drug arrest. He was desperate. Max was his wealthiest client, old and in ill health. And someone wanted to get rid of him, probably because Max had been poking around Edu-Pub. Do you know anything about Edu-Pub?"

"Reggie's father used to be on the board, that's all I know," he said stiffly.

Ah, finally, confirmation that Reggie had access to the cartel Max was investigating.

"Well, you'd better start preparing your statement before the police come around," I said blithely. "I assume Reggie told his father's associates about Max's investigations. They decided it would be a good thing for all to dispose of Max and scoot Reggie out of the country, thereby killing two birds with one stone."

"You're saying Reggie killed Max because of some textbook company?" Blackwell asked, appalled and fascinated.

I shrugged, keeping an eye on the candidate and his entourage while I continued spinning fantasies. "Reggie killed him to get enough money to leave the country. The people behind Edu-Pub have other issues, including money-laundering. And because Tex's office has been investigating the company, I think they've decided to do away with him, as well. Now, whose side would you like to take? I've already notified the authorities, and they're investigating as we speak." Wholesale lie, but it occurred to me that if Max could get killed and EG kidnapped, I was just dust in the wind to them. They could blow me away no matter what I said to whom. "Spill what you know, and you'll probably be called hero."

I didn't tell him about EG. I didn't want to sound helpless, and I didn't want to reveal that I was clueless. I was taking a chance that Blackwell wasn't the kidnapper, but I was betting he wasn't a man of action. He liked knowing things, not doing them.

"I don't know much," he said gruffly, not looking at me again but searching the room with an uneasy expression. "I don't want my name involved."

"That's easy. Tell me what you know and I'll nail the research and pass it on, but you'll miss your opportunity to be a hero."

"Who the devil are you?" he demanded.

"Max's granddaughter," I said simply. "I'm finishing what he started."

"And Graham has nothing to do with this?"

"I think he's doing the same thing." I hadn't fully realized it until now, but as I said this, I was sure of it. Graham had other agendas for him to set up that sophisticated operating room, but right now, I was certain he was helping me find out about Max, his mentor. I'd never had a partner before, but if I had to have one, a crazy one worked well.

"And you think Max was investigating Edu-Pub?"

"I know it. I have evidence of why he was interested as well, and the police are already investigating the tie-in with Mindy's death. It's either me, or the cops."

Blackwell rubbed his forehead and spoke while his hand covered his face. "Reggie's father belonged to a group of men who think the country needs to be run by a more educated class of citizens. The group calls themselves Top Hats, and they own stock in companies they consider conducive to their goals. After Reginald died, Reggie tried to sell out his father's shares. After that, he received visits from people who weren't clients and who emerged from Reggie's office in a state of agitation. I don't know any more than that. You'll need to find Reggie for answers."

"Oh, I know where to find Reggie. I'm just biding my time until I have all the facts," I said with an insouciance I didn't feel. "I'd suggest you write down everything you know and put it a in a bank vault and tell your loved ones to open the vault if anything happens to you. That's how they do it in movies, isn't it?" I shot him an evil smile.

"You're the one who is likely to end up dead." He started to edge away as if I had cooties.

He hadn't helped me find EG, but he confirmed enough of my suspicions that I wasn't letting him get away just yet. "Which of those men up there is Rose's fundraiser?"

That stopped him cold. "Ed O'Reilly, the one with the bald head and gray fringe."

I could see the wheels of his mind spinning. Presidential candidates, fundraisers, and wealthy financiers who want to change the world. Alarm crossed his face.

Don't ask me why I'm suspicious of money men. My mind just works that way. "Tell Ed I have something interesting he'd like to see. I'll meet him in the library at nine."

"Senator Rose speaks at nine," Johnson said, apparently hoping to distract me.

I patted him on the cheek in a definite Magda-ism. "Then make it a quarter till nine."

Praying Magda's tactics worked for a five-two dominatrix, I put more wiggle in my walk as I turned away. My adrenaline—aided by two glasses of wine—had reached such volcanic proportions that I'd have flung the kidnapper over my shoulder and into the punch bowl if he'd approached. Fortunately for both of us, he continued to torture me by not showing.

Sean had yet to put in an appearance either, but he probably wouldn't until it was time for the candidate to speak. I've known a few journalists over the years. Punctuality isn't one of their finer qualities, especially if they're Irish and there's a bar nearby. I don't mean to sound narrow-minded, but stereotypes exist for a reason, and I shouldn't have to point out the basis for this one. I was quite willing to be pleasantly surprised if I was wrong.

I had my next victim already targeted. I sidled up to a pleasant looking Korean businessman who'd spent more time than most talking to Pao. "I know a gentleman who has an interesting proposition for Sak Thai Pao," I whispered to him. "If he's interested, tell him to stop by the library at a quarter 'til nine. It won't take long."

I slipped away before he could recover his tongue and ask questions. I figured I was wearing enough perfume to choke my victims into near unconsciousness, thus increasing my chances of escape.

I made several similar stops to cover all known suspects before checking the smoke-filled bar set up in a back room. If Sean was there, I didn't see him, which was probably a good thing. He might have noticed my evil smile when I recognized Hagan at the bar. I hadn't thought mid-level underpaid government employees could afford black-tie affairs like this—unless skullduggery was afoot. That thought made me more mad than afraid.

I couldn't use the wink and a promise technique with someone who knew me, so I waited until the man Hagan was talking to left the bar and came my way. I approached him and gave him a different line than I'd given Pao. A man like Hagan would have ego wrapped up in his physique. He would heed the call of sex faster than business. My accomplice looked startled at my suggestion and hesitated long enough to let me slip out.

To prove I wasn't entirely insane, I'd scouted a place for my confrontational theater in my earlier search for EG. I'd discovered the library had a lovely little MacBook tucked into a fold-down desk in the bookshelves. One of the dirty little tricks the guards at the door hadn't appropriated from my purse was my keychain thumb drive. The innocent-looking fob contained the best hacking program money—and my hacker half-brother—could buy. Tudor had his uses.

It was half insane and half brilliant to wait until the last minute to call up Graham on the Mac after I'd hacked into it. If I'd called him earlier, he probably would have summoned the men in black to haul me out by my frivolous hairdo. Waiting until the last minute chanced his not answering, but I figured that was the lesser of two evils.

At eight-thirty, I stopped at the computer, powered it up with my stolen password and typed, *In fifteen minutes, Pao, Ed O'Reilly, Thomas Hagan, and aides from the congressmen with shares in Edu-Pub will be meeting in this room. I'll be watching from outside. The ball's in your court. Have fun."*

I IM'd Graham with my teleconference invitation. He was online. All he had to do was hit the video conference button I sent him, and he'd be hooked up to the library. I ran before he could accept with an irate reply. Or rather, in those heels and tight skirt, I minced out.

It was past eight-thirty by the time Nick found me opening a closet door in the foyer. The party was just hitting its stride. The kidnapper still hadn't contacted me, but that might be because I hadn't stood still.

"I thought you were staying at the buffet," Nick said angrily, catching my elbow. "What the devil are you doing?"

I turned, and recognizing the frowning senator beside him, I applied my evil ruby smile rather than explain myself. "We meet again, Tex. Did Nick tell you we have plane tickets waiting at Reagan?"

I wanted to believe EG's father wasn't involved, but it would be simpler dealing with him than a group of killers. His lined face pulled into a deeper frown, and I knew he hadn't done it.

"If this is Magda's idea of a joke—"

"Magda isn't here. I've looked," I informed him coldly, just in case I could make him angry and pry his secrets out of him. "And none of her friends have approached me with ransom demands. That leaves you and yours, senator. Who else knows about EG?"

High as I was on adrenaline and wine, I could have confronted lions without flinching. I twirled my wine glass and let Tex look stunned. I'd spent the last half hour learning what perfume and a little cleavage could do. The undergarments Nick had bought for me were excellent. Power was mine. Except Tex wasn't buying it.

"Ah'm not that enterprising," he said wearily. "Ah told Magda I'd pay for the girl's education in that pricey school in Switzerland. This isn't my way of backing out of a promise."

The senator was losing his hokey drawl again. I couldn't tell if it was out of concern for EG or for the possibility that the secret of her existence might leak to the press. Nick's expression remained neutral.

"EG sent me an e-mail this afternoon," the senator continued wearily.

That got both our attentions.

"She wanted to meet with me, but I didn't read the e-mail until well after school was over." He held up his palm to hold off our questions. "Anyone in my office could have read it. She didn't know my private e-mail address."

We understood instantly. Anyone in his office could have read EG's note and passed it on. Anyone could have known she was waiting for Tex. The kidnapping field was wide open, and my terror multiplied a hundredfold. I hadn't believed Tex was a kidnapper, but I'd wanted him to be, because EG would have been safe with her father.

"I found her history book in the main room," I told them, studying the senator's reaction. He was a practiced politician trained to hide his emotions, but right now, he looked just as worried as we were. "She signed it. It's hers. She could be in this house right now. I want a search organized."

Even Nick looked ready to object to this. I shook my head at him. "A quiet search. No one's approached me. They may not be here yet. EG might not be either, but I would rather find her than confront kidnappers. How long would it take to search the rooms upstairs? I've already looked down here."

It shows how anxious they were that they took me at face value. They even seemed to think I made sense. Little did they know that I'd crossed the family line into insanity by setting up the little seminar in the library.

"I'll have one of my aides keep an eye on you while we search upstairs," the senator suggested. He glanced at his watch. "Tell us where the table is with the book, and we'll meet you there after Paul gives his speech. If the kidnapper shows up before that, send Zeke after us." He nodded toward a lanky fellow in a tux watching us anxiously.

Zeke was a stupid plan. I didn't want anyone I didn't know shadowing me. I nodded solemnly, playing the part of docile female with a vengeance. Nick shot me a suspicious look. He understood the vengeance part.

"If EG is found safe, your secrets are safe with us, senator." I meant that, I thought. Blackmailing Tex into doing right by EG probably wouldn't work. "But if someone in your office is responsible for this, I'm taking them down."

"My wife said you know something about Mindy." He looked scared and concerned more than threatening. And he was following my path of thought.

"Did you know Edu-Pub may be laundering illegal campaign funds?" I asked.

He looked uncomfortable but desperate. "I didn't when I signed on. An influential group asked me to join the board, and I was flattered."

I gave him my stolid cat-eye stare. He glared right back. "That's how politics works—networking with the rich and famous. Mindy was the one who discovered the problems with the textbooks. She was outraged at the propaganda. I'm not much on history, but I started looking into things. You aren't telling me that a group of men as wealthy and influential as that would kidnap a child?"

I heard his disbelief. It's always easier to believe drug addicts and career criminals commit crimes. White collar crime is rampant but much more subtle and difficult to discern—until it runs to murder. "If I'm right, whoever set you up to take the fall for Mindy may have murdered others. My knowledge may be the reason EG was kidnapped. I don't want her to be the next murder."

"I'm calling the police." Nick turned around and started to stalk off.

I shouldn't have hit him with that theory so abruptly, but I'm new to the spy and spook business. I grabbed his elbow and jerked, hard. He glared. "Let's not alert the bad guys yet," I told him. "Look for EG first. Quietly."

I could tell they didn't like it, but they didn't have any better ideas.

"This is outrageous," Tex muttered. "I ought to call the FBI."

"The FBI is way too obvious. The kidnappers would see them coming and haul tail, taking EG with them," I said, hoping to stall him. "Search upstairs, then get back to me."

What I was actually doing, they should worry about, which was why I didn't tell them. I didn't think they'd take lightly to my blowing up every single suspect on my list at once.

Nick and Tex hurried out of sight, taking the backstairs so they wouldn't be noticed from the wide front hall where I stood. People were still arriving, although the crush at the door had reduced to a trickle as guests jockeyed for a position in the big room where Rose would speak.

I smiled at Tex's flunky. He tugged his tie knot and nodded.

Then I stepped into the coat closet and closed the door.

I probably didn't mention the reason I chose to live in a small dark windowless apartment. I could have afforded better, but small dark closets are my idea of security. My therapists called it regression to the womb, but they didn't really understand. My curiosity was developed as a form of self-defense against Magda's chaotic world, and closets were the best method of satisfying my curiosity.

I'd caught Magda in a closet once and tried it for myself. Now that I understood Magda was a little more dangerous than I knew, I realized she probably wasn't playing nooky in there. At age six, I just thought it looked like fun. By ten, I was a confirmed closet inhabitant.

Closets have lots of other advantages when one wishes to hide from nannies, tutors, and pestering siblings. I'd even learned to look for false walls after I discovered the entrance to an earl's pornography collection behind one. I have an interesting education. But closets attached to libraries and studies are the best. In old houses like these, they almost always have peepholes.

I didn't speculate on whether servants or spying employers or scheming politicians installed the holes. Knowing human behavior, I'd vote for all of the above.

All I knew was that I'd done a quick search of the ground floor, found no sign of EG, but I'd discovered the coat closet had an excellent view of the library.

Chapter Twenty-six

Ana gets caught in her own trap

IN AUGUST, coat closets tend to be spacious. A moth-eaten muffler left over from the prior winter and someone's raincoat occupied the space with me. My boot heel caught in a pile of cloth on the floor that I assumed was a sweater fallen from its hanger, and I shook it free.

I didn't waste time worrying about what Tex's aide would do in the foyer while I was in here. That was his problem. I found my peephole and studied the situation in the library.

The representatives from Congressional offices were standing around with their hands in their pockets, probably discussing ball scores or the women they'd had last night. They didn't look unduly concerned about sharing my theoretical business proposal.

The long library table had been covered in white linen and decorated with candles, humidors, and assorted important looking tomes that I assumed some designer bought by the foot in a used bookstore. I'd left the library computer on, but it only played a screensaver at the moment. They should have been suspicious of that, but they were all clueless.

I smothered an incipient sneeze at the same time I heard a distinct mewling near my feet.

Like my namesake, I live a doomed life, and at the rate I was going, I was probably destined for a short one. I couldn't see the floor in the dark, but my nose told me all I needed to know. Some damned cat had left a nest of kittens in the sweater on the floor.

Trying not to breathe, ignoring a miffed meow outside the closet, I tried to keep my eye focused on the peephole. I thought I saw Hagan in a group of gray suits on the far side, but it was a corner I couldn't see well from this angle. If I wasn't mistaken, Blackwell Johnson was in the same group. I hadn't invited him. Interfering bastard.

Ed O'Reilly entered, glanced around at the company, checked his watch, and decided to stay for a few minutes. He moved to the wall where I stood, bringing one of the aides with him.

They were discussing which members of the media they'd allow near their candidate when Pao entered. O'Reilly said something that sounded like *shit* before I sneezed so loudly, the closet door flew open.

Maybe it didn't fly open so much as get yanked. As I hurried out in hopes of escaping anyone within hearing of my sneeze, I stumbled into Sean. Zeke was nowhere in sight.

Sean caught my elbow and hauled me through the crowded foyer as if he had a good idea of what I'd been doing hanging in a coat closet. I rubbed my watering eyes and sneezed relentlessly, unable to even send a baleful glance at the mama cat returning to the closet.

Sean looked gorgeous in a tux obviously tailored just for his wide shoulders. Unlike Nick, he played it discreet with white and black, but he looked beyond dashing. And angry.

"Well, now I know where to look for you when I want to find you," he said, all but shaking my arm. "I'm supposed to be reporting on Rose's speech, but I don't suppose that's why you're in a closet, is it?"

He handed me a handkerchief. I adore men who carry handkerchiefs, but I was getting damned tired of gorgeous, mysterious men who thought they were omniscient. I rubbed my streaming eyes and blew my nose and kept the handkerchief. I'd send him a new batch as soon as I saw his byline on a newspaper and knew where to find him. I had my doubts about ever seeing that byline, and I was wondering what he'd done with my bodyguard.

"You know what I'm doing," I answered in the same tone as he used. "Although how you know is highly questionable unless you're the kidnapper."

He dropped my arm like a hot potato and walked off. I'm really good at self-defense—and sabotaging relationships. I didn't have time to question why he got to be angry and suspicious and I didn't.

I had to get inside that library before Graham started speaking.

Ignoring Sean's departure, I hurried down the hall to the library door just as Pao stepped out. He saw me but apparently had no reason to recognize me, thank what few lucky stars I might possess. Ed was hot on his trail, probably attempting to locate my sneeze. Or given his reaction to Pao earlier, maybe he wanted to take him down. Maybe blowing up the Edu-Pub warehouse and its contents hadn't been a financially wise move for one of the parties involved.

I hurriedly tucked the handkerchief into my purse and sauntered down the hall as if searching for a restroom. I could hear Graham's voice begin to speak in the library. Both Pao and O'Reilly spun back in apparent surprise and returned to the room.

Interesting reaction. Had they recognized Graham's voice or just responded to the note of authority in it? I didn't have time to ponder before Sean stepped out of the doorway he'd hidden in and fell into step beside me again. Maybe he hadn't been mad at me but hiding from Pao. Maybe, should I survive this, I'd give relationships another chance. Maybe.

"And they call your sister the evil genius in the family?" Sean asked incredulously. "Did I just hear Amadeus Graham in there?"

His incredulity warmed my wicked heart. He didn't wait for me to answer but halted in the doorway O'Reilly had left open. Since I already knew the players inside, I opted for staying in the hall and listening.

The computer was on the far wall. I recognized Graham's mechanical inflection, but I could only catch a few words. I needed to be closer. I should have turned the speakers up to blaring, but then I figured we'd collect a crowd. I wagered the men in the room were drawing closer to the computer to hear, within convenient range of the video camera in the monitor.

The corridors back here were empty. The rest of the guests had all crowded into the front foyer and reception hall to hear the candidate's speech. "Where did you send Zeke?" I whispered to the James Bond wannabe straining to hear through the open door.

"After Nick and the senator," Sean whispered back before hushing me with an annoyed gesture and pressing me back against the striped wallpaper with one arm.

Sending for family at a dangerous moment like this wasn't smart, and holding me back was cause for maiming. I'm the oldest. I get to play the stupid superhero part.

I stomped Sean's instep with my heel to remind him I was Brody's daughter, and sashayed past him when he grabbed the door to keep from keeling over in pain. How dangerous could a bunch of congressional aides be if a dead man could worry them?

A few of them looked around at Sean's groan. Their eyes widened at seeing me, but I simply smiled, gave a little wave, and settled on the end of the library table, crossing my knees and swinging my boot heel into the floor-length cloth. My skirt rode up to nearly invisible. They swallowed and returned their attention to Graham. The computer monitor displayed an American flag, I noted with interest. He wasn't using a video camera on his end.

I'd missed the introduction and came in as Graham announced, "The Carstairs report indicting the profiteering of the textbook publishing cartel will be released to the media shortly. If you were called here tonight, it's because your congressman was named in the report as part of the syndicate. Those of you aware of the cartel's underlying interests might take this opportunity to come clean while you can, before the scandal hits."

Even past all the high-flying words I caught the threat. Underlying interests? Besides making money? I'd read far enough into the encyclopedia to grasp the purpose of monopolies—greed and control—although I found it hard to believe textbook publishing was a money maker. Which meant... Hell if I knew. I tried to concentrate on Graham's authoritative discourse.

"According to my sources, Sak Thai Pao's laundering of soft money campaign funds through the distributor he formed for your use is currently under investigation by the bureau of Homeland Security. His connection to the publishing cartel is imminent, and his reputation is questionable. If you wish your candidate to survive, a housecleaning is recommended."

O'Reilly looked thunderous, but Pao remained complacent as the American flag disappeared, and Graham's voice fell silent. I suspected the speech had been taped.

Blackwell Johnson nodded knowingly. Apparently that little diatribe confirmed what he'd told me earlier, although he hadn't mentioned Pao. None of this was finding EG.

I didn't see Hagan any longer. Had he escaped while I was lingering outside the door? I glanced around the library and discovered a servant's door to the back hall disguised in the paneling. *Shit.*

Should I see where he'd gone? If there was any chance that EG was in the building, I didn't want any of the presumed bad guys near her. But Nick and the senator were out there. The house was full of people. Surely nothing bad could happen. Yet.

Several of the aides looked puzzled at my arrival. Most of them didn't know I'd instigated the gathering, but they studied me surreptitiously anyway. For the amusement of it, I helped myself to a cigar from the humidor and began peeling the wrapping. The few who recognized me turned in my direction with expectant expressions.

"Who are you?" O'Reilly demanded. "Why have you resurrected that paranoid schizophrenic?"

Interesting phrasing. I assumed the insult meant he'd recognized Graham's voice and knew who he was. Or had been. This could be an enlightening evening in more ways than one.

I raised my arched dark eyebrows and twirled the cigar in the crotch of my fingers. "Me? I'm just looking for my little sister. She looks a lot like me, only younger and smaller. If any of you have seen her, I'd appreciate knowing where. Our plane tickets are waiting at the airport."

All appeared puzzled, except Pao. Expressionless, he eased toward the servants' door. Fear clenched in my throat. I wished Nick would hurry up. I needed to know EG was safe.

I was lousy at this cloak and dagger stuff. I should have noticed that door and stationed good old Zeke there.

I was aware of Sean lingering just inside the main doorway, but I had no reason to trust anyone, especially if Graham had taped that speech so he could be elsewhere right this moment.

Noticing Pao's impending departure, O'Reilly diverted his attention from me. "Wait a minute, Pao. I want to hear about this money laundering gambit. I don't need the media down my back on that." He angled his head to indicate Sean's presence.

Ah, so he actually was a journalist. Score one for the boy. I relaxed a trifle now that Pao was cornered by someone more powerful than me.

"As you say, this person on the computer is mentally deranged. All investments are audited," Pao replied politely.

I had a feeling this was a performance for Sean's sake. My only concern was in finding EG and getting the hell out of there. I had to keep an eye on all parties present until I knew EG was safe. I'd certainly made my presence known if the kidnapper wanted to contact me.

To my interest, while O'Reilly was shoving past his comrades to reach Pao, Blackwell Johnson came out of his daze and eased in my direction. The man was a greedy shyster, but he wasn't on my suspect list. Only, as determination replaced his earlier deer-in-the-headlights expression, I started having second thoughts.

Maybe this wasn't about Mindy's murder or Graham. Maybe this was about *us*. How stupid can one person be? Who else would want us out of the country except the guy we were suing for all he was worth? Not that it would do him any good. We'd come right back. So chances were good that his intention wasn't to put us on that plane.

I leaped down from the table and eased toward Sean and the doorway. Caught up in their own discussions, glancing at their watches, no one else noticed, or if they did, they didn't care.

"I don't know what this little production was about, Miss Devlin," Blackwell said calmly enough as he caught my elbow and blocked my exit, "but it's time we had a chat."

* * *

Muttering under her breath, EG attempted to shake the window mullions loose from the frame, but this was an old house, built with real wood and nails and not plastic pop-ins. She'd smashed all the panes but not a single person in the parking lot below had noticed. She'd hoped at least the smokers would look up once the chaos steadied and everyone was inside, but breaking glass outside a kitchen apparently didn't capture anyone's interest.

She could be left up here to starve and no one would notice. All her genius was useless without any tools to apply it to.

Panic was rapidly turning to hysteria. Her new knee socks were filthy from crawling around the floor looking for trapdoors or loose boards. Hating acting like a baby, she'd rubbed at the tear stains on her cheeks, but all she'd succeeded in doing was smearing the dirt from her hands onto her face. She couldn't see herself in the mirror now that it was dark. The light bulb had been removed from the ceiling socket.

She'd come to a few conclusions over the hours, and none of them were pretty. Anyone who knew about her nonexistent millions would know Reggie had them and that she was worth nothing. Tex wouldn't kidnap her to get at Magda. Even if someone knew Tex was her father, they had no reason to kidnap her when he'd already been framed for murder. She was insignificant in the scheme of things. Unbelievable as it seemed, Ana was the key. Everyone who knew Ana would know that she would tear down mountains for her family.

Someone wanted Ana to come looking for her.

Crying again, EG shook the doorknob one more time and pounded the heavy paneling. She was small and couldn't make much noise. And the noise of the crowd downstairs was much greater than anything she could accomplish. She hated herself for being so stupid. Ana and Nick would never forgive her. They'd never let her stay with them again. She wept over that more than anything.

None of it would matter if she and Ana were a pile of bones when they were found.

She pressed her ear to the panel in hopes of hearing footsteps, voices, anything to indicate someone was coming for her. She hadn't been able to rip off any chair legs like they did in the movies. She didn't have anything to use as a weapon, except the roll of quarters in her backpack. Ana had taken away the first roll, but EG knew how to go to the bank and get more. She just didn't think they would work very well on a man a foot or two taller than she was. She'd have to stand on the bed to hit an adult jaw.

Voices!

Now that she heard someone talking, she didn't know if they were good guys or bad ones. It didn't matter. The bad guys knew where she was. The good ones wouldn't.

Screaming at the top of her lungs, she slammed a straight-backed wooden chair against the door.

"Eezhee!" a familiar voice cried from the other side of the panel. *Nick!*

"In here, in here, hurry up," she called. She knew she was being senseless. He didn't have a key. He couldn't beat down a solid door. But she couldn't help it. Sobbing, wiping her eyes, she tried to think of helpful things, but she was all out of ideas.

She heard a whispered consultation outside the door. *Ana!* Ana must be out there, too. Ana would figure out how to rescue her. Ana was safe. Everything would be all right. She would never, ever do another stupid thing in her life.

"Step back from the door, Eezhee, we're coming in," Nick warned.

Recovering enough aplomb to realize that wasn't too bright an idea, she backed off anyway. Ana couldn't break down doors. Nick wouldn't like messing up his clothes or his hair. Had they found a battering ram?

Something exceedingly heavy slammed against the door near the knob. At the same time, something else slammed into the middle of the door. The dual pressure cracked the frame near the lock, and her heart did a little leap of delight.

One more dual blow and the lock caved. Nick came tumbling in—followed by Tex.

"Daddy!" Weeping uncontrollably, EG threw herself into the strong arms open and waiting for her.

Lifting her to his shoulder, Tex snuggled her close, and she sobbed harder, this time as much in joy as relief.

Rising from the floor, Nick flicked the dust from his polished shoes with a handkerchief and brushed a wave of hair out of his eyes.

"Euell?" a woman's voice called uncertainly. "Are you up here? The senator is looking for you."

A slender, polished woman in an evening gown appeared in the doorway and stared at EG in Tex's arms. For a brief moment, EG stared back at the woman who didn't know she existed, and then her brain kicked into gear.

In a flash, EG scrambled to get down. "Where's Ana? I think he wants Ana."

* * *

Sean left his post at the oak roll-top desk near the doorway and sauntered in my direction when Johnson caught my arm. Several of the aides checked their watches as it became obvious Graham wouldn't be returning, and that I didn't have anything to add to the meeting. It was already after nine. The speech should be starting, but I hadn't heard a roar of applause yet. My inspired confrontation hadn't uncovered terrorists or kidnappers—only one scared lawyer.

Johnson couldn't see Sean approaching from behind him. "I don't think you have any idea what you're doing, Miss Devlin. You're new to D.C. You don't know who the players are."

Damned right. And if he didn't let go of my arm, I would never learn. "Where's EG?" I demanded. I could take Blackwell out in an eye blink, but I had to know where EG was first.

"EG?" he asked, jarred from whatever tirade had formed on his tongue.

"EG, my sister, Elizabeth Georgiana." Did he think I was dense? "Isn't that what this is all about? You want us gone, so you took her? The tickets are at the airport. You know we don't have the money, but if you'll just bring her safely to me, we're out of here."

"I was talking about Graham..." A look of horror twisted his Botoxed face. "Your sister is missing?"

"Exactly. If you don't know where she is, then I suggest you get out of my way." But what if I was wrong? What if Blackwell really had our best interests in his narrow little mind? "What do you know about Graham?" I was in such a panic that I could suspect anyone.

"That's what I've been trying to tell you. He's paranoid. Along with the injuries he sustained trying to save his wife in the Pentagon crash after 9/ll, he suffered post-traumatic stress. He saw conspiracies around every corner. After he accused the vice-president of conspiring with terrorists, he was quietly removed from the White House and tucked in a sanitarium, leaving everyone to think he'd died. He's ex-CIA. If anyone is capable of kidnapping your sister—"

"She's in here!" a male voice shouted from down the hall.

Since I was the only *she* in the vicinity, I had a vested interest in that shout.

I was desperate to hear all about Graham, but EG was my focus. I didn't know whether to break Johnson's arm right now and escape, or use him as a shield if someone was after me.

Sean had apparently seen no threat in my lawyer's attention, but with the shout outside, he placed himself between me and any sign of attack from outside. Brave man. I was more dangerous than any attacker, and Sean turned his back on *me*. Brave, but foolish. Wrapping my fingers around Johnson's wrist and squeezing a painful pressure point, I nearly broke a bone until he released me with a cry of pain.

I started to shove past him when EG burst through the door.

Dressed in her school clothes, tear-stained but unharmed, she scoped out the room and dashed directly toward me. With more joy than if I'd been given the mansion and the millions, I crouched down and hugged her harder than I'd ever hugged anyone. Her small body felt frail and warm and good in my arms. Unexpected moisture pooled in my eyes.

Nick and the senator raced in on her heels—followed by the senator's impeccably coiffed wife in mid-harangue. "I swear, Euell, if you'd just confide in me occasionally, we wouldn't have to go through this every time one of your peccadilloes—" Apparently realizing a reporter was in the room, Marjorie clammed up and forced a brittle smile.

I was so thrilled to have EG back that I almost forgot Johnson and his cohorts. While I hugged EG, I caught movement out of the corner of my eye.

I looked up to see Johnson ignoring us but scanning the room. I caught the direction of his look and saw Pao easing toward the hidden exit. I didn't have time to ask questions. "*Pao*." I shouted, pointing at the departing businessman.

Since *Pao* sounds exactly like *Pow*, several people gave me odd stares, but Nick caught the implication and sprinted across the room without question.

I, unfortunately, didn't have a chance to watch the flashy pyrotechnics when Nick caught him. A cold barrel of steel suddenly rubbed against my spine from beneath the tablecloth.

"If you'd simply waited instead of stirring up trouble just like the old man, we would be on the way to the airport now, Miss Devlin."

I do not react well to terror. Like a possum, my first instinct was to fall flat and play dead. Barring that, I get physical. With EG in my arms, falling flat was out of the question.

The crowd outside in the reception hall burst into thunderous applause, presumably at the candidate's appearance. The gun barrel shoved at my spine, urging me into action.

"Be sensible, and I'll fix it so no one gets hurt. Stand up slowly and start moving for the door," my invisible assailant said under cover of the distraction.

Sensible did not begin to cover my rage.

Instead of standing as prompted, I pitched EG at Sean who nearly fell backward catching her. In the same motion, I rolled to one side and lashed under the table with my spiked boot. Good thing I was wearing excellent underwear because my mini rode straight up to my hip. My purse with all my valuables flew across the room with EG.

Since I couldn't see beneath the tablecloth to aim my kick, I could only aim for where I'd last felt the gun. From the crunch of bone, I assumed I'd hit my assailant's wrist. The gun roared. Over the applause of the crowd in the other room, Tex's wife screamed.

Damn. The idiot had the safety off, and the gun hadn't flown out of his hand like in the movies. I prayed no one had been hit by the stray shot as I scrambled for a better position.

Sean was hauling ass toward the door, carrying EG with him. I don't know where Johnson went. Maybe he was gun-shy.

I heard a muffled commotion in Pao's last known location that involved fists and grunts, but my attention was fixed on the long library table. In my estimation it would be too heavy to lift even if the frozen dickheads near the computer had bothered to come forward to help me, which they didn't. The gun and the villain had disappeared beneath the cloth, and I truly didn't want to crawl under there after them.

While I studied the table, Tex did his fatherly duty and ran to grab EG from Sean. But knowing my propensity for violence, EG had already escaped and rolled under the heavy oak desk before Tex could reach her. We'd taught her well.

Sean was now shoving the hysterical Mrs. Tex out the door, and since no one else had the guts to approach me, that left Tex in the awkward position of the man between me and the exit. He either had to haul EG from under the desk and run, or help me, or personally go after the gunman under the table. Approaching a trapped animal is seldom wise.

Ignoring Tex's predicament, I stayed down, grabbed the tablecloth, and whipped it off, sending humidors and books flying. A gray suit emerging from under the far end of the table stood up and spun with military swiftness. He might have blended right in with the rest of the crowd at that end of the room had he not been holding his wrist clutched to his chest. When the tablecloth unmasked him, he grabbed for his coat pocket.

Hagan. And he still had the gun. Any kidnapper would have had to smuggle EG in here before the security was in place. He could have planted a gun then. Heck, he could be security.

I didn't have time to castigate myself for not realizing that until now.

EG screamed as she caught the problem before I did—Tex was the only man standing between me and a bullet.

It wasn't fair to have her daddy rescue her only to watch him die. Instead of going into action mode, I froze like an opossum right where I was on the floor. Nodding approval, Hagan grabbed Tex's arm and hauled it behind his back, lodging the gun at his back.

"Get up, slut, and nobody gets hurt."

Somebody watched way too many action movies, I thought, scanning the room as I grabbed the back of the couch and reluctantly pulled myself up. Looked like I was the only slut in here. Even the senator's wife had gone quiet out in the hall.

"If it was me you wanted, you should have asked," I said, adjusting my skirt and pretending to have difficulty standing. "You didn't have to frighten a kid like that."

"You're a hard person to pin down, and the kid wasn't," Hagan replied without remorse.

Admittedly, I'd not stayed in place today. And even if I had stayed at my computer, he wouldn't have been able to get at me through Graham's security. I'd left EG vulnerable.

Sean was out in the hall with Mrs. Tex. Nick had Pao's Cambodian neck bent backward so he couldn't move, but he was looking at Hagan as if he'd rip out his throat if he only had two more arms. Good old Nick. He was too far away to help me. All the politicos were easing as far from the scene as they could without walking through walls. That left me and Tex and Hagan.

They all waited to see what I would do. I *hated* being the center of attention.

"Were you the one who sent poisoned envelopes to my grandfather?" I asked, trying to brush myself off with a hand shaking so badly that I wanted to punch something just to stop it.

"Max was becoming a nuisance." Keeping Tex's arm behind his back, he pushed him toward me. "But all I did was provide an asshole with the motivation and the means. Brashton did the dirty work. The government pays me to learn these things." He looked over his shoulder at his frozen audience. "Someone get word to the schizoid that I have his little whore as insurance. If I'm going down for this one, I want protection."

Verifying my suspicions, I didn't turn my head to look at Nick. Our grandfather had been murdered by Reggie, incited by Hagan. Reggie would have done it for the money. Hagan did it because of Mindy's report. But to save whose hide? He was a flunky. I couldn't imagine him doing it on his own. Someone in the cartel had to have ordered Max and Mindy eliminated.

Sweat beaded Hagan's waxen brow. I figured I'd cracked a bone in his wrist with my kick, but he was holding the gun steady enough to blow Tex away. Now that I'd got over the first blur of adrenaline, I could think a little straighter. Hagan didn't want EG or Tex, he wanted me—to get at Graham. He must have known Graham had taken up Max's investigation. Tex's credibility had been destroyed by being made a scapegoat for Mindy's murder.

As expected, Hagan shoved Tex away when he was close enough to grab my arm. Just because I had my thinking cap on didn't mean I wouldn't react to being grabbed, but I restrained my instincts for a change. There were too many people who could get hurt by flying guns. "Why would anyone kill Max?" I demanded, dragging my heels and searching for escape as Hagan's fingers dug into my skin.

"Why does one flatten gnats?" Holding my elbow, he dragged me toward the door with the gun in his injured hand swinging back and forth to warn off the sheep staring at us.

"Was Mindy a gnat too?" I did my stumbling best not to move quickly.

"A fat mosquito," he snarled. "One who couldn't leave well enough alone."

He'd had Mindy and Max squashed because of textbooks? I couldn't think of another damned thing to say after that.

Apparently into drama, Hagan managed the conversation without me. "I took care of your bosses," he told his stunned audience. "Now it's time for them to take care of me."

Bosses? All the men I'd invited in here were involved? Or the senators who paid the aides, at least. I didn't have time to process it. Hagan was still dragging me toward the exit. Concentrating hard, I didn't look at Sean as we passed.

"Keep this quiet, and we'll all live happily ever after," Hagan promised in a voice that sounded assured, not scared. "I want an attaché case filled with hundred dollar bills waiting for me at Reagan. If Miss Devlin did as asked and brought her passport, I'll do everyone a favor and take her with me."

Maybe if I was more cool at this spy game I'd have been assessing the reactions of the various officials around the room, looking for the guilty parties to whom he was talking, but I was too busy scheming ways to save my neck. In a couple of moves I could have flung Hagan over my shoulder and smack into the bookshelves, but he still held a gun. I didn't have a lot of experience with guns. I'd trained in the martial arts for anger management and exercise, not assault. I didn't want flying bullets to hit EG or Nick. Beyond that, as far as I was aware, everyone else in the room could be involved with Hagan and could go down with him.

To my immense relief, Nick whistled sharply. That was an old signal we'd worked up once in Istanbul. The whistle meant he was okay and about to start a distraction.

Hagan was so sure of himself that he'd only grabbed me by my upper arm like some old time movie bully hauling the weak, screaming heroine around. If he was ex-military, he hadn't dealt with too many female commandoes in his line of work. I didn't tense but stumbled weakly so Hagan had to pull up hard on my arm.

Without further warning than the whistle, Nick tossed Pao in a neat backflip at the group of suits, scattering them. My tablecloth trick had littered the floor with cigars and candles, and several of the less fleet of foot did somersaults and belly flops in their haste to escape a flying Pao. I might have been amused at another time. Right now, I had two seconds to act.

To the accompaniment of crashing bodies in the library and the roar of applause in the reception hall as Paul Rose approached the podium, I sliced downward on Hagan's already injured gun arm with the side of my free hand—the one that could break two boards. He howled and dropped the gun. Even though he kept his grip on my arm, that was worse than letting me go. I shifted my feet to brace my stance, grabbed his coat collar, twisted my captured arm, and flung him head first into the library table.

A big man, he flew solidly, hitting his head on the solid oak with a lot of force behind the crash.

Only then did we notice the scream of sirens in the drive.

Chapter Twenty-seven

The bad guys are caught with their cigars down

THE REST of the party was a bit of a blur. Gray suits stumbled to their feet amid crushed cigars to surround Pao, although they probably didn't know why except that he was down. If he was Hagan's partner in crime, he was maintaining his Oriental inscrutability.

More intelligently, Nick grabbed the gun, sat on Hagan, and held the barrel under his captive's chin. If Hagan had any inkling that Nick was gay, he'd probably pass out at this compromising position.

Tex performed his best Texas drawl trying to reach his hysterical wife.

Blackwell Johnson straightened his tie and slipped out. I figured I knew where to find him when I wanted him. I had so many questions, my brain froze.

Blue suits burst into the room and avoided Keystone Kops antics on the rolling cigars by the simple expedient of deliberately mashing them into the expensive carpet with their polished clodhoppers.

Needing a moment of sanity, I crawled under the desk to hold EG who was nearly as hysterical as Marjorie, except EG was shaking with laughter, crying, and demanding to learn the chopping trick. She's a great kid, and I was proud of her.

Sean had apparently abandoned Mrs. Tex, seen me with EG, and gone to interrogate Pao before the cops interfered. Now, he tried to shove his way back to us—I hoped with answers to all my questions—but security and the men in black followed the cops in, and the crowd from the reception spilled into the halls and library, blocking Sean's progress. Paul Rose would be a little ticked at the distraction from his no doubt groundbreaking speech promoting flags and apple pie.

I was tempted to imitate Hagan's trick. The library table was unmasked, but we could cower in the cubbyhole beneath the desk until the room cleared. Or someone remembered us. I feared the latter was more likely.

"If this were a really good movie, we'd find a trapdoor in here," I muttered.

"Yeah, but in the movies, you'd miraculously retrieve your purse without crawling under people's feet," EG thoughtfully pointed out.

I hated to lose that hacker program, especially if any of the men in black were FBI or whatever they called themselves these days. I had sacrificed my invisibility this evening, and with a passport like mine, I could easily become a Homeland Security target.

I peered around the corner of the desk just as a black-suited arm reached down to recover the elegant little bag Nick had picked out for me. The diamond cufflink winking on the white cuff beneath the black caught my attention. How many FBI agents wore diamond cufflinks?

Suddenly eager to see the owner of that arm, I scooted out from our hiding place. And ran headfirst into Sean's knees.

He wasn't wearing cufflinks and didn't have my bag. Using his knee to pull myself up, I didn't bother admiring his crotch in my haste to see the diamond man. Sean grabbed my elbow and hauled me upright. I strained to see past his wide shoulder but I was too short. Elbowing him out of my way, ignoring his *oof* at the sharpness of my elbow, I sought the purse thief.

The room strained at its plaster seams with men in black and blue and gray, mixed with a few women in sparkly gowns. No diamond cufflinks winked back at me. The thief had taken my purse, my hacker program, and my passport, *damn him*.

"I've got a car," Sean said, gripping my arm with less than gentleness, probably to keep me from elbowing him again since I was frantically trying to escape. "Let's get out of here."

Getting out of there sounded like an excellent idea, but I wasn't ready to go with *him*. I had a driving need to see Diamond Man. "Why, so you can pump me first? Did you get anything out of Pao?"

"A few Cambodian curses. Let the authorities work out his financial shenanigans. Homeland Security knows about his website. They'll check him out. We need to get you out first."

Helping EG from under the desk, I pushed her toward the door, searching for Nick. Just as I caught his eye in the doorway, a familiar formidable figure in boiled shirt stepped in front of us.

"If you'll come this way," Mallard said formally, "I believe we can leave while the senator's wife is still shrieking."

He didn't have to ask twice. Although Mallard's bulk nearly blocked us from view and Sean added to the barrier, there were far too many officials in here for us to disappear into the woodwork. Heads were already turning our way now that we'd departed our hiding place. I felt naked without my purse and passport.

Holding on to EG, I eased along in front of Mallard, following Nick's lead and aiming for the exit. Sean shouted "*Wait!*" as the crowd closed in around us, but I didn't linger. I didn't check to see how Mallard cut him off either. All I saw was the door out, partially blocked by curiosity seekers being pushed back by the men in blue.

"Oh, excuse me, old man, it's such a crush, isn't it?" Nick's fruitiest British accent drifted toward us, followed by "Oh, my, do that again," in a lascivious tone. Humanity suddenly surged around us as manly men backed out of his way.

"There you are, Jeeves, old fellow. Lead on, I feel positively *faint*." Nick draped his arm over Mallard's broad shoulders and surreptitiously shoved us faster out the door.

A gray suit hustled to halt us before we could push past the cops guarding the exit. I dodged his steely gaze and hastily sought a distraction to get us out of here. I *really* didn't want to have to answer any questions right now—probably because I wasn't the one with the answers. Machiavelli was, and he waited back at the mansion, safe from hoi polloi.

Without warning, Sean muttered near my ear, "You're gonna owe me for this." I could smell the subtle scent of his spicy aftershave and see the bristles of his five o'clock shadow as he pushed off the wall.

I had no idea how he'd managed to navigate the crowd, and no time to question as he pointed at the window on the opposite side of the room.

"Look, he's getting away! Catch him!"

Gray suit glanced away. The cops surged around us. Mallard and Nick shoved from behind. EG and I popped from the library like eggs from a bird.

Well, there were more representative metaphors, but I've already overused my favorite swear word.

With Mallard running offense in front and Nick handling defense behind, we shoved past the crowd in the corridor in the opposite direction of the front exit. I knew this tactic and didn't hesitate in their choice of objective. We hit the servants' hall running.

Mallard had drawn the Phaeton under the old-fashioned portico in the rear of the house. I had no idea if this was still a driveway or the kitchen garden. I merely dived into the back seat after EG when Mallard opened the door, while Nick took the front.

The back seat wasn't empty.

"To the airport?" a pleasantly warm male voice inquired. A diamond cufflink winked as he handed me my purse.

Shock hit me. I smacked the roof looking for a light switch so I could see the mystery man, but this was an antique car and not a modern limousine. My next reaction was to grab for the door and escape as Mallard guided the enormous vehicle past—rosebushes? Definitely not a place to jump out. Tearing my astonished gaze from the window to the silhouette of the man in the seat across from us, I narrowed my eyes against the darkness.

"Graham?"

"An admirer," he corrected. "That was an amazing performance. Although your rashness should be condemned, I congratulate you on your efficiency and quick thinking under pressure."

I could actually *hear* the admiration in his voice. It went down amazingly well. Few people offered appreciation for my somewhat obscure and often inappropriate abilities.

Walled off by glass, Nick hadn't realized anything was wrong. I could see him leaning out the front window, directing Mallard past whatever obstructions remained in the backyard. I prayed they were heading for a gate and not a crash.

Beside me, EG caught my hand but wisely remained silent. If this was Graham, we were cruising for a showdown, despite the flattery.

His warm, very human voice didn't have the mechanical quality of the intercom. He called himself an *admirer*. And the way he said it had elicited shivers up and down my spine and to other places best not mentioned in front of impressionable nine-year-olds. I inhaled the spicy male scent of him and wished wistfully for a man I could trust, but who could trust a man who wouldn't admit his identity?

We had three airplane tickets waiting for us at the airport. I had my passport back if Mystery Man hadn't removed it from my purse. If we could snag EG's passport, we could get the hell out of D.C. before everyone from the FBI to Homeland Security came down on us, asking questions we couldn't answer.

EG's fingers squeezed mine, and I slipped off my frightened cloud and back to earth as I remembered our reason for being here in the first place.

EG needed her father. Tex had just risked his life and his reputation rescuing her.

I wanted to go back to being the sane one in our family. Not the brilliant one or the gay one or the eccentric one or any of those other appellations attached to my weird and wonderful half siblings. I am invisible, unostentatious Anastasia, the family doormat.

Not anymore, a small voice inside my head said. Much as I wanted to go back, I couldn't. I had family now, and responsibilities. And a mystery man who admired my *performance*. I was feeling very, very visible. "Why did they kill Max?" I asked in resignation.

A stranger would have no idea what I was talking about. The man in the diamond cufflinks didn't hesitate. "He knew too much and had too much power." The velvet voice continued without inflection. "As did Tex. Max persuaded Tex to make a report to Congress, and the textbook cartel found that unacceptable. Any evidence of wrongdoing will be destroyed by now. Computers are being wiped as we speak. Hagan and Pao will go to jail for the murder of Mindy Carstairs. The best lawyers in the country will look after them to be certain there is no mention of the textbook matter. It's over. There is nothing further that can be done here. The car is at your disposal. Mallard believes he is taking you home, but he can be dissuaded elsewise."

He waited silently for my decision.

I was suffering the exhaustion of the introverted after immersion in too much socializing. I was so totally depleted that I would crawl under a rock if I could. I was coming down from my adrenaline high so fast that a crash was inevitable. I wanted to go home, to my computers and my silent clients.

To my grandfather's mansion and The Whiz. My eyes teared up in desperate desire for the security of a real home.

If this was Graham, was he offering to take us there? Or throwing us out?

The broad-shouldered silhouette looked mightily like the one I'd seen upstairs against the background of computer monitors. Who else would be in the Phaeton with Mallard?

I needed time to mourn my grandfather, a man who had tried to help me and had turned to me in his dying moments. That last frantic e-mail must have been a warning. He must have known Pao was a killer. Johnson had said Top Hat was the cartel. The cartel doctored textbooks and hired Hagan as muscle and Pao as their financial finagler. And Diamond Man was saying we couldn't stop a cartel so dangerous it had killed two people and kidnapped a child.

I'd found EG and helped find Max's killer, but I'd still not saved the inheritance he'd intended for us. Revenge didn't warm me any.

I wanted the house, a stable home for EG, a haven for our siblings. A refuge for Nick when he needed it, as he surely would, given his penchant for drama and bad lovers.

Max's will had offered all of that. I'd missed my family these last lonely years. As a man who'd driven off his only daughter, had Max understood what the house would mean to us? Tears sprang to my eyes as I crushed EG's fingers in my own.

I might still be Anastasia the Doormat to my family, but I'd proved that I could hold my own against Magda or school officials or government hacks. I'd captured a murderer—I thought. I needed to find out just what the hell I had done tonight.

"EG needs a home of her own," I replied, not as boldly as I would have liked, to Diamond Man's offer to take us to the airport. "She needs a family, not a boarding school."

"My dad thinks I look like Magda," EG said quietly.

"Did he tell you that?" I asked, curious about how Tex had found her.

"No, I just know it," she said with the same firmness she used to tell us our grandfather wouldn't be in D.C. to greet us. At least this was a positive message. Who was I to argue?

"Who kidnapped you?" I asked, aware of the stranger listening.

"I didn't know until I saw him in the library with the gun," she admitted.

Hagan had been the only library occupant with a gun.

"When he came and got me," she continued, "I asked if my dad had sent him, and he said yes. I knew Tex couldn't come himself. I thought maybe he was waiting in the car."

I glanced across at the stranger, waiting for him to question this.

But the stranger merely waited for EG to continue her story, not interrupting or interfering in any way. That didn't sound like Graham. But if it looks like a skunk and smells like a skunk, did it matter if it didn't act like a skunk? Maybe he was rabid.

I recognized the defense mechanism kicking in. I was trying to disassociate myself from hoping that this man could be more than an outsider.

"You followed a stranger?" I finally asked in incredulity. Hadn't Magda taught her better than that? No, Magda had taught her that strangers were all around her, and she should use them.

As I'd been using Graham and Sean.

She shrugged her small shoulders. "I knew he wouldn't hurt me. I thought it was because of my dad, but later, I figured it was because he didn't care who I was. He wanted you. And I knew once you found me, it would be okay."

I wanted to sink down in the cushy leather seat, cover my eyes, and make the world go away. She trusted her instincts. She trusted me. How reliable were either of us?

"Hagan locked you upstairs? Why?" I wasn't about to argue with EG's confidence that everything would be all right once I showed up. I had worked at assuming an invincible attitude for the sake of the kids. I didn't think EG actually *believed* it. The kid was too smart for that.

The kid knew things I didn't.

"I think he wanted people to believe my dad was guilty of kidnapping, so he set it up to frame him and to get at you." She had the grace to look guilty as she admitted. "I used your computer to send him an e-mail. He must have traced it."

And I'd compounded his fear by showing up in his office this morning. I couldn't berate EG for doing something stupid if I'd done the same.

"Hagan wanted the hard drive with Mindy's report on it," the stranger offered. "His pal in Tex's office tried to get it this afternoon, but the drive had been replaced. They must have assumed you were the one who took it and panicked. Hagan couldn't get at you, so he settled for Elizabeth when her message arrived at the office."

"Who *are* you?" I demanded again. The question worked whether he was Graham or not. Who in hell did he think he was?

"A believer in democracy and free enterprise," he said with a sexy resolve that made me shiver with need and want to reach over and slap him for his evasiveness at the same time.

But I was too wiped to slap anyone. "Democracy and free enterprise—as opposed to Senator Rose and his textbook monopoly?" I hazarded. The amorphous shape of the plot formed a sharper picture, although I still couldn't identify it. I had a strong suspicion Hagan and his pal were only bit players in a bigger production. The argument between Pao and O'Reilly proved there were connections within connections.

"There is no evidence that Senator Rose is aware of his investments as anything more than a stock portfolio," he chided my ignorance. "Should he become president, he would have to divest his interest in them."

That wasn't an answer. Why did I think the stranger had an answer? Why should I care? Magda was the one who dabbled in politics, not me. Had Max died because of *politics*?

I reverted to my main concern. "But Rose hires goons who think it's okay to kidnap kids to trade for what he wants?"

"You're the one who mentioned Rose, not me," he answered without reproof. "Hagan was intent on framing Senator Hammond for the kidnapping as well as the murder of Miss Carstairs. The Carstairs report would have cost Hagan his job and undermined all the work of putting together the cartel."

That made a great deal of sense. Some shady senators had cooked up a monopoly, bribed a government lackey to recommend their products, and Hagan would have been the sacrificial turkey if the plot went down when Mindy's report hit Congress. Pao had used the whole illicit scheme to harbor his money-laundering. Had Hagan known that?

"Pao and Hagan gave each other alibis for Mindy's death," I argued. "Did Hagan or Pao murder Mindy?"

"I assume the police will sort that out with forensic evidence, although providing an alibi is more Pao's style than murder. Pao is a financier. He is the one who set up the dirty web of Edu-Pub. Hagan was decorated in Vietnam and released from service with a psychological discharge which prevented him from working in higher office. His bank account received a large deposit last week. It's quite possible someone convinced him that Max and Ms. Carstairs were not only a threat to his job, but to national security."

I tried inhaling that and choked. "Bad textbooks are a matter of national security?"

"Some spiders weave large webs," he answered enigmatically as the Phaeton rolled to a stop in front of the mansion. "You have rooted out the murderers. Your job is done. The plane tickets remain at your disposal. I bid you good evening."

The back door opened and Nick stuck his hand in to help us out.

In the light of a streetlamp, I caught the flash of a diamond against the stranger's starched cuff before Nick hauled me to my feet.

EG scrambled out after me, slamming the car door, and the Phaeton glided away—leaving us in front of grandfather's mansion.

Home, or was it?

Chapter Twenty-eight

Ana waits for Graham and finds a home

GIVEN my agitated state of mind, I figured Nick would be much better at calming EG than me. I left them alone and proceeded directly to the third floor. All the doors were closed and the hall lights were out. Not even the cat came to greet me.

I opened the door to the computer room. The monitors played their eerie pictures of the house interior and exterior. One screen monitored the front door of the reception hall we'd just left. Its drive was still lined with police cars. Another showed scrolling texts and websites I didn't recognize. No one sat in the big chair in front of the screens.

Convinced I had the conniving—not crippled—spider this time, I returned to the staircase and sat down on the top step to wait—which left me with entirely too much time to think.

Johnson had said Graham had been in a mental institution. Did I really want to sit here and wait for him? Yep. I did.

Except I'm better at researching than sitting still. I wanted to go down to the Whiz and run Hagan's profile, find his connection to the other congressmen in the *cartel's* board. Leave it to Graham to come up with a word that sounded like a conspiracy instead of a good old-fashioned greedy monopoly. They'd doctored textbooks, produced crap for next to nothing, and sold them for a fortune to school districts across the country after bribing government officials to recommend them. Looked like a nice profit-maker to me.

Why the greedmongers wasted time twisting history to make rich people look good and unions and environmentalists look bad were questions a psychiatrist would have to answer.

My thoughts were more practical. I hoped the cops had enough evidence to nail Hagan for murder because I really didn't want to have to report EG's kidnapping. No more cops and robbers, sleuths and superheroes. I just wanted to know if we had the weekend to move out or if we could stay so I could register EG at the alternative school for the gifted on Monday.

Now that EG had found a father, I knew we wouldn't be going back to Atlanta. I was okay with that.

I wasn't okay with a mysterious stranger living in the same house with me. So I waited.

I didn't know where Mallard had taken the car or his passenger, who had to be a walking, talking Graham—a man whose voice alone was dangerous to my libido without considering the whole package. A man

Mallard had denied knowing, the liar. Mallard had been here for decades and if Max had been Graham's mentor, he knew him as well as he knew my grandfather. Military attaché to an ambassador, my foot and eye. Mallard was retired CIA, or I'd eat my boot.

I listened but didn't hear anyone return. As far as I was aware, the Victorian had no drive or place to park a Phaeton, so I supposed they had to walk back from whatever garage it was parked in. I heard Nick and EG murmuring for a while, then the lights went out in their rooms. I sat in the dark, beginning to wonder if I was an idiot. Maybe if I opened all the doors up here, I'd find Graham safely in his bed.

A security light along the baseboard lit in the upper hall behind me, and the door to the computer room opened.

"You might as well come in," Graham's mechanical voice intoned.

Maybe he wasn't just an invalid. Maybe he was a robot. Maybe he had one of those larynx implants.

Maybe he was a bloody liar trying to make a fool of me. Which wouldn't be very hard to do, given how much I wanted diamond man to be Graham.

There was no way diamond man could have got past me unless he wore a cloak of invisibility.

I stalked down the hall and leaned against the doorjamb, cocking my hip at an angle and crossing my arms to push up my breasts in a Magda pose. Still wearing my stilettoes and thigh-high little black dress, and backlit by the hall light, I assumed I was woman enough for him.

Graham turned his chair to face me. Maybe it was wishful thinking, but I thought I saw his hands freeze on the chair arms, and felt the lust factor soar to palpable. If I'd thought for certain he was Diamond Man, I'd have sashayed in and kissed him until his chair spun.

I could see his silhouette against the monitors. Lights from the multiple screens lit his wrist. No diamond. No cuff. He was wearing a short sleeved black T-shirt, and I could see the glitter of his gold watch on a fairly muscular forearm. We were back to Robot Man.

I focused on his face now that I knew Graham had, indeed, been injured in 9/11. Was that a scar shadowing the side of his jaw instead of just the result of flickering light and good bones?

"Explain the cartel." I hadn't known what I would say until I said it. Sometimes, my subconscious works in mysterious ways.

"You didn't accept the plane tickets," he intoned in disapproval.

I looked for a microphone that might have disguised his voice, but it was too dark. Microphones come small these days.

"No. We're staying in D.C," I informed him. "You can have us thrown out, if you like, but I've found a school for EG, and Nick has a job he likes. I can work anywhere, but I'm staying with my family."

He nodded and steepled his fingers. I didn't think he was praying. Bracing elbows against chair arms and pushing fingertips against each other is an excellent aerobic exercise that I use often.

"You won't leave Max's death alone, will you?"

I let stony silence answer for me.

"You don't know what you're asking for," he replied.

"If you'd tell me about the cartel, I might know more." I shrugged. Two could play at this game of nonchalance. "But it won't change my mind. We're staying. D.C. is the world Magda raised us for."

Wow, I didn't know where that had come from, but I knew I was right. In her own roundabout way, Magda had showed us all we needed to know to survive in her world. She didn't force us into it. She let us choose for ourselves. And here we were, gravitating to the play of power and politics.

"Gauging by your energetic performance this evening, you may have taken her training a little farther than she imagined."

I thought I detected amusement behind that cryptic comment, but I wasn't biting. I wanted something, but I wasn't asking for it. "How much danger is EG in if we stay in D.C.?"

"Excellent question. I had a talk with Senator Hammond. He will be selling his stock in Edu-Pub and removing himself from oversight of the education committee. The shooting episode was a reminder to back off even if he beat the murder charge. He's backing off."

Which didn't answer my question but raised a dozen others. "And I suppose you've talked to the cops and the FBI and know if Hagan is going down for murder?"

"I believe the DNA from the hairs caught beneath Ms. Carstairs fingernails will prove his guilt, yes."

Diamond Man hadn't mentioned DNA. But then, there had been plenty of time since the car had returned us here for him to have checked his sources with the police. "And Pao? What do they have on him?"

"Unfortunately, Pao is a trifle more elusive. He will no doubt be deported under any number of domestic security acts, but it's unlikely that evidence will be found to convict him of any crimes unless they can prove conspiracy in providing Hagan's alibi. The warehouse and all its records are gone. If the company laundered money, the evidence has been destroyed. I'm sure suitable personnel will be alerted to examine related bank accounts in Indonesia. It's uncertain how Pao's government will greet him."

"Did he murder Max?" I demanded.

"The analysis of the poison isn't in yet, but the symptoms point to a poison from Indonesia that would have been available to him. Reggie regularly ordered Max's supplies. We will have to wait for Hagan to explain how he persuaded Reggie to give him the delivery schedule, but I think we both know that as a coke addict, Reggie was easily blackmailed."

I knew he was right, but I felt a strange letdown, and sagged against the wall. I'd found Pao. I'd done my job. I just didn't know what the hell that job had been. "I'll never know for certain what this was all about, will I?"

He tapped his fingertips together. "Under the circumstances, if you insist on staying in D.C., it might be wisest if you stayed here, where the security is unassailable and your unflagging curiosity and inimitable efficiency can be monitored."

I straightened up so fast I almost conked my head against the wall. "Here? In this house?" I ignored all other references and zeroed in on the important one. "With EG?"

Not a single sign of reaction, but I had the feeling every word was being wrung from him the hard way. He didn't want me here, but maybe it was because he didn't want us hurt, not because he didn't *like* us. Obviously, I was very tired.

"Max wanted his family looked after. For your own safety, I believe that living here would be best for both of you. However, there will be no more smashing of security cameras."

"There will be no more placing of said cameras in my bedroom," I countered, hands on hips as I drew my line in the sand, while my heart skipped in an excited cha-cha.

I can be honest with myself upon occasion. I realized it wasn't just the house raising my hopes—it was the man in front of the monitors, a man I knew somehow had to be Diamond-Cufflink Man, a man more elegant, more sophisticated, more exciting than any man Magda had ever dragged home. I didn't want to leave him. I was officially insane.

"A camera must be placed on all entrances and exits," he continued, oblivious to my brain explosion, "and the window to your chosen room is vulnerable."

"Then I'll find a closet!" I should have been jumping up and down with joy, but I wasn't letting him know how much I wanted this. My curiosity overfloweth, but I hid it well.

"There is a large closet in the chamber next door to yours if you want to put a bed in it," he said in irritation, "but you cannot work in a closet."

"We're still hiring Oppenheimer to get our house back," I warned. Graham might be into living in shadows, but I believe in being right up front. We needed ground rules.

"You may try your best," he murmured. "I believe Brashton is within a day's sail of St. Kitts."

Now I wanted to jump up and down and scream with joy. Nick could fly down and retrieve our millions. We could do *anything*.

"Why are you really doing this?" I asked, perpetual curiosity and optimism winning out.

"Because I owe your grandfather a great deal, and he would want me to protect his disastrous offspring if they insist on staying in D.C.," he said with familiar dryness. "And also because I can use your network of contacts—if you promise to leave the non-computer investigating to those who know how to do it."

For all I knew, I was listening to a paranoid schizophrenic. And I didn't care. He was telling me what I wanted to hear, so that made him sane in my world.

"I've had all the detective work I want," I told him. "All I need is privacy for my computers. You wouldn't happen to have an attic over this floor, would you?"

He sat silently tapping his fingers until I thought perhaps I'd pushed him far enough. I might dream of Diamond Cufflink Man. That didn't mean I had to believe in superheroes.

"That is a possibility I will take into consideration," he finally said.

I grinned so wide I thought it would split my face. "And if Patra shows up, I'll give her my room."

"Patra?" he asked with what passed for alarm in Graham's world.

"Or Tudor, or any of the others. Where I am, they go."

I thought I detected a highly unsuitable curse muttered under his breath, but I was adamant. I wouldn't be living in hog heaven and shutting out the opportunity for my family to enjoy the same.

"I'm sure they all have far better things to do than come here," he conceded with more grumpiness than any other emotion he'd ever expressed.

I didn't tell him Tudor was expelled from school regularly, and while only EG of the younger ones had shown any adventurous aptitudes, the next eldest half-siblings all possessed Magda's wanderlust. They'd show up just to see what I'd fallen into.

"Good-night, Ana," said Robot Man.

He didn't have to let us stay. He didn't have to be concerned about our safety. It wouldn't hurt to show appreciation for not throwing us out.

But a mere thank you simply wouldn't suffice. Before he could spin his throne back to the monitors, I stalked across the office, clapped my hands on the chair arms, and planted my mouth on his.

He was alive and not a robot.

After a moment's hesitation, I realized just how alive he was. My hair was standing on end by the time he'd hauled my head down to his and kissed me so thoroughly that I wasn't certain I could walk away. Then he clasped my face in his hands, set me back where I belonged, and after briefly running his finger down my jaw, swung back to his keyboard.

"I like your new fashion statement," he murmured in what sounded like genuine appreciation, "but boot heels are not suitable for wood floors." He leaned his chair back to examine a screen well above my head, effectively dismissing me.

I refrained from pounding my boot heel against his hard head. I knew the need for distance after a mind-blowing experience.

And I'd been right. His cheek was badly scarred. I'd be able to identify him anywhere.

With anticipation, I closed the door and let him return to his web. For now.

* * *

The heat in my room woke me the next morning. Sunshine poured through the big front window. If I was staying here, I was definitely relocating to somewhere dark. Maybe I could move Mallard out of the basement.

As if recognizing that I was awake, the intercom intruded into my morning attitude adjustment. "Mrs. Euell Hammond on line one."

Euell. No wonder the guy called himself Tex. I kicked off what remained of my sheet and stretched full length in front of John Quincy's camera. I wore a T-shirt that stopped at my midriff and a pair of black panties and nothing more. If Graham had repaired the camera, I hoped he'd swallow his teeth. My hours at the gym hadn't exactly been wasted, and my taut abdominals reflected it.

I hit the telephone button and tried not to snarl too obviously. "Yes?"

"The Senator and I would like to invite you and Elizabeth you to dinner this evening," Marjorie said in her oh-so-polite diction.

"And Nick?" I yawned and rubbed my eyes, not awake enough yet to care if I was being obnoxious. I'd probably regret it for EG's sake if Marjorie withdrew the invitation, but I had no interest whatsoever in hobnobbing with the rich and famous.

I'll give her credit for only hesitating a moment. "Yes, of course. The senator would prefer that he has time to get to know Elizabeth before the press finds out about her, but we are prepared for all eventualities."

"You are a good person," I told her. How many other wives would acknowledge their husband's bastards? "I would have cut the man's throat."

The intercom made a loud harrumph warning me that I had gone too far. I smashed the side of my fist on the intercom's buttons, and the machine emitted an unholy screech. I wanted Graham to drool over my bod, not interfere with my social life. But the knowledge that he was there, watching me, heated my already charged hormones.

The lady took it all in stride. "You're young and idealistic. You'll understand better when you're older. At seven then? We'll send Boise to pick you up."

So, there we were. Not only had EG's father accepted her existence, but his old lady was accepting her as well. Mission accomplished. I should cheer in triumph, but I was more interested in the spook in the attic than the walking wounded like the senator. Between the murder accusations and EG's presence, Tex was a lame duck without a tail wind.

Before she could hang up, I remembered another dangling puzzle piece. "Has the senator figured out who told Hagan about EG's message?"

She hesitated a little longer this time. "We believe it was Nick's young friend. He handed in his resignation yesterday."

Oh, shit. I let her hang up while I thought about that. Maybe Nick's heart wasn't involved this time, but chances were about even that he'd not kept EG's parentage a secret if he'd trusted his lover. I didn't think I'd take up newspaper reading just yet. Tex was about to get barbecued.

It was definitely time for Nick to be given a hero's job of nabbing Brashton.

I gazed thoughtfully at John Quincy. My Grateful Dead poster had been removed to another wall. I had to assume the camera had been repaired.

"I'm getting my own phone line," I announced. "And I'm hunting for the attic."

"That's a shame," the intercom sighed. "Your choice of nightwear is revealing."

I'm sure it was just my wishful thinking hearing a sexy chuckle emanating from the intercom as it switched off.

I grabbed my new silk halter and capris outfit so I could race downstairs and tell Nick he was off to St. Kitts to rescue our money and drag home Max's murderer. We were *so* not going to put up with Graham's nonsense forever.

Author Bio

With several million books in print and *New York Times* and *USA Today's* bestseller lists under her belt, former CPA Patricia Rice is one of romance's hottest authors. Her emotionally-charged contemporary and historical romances have won numerous awards, including the *RT Book Reviews* Reviewers Choice and Career Achievement Awards. Her books have been honored as Romance Writers of America RITA® finalists in the historical, regency and contemporary categories.

A firm believer in happily-ever-after, Patricia Rice is married to her high school sweetheart and has two children. A native of Kentucky and New York, a past resident of North Carolina and Missouri, she currently resides in Southern California, and now does accounting only for herself. She is a member of Romance Writers of America, the Authors Guild, and Novelists, Inc.

For further information, visit Patricia's network:
http://www.patriciarice.com
http://www.facebook.com/OfficialPatriciaRice
https://twitter.com/Patricia_Rice
http://patriciarice.blogspot.com/
http://www.wordwenches.com

Reviews left with on-line booksellers such as Amazon and B&N will encourage advertising promoters to discount this and related books in the future!

www.ingramcontent.com/pod-product-compliance
Lightning Source LLC
LaVergne TN
LVHW091534060526
838200LV00036B/606